Diamond Blood

Diamond Blood

S.R. WALCOTT

ISBN: 978-1-0686113-0-8 (paperback)
ISBN: 978-1-0686113-1-5 (ebook)

Book design by Wordzworth
www.wordzworth.com

Contents

ONE

It had been many, many, years since I had felt so alive. Well, as alive as one would expect for a vampire. I am at fault and expect no pardon for my self-inflicted ruination. As they say, the soul is willing, but the flesh is weak. So, here is my story. And so, it began.

My name is Estella Vincent. I have walked the earth for two hundred and forty-two years, and twenty-five days. Do not be alarmed. I know, it sounds like an eternity. But what's the concept of time when you're the undead? I was once a proud vampire. But, as they say, all good things must come to an end. Consumed by raw lust, I was unscrupulous and yearned for his sordid touch. Now I know I should have turned around when his shadowed silhouette appeared at the window. But I was weak, and the intensity of my infatuation had become way too strong.

The guilt had already dissipated. He had already undressed, standing there with his chiselled perfect six-pack on display. He pulled her in closer.

'I am addicted.'

'Good. You belong to me now.' He whispered.

His voice was breathy, and his breaths were heavy. He kissed her gently, circling her neck with his lips. She closed her eyes. Her body relaxed and became his, as his bare chest rubbed hot against hers. He tenderly nibbled her ear, encouraging her to wrap her slender arms around his neck. Cold hearts, but the desire for each other was as hot as fire. Their ice cool bodies entwined, locked together in a tight embrace. His yearning for her was evident, hungry and intense. For a moment, Estella forgot who he was. It felt good, it felt forbidden, but most of all, she unashamedly enjoyed it. Hot kisses caressed her body, igniting waves of pleasure. But why didn't she feel this way with the man who loved her? With little hesitation he lifted her skirt, exposing a bare slender thigh. She wrapped her legs taut around his waist. Her cold heart pumped a thousand beats, against his. His hot breath pricked against the skin of her neck, arousing her senses. She bared her teeth with gratification, then promptly reached for his crotch. His excitement was obvious. Making love to him was a game changer, and frankly, this worried Estella. Would she ever feel this good again? This was her third encounter with the stranger, and each time more intense than the last. Her razor-sharp nails slashed across his back. With bared fangs, she lustfully bit into his neck, although, he hardly made a sound. Estella enjoyed the sight of his deep red blood oozing from the fresh wound but was discouraged to indulge. The smell was musky and weird, sour almost. But what was pleasure without pain? He grunted, several times, and it was over. She held her head back in ecstasy, enthralled by the passion.

'Estella?'

The voice was familiar. Too familiar.

'Quick, he's coming.'

Her voice trembled to a whisper. She felt like a tawdry whore but enjoyed the thrill. Panic-stricken, the pair hurriedly got themselves together. Estella's blouse lay at her feet like an old piece of rag. She sheepishly snatched it from the floor, fastening it swiftly back into place. Estella looked over at him with lustful eyes. He had already dressed. Their gaze studied each other. She was satisfied, and so was he. His intense green eyes pierced through her skin. Estella froze on the spot, mesmerized by his charm. He licked his thick lips; his thirst had been quenched. He leaned into her ear. His scent was musky and raw, causing a shiver down her spine. Estella closed her eyes, ingesting the arousing aroma of his natural odour. Another flash of excitement flushed her cheeks.

'Do not look for me,' he whispered.

Estella studied his expression. Like a Greek God, his handsome face made up for his shortcomings. His masculine 6'2 frame towered over hers. She opened her mouth to protest, but he had already disappeared through the bushes. Estella made ill attempts to relax her dark curly hair back into place. Long brunette wisps hung down the sides of her face, curling at the temples of her head. Estella was stunned. He appeared to have already tossed her away like an old cast-off. She felt used and inadequate, then questioned her own self-esteem. However, despite her obvious distress, she prepared to act seemingly normal.

'Estella, what are you doing out here?' He seemed anxious, placing his arms squarely around her shoulders. Estella hung her head in shame. She struggled to obtain any decent eye contact and wished he would stop mollycoddling her at every opportunity. 'Are you ok? You look flustered.'

'Yes, I went for a walk,' She replied flatly.

'You know, you should have asked me first. There's a lunatic lurking. You cannot simply wander at will.'

'I know. And for that, I'm sorry. I needed air.'

Marc caressed her hair. He ran his fingers through its length, winding her brunette curls taut around his index finger. 'I know, it is hard for us nightwalkers to be confined like a rabbit in a box, but, until we know what we are dealing with, this has to be the way. I promise you things *will* settle down as soon as the culprit is caught.'

Marc kissed her lightly on the forehead. Estella was riddled with guilt. She would feel better if he got angry or behaved irrationally. However, he was so attentive and agreeable, he'd be mistaken for human. Marc was understandably distraught. Estella wasn't surprised. She had disappeared for several hours and was still amazed that not one of them had bothered to check the thick shrub of bushes behind the back of the mansion. She was right under their noses. Mid-tryst, she had seen the elders marching throughout the front grounds, desperately trying to find her. As usual, they dismissed the back of the courtyard. She knew they would. Orders were given by the elders to restrict access to the back of the mansion for safety reasons, including the courtyard, of which, was completely off bounds. You see, unlike the movies, vampires didn't die an ashy death, whittling away to little more than ash. There were only two ways to kill a vampire. Either pluck out the heart or chop off the head. There had been six deaths within the community that week. Every corpse found, was beheaded and ripped to pieces. It was apparent they were possibly hunting one of the deadliest creatures known to vampires. Though there were clear separation between the species, werewolves lived amongst vampires in harmony for years. It was part of the treaty rules. However, for the most part, they got on, keeping their own close boundaries, never straying beyond their own perimeters. But these deaths were not caused by werewolves. After a thorough analysis of the last unfortunate creature, Marc was stumped to discover there were no obvious werewolf markings nor residue to be found. For extra protection, Marc had called in some of the older, more seasoned vampires. The old brooding board members, also known as, The Elders. Reluctantly, they had agreed and had flown several hundred miles from the confines of Castle Dravenherd to offer extra protection to the couple. They would lodge with the lovelorn pair, at least until safety had been established. Marc was particularly fearful for Estella's wellbeing, especially as he had stumbled upon the last corpse discovered three nights ago, beheaded on their grounds. The body was identified as, Merl. A young vampire with bright red hair, and a heavily freckled face. Marc felt it to be a warning to them all. Ever since, he hardly let Estella out of sight.

TWO

Marc was a good man. He protected Estella at every opportunity, handling her as if she were a delicate muse. She wanted for nothing. However, as the years rolled by, the passion had dwindled. The twenty-year age difference became increasingly apparent. A hundred and fifty years ago, he was the love of her life. She was barely twenty, and had been captivated by this older, handsome, vampire. With his dark hair and chiselled good looks, he was a good catch. And he, was enthralled with her beauty. To be fair, he still was. At the time, Estella was barely human, enjoying her new-found immortality and the freedom it offered. Marc had introduced her to a new underworld. The vampire life.

Estella remembers her fate as though it were yesterday. Back then, the year was 1775. It was a particular-Sunday evening. The atmosphere was weirdly euphoric. Once again, Estella was sent out to the barn at her father's request. He sent her out regularly, perhaps several times a day. Estella hated her role of housemaid but had little choice in the matter. If she protested, she'd be beaten severely, as he had done once before. However, on that occasion, Estella was grateful to get away from her father. His mood temperamental, more so than usual. For the entire day, he'd been unbearable to be around. Estella decided, she would stay out at the barn longer than necessary and was relieved to have a moment's break without his overbearing presence. Back then, in the sleepy English town of Marlow, there had been widespread panic fuelled by reports of unusual deaths. A child was slaughtered. Hung and found with bite marks around the neck. Others were also killed, found with identical bites around the neck in particular. Reports of an unknown wild animal surfaced. Within weeks, the town grew paralysed by fear. Several weeks later, such accounts were quickly dismissed as two locals claimed to see a peculiar looking man with pointed teeth and wild eyes, wandering around at night. Many in the community spread the news like wildfire. However, a fair few thought it to be fictional nonsense. This done little to ease the fears of Estella's highly strung mother, who worried frantically about her wellbeing. She done everything to shield Estella away from it all. But, her father, he was a non-believer, diplomatic in approach. He presumed the locals were mad, refusing to entertain any thought of such nonsense. Life carried on as usual. Her father continued to send Estella out to the barn all hours of the day and night. The animals had to be tended to. Her father relied upon the milk and eggs to make a living.

Unfortunately for Estella, that would be the day she would never forget. The day, which changed her life forever. On that fated Sunday evening, with exception to the animals, Estella wasn't the only occupant in the barn. What transpired next, the details of which were still unclear. Or perhaps Estella chose not to remember the horror she had succumbed. It happened so quickly. She was savagely attacked by a rogue vampire who had trespassed into her father's barn. Unfortunately, the brute was never captured. At first, Estella thought it to be the kiss of death. Her body grew weak and sickly. Ghastly changes took place. She struggled to conceal her infliction from her mother, too afraid to reveal the truth. Estella often wondered why the vampire didn't just kill her and be done with it. Instead, he gave her the gift of immortality. He must have known her pain and suffering and granted her another way out. Estella wished he had cut her heart out. She was turning into a monster, and there was little she could do about it.

Exactly eighteen months after the incident, Estella's mother succumbed to poisoning. Accused of adultery, Estella's father beat her black and blue. Estella found her mother's lifeless body in bed the following morning, having suffered significant trauma. Estella's world was shattered forever. Her mother's death struck hard. Estella had only one regret. She wished she had given her mother the gift of immortality. Being an only child, Estella was as close to her mother as any daughter could be. But her mother wasn't happy. All her life she had suffered at the hands of her husband, a merciless man who wanted things done his way, and would often punish the two accordingly. Soon after her mother's death, Estella's grief pushed her to the edge. She vowed to kill her father, but unfortunately, he beat her to it. Fifteen days after the discovery of her mother's body, her father was found dead in bed. A heart attack, they said. With a sorrowful heart, Estella ran away to a neighbouring town, vowing for a fresh start. She was seventeen. Like most other young women her age, she should have been married already, but Estella wanted to pay her way and earn a living instead. But that didn't come easy. Her body was ever changing. Estella burnt in sunlight and had to find other means of earning a living.

One night, Estella stumbled across a well-dressed lady. Articulate and friendly, she told Estella what a pretty little thing she was. Your beauty is to be admired, she said. And then, the introduction began. Estella was acquainted with a different kind of life. She worked at night, for the gentlemen. Soon enough, Estella became friendly with a local girl. It wasn't long before the pair became firm friends. Her name was Anna. Tall, blonde, and good-figured. The men flocked to Anna in droves. Between the two, the girls earned a good living. They housed together in a three-bedroom home with an older woman, living amongst the rich. Tailored dresses and hearty meals became a way of life. However, Estella never ate a morsel. She was violently sick every time she tried. Her stomach would refuse it. Raw meat sparked her hunger; a bizarre craving she hid from Anna. It became a regular occurrence for Estella to excuse herself from the dinner table, citing reasons to eat alone in her room. Food would be hidden under the bed until discreetly disposed of. With the exception of this problem, life carried on seamlessly. However, unbeknown to Estella, Anna grew suspicious. Estella seldom left the house before nightfall, blaming sun sensitivity and a rare skin condition. However, Anna was weary. A year later, gossip spread. Estella was thought to be a witch. She was confronted by Anna who scrutinized her eating habits, demanding she be supervised at every meal in order to prove she wasn't a witch. Estella was stunned; Anna had changed. She became cruel, with an insidious streak, and would manipulate Mary to taunt Estella at every given opportunity. Weeks later, the town issued a summons for Estella's hanging. Anna's betrayal cut deep. Days before her trial, Estella done the unthinkable. She still recalls Mary's screams echoing through the house. Anna's mutilated body was found outside the front door. Every limb missing from the corpse. Somehow, Estella managed to escape all accountability. Fortunately for her, the blame was placed squarely upon the young man with whom Anna was courting. His name was Tom. Burdened with guilt, Estella ran away to a neighbouring town. She learnt to live discreetly in the shadows, hunting only at night. She slept rough. Sometimes in bushes, at other times, in old derelict buildings, or underneath horse carts. Soon enough she learnt to adapt and became somewhat comfortable with her way of life. She knew her body was sick. *Something* was gravely wrong. Little did she know, the monster she had become.

It was 1803 when Estella met Marc. Handsome, magnetic, with a shimmer of mystery in his eyes, Estella was instantly drawn to him. Together, they became inseparable. It was then Estella learned of her infliction. She was a vampire. Blood suckers, who roamed at night and were intolerant to light. During the days they slept and would rise at the stroke of ten. Marc said, destiny that had brought them together. It wasn't long until Marc and Estella formed a close companionship. Sixty-two days into their courtship, Estella left the town behind. On Marc's insistence, she returned to his residence as his wife. Despite this, Estella was resistant to Marc's pleading of intimacy. She would refuse his advances and often tensed when touched. Estella blamed it on her childhood. Traumatised by relations between her parents, she had witnessed her mother's rape several times, followed by vicious beatings. However, eighteen months after the day she moved into Marc's great big house, Estella allowed herself to be loved. The first time they were intimate, it was electric. She remembers as though it were yesterday. Marc's ravishing blue eyes made her weak at the knees. He was so tender. Their love making, was fire. They couldn't keep their hands off each other and would be at it several times a night. His thick dark hair defied his age, perceived to be a lot younger than the three hundred years he had walked the earth. But Estella was no longer in love with Marc. As the centuries rolled by, unfortunately, so did her craving for him. Estella craved her own freedom. She wanted the spark back. Many times, Estella would conjure the courage to tell him how she really felt but was too much of a coward to carry it out. Ever since becoming a vampire, Estella's undead existence was one of gluttony and luxury, evidently, she had a lot at stake. Truth be known, Estella felt like a traitor, but decided it best she kept quiet for both their sakes. Many a times she came so close to revealing the truth but would back away for fear of being thrown out of the treaty with nowhere to go. She also felt a sense of obligation to the man who had taken her in all those years ago. He had her soul. He made her a woman. Unfortunately, lately, intimacy had become strained. At least on her part. Estella grimaced at his touch. Their relationship was monotonous, although Marc preferred to pretend otherwise. Estella learnt to play the dutiful wife. She mastered magnificent displays of satisfaction and admiration, although had little real interest. Unbeknown to her, Marc had noticed her disinterest; but he wasn't a talker and observed more than he spoke. His love for Estella had consumed him, so much so, he done little to rock the boat. Estella often questioned her loyalty. Why couldn't she just love him? Marc done all the right things. He was a good man. She knew he deserved better and hated herself for being so weak.

More recently, Estella had another secret. One she would keep for an eternity. Ever since her first encounter with the handsome stranger, there was a change within. Initially she questioned her own sanity. It was subtle at first. Then, things became really obvious. For example, she craved sleep at night, then began waking at dawn. Lately, her stomach felt as though it may explode. The pain was unbearable. Ten days ago, Estella's condition took a turn for the worst. She couldn't keep her eyes open past midnight. And then, there was the sun. Three days ago, she woke in terrible agony. It was daylight. She had wondered out to the landing, and then, she blacked out. She woke with her head struck half-way out through the shattered landing window, feet dangling like a corpse. It was the middle of noon. The sky was as blue as the sea. The sun was out, birds sung in sync. Panic stricken Estella had reasonably expected to burn to a crispy ash. However, she was unscathed. This should have been impossible, yet, she had no plausible explanation for the unusual phenomenon on that peculiar Thursday afternoon. That night, Estella's mind was unrest. She knew something was seriously wrong. Discovering she was suddenly immune to daylight made no sense. Not to arouse suspicion, Estella kept quiet. Then, there was something else. Her bizarre desire for meat. Recently, she would stroll past the blood machine several times a day but had little interest in it. Instead, Estella yearned for thick fresh slabs of raw flesh. Her thirst to kill became intense. There were other signs. Like her eyes. They had been steadily changing colour, much greener than before, and definitely noticeable. Paranoia crept in. Estella found ways of having less and less eye contact with Marc. Lastly, the pains in her stomach felt like a truck was crashing into her abdomen headfirst. Not to mention the ghastly hairiness she was experiencing. Estella done her best to conceal it, but it was challenging and became more difficult with each passing day. She couldn't be certain if Marc had noticed any of it. However, she knew that sooner or later, he *would* find out.

Marc walked Estella back inside. He made sure to firmly bolt the back doors with reinforced slabs of timber as though preparing for a storm. The elders were sat in the grand foyer cross legged on tall back chairs, drinking blood from large, frosted glasses. Edgar, one of the elders, greeted her with a nod.

'Good day, Estella.'

Estella managed to muster a stiff smile. Marc took hold off her hand. He examined her delicate slender face, then leant in to sniff her cheek. Estella froze. She reeked of *him* and prayed Marc wouldn't smell his odour lingering over her like a bad scent. Fearing he would sense her nervousness, Estella made swift excuses to retire for the evening.

'I'm tired. I need to rest.'

'Have you bathed?'

Marc's tone was concerned. Estella stiffened her stance. She could've died of embarrassment. Her personal hygiene had always been immaculate, and Marc's sensitive inquisition made her feel like some dirty sordid animal.

'Yes, of course. Why do you ask?'

'Sorry, just my delicate nose. You smell a little musky, that's all. Perhaps my scent isn't what it used to be.'

Marc kissed her lightly on the forehead. He proceeded to usher her up the large twirling staircase with his right hand. Estella didn't tally. She ran for the stairs, eager to get away from prying eyes. She feared it wouldn't be long before her life would soon be in danger. Once upstairs, she darted to the bathroom, locking the door firmly behind her. Panic suddenly set in. She was breathless. Her veiny hands shook like a leaf. Perhaps it was the changing, or perhaps it was just her guilty conscious. Whatever it was, it was a symptom of her promiscuity and had only gotten worse over the coming days. Dropping the contaminated clothing to the floor, Estella stripped bare. The wide oval mirror glared back at her. Designed fit for the undead, this was no ordinary mirror, allowing her to inspect her pitiful reflection. Engraved in solid yellow gold, centuries old, with a long, jagged line across the middle. She stood motionless. Her strained face looked back at her. Her carefree demeanour had changed, replaced by a silent solemn mood, and lack of compassion. The only thing she desired, was him. He, who had marked her. He, who had turned her life upside down. So obsessed had she become, Estella couldn't imagine her existence if he were no longer a part of it. Like a drug, she was addicted. He seemed to have a hold over her, one in which she couldn't comprehend. Estella turned to her deathly white reflection. Whilst scrutinising her slender back, another daily habit which had become more ritual than casual, Estella was met with the horror of tufts of fuzzy brown hair which sprouted from the middle of her spine as if she were an exotic wild animal of sort. With swift precision, Estella aptly removed the offence with one quick tug. Seconds in, she had peered down at her shaky palms to examine the offence. There it was, at least an inch long, brittle and coarse, and appearing to have belonged to a werewolf. Estella couldn't be sure if this some sort of new-age puberty, or perhaps some terrible infliction she had come on upon. Whatever it was, Estella hated this recent discovery, and hoped if she ignored it long enough, it may go away never to return. However, the absolute worse was concealing it all from Marc, whilst trying to maintain a modicum of sanity. Estella disposed of the offence, attempting to soothe the anxiety erupting within her chest. Feeling eerily strange, she scrutinized her eyeballs, a ritual she had taken to every day for the past week. There was a recent development, so bizarre, Estella didn't know what to make of it. Her hazel eyes were suddenly speckled like an emerald, steadily becoming greener with each passing day. Estella knew it wouldn't be long before her eyes were the colour of a meadow, at which point, she would have some explaining to do. Despite it all, Estella had no desire for a pity party. She had broken treaty law. Dire consequences were in place for vampires fornicating with werewolves. But there was another issue. Xavier wasn't merely a werewolf. He was a hybrid. Half werewolf, half monster; so, he said. No matter how she pried, Xavier was coy of his identity. Thinking it to be a joke, Estella dismissed his claims. Suddenly, she wished she hadn't. She had been far too distracted with his manly charms to give a shit about his genetic makeup. But now, once the fun had ceased, Estella's intuition knew something wasn't right. Curiosity had turned to fear. Furthermore, Estella suspected Xavier may have a part to play in the recent murders. Suddenly, there was a knock to the door.

'Estella, are you ok?' Marc's voice echoed from the other side of the door. Estella rolled her eyes. She had grown intolerant to his constant petting.

'Yes, I am fine.' She snapped back.

'You've been in there an hour.' He declared.

Estella said nothing. She wished to be left alone. After a moment of shuffling, she heard his footsteps walk away. Feeling relieved, Estella ran a bath, then sunk herself deep inside the tub. The ice-cold water felt amazing. With her head leaned against the sturdy acrylic bath. Estella closed her eyes to the sound of the sea. Her thoughts turned to Xavier as though he were a record on repeat. Her breaths grew heavy as she reminisced his touch. The feeling was so intense, she could almost feel him all over again. Waves of pleasure evoked through her slender body. Although Estella knew little of the handsome stranger, her appetite for his touch was insatiable. Suddenly, the footsteps returned. They paced back and forth outside the door, impatiently awaiting her departure. Not wanting to cause a scene, Estella dragged her soaking wet body out of the tub, quickly fastening the royal blue towel on the door around it. She dilly dallied longer than necessary, and by the time she pulled the door open, Marc had already gone.

The walk to the master bedroom was a long one. The corridor spanned twenty feet, bypassing several rooms on either side. As she approached the landing, the elders could be heard in the galley, ruminating in fits of laughter. Their gruff voices echoed up the hall like a burning candle. They would stay up until dawn, eventually retreating for rest in quaint wooden boxes which they would bury themselves into. Speaking of which, those coffins were some of the most prestigious Estella had ever seen. Centuries old, built from the finest craftsmanship, only the wealthiest vampires could afford such luxury. With their solid mahogany finish, they were certainly built to last. Their vampire rhythm had become a source of envy. No matter how hard she tried, Estella's body danced to a different beat. Feeling like an outcast, Estella begun to crave sleep at conventional hours. Marc was suspicious, as were the elders. Convinced Estella to be gravely ill, Marc had ushered in specialists for the undead. Each visit was futile as Estella refused to be seen.

The bedroom door was ajar. Estella crept in with a shiver. The chill in the air circled her shoulders. Vampires loved the cold. But it was almost freezing. Marc's dark figure stood over at the window, his back turned in ponder. His shadow reflecting by the light of the night sky. He had done this all week. Stood deep in thought, his eyes alert and wandering. Killing a werewolf was not particularly difficult, but these deaths were strangely unfamiliar. No claw markings left behind, nor were there any obvious bite wounds. The victims appeared to die from strangulation, although, this was merely speculation. One thing was for certain; these deaths were not the works of vampires, and there were doubts the blame should be cast at the werewolf's feet. Nevertheless, without sufficient evidence, the four-legged species were the likeliest suspect.

'Hello, Marc.'

Marc ignored her presence. He just stood there, silent and strong. Evidently, he had a lot on his mind, mostly thoughts of Estella. He wanted to protect her but feared he had already failed. Marc knew she no longer craved his touch. And, truth be known, this bothered him. Despite his woes, Marc was unconfrontational. He preferred to ponder, rather than have an honest discussion. That being said, Estella she was under no illusion. As much as he loved her, if Marc found out about her tryst with Xavier, she would become the hunted, and him, the hunter. Fearing it was only a matter of time until he learnt of her deceit, Estella had a hard decision to make. You see, Marc was a proud vampire. The spoke of the werewolves as though they were little more than ravaged dogs. He thought they were beneath him, as most vampires did. Deceit with one of their kind, would be the worst kind of betrayal. Estella would be discarded to the streets like a bag of old rubbish, or worse, she would be killed. As her guilt swallowed her up, menacing thoughts plagued her mind. Estella walked over to the dark mahogany wardrobe, then pulled out a shimmery black dress. She delicately slipped her freshly washed body inside of it, then headed over to the incredibly large bed with its surrounding columns stood at every corner. Evening had set in. Like the disease consuming it, her body grew tired, fast. Her vampire DNA was steadily becoming host to something uncanny, of which, Estella had no idea what that could be. Whatever that case may be, she felt she was 'marked', and no good could come off it. As her head spun with deliberating thoughts on what her next plans should be Estella closed her eyes, allowing herself to doze off.

'Sleeping?' Marc's voice was tainted with suspicion. He peered over his shoulder as her head hit the pillow.

'I must rest.' She mumbled; face buried within her soft Egyptian cotton pillow-case.

'You're a vampire for goodness sakes. I fear you have contracted a deadly plague of some sort. Similar to the one that killed several vampires back in the 1600's. Please agree to bloodwork. You have slept at 10pm every night, for a fortnight,' he said.

'I assure you I am fine. Just tired.' she lied, forcing herself to converse, wishing he would stop fawning over her as though she were a helpless child.

'Estella, I know you better than you know yourself. I will arrange for you to get a blood test from the board. This, is bizarre.'

Estella felt irritated. She scowled. 'Marc, I am absolutely fine, and I certainly do not need a blood test. I think it's all that synthetic stuff. My body is rejecting it. I need a real meal.'

Marc stood over the bed with worry in his eyes. He peered down at her as the lines between his brows intensified. Estella knew he was worried sick. However, the more he worried, the more he aroused her own fears. Soon enough his worries would grow to suspicion. They had practically lived off manufactured blood for the last fifty years, with little to no trouble. Estella's sudden new development was the subject for discussion most nights with the elders. Often, the three vampires could be heard downstairs deep in intense debate, reasoning all the possible explanations for her new affliction.

'Ok. I will discuss this with Edgar. Perhaps that retched machine needs a new filter.'

Marc's voice was shaky. His tone, unsure. His love for Estella was as strong as the day he had laid eyes on her. His biggest worry was mustering the strength to go on if he lost her. Although Marc spent most of his nights with the elders down in the galley, since Estella's mysterious illness, seldom had he left her side. Night after night, he stood by the window watching her sleep, steadily becoming a torn man.

There was rustling at the window. It was daybreak. Like a mechanical grandfather clock, Estella woke on the hour. She grabbed the dark cotton blanket, pulling it taut over her head. She turned to her right. Like a cocoon, Marc was well wrapped within the deep layers of the blanket. It was a sour myth that vampires slept in coffins. Estella had never spent a night in one. Not once, in two hundred years. She tried it briefly, and quickly felt suffocated, refusing to ever do it again. Marc couldn't convince her otherwise, so he made the painful decision to refrain from sleeping in one himself. Although on occasion, he would succumb to his tradition, usually once every other month. He had a special one. Handcrafted with the finest wood, polished to a deep rich mahogany. Estella had one, too. Hers white, patterned with real gold. Like a prized possession, it was barely touched. Kept in the cellar, the two were neatly positioned side by side, gathering dust with each passing year. The tapping at the window continued. Estella sat up bushy tailed and wide eyed. No matter how she tried, she struggled to sleep as the sun had risen. Like a tortured soul, she felt trapped within the confines of her own home. The tapping at the window grew louder. Two, three, four, until she was forced to leave the bed. With a heaving sigh, Estella glided towards the wide bay windows, feet barely touching the floor. She shifted the dark heavy curtain an inch apart, peering out onto the back quarters of the mansion. The high shrubs and thorny trees disguised a lot. Like an intruder of the mind, flashbacks of her sordid tryst played blackjack with her conscience. The guilt was agonising. The back of the mansion was the perfect hiding place for any trespasser, vampire, werewolf, or the like. To her dismay the grounds were empty. With the exception off a murder of crows which littered the yard, mostly high up on the willow trees, there wasn't a soul to be seen. Secretly, Estella had hoped that Xavier had come back for her. It was unlikely, but she was addicted and craved him as she craved flesh. She hoped he had a change of heart, perhaps realising just how great she really was. After all, she had risked everything for him. Feeling flattened, Estella drew the curtains then returned to bed.

THREE

Daybreak set in. As usual, Estella was alone with her thoughts whilst the vampires slept. Despite the blackened windows, the early morning sun was forcing its way through. Nostalgia returned. However, Estella knew things would never be the same again. As she turned to observe Marc on the bed, something she found herself doing rather a lot, lately, Estella was stunned to find herself alone. In a state of flustered panic, Estella gasped at the empty spot where Marc should have been. She knelt and peered underneath the bed, expecting he had found a better place to sleep, but was met by still blackness. A sudden chill ran down her spine as her mind played overtime. Convinced that Marc had discovered her betrayal and had left her for good; Estella ran out of the bedroom in frantic hurry, sprinting down the hallway. Truth be known, she didn't want to lose him despite her deceit. As Estella flung open the doors for all six rooms along the first floor of the house, each time becoming more worried than the last, the reality that her husband may have left her, set in.

'Marc?'

Estella's voice echoed as she levitated down the twirling staircase at lightning speed. On approach to the maid's quarters, she noticed the Elders. As always, their coffins were firmly jammed shut. Estella peered in the kitchen with hopes to find her absent husband. Even his familiar woody scent had disappeared. As usual, the kitchen was cold and clinical. Rows of blood-stained glass beakers stood upon the oblong oak table evident the elders had a feast the night before. Estella sobbed with anguish. She gripped one of the chairs to steady herself. This was all her fault. Marc had worked it all out and gone. Or worse, he was somewhere preparing her death. As Estella's mind became seeped with dark thoughts, her frustrations grew. In a state of hysteria, she banged hard on the table with her fists, to which some of the beakers went flying. Her life was a mess. She wasn't a vampire. She was a monster. A monster who had driven her husband away. In angst, Estella picked up one of the remaining glass beakers and smashed it to the marbled floor. It was weirdly therapeutic as the shatter of glass soothed her anxiety. She picked up another and hurled it on the floor. It shattered violently, smashing to a thousand pieces. Her breaths quickened. She was enjoying it. It was an odd release and aroused a familiar satisfaction to her tryst with Xavier. As she flung the remaining glasses towards the kitchen walls, the adrenaline pumping through her veins was at bursting point. It wasn't long before the marbled floor was covered in equal amounts of glass and blood, which dressed the floor like a creative portrait. Estella was stopped in her tracks as the knocks to the door came quick and fast. Suddenly, the kitchen door flung open. Marc stormed in with rampant rage. With bloodshot eyes, his face twisted with red hot fury. He bared his bite, then lunged towards her with arms outstretched. Like a frightened rabbit in a hamster cage, Estella backed away. Her hands trembled like a leaf as she prepared to meet her demise. She knew, she deserved this. With nails like claws, Marc showcased his talons. His breath was sickly sweet as he reached for her throat. Estella gasped, legs dangling inches off the floor. Suddenly, she was thrown against the wall as though she weighed little more than a bag of sugar. And then, it was still.

Estella jumped out of bed. Her cold hands trembled like a leaf. Her dishevelled brunette manes wispy strands stuck to her forehead like butter to a hot pan. Shockingly, there was an offending patch left behind on the bed. Estella grimaced as she ran her hand over the cold, wet spot. It was sooty blackened liquid, unfamiliar to anything she had experienced before. Estella grew worried. It was nonsensical. Vampires didn't perspire. This was only vaguely more puzzling than the roaring pain piercing through her head. The thought she might be 'reverting' back to a mortal being, had plagued her mind more times than she cared to admit. Estella peeped over at the other side of the bed. And there he was. Marc's cocooned body was still snugly wrapped inside like an enslaved caterpillar. It had all been nothing more than an awful dream. In fact, it was a complete nightmare. Estella was convinced this was nothing other than a pre-empt vision of what was to come. Like a slow torturous death, she was losing her grip on reality. For every day she spent at Heath Hall, a part of herself was slowly dissipating. She *had* to get out of here. Like a thief in the night, Estella quietly crept out of bed with intentions to escape. Feet barely on the floor, she slid over to the old mahogany-polished vanity with the long rectangular mirror. Hands sprawled crazily until she found it. And there it was. Her centuries old pocket watch, buried amongst different bottles of perfumes and potions, as well as a plethora of blood red lipsticks. It was six in the morning. The sun had already risen. Estella's body no longer ticked to the vampire rhythm. For the past week, she would wake around the same time, and potter about the mansion like a carefree housewife. Marc was none the wiser. Nor were the elders.

Estella flung open the creaky wardrobe door. Piles of black and red garments stood in neat orderly rows like an upmarket boutique store. Estella had a dislike for almost every other colour. Scurrying about in a frantic frenzy, Estella grabbed the weathered brown leather bag sat at the bottom of the wardrobe, then stuffed as many pieces of clothing as she could into it. She glanced over her shoulder. Marc was still buried deep inside the thick duvet. He'd be cocooned in there till night, allowing her plenty of time to carry out her plan. Once she had finished, Estella chucked several bottles of unnecessary 'stuff' at the top of the bag, before finally zipping it taut. She threw the black gown to the floor, then prised herself into a pair of slender black trousers teamed with a sheer red blouse. Estella gasped. She grimaced at the tufts of downy brown hair which had seemingly sprouted upon the tops of her shoulders overnight. Convinced she was becoming a wild dog on a full moon, the hair increased in small amounts every other day. Devastation set in. Estella ejected her nails, pulling the offensive with one swift tug, as she routinely did. Convinced she really *was* turning into some sort of creature, her mind raced, eager to escape. Estella grabbed Marc's old, tinted sunglasses from the dark wooden cabinet, then slipped them frantically over her face. "I stole them from a dead man", he had said, proudly displaying the tinted eyewear neither of them was accustomed to. Without hesitance, Estella left the home she shared for two hundred years, the safe place that was once her refuge.

Outside, the air was calm and tranquil whilst trees cast eerie shadows on the ground. Ignoring the unsettling lump welling in her throat, Estella turned to Heath Hall to bid her farewell. The mansion spread across several acres, looking more like a palace than a comfortable family home. Nevertheless, she had spent many comfortable years there and would likely never see it again. Her tearful eyes cast over its bare extravagance. Though in need of a lick of paint, the large black and white house still oozed buckets of presence and appeal. Self-pity was pushed to the back of her mind, accepting this was all her doing. Estella teleported to a mist through the hedgy path, towards the front entrance. Resisting the urge to look back, she sprung through the air, travelling as fast as she could. Spanning acres of greenery, Estella flew ten miles with no real destination to hand.

Her mind was busy, plagued with the reality of her own immortality, and the decades of undead existence she had left to endure in this prison of a body. The poison running through her veins was steadily becoming stronger, and her hunger, unbearable. Without the comfy convenience of Edgar's blood machine, she would soon crave human blood. This, Estella feared the most.

It wasn't long before Estella arrived at a quiet rural road, neat quaint houses scattered around. She lowered herself to the ground, straightening her blouse on landing. Suddenly, she was gasping for breath like a human with a twenty a day smoking habit. A small white car crept towards Estella on the other side of the road, and there in it sat a woman with a face like thunder in the passenger seat. Humans. Estella smelt them a mile away. With dead eyes, the woman looked out with a fixed expression. She was doused in fear and hopelessness, disparity, and loneliness. Her aura was so black, Estella felt fraught. In fact, the stranger's entire life flashed before Estella's eyes like a well-read book. The woman was living within an abusive relationship. Several times she had tried to leave the marriage but was threatened on each attempt. Fear kept her rooted to a man she loathed. Suddenly, the car picked up speed, accelerating faster than before, wheels screeching madly on the tarmac ground. Within seconds it had gone. With wild eyes and nothing more, Estella stood patiently on the side of the road, hoping some poor soul would take pity on such a lonely figure of a woman. With a rampant mind and limited options, Estella ruminated on her very existence, pondering why on earth she had thrown everything away for a short bout of excitement. After many years of reckless titillation, living a life she could have never hoped for, she was now at war with her conscience, standing on the corner of a derelict road in the middle of the day like a hitchhiker without a plan. Although the sun was hidden behind a cloud, the temperature was far warmer than one would she expect for the autumn season, and far too balmy for a vampire. Suddenly her thoughts were interrupted by a shadowy flicker at the corner of her eye. A sleek black car pulled up. Shiny wheels and much more sizable than the little white car gone by, this car had an air of authority to it. Estella was surprised when it came to an abrupt stop. A dark-haired man with a rounded pleasant face, greeted her at the window.

'Hey, hop in.'

Estella starred at the human in awe. Once again, that little vampire trick went to work. His entire life flashed before her eyes. She already knew he had two legitimate children. A boy and a girl, whom of which, was the splitting image of her deceased mother. The man was widowed a while. Sadly, he would be dead at the tender age of fifty-seven, having succumbed to a stroke. Estella smiled sweetly, hoping her pouting red lips would do the trick. Of course, he knew no better. He thought she was human. Estella tugged at the car door, then promptly got in. For a while they drove along in sweet silence. Driving through hedgy paths and narrow lanes, Estella closed her eyes as she enjoyed the ride, a welcomed distraction from the current situation she was trying to shove to the back of her mind. Never had she driven in a car before and was grateful for the stranger's discretion. She certainly wasn't in the mood for small talk. And then he spoke.

'So, where exactly is a lovely young lady like yourself going?'

Estella shuffled uncomfortably in the seat. That could've been the worst question possible, as she had absolutely no idea where she was going. The man glanced at her, not impressed by her silence. Estella twirled a chunk of her dark hair around her index finger, while softly chewing on her bottom lip, pondering whether to tear him apart, but quicky deciding not to.

'You do not strike me as shy' he probed.

'Shy? I'm not.'

'It's ok, I can drop you in town if that is good for you.' The driver sensed Estella wasn't in the mood for small talk. Estella turned to the human.

'Why did you pick me up?' she asked.

The man frowned. He seemed slightly perplexed by the question. 'Why? well It wouldn't be courteous to drive past a beautiful woman in need of a ride, would it? There are bad people around here, lady. Have you not heard? There are recent reports of strange wild animals ripping people to shreds. Wolfdogs, they say.'

'Oh, really?'

The man was intrigued by her cool exterior. 'You seem…aloof. Are you angry? Is it…a man? If I had a woman like you…'

'Why would a man anger me? I am fine, thank you.' She interjected.

'Ok lady. I didn't mean to upset you. Just trying to make small talk,' he said.

Thankfully for Estella that was the last word he uttered. Her mind was focused on Marc and had little room for anything else. Thirty-three minutes ago she had walked out on her husband. The centuries they shared, suddenly seemed meaningless. The lump in her throat welled up as she fought back cold as ice tears. She had no idea where she was headed but knew her life would never be the same again. Undoubtedly, Marc would call out a search party. Within the small vampire community, she couldn't be too hard to find. It wouldn't be long before she was hunted. Probably a few weeks at most. It would take that long, at least. But of course, there was the possibility she could be almost unrecognisable by then. Her body was destroying itself from the inside out, making her an abomination of the worst kind. There was something sinisterly wrong, and Estella, had little power to stop it. The car suddenly came to a screeching halt. Estella turned to the burly man sitting in the driver's seat. He wore a thick grey jumper with an odd blue tie, tightened so taut, it appeared to be choking him.

'I can't go any further than here,' he said.

Estella looked at him with empathy. His blood was sour. He was a heavy smoker, or sick. One or the other. Estella sensed the man's obvious discomfort. He cleared his throat loudly, perhaps hinting for her to leave the vehicle. After an awkward silence, Estella stepped out of the vehicle.

'Thank you.'

Without a moment's hesitation, the car sped off with the passenger door still ajar, almost knocking her over. He couldn't get away fast enough. Estella rolled her eyes. Perhaps she had freaked him out a little. Although, that wasn't her intention. Maybe her reluctance to converse had ruffled his feathers. Unfortunately, vampires weren't good conversationalists. She hadn't failed to notice his jovial manner had turned serious. Estella realised she had to perfect her humanness with a little more finesse. At this rate, she couldn't convince a fool.

Estella studied the sleepy town. Crowds of humans walked around aimlessly, like sheep in a herd. Always in a hurry, with nowhere to go. Estella lifted her chin, narrowing her eyes. There were an eatery and several shops along one side of the road. On the other side, was a gas station, and a bunch of tall buildings. She looked around in wonder. Never had she seen so many humans. The sun now shone brightly upon the small dusty town. Estella reached for the special jagged edged pocket mirror in her brown bag. Her porcelain-white hands trembled as she held it face level. No ordinary mirror, it made the impossible, possible. Her face was pale, exceptionally so. Even for a vampire. Her deep-set green, emerald eyes were rather startling. Her face had become gaunt, anxiety and uncertainty etched all over it. Estella barely recognised herself. Her hazel eyes and neatly arched brows were a distant memory. And then, that familiar pain kicked in. Gruelling and intense, Estella gripped her stomach, doubling over in agony. Vampires didn't feel pain, but this, was like nothing she had experienced before. Like a hot skewer poking its way around her ribs, her abdomen was tender to touch. In fact, since becoming immortal, pain had been little more than a distant memory. Estella shuffled about like a penguin, hobbling from one foot, to the other.

Sinister thoughts danced about in her head. Her rock-hard stomach protruded. Estella was almost certain she had vividly felt movement. Was there a monster eating at her insides? If she hadn't known better, she would be forgiven for thinking this was some bizarre supernatural pregnancy. Everyone knew vampires couldn't reproduce. The only snag was that Xavier wasn't a vampire. Forever coy about his linage, he had always said very little. Their causal dalliances were never followed up with small talk. Before she had managed to button her blouse, he would disappear as fast as he came. His mother was a werewolf, he would proudly proclaim. But little was said about his father. Whenever talk of his father was mentioned, Xavier became tense and defensive. The best he could muster was.

'My father is something other' behaving as though it were a dirty secret, leaving Estella's mind to come to its own conclusion. To be honest, it plagued her mind often. Trying to guess the other half of Xavier's genetic makeup, had become something of a pass time. The werewolf's greatest talent was their extraordinary ability to shape shift with grand superiority. Xavier's case in point. How on earth could such a handsome specimen of a man turn into nothing more than a rabid dog within milliseconds, was bizarre in itself. Estella was fearful. She knew he was hiding something, and now, she had become inflicted. Ever since their last encounter, Xavier had become increasingly hard to track down. She could no longer smell him, nor could she sense him. His whereabouts was one of wonder. Estella felt a fool. Used and tossed to the side. Fornicating with a werewolf who clearly had little real interest, in her. And now, she paid the price.

Estella gently pushed open the weathered glass door. The smell of cheap sausages and greasy eggs made her gag, akin worse than death. How on earth could they eat such rubbish, she thought. Unfortunately, this was no time to be disproving of the human palate, as Estella desperately needed a seat. Never had she felt so un-vampire like. Her legs had almost buckled. She had lost all control of her limbs. There were a few discreet gasps as she entered the café. Estella eyed the curious humans. Blissfully eating their poison, living their pitiful existence, completely unaware there was a bigger battle going on. And they, were bait.

'Miss, are you ok? You look a little pale.'

Estella looked at the balding, overweight man. She admired his kind gesture. He wore a greasy apron and looked rather unkempt. With chubby fingers, he swiftly pulled out a chair. Estella eyed him beneath her glasses. He seemed genuinely concerned. Who said vampires had no heart? She was touched. Obviously, the presumption she looked dreadful was an obvious one, why else would he be so concerned. Still, the balding man smiled sweetly without judgement.

'Cup of tea, Miss?'

'No thank you. I prefer something a bit more…full bodied.' she snorted back.

The man walked away. He smeared his greasy chubby fingers along the dirty stained apron. Estella closed her eyes to the buzzing of human clutter and chatter. She heard their veins pulsing loudly in their necks. The sound of blood oozing around their bodies was an odd kind of comfort. Feeling aroused, her teeth began to poke its way beneath her top lip. Her hands grew shaky with a soaring appetite. Just as she felt she was losing control of herself, threatening to pounce on the nearest human, the café door suddenly flung open. An injured woman fell to the floor.

'Quick, get help.'

The unidentified woman was unconscious, covered in blood. The young girl sat over to the corner eating a breaded roll became hysterical. Her scream echoed around the café like an annoying banshee. Like a discarded piece of meat, the woman's lifeless body lay motionless. There were distinctive slashes across the chest. She was killed by werewolves. Vampires were too dignified and graceful to kill a human in broad daylight. Killing humans was no longer the rage it used to be. In this day of civilization, most vampires lived off synthetic blood, and for the most part, enjoyed it. Few gave in to their natural urges. Vamp children would sometime kill for fun. But this, was not the work of a vampire. The greasy fingered man in the apron, became frantic. Two men got up, attempting to revive the dead woman on the floor. Seeing so much blood oozing from her wounds, made Estella giddy. Since Marc's introduction to the blood machines, human blood had been off the menu. However, the recent spike in her appetite for human blood, made her uncomfortable. She found herself gazing at the bloodied shirt clenched to the woman's lifeless body, wishing to indulge. Usually too dignified and regal, it would have been a no go. But now, something had taken over. The struggle to control her natural desire became uncontrollable. Estella's hands trembled like a leaf, fearing she may attack. She *had* to get out of there. The thin woman behind the counter yelled.

'Call the police.'

Back outside the café, quite a crowd had gathered. An anxious woman in a plaid jacket and brightly-coloured trousers bawled loudly. Her face pallor and distressed. She stood beside a middle-aged man in a green jumper. He had a thick grey moustache and placed a comforting arm around her shoulders.

'Patrick, who could've done this? Susan wouldn't hurt a fly.'

'I don't know, Maud. Hopefully, they will find the culprit.'

Maud buried her head into Patrick's chest. Estella took pity. Little did they know the dangers that lurked. Soon, there would be a bloodbath. She could sense it coming. Like a moth to a flame, Estella was drawn to despair and destruction. Feeling disgusted with thoughts of mutilating Susan's already maimed body, Estella made attempts to sneak past the gathering mass of people. She wanted to gag. Her stomach churned. She felt ashamed. She was becoming a killing machine, housing a desire she had never had before. Estella sheepishly walked away from the café. Her brown holdall tightly gripped in hand. One human death made little difference to her. A hundred years ago, it was commonplace. Humans lived in fear and were savagely hunted. And still were to some extent. Now, with the inclusion of the treaty, vampires had to choose their sides carefully. Plus, whose side was she on now, anyway? She couldn't be sure. Like a rebellious schoolgirl, here she was like a rouge outsider who had ran away from the safe confines of her own community. Would the werewolves want her alliance? Was she now one of them? the questions were endless, none of which Estella could answer. Her only certainty was the thing that grew within.

FOUR

Disgruntled and despairing, Estella caught sight of the bright red building opposite the café. A motel, offering bed and breakfast. With a slither of promise, and not much hope, Estella paced towards it. She strolled up to the entrance, looking up at the badly designed architecture. At least a hundred years old, however it weathered far worse than Heath Hall, which had been around for several centuries. The dated blandness was in need of fresh paintwork. A young man with a brown suede trilby walked out through the doors. He was smartly dressed, with a cigar in hand. He looked over at Estella, then startled. He was a werewolf, and possibly the same one responsible for the gruesome scene back at the café. Estella was surprised when the man suddenly became flustered. He knelt before her as though she were a vampiric aristocratic figure.

'Oh, good grief. Please don't kill me.'

He removed the hat from his head, placing it on the gravelled ground by his side. Estella was stunned. Reeking with embarrassment, she eyed him suspiciously. Unsure of what to say, she looked around for prying eyes, hoping he had not brought unnecessary attention to her.

'What the hell are you doing?'

The man seemed mortified with Estella's question. He became flustered even more so than he had already been. 'Err…I've never seen your kind before. Not in real life. They speak of you as though you are only folklore, usually to frighten naughty wolves before bed.' He stammered nervously, like a pubescent school-boy caught cheating an exam. The werewolf became rigid. He put his hat back on. 'We thought they were lying. You're not folklore at all…'

Estella was mortified. Honestly, she didn't know what to think and wouldn't allow herself to give in to the creeping paranoia which was steadily plaguing her mind.

'Have you wolves lead such sheltered existence that you've never seen a vampire? You ought to get out more.' She snapped.

The werewolf seemed confused by Estella's statement. 'A vampire? But you're not…' His voice trailed off before he could finish his sentence. His nose wrinkled with confusion as he ran his hand through his hair trying to work out what had been said. Eyes wide, he shook his head.

Shock rippled through Estella's body. She was wrong. He wasn't some weird, sheltered werewolf with a hapless delusion. No. Of course he had seen vampires and fought many. That was seen as clear as day. The problem was, he thought *she* was something else. An eerie blackness took over. Waves of anxiety rippled through her body. If she wasn't turning into a ravished wolf, what the hell was happening to her? With legs like jelly, Estella scurried away from the man, wishing the conversation had never happened. As she approached the motel door, she glanced back over her shoulder. His face was puzzled, his eyes wondering.

The motel hallway was dark and dingy. Its bland dated interior was reminiscent of her childhood home. After a short walk, Estella arrived at a dimly lit reception area which lingered with the stench of stale cigar. She eyed the dated large red polyester sofa over to the left of the room, in which sat a dark-haired woman with a young child on her lap. They were engrossed, attempting a crossword puzzle of some sort. They were so distracted, they hadn't noticed Estella's arrival, despite the noisy chime as you walked through the door. A short, robust woman with dark wiry hair, stood behind the desk wearing a high-necked orange jumper clearly several sizes too small. She eyed Estella over the thick rimmed glasses that perched along the top of her upturned nose. Estella could smell her cheap perfume a mile off.

'Hello. Can I help you?' her tone was half-hearted and rather nonchalant.

'Err, can I have a room.'

Suddenly, the little boy said aloud 'That woman is a monster.' He was pointing directly at Estella, whilst his mother done her best to hide her embarrassment. 'Don't be silly, Matthew.' She scowled.

'That *is* a monster.' He whined.

Estella couldn't believe it. How could the human child know such a thing? For a moment, a slither of panic ran through her veins. She eyed the woman behind the counter, then glanced back at the whinging child. His mother looked at Estella coyly. She shrugged her shoulders while uttering a quiet apology. Estella looked at the boy. He clung onto his mother, burying his head into the crock of her armpits. He then demanded to go home.

'Matthew, can you stop this at once. Now, apologise to the lady.' She demanded.

'No mum, she's a monster. I want to go home.'

The child hugged his mother tightly. His face firmly snuggled within his mother's bosom. Estella grew uncomfortable at the attention. However, the woman behind the counter seemed bemused if not a little perplexed. Estella cleared away any unpleasant thoughts of eating the boy alive, Instead, she smiled sweetly at the boy's mother, gazing deeply into her brown eyes as if draining her soul away. Suddenly, the woman stood up in a trance like state. She lifted the boy from her arms, placing him to stand on the floor. Without another word, she marched out of the hotel lobby not bothering to look back for her crying child. Her deadpan face was unknowing of the mind trickery she had succumbed to. The red-faced screaming child hurriedly ran behind his mother, attempting to tug at her skirt, but was ignored as she took long, swift strides. The motel owner looked horrified, she turned to Estella.

'What kind of mother walks away from her child? What has gotten into her? She should be reported.'

Estella rolled her eyes trying not to chuckle. Her conscience was clear. Humans were no longer a concern to her. They were little more than cattle, and she couldn't see what all the fuss was about. Also, it would teach the little brat a lesson. He should have kept his mouth shut. Estella looked at the woman blankly.

'Reported? Can you blame her? If I had birthed a little brat like that, I would have been tempted to walk away from his little shitty arse as well.'

The woman's mouth fell open at Estella's vicious attitude. However, Estella was too busy sizing her up to care that she was being ogled with vapid disapproval. Like a ravished dog, Estella discreetly sniffed the air. Death lingered. The woman behind the counter was fifty-five at most. Unfortunately, she would have a fatal heart attack within a year, leaving her only son behind. High cholesterol to blame. Estella only saw death, never anything pleasant.

'Are you ok?' The woman looked concerned.

Estella paused, realising she had a habit of gazing. It was a vampire thing. Gazing into the past or future, seeing events as real as day. It was also a way of communicating with each other, as vampires preferred to acknowledge each other with intuitive stares, rather than verbal greeting. It was a gift that chose you at random. Some vampires had it, and others didn't.

'I'm fine.' She said, after a moment's hesitation. 'I will have a double, please.'

The woman handed her a crumpled book to sign. She looked annoyed, hesitant almost. What sort of uncaring human being was she? Those were the woman's thoughts. Refusal of service was on her mind, too. Estella had little choice but to influence her thoughts as though they were her very own. She needed somewhere comfortable to stay the night and really didn't want a night on the streets. Suddenly, the woman's demeanour softened.

'That will be forty pounds for the night. Check out, is noon tomorrow.'

Estella looked down at the rusty Pegasus coin buried in the fold of her palm. She had no human currency for a room. In fact, she had no choice but to succumb to her vampiric charms.

'But I have already paid for my room, remember?'

Estella spoke in a whisper. She locked the woman within her gaze as though placing her under a spell. With that, Estella slid the book back towards the woman, not bothering with a signature. The woman smiled broadly. Her deep brown eyes were inviting, yet unknowing. Like a puppet on a string, her brain was being manipulated for Estella's own gain.

'Uh, yes, of course you did. Here's your key. You're in room twenty-three. Enjoy your stay. I do apologise.'

Estella reasoned with herself as she walked the narrow corridor towards some equally narrow stairs. She didn't particularly enjoy being a thief, nor a master manipulator. But she had to do, what she had to do. Her sympathetic nature was steadily being erased for something far less forgiving, and a lot less sympathetic. The walls were lined with black and white pictures, hung behind dusty glass frames. There was a narrow staircase at the end of the corridor. On arrival, Estella took to the stairs, two at a time. Seconds in, she arrived at the second floor. With its psychedelic wallpapers, the motel was reminiscent of another era. The key rattled eagerly as Estella tried to open the door. After a short struggle, the lock clicked loudly. Ever so slowly, the door creaked open. The smell of mould and mildew danced beneath her nose. Not what you would expect for £40 a night. The room was dimly lit. Bland brown carpets with matching brown curtains made the room appear even smaller. A small double bed with faded floral sheets sat over at the right side of the wall, along with two equally sorry looking pillows atop the sheets. A shabby brown throw was also draped over the side. Estella ran her hand over the cheap polyester. She studied the mahogany hanging rail standing solo, inches from the bed. A thick grey robe hung from its rails. Every detail was delicately scrutinised under Estella's magnified eye. There was another door overlooking the bed at the opposite end of the room. The paint chipped, its handle loose. Estella was greeted by a bathroom the size of a shoebox. With a small shower cubicle squashed against an equally small toilet, it was arguably the smallest bathroom Estella had ever seen. And, she had seen a fair few. Admittedly, she had become rather spoilt grazing the floors of antique mansions. This was somewhat squalid living conditions. Like the rest of the room, the bathroom's bizarre blue tiles were dated and tasteless. Lacking any real warmth or comfort, the room appeared almost as cold and lifeless as she was. Estella spun around to the windows. She walked over to the curtains, swiftly pulling them open. A badly shaped grey building bellowed clouds of smoke through the top, along with an unpleasant smell of burning coal. Estella watched with intrigue as thick grey puffs evaporated in the air. Deciding it to be some sort of factory, Estella drew the curtains taut. Not quite knowing what to do with herself, Estella strolled back over to the dingy bathroom. The tiny lavatory was merely adequate for a small child. Thankfully, she wouldn't need it. A cracked squared mirror hung upon the blue tiled wall. A human mirror, of course. Her reflection was non-existent as though she were a ghost. Suddenly, she fell to her knees. As it had done before, she felt as if someone was pulling at her insides. Estella hung her head as she bent over like a wounded cat. She bared her fangs as she fought the pain. Her nails scratched along the chipped porcelain in an attempt to steady herself on the sink. Her stomach was swollen and tender, seemingly protruding far more since she had left the café. Estella thrashed out as the pain kicked in. Her empty stomach growled with hunger reminding her she hadn't eaten anything in days. The thought of synthetic blood made her want to retch. But with limited food sources and a steadily growing appetite, her options would soon be scarce. The problem was, Estella no longer craved blood. She craved human flesh. And lots of it. She sat crossed legged staring at the bathroom wall, fearing she was losing her mind. This was surely a punishment for messing around with a werewolf and was evidently paying the price for her lustful ways. However, Estella felt like a hypocrite. Truth be known, she had enjoyed it. More than she cared to admit. In fact, Estella felt she had no room to complain and should therefore endure her fate. As she closed her eyes with her head back against the wall, a cold tear trickled against her cheeks.

The sudden knock to the door made her startle. Estella slowly opened her eyes, looking out at the blackened room. She froze as another knock came thick and fast, louder than the first. She turned to the window. The sun had disappeared, evening set in, reminding her she must have slept for hours.

'Room service.'

A dull monotonous tone called out on the other side of the door. This voice somewhat dissimilar, it certainly didn't belong to the lady behind the counter. It was a contradiction. Estella was sure there was an obvious sign displayed behind the counter written in bold letters, clearly marked, "**No room service**". Perhaps it was an old notice, invalid and mislead. However, there was something vaguely suspicious about the caller. Her vampiric intuition knew something was not quite right. Quietly Estella crept towards the door. She sniffed the edges, twitching her nose like a wild animal. Ah, she was right. The caller wasn't human. Nor was it a werewolf. In disbelief, she took a step back from the door. A vampire had tracked her down. The funny thing was, she knew it wasn't any of the elders, and it certainly wasn't Marc.

'Who are you, and what do you want?' she called out.

'Oh Estella, stop being so angry. I am here to help. Please open the door.'

The voice was uncanny, yet it couldn't be placed. 'Tell me who you are, or I am not opening this door.'

'You were always so damned stubborn. Fine, it's entirely your choice. But, let me warn you. If you do not open this door, you will regret it.'

Estella bit her bottom lip. What was he talking about? She pulled a nervous frown. Her hands shook. Hunger had kicked in, though was masked by the gushing adrenaline in her agitated state.

'I am the only one who can help you now. Open this blasted door at once!'

The anonymous voice became loud and angry. Estella pulled her head back. She glanced up at the stained ceiling. There was no denying the forceful rage threatening to erupt from within. The contamination running through her veins, now desperately wanting to break out. Estella gasped. Bulging green veins ran the length of her paper white arms. Her fangs grazed her bottom lip. Her fingers tensed. Estella really didn't want a massive showdown. Not here, and not now. Unfortunately, the vampire on the other side of the door seemed to have other plans. Determined, he grew irritated and angry, as did she. Pulling the door open with vexation, she froze.

'Apollyon! What are you doing here?'

The tall dark figure gazed at her in silence. The black robe covering his head, concealed most of his face, though, his scent gave the game away. Apollyon was one of the board members. However, he was also a friend. A friend Estella hadn't seen in a hundred years.

For the immortal, a hundred years was no time at all. Estella stood aside as Apollyon stepped cautiously into the room. At six-foot-five, he cut a chilling figure.

'I may as well cut to the chase. I bare bad news, Estella,' he said.

Apollyon removed the hooded robe, showcasing thick blonde hair slicked back to his nape, easily defying his four thousand years on earth. Although one of the oldest vampires, age showed no mark on him. Estella gazed straight through him.

'Estella, are you listening?! You're miles away.'

'Huh. I'm so sorry, Apollyon. I haven't been… myself.'

'Literally. This, I know. Your lust overcame you, and now, you pay the price.'

'How do you…'

'Shh, I know everything.'

Apollyon's voice was deep and flat, echoing around the little room like a lion's roar. Estella hung her head in shame. She should have known that someone was bound to find out. After all, they were vampires.

'Apollyon, what is happening to me?'

Estella's voice grew shaky. Regret bore every corner of her face. She would literally kill to turn back time. Estella's betrayal to Marc would haunt her forever. Suddenly, the yearning for him became immense.

'I want Marc. I need him.'

Apollyon turned a blind eye to her sobs. Not one to sugar-coat his words, he made his opinions very clear. 'Best you forget about him. Once he learns of your betrayal, he will certainly forget about you. At the very least, put a bounty out for your death.'

'Tell me what is happening to me! What do you know?'

'I must be frank, Estella. You're no longer one of us. Ten days, maybe more. You don't have much time left. Tell me, how much do you know about the stranger?'

Estella was speechless. Her suspicions confirmed. She was turning to that of a ravished dog. A werewolf. Apollyon read her fears. 'No, you are not becoming a werewolf, Estella. I am afraid, it is a curse far worse than any four-legged monster.'

Estella was stunned at Apollyon's revelation. She pleaded through silent tears. 'Am I dying?'

Unfortunately, Apollyon offered little sympathy. 'No, you are not dying. However, the vampire life you know and love, will become no more. I am afraid I cannot say any more on the matter. That being said, I am intrigued by the… stranger. Do you know his name?'

Estella gasped. 'Why do you care? You refuse to give me any real answers. Why are you here?'

'To warn you.'

'You don't have to warn me. I already know that nothing good can come of this. As you can see, I have fled my home.'

'You're becoming a daemon.' He spat.

Estella froze. Goosebumps crept along her skin. She trembled as the blood drained from her body. An insidious fear engulfed the room. If there was anything worse than the undead, it was the Daemon. Once considered folklore, and nothing more than a bedside fable for naughty young vampires. Quite simply, the Daemon was the worst kind of monster imaginable. A supposed mythical muscular humanoid beast, hairier than ever, fourteen feet tall, descended from demons. Folklore maintains, the Daemon was hideously repulsive in nature and even draped himself in animal skins to keep up his unpleasant and intimidating appearance. And like every good magic trick, they could shapeshift at the drop of a bottom, morphing to and fro at will.

'How is that possible? Xavier, for all his faults, he's certainly no daemon. I would have smelt him…surely' Her voice trailed off. 'If he is, I would like to know what kind of sorcery he's working with'?

'Sorcery? Didn't you know? Daemons are the creators of deception.'

Apollyon observed her as though she were dull-witted. 'Estella, I realise it's a bitter pill to swallow. But the sooner you know the truth; the sooner you can take precaution. I'm no werewolf geneticist, but I've been around long enough to have studied a thing or two. Here's the deal. If Xavier was simply a wolf, none of this would ever happen. Though not incredibly common, and certainly not encouraged, however vampires and werewolves have, on rare occasion, been intimate. But never has the two species genetically crossed the barrier of the other's genome. Consuming the genetic code of another species whilst being passionately intimate, is largely impossible. You're either a vampire or a werewolf, and bloody well stay that way. Unfortunately, Estella, the daemon is a totally different species. One we know very little about. What I do know, is that their genetic material somehow attaches to the other hosts and disrupts the coding of selected cells. Basically, it consumes the other. In fact, the female daemon is known to eat her mate. Though, not always. It's usual to have a rapid gestation. They can deliver within weeks.'

Apollyon's words swam around Estella's head like a bright neon warning. Estella thought she might lose her balance. Her stomach danced; her head spun.

'You may as well stake me in the heart and be done with it. I'm a bloody abomination.'

Estella fell to her knees in anguish. Head lowered to the floor. She reached out and grabbed onto Apollyon's ankles, piercing his skin with razor sharp nails. She was angry. Mostly with herself. 'So, does that mean I, am more powerful than you? I could probably kill you now.' she snorted.

'Estella, release your hands at once. What are you doing?'

'Apollyon promise me. Promise me you won't reveal any of this monstrosity to Marc, or I will find you, and eat your heart out.'

'Are you insane? The board will know, sooner or later. In fact, a bounty will already be out for your head on a stick. Marc, would have certainly alerted the board about your disappearance by now.'

Estella's face was frozen. 'Apollyon, how did you know my secret? Tell me. Even for a vampire, your power super exceeds you.'

'Ok, enough about me. My supposed greatness, often comes at a steep price.'

Estella released her grip on his ankles. How could she kill a vampire? A friend. She wanted nothing more but to burrow herself within the ground so deep, she would never be found.

'Estella, when the board gets wind of your affliction, they will hunt you by the dozens. Daemons are a dangerous threat. Vampires will be sticking together. I suggest you go to America. There is a very small daemon community in Salem. You will be safer there.'

Estella's eyes widened in disgust. 'No way shall I leave the country. How dare you suggest I do. I thought, you wanted to help me?'

'I *am* helping you. That is your best option. And it's the one that will keep you alive. I'm afraid there is nothing more I can do. You're marked. I am sorry, Estella.'

Distraught and fraught with devastation, the reality of her situation hit hard. Estella was no longer a vampire. Ten minutes of rampant fornication had wiped away two hundred years of history. She had no one else to blame. Staking her own heart would be the easiest thing to do, but Estella was a coward and couldn't face the thought of taking her own life, no matter how much she hated herself. But faced with the prospect of becoming a daemon sent shockwaves of fear throughout her body, death seemed a likely option. Apollyon made strides towards the door.

'Goodbye Estella, I wish you well. Take care of yourself, and the thing growing inside of you.'

Estella snapped out of her dark thoughts by the time Apollyon had disappeared. It was confirmed. Something hideously grotesque grew within. She ogled the fine white mist left behind on the spot on the floor where he'd stood. She looked around the darkened room. The garish wallpaper was claustrophobic. The miniscule bed was barely sufficient for a fully grown adult. Suddenly, Estella's stomach felt as though it was eating itself from the inside out. As she crawled to the bathroom in agony as the pain reached a level of intensity so traumatic, she thought she may pass out. Once inside, Estella slammed the bathroom door shut. It felt safer in there. She shook like a leaf as trembling hands curled over, rigid and hard. Completely overwhelmed with raw emotion, Estella rocked her wreckage of a body back and forth, toing and froing in slow steady motions. Her eyes gently closed.

'Madam, is everything ok? You should have checked out forty minutes ago. You know, I will have to charge you.'

The plump woman's grating voice was unmistakeable. Estella struggled to open her eyes. She looked at the floor beneath her. She was in the bathroom, face down, exactly where she had sat yesterday evening. Her entire body ached as though she had been run over by a truck. Estella slowly stood to her feet. She fought against the dull throbbing in her temple. Reaching for her trusted mirror, she was horrified at the face looking back. She was barely recognisable. Her hair a matted mess, though, that wasn't the worse. Her iced-white vampire complexion, had become sallow, highlighting the dark rings around her eyes. Tuffs of stray hairs threatened every corner of her face. Coarse hair ran along her cheeks, and in between her eyebrows, creating a sinister weird unibrow. This was only vaguely better than the blood she excreted every other day. Her green, emerald eyes, deep and intense, was certainly more startling than the hazel brown she was used to. Estella couldn't quite believe how quick this thing had taken hold. She *had* to find Xavier. They would battle, or make love, but there were too many questions unanswered. He should have loved her. Instead, he gave her a life of turmoil.

'Madam, if you don't open the door, I will have to let myself in.'

The woman's voice became impatient. Like a foghorn, it was increasingly high pitched and irritating. She banged on the door several times, venting her frustration. Fair play to her. It was a family-owned business. Estella saw her point. Begrudgingly, Estella shuffled towards the door and pulled it open. The woman jumped back with a gasp. She clutched her chest with fright. Wide eyed and visibly shaken, she eyed Estella as though she were a monster, though indeed she was.

'You ought to put some clothes on.' The woman stammered nervously.

Estella looked down at herself. Indeed, she was half dressed, wearing only a stained white t-shirt that barely covered the tops of her thighs. Estella had no recollection of anything. She could have sworn she had been fully dressed, adorned in her slinky sheer red blouse and pressed black trousers. 'I best get dressed.' Estella's tone was low and flat, devoid of any emotion. She slammed the door. The motel owner stood on the other side, red faced and stiff. Sheepishly, the woman made her way back down to the counter. Estella hoped she hadn't given her a scare but toyed with the idea of staying for a while longer. She needed somewhere safe to lie low until she figured it out. It was the easy option, after all. Taking the poor woman's mind hostage and possibly staying for another month seemed like the best thing to do, but then Estella had a blow of morality. She felt too dignified for such trickery; her pride went against it. Hair scraped back like a convict mugshot; Estella pulled on an all-black ensemble. Dishevelled and unkempt, intense green eyes with black ring around them, complete with sallow dull skin, Estella looked like an entirely different person.

'Thanks for the stay.'

Estella chucked the key down on the desk. She strolled out of the motel, stomping feet with long strides. She didn't look back. The plump woman was motionless, her face indifferent. It was evident she had no recollection of the morning's events. Estella made sure of that. The morning sun had already risen. The streets rapidly filling with life. Busy bodies intermingling inches from one another. Estella pitied them, for they knew no better. They would simply serve and die, mostly living a life of suffering and hardship. If only they had a taste of the other life. The vampire life, they would soon learn what living was really about. The taste of immortality was one of the sweetest tastes Estella had known. The smell of death was rampant, almost indescribable.

FIVE

Estella walked through the sleepy town, analysing the dull humdrum of human existence. Her pale skin tingled with the beam of the sun. Still, she was grateful. It was far better than being burnt to a crisp, and probably the only real drawback of her vampiric DNA. Estella pondered about the underworld. If vast humans managed to intermingle harmoniously amongst each other, why couldn't other species, too. Of course, she wasn't expecting some undead utopia, but an underworld in which werewolves, vampires, and even the dreaded daemon could somewhat co-exist in harmony. As unlikely a thought it was, nevertheless, it gave Estella some comfort. Hope that one day, it wouldn't matter what specie you belonged to. To the humans, they were all feared, and equally misunderstood.

An old woman wearing a black headscarf walked hastily past. Their eyes met. She was a werewolf. The second wolf Estella had seen in this town. The old woman had killed last night. The stench of fresh human blood lingered off her, long after she had walked past. Still, Estella walked on by as though oblivious to her presence. Her secret was as good as any other. There they were, creatures of the night, intermingling with unsuspecting human folk. A day like any other. Estella walked ten miles until she came to a busy main road. The 'change' was draining every ounce of energy she had left in her wreckage of a body. Weak and tired, she had little strength to teleport, nor levitate. Nonetheless, Estella continued her journey, determined to get as far away from Heath Hall, as possible. Fast cars sped in intersections. Weaving in and out, within an inch from each other. Estella had never seen so many cars all at once. Over to the left, there was a quiet road adjacent to the traffic. It was secluded and discreet, and a perfect escape away from the noisy bustle. Her supernatural ear faring to be far too sensitive for so this level of stimulation, Estella took to the path, unsure of her destination. It was eerily quiet and just how she liked it, Estella's feet rustled against the rough gravelled ground as she walked. Suddenly, something caught her gaze. Two robust human men dressed in leather jackets and heavy black boots, walked towards her. Both bald headed and heavily tattooed, Estella studied the humans with suspicion. The sight of a lone dishevelled female must have sparked their curiosity, as the men began to laugh amongst themselves, eyeing her as if she were a prized trout. On approach, they smirked through leering eyes with wry smiles, desperately trying to garner her attention. Estella, being the supernatural night walker that she was, walked on by with unfazed confidence, not allowing herself to be intimidated by a couple of humans. She was suddenly grabbed by the arm by one of the men. He was the biggest of the two, and built like a house, towering over her modest statue.

'Not so fast. Why's a beauty like you walking these mean streets by yourself?'

Stale cigar and alcohol reeked from his breath. Estella struggled to shake her arm free, but he tightened his grip. To her horror, the other man stood with arms outstretched blocking her path. He then began unzipping his trousers, grinning like a Cheshire cat. Within seconds, the man holding her arm grabbed her from behind, crushing her with his heavy weight and sheer size.

'Get off me, you beast. I can take you out with one hand.'

The men laughed at her admission. Clearly, they thought she was a deluded human who posed little threat. Estella attempted to throw the pair off her back, but she couldn't. She struggled desperately but her strength had dwindled. Estella grew frustrated that her body wasn't cooperating as it should. She managed to kick the second man on the shin. He hollered and yelped. Unfortunately, she was then slapped across the face and restrained by the other. Panic set in. Hysteria took over.

'She thinks she's got powers. Poor thing. We have all the power now, baby. You're all ours.'

Estella fought as hard as she could. Unfortunately, the metamorphosis had literally drained every ounce of strength from her body. No longer had she the privilege nor strength of a supernatural. Her body transforming to its new composition, would take several days to fully regain its physical peak. Estella fought her hardest. However, the fight was not one she would win. She was pushed to the floor and forced to her knees. What happened next, was horrendous. She was reduced to a morsel of a being. Treated with such contempt, she would have preferred to die a gruesome death. The men took turns as though she were a piece of meat. Like an object to play around with, she was forcefully assaulted, one after the other. Eyes squeezed shut, knuckles red raw. Placed in a delicate state of disarray trying to escape the torturous brutality of what was happening, Estella had never felt so violated. Flashes of gruesome images played out in her head. Not quite sure if they were a memory, or simply a premonition. Dead human bodies scattered everywhere. Some old, and some young. Most limbless. It was a slaughter. Blackness fell everywhere. This went on for several minutes. Then, came the calm. Still, Estella couldn't shake the gruesome images out of her head. Images she's never had before. Perhaps it was a dire projection of the literal pain and humiliation she had endured. Once the men were done with her, Estella was repeatedly kicked in the stomach. Left for dead in a bloodied state sprawled upon the ground, with nothing more than a ripped black shirt barely covering her modesty, she was stripped away of her dignity. Revenge would be sought. They would be hunted and killed in the most insidious of ways. First, the daemon had to arrive. Upon her newfound strength, finding the culprits would be easy. Unbeknown to the men, Estella had traced their smell and was eagerly tracking their every move like computerised data in her head, as if it were an electronic storage device. She knew where they lived, even the vehicle they drove. They would pay for their actions.

As she scrutinised the paved ground, Estella caught sight of her delicate black underwear carelessly abandoned like an old piece of rag. The blood dripping between her legs was ice cold and nearly black. There was something to be said about the sight of one's own blood. Estella's stomach churned as nauseated nostalgia kicked in. The temptation to sample her own suddenly became intense as the beast within couldn't resist. She retched at its bitterness. It was horrid. Like bitter bile, nothing compared to the freshness of human blood. In all honestly, the synthetic stuff from Edgar's blood machine was much more palatable. Getting changed was a challenge. Her bag had disappeared. Her clothes were missing. Estella stood with shaky feet eyeing the derelict bareness. There was a huge industrial bin on the other side of the wall, about ten feet away. Estella gazed at it. She already knew her bag was amongst the rubbish. Evidently, the men had hoped to find money and were hugely disappointed.

Nearly an hour since the attack, Estella felt no better. There she was propped up against the wall, knees bent, head down. She shook as though she had ingested a gallon load of illegal substances. Somehow, after her rubble through the bin, she had managed to throw on a long black dress to protect her modesty, being the only piece of clothing void of any dirt and pieces of stale food. Estella examined the pale skin on her forearms. Bulging blue veins were at bursting point. A suspicious patch of thick dark hair sprouted effortlessly from one arm. And then, her undead existence took on a whole new meaning. It was sudden and spontaneous, Estella had little control of what was happening. She growled loudly, then gasped with horror at the sound coming from her mouth. Then, it happened again. Only this time, louder than before. She peered down at her rock-hard stomach. Shallow indents ran the length of her stomach. Whatever was in there, were now ready to come out. Estella wailed moany deep grunts like a pig to slaughter, she made a warthog look graceful. She looked around thankful the secluded path was scarce. The horror of being discovered mid-birth, legs up, bottom exposed, would be worse than the act itself. Several minutes of panting and groaning ensued, and then, came the urge to push. Words couldn't describe the horror of events that followed. As her body prepared to birth the unknown, Estella trembled uncontrollably as hot searing pain rippled through her body. She had endured plenty in her time, but this had to be the worst. Feeling the urge to push, Estella bared down as though she had done it before. Twice, three times, then all was still. After several difficult minutes, it was over, with little more than a two-month gestation period, and a slight hint of a baby bump. She had done what she needed to but couldn't bring herself to look at the *thing* on the ground. It would be easier to walk away, pretending it had never happened. Vowing not to look at what she just delivered, Estella managed to cover it over with a discarded carboard box lying a foot away, whilst peeping at it with one eye open. Some things were best left unknown she told herself. With shaky legs, she stood to her feet, hobbling about as if her world had just been turned upside down. Estella knew she had to pull herself together but couldn't deny the urge to get away was intense. She had to continue her journey to nowhere, preferably alone. With daemon DNA now contaminating her blood, levitating was awkward and clumpy. Just as she geared herself up for a third attempt, Estella was stopped in her tracks.

She turned to the loud pitched wail coming from the bundle on the floor, which couldn't be ignored. Shock sent shivers through her body as she prepared to face her fears. Then, it hit hard. She was leaving her baby behind. A hybrid monstrosity, the child would be feared by most and likely hunted by others. Supposedly, the first of its kind. However, it was her child, and her responsibility. Estella questioned her unscrupulous behaviour. The child would be killed within days if discovered by a vampire and wouldn't fare much better if werewolves found it. That was the moment Estella knew she had to protect it. Grief-stricken, Estella felt empty. Her stomach was in knots. Swallowing what little pride she had left, Estella crept back over to the screaming bundle on the ground. Her mind raced with the unknown. Would she love it? Could she love it? Estella knelt before the bundle; she gasped as she lifted the box. Her lip trembled as she forced back tears. With a mop of brown hair and chubby red cheeks, the baby looked like any other new-born. With pale pink lips, shaped into a neat cupid's bow, the baby eyed its mother with a knowing that couldn't be described. Its intense brown eyes were eerily deep. Like the ocean, they had a way of drawing you in. Estella felt scrutinised. As Apollyon had said, the child appeared much older than it was, already the size of an infant several months old. Estella became mesmerised. For an entire ten minutes, she couldn't pull her eyes away from the spectacular being she had created. Estella studied her perfectly formed little hands. She gazed at her feet. Like a duck, her toes were webbed. However, that didn't matter. The love she had for this miracle, was more than she could have imagined. The stark realisation hit hard as she fought back the pebbled lump dwelling in her throat. Tears fell against her cheeks. She took pity upon the poor little thing. Innocent and vulnerable, with a whore for a mother, Estella felt unworthy of such a special gift. A gift, which had undoubtedly changed her life forever. At that moment, Estella knew her very existence would never be the same again. It was a bittersweet moment as she wrapped the child snugly amongst bits of cardboard and various pieces of soiled clothing in an attempt to keep it warm as she placed the baby at the bottom of the worn brown holdall.

A chill circled the air. The sky was dusky. With numb feet, Estella picked up her brown bag. The ground was cobbled and dusty as she jumped around trying to avoid massive potholes. Fresh pain seared through her legs. It wasn't long before Estella left the secluded alley-way and stepped out onto a beaming main road where cars weaved in and out, inches from one another. The noise of chaos was excru-ciating to her delicate ear. With little direction, Estella allowed her instincts to lead the way. For the baby's sake, they needed a safe place to stop. With little strength to levitate her legs struggled. Estella, determined to get away from this place by any means necessary, wouldn't be deterred. A quick peer at the brown bag, caused a dread of panic threatening to churn her stomach. Estella was no longer a priority, and such a thought caused great ill-ease. With unsteady feet, she stepped out onto the road. Horns sounded at full blast. Cars swerved, desperately trying to avoid her, and each other.

'Watch where you're going, stupid woman.'

A dark-haired man was raging, yelling through the window. His eyes were wild; his face twisted in anger. Estella eyed him vengefully. She wouldn't allow another human to abuse her again, nor speak to her as if she were two-years old. Maybe it was adrenaline, but Estella found an inner strength like never before. She darted over cars, leaping two at a time. With one hand, the man was dragged out through the driver side window as she gripped him taut by the neck. The woman in the passenger seat screamed loudly.

'Argh! That's my husband. She's taking my husband!'

There were gasps and shrieks from a young lady in the car behind. Estella eyed her with an insidious smile. The women became pallor with fear, then slumped over the wheel. Estella sprinted over cars a dozen at a time, she leaped with great speed, narrowly swerving a bus, to which it then collided with a large utility vehicle.

'Argh, get off me.' yelled the man, red-faced with hysteria. Estella held him by the scruff of his neck. She flew to the other side of town. The noise of carnage and chaos, and screaming human's, aroused an unfamiliar satisfaction. Her dutiful nature towards humans had been tainted, and now, the only thing she remotely cared about was her own wellbeing, and of course, the creature she carted around in her brown bag. She had lived her life purposefully avoiding humans, not wanting to tantalize her vampire instincts, cautiously feeding from Edgar's synthetic blood machine like a good little girl. She had made a promise to Marc that she would never kill for food, now feared that promise couldn't be kept. Not anymore. She was longer a vampire, so her loyalty to humans had ceased. With no governing by the treaty, she would therefore torture and kill to her hearts content if she so wished. Estella tightened her grip around the shrieking man's neck, puncturing an artery. She salivated at the texture of sweet blood dripping through her fingers. It felt good. Feeling elated, she then tossed the man in the air, dropping his lifeless body amongst some nearby rubble. Estella had one final look over her shoulder, realising she had little remorse for the mayhem caused.

SIX

The sky was cloudless; the afternoon haze was misty and refreshing as the windy air danced along Estella's face. She had travelled eleven miles with little direction, and only when the child strapped to her back begun to slurp on her own fingers, was she inclined to stop. Teleportation wasn't for the faint hearted and was certainly more work than one could imagine. Estella levitated as she eyed the scene on the ground. There was a mighty mass of people, almost all presumably human. It appeared to be some sort of fair. There were people everywhere, some buying, some selling a variety of things. Estella peered behind a tree whilst her mind ticked over like a clock. Nowhere would ever be totally safe for a hybrid daemon baby, but there was something about this place that felt vaguely safer than the last. Without the familiar werewolf residue, it appeared unscathed from the infiltration of the creatures of the night. Nevertheless, Estella knew all too well to act with caution, lying low, watching and waiting. Vampires could be anywhere. It wouldn't be too unusual for a young, rogue, vampire with nothing to lose, wandering around a city like this one, on the hunt for a kill. After some thought, Estella decided to see what all the fuss was about, gently lowering herself to the ground. She stood twenty feet away from the crowd, embedded by grassland and open space, watching the humans as though they were a buffet feast. She sniffed the air; their hot blood was sweet and tempting. Their flesh smelt even better. Out of nowhere, a young man trudged towards her path, his shadowed figure crept closer into focus. Appearing to be in his own world, he ignored Estella entirely, brushing her gently on the shoulders as he strolled on by. Tall with dark curly hair, he couldn't have been older than eighteen, maybe nineteen, and bared an uncanny resemblance to Marc. With his thick dark hair and striking blue eyes, Estella studied him with the same intrigue she applied to all humans. One of wonder, and one of lust. She could smell his blood a mile off. The young man, oblivious to her scrutiny, continued his pace, walking along with a deadpan face. Estella spent several minutes deciding whether he was worth the kill. Perhaps he was spared by his likeness to her former spouse, as after some thought, Estella decided to continue with her journey, trudging further along the meadowed landscape nestled within rows of old derelict buildings that formed a neat line around it. It was here Estella decided to stay the night, or as long as necessary. The baby grumbled loudly, just as Estella's own stomach growled to be fed. She sang to the child, hoping her off-pitch lullaby would soothe her daughter's misery until she found something suitable to feed upon. However, Estella couldn't ignore the intense smell of human flesh, which was seemingly provoking her appetite. Vowing to make a kill once the sun went down, Estella found a secluded place where the ground was raised and cobbly. There were no houses, no humans, and definitely no supernatural creatures, this town seemed like a safe enough spot until she worked out a plan. With her back sat against an old barren tree, Estella placed the weathered brown bag along the thick grass. The thread on the handles was unravelling; the worn leather was fading, all of which was to be expected as it had been used as a rucksack. Estella lifted the weary baby from the bag, placing her aptly upon her leg. Estella caught a whiff of her own armpits, and gasped. She smelt vastly different. Now a rogue outsider, she was an anomaly of the worst kind. Hunted, and yet feared, silent tears fell to her cheeks. If not for the child who was solely dependent on its mother, Estella felt she would be better off staking her own heart. The child was innocuous and deserved a better mother. The infant's loud piercing shriek jolted Estella away from her own thoughts. She peered down at the bundle wrapped up in the crock of her left arm. Truth be known, Estella had no real idea what to do with it, and it wasn't long before Estella became the class clown, pulling an assortment of faces in an attempt to soothe the crying child. Thankfully, it worked. The bawling came to a halt. The baby gurgled at her mother with a wide drooling grin, to which Estella snickered. There was a sudden rustling in the trees. With tensed shoulders and eyes wide, she tightened her grip on her child. Seconds in she was relieved to see three crows. The birds perched directly above on a thick bendy branch, then begun to caw. The curious baby giggled at the spectacle, wriggling her toes. Apollyon was right. The daemon's growth was astonishing. Although merely two hours old, the infant could easily be mistaken for a four-month-old baby.

'If you continue growing like this, I will have a toddler within weeks.' Said Estella.

The baby looked at her mother with unblinking eyes, then shoved her finger in her mouth. The gushing of the wind was blissfully soothing, providing a different kind of comfort. With her back against the tree, Estella closed her eyes in meditation, ruminating upon her life. The last two hundred years begun to pale to insignificance. After all, she had spent a fair chunk of it confined to the walls of Heath Hall. Despite the obvious hurdles ahead, the reality she had succumbed to, was weirdly rather freeing. This was a funny kind of privilege. Now and again, Estella would peer down at the baby, who seemed happy enough. Whilst admiring the innocent bundle on her lap, Estella had to accept the reality of the situation. Her child was hot commodity for both species and would be pursued by many. A powerful hybrid, both freak and threat, the burden was overwhelming. Nevertheless, with every gleeful gurgle and innocence babble, Estella vowed to protect the infant at all costs,

Evening had set in. The air steadily becoming icy cold. The thriving offspring was sucking her own fingers, happily and content, but which aroused a pang of guilt within Estella. The child hadn't been fed and was likely trying to eat her own flesh. Estella had been too consumed with her own woes she had forgotten to feed her. Whilst fighting her inner demons, Estella was reminded of what a terrible mother she was. The tall grass bellowed with the wind, dancing to its rhythm. The brisk air prickled her cheeks, its coolness allowing a tranquil calm to convey. A brown bird caught her eye. Its little wings fluttered as it came to a standstill, hobbling around on broken tree limbs. Grey markings covered its back. Like a crouching tiger on all fours, Estella positioned on bended knee, her gaze intense. Laying the child on its back, she quietly crept along, lips pursed tightly. Three, two, one….it happened so fast. The squealing bird took its last breath as Estella tightened her grip around its little body. Seconds later, she held the limp bird between clenched fists, waving it at the baby, of whom didn't seem amused. She looked up at her mother with those big brown eyes, then switched her gaze to the bird. Estella shrugged as she began to rip the bird apart, pulling its little wings away from its body. As she tore at its head, a feeling of elation set in. It wasn't long before the carcass was in pieces. Estella slowly teased small chunks of the bird into her offspring's mouth. Surprisingly, the baby gobbled it up sprightly. Eight minutes in, the bird had disappeared, leaving only feathers behind. It wasn't long before the baby slept in her arms.

Darkness transcended as night fell. Estella's thoughts turned to Marc. She wondered what was happening back at Heath Hall and unsuccessfully tried to gaze. Unfortunately, she was stopped by the pain in her head as a warning not to. It hurt too much. Already, her vision had become hazy. No longer a vampire, she was revoked of its privileges. Always at the back of her mind, her betrayal never left her conscience. They say, love is blind, but she often wondered if Marc chose to turn a blind eye. There were no doubts in her mind he would be plotting some elaborate plan when learned of her deceit. After all, she was his princess and could do no wrong. Catering to her every whim was a pastime he frequently enjoyed. Indeed, he had spoilt her rotten. Perhaps, that was half the problem. He gave her *everything,* and she wanted for *nothing.* Maybe if he hadn't been so predictable. Of course, blaming him made her feel better. At least, it lessened the guilt. Her thoughts drifted; her eyes became heavy.

Estella stirred. The morning sun was still hidden behind thick clouds. The birds begun their song, singing in sync within the trees, disturbing her sleep. Estella peered down at the sleeping child. Its little webbed feet stuck out beneath the badly wrapped cloth. Her willowy brown hair was plastered to her little round head, which made Estella smile. As if butter wouldn't melt, who would have guessed this delicate little thing, could be so…dangerous. Could this baby really pose such a threat to the underworld? Her perfect pink lips formed a neat pout as she laid deathly still on her mother's lap. Estella was awe, though, it was short-lived. Overwhelmed by the crushing responsibility of caring for something so defenceless, Estella's awe turned to grief. She knew, their contentment wouldn't last forever, nor could she live a life like this, running and hiding. Very soon, they would be hunted. A hybrid would never be accepted by either species, so would inevitably live a secluded existence. While dark thoughts took up space in her head, Estella caught sight of her own hands. Hair free and relatively normal in appearance, it was a welcome surprise to the torturous arthritic substitute that had replaced her hands over the last few weeks. Even the crippling pains in her legs had ceased. With renewed confidence, and gratitude to not having turned to a wild dog, Estella felt the transition was over, she had her body back. Here she was, a daemon. The vampire life she once knew, was over. Although considered to be an utter monstrosity, Estella never felt better. Her strength had returned, stronger than before. She felt good again and welcomed the return to her old self. Just then, the baby stirred. Her little webbed feet wiggled around in the warm depths of her mother's lap.

'Look at you. As cute as a button. Pity, you haven't a clue of what lies ahead of you.'

Estella spoke in a whisper. The baby opened her eyes. She gurgled sweetly, seemingly disagreeing with her mother. With sombre thoughts filed away to the back of her mind, Estella decided motherhood actually was not such a bad thing. As she cradled the baby within the crease of her arm, Estella spotted a shallow lake hidden several feet away between dense bushes. Her eyes lit up. Although not quite the same luxury as an icy cold gold-rimmed bath, it was a welcomed surprise. Estella, loved water, the colder the better. With the baby in hand, she strolled over to the stream, eyes beaming. Estella dipped her hand in. The water was murky and lifeless and probably embedded with dead weeds and grown toads. Nevertheless, Estella stripped off and stepped inside. With her offspring tightly embedded within the crock of her arm, she gently lowered her body into the stream. A few drops of dirty water couldn't possibly do much harm, she thought. Estella took handfuls, splashing it cautiously over the infant's back. The infant seemed indifferent. She barely flinched. Once she had finished, Estella placed the baby along the spongy river edge. With one eye on the infant, Estella splashed around like a carefree child. The temperature was near freezing, perfect for the undead.

The moment at the lake was rather satisfying. For the first time since leaving Heath Hall, Estella felt liberated. Her life had taken her by surprise, but now, she welcomed it with open arms. No longer fearful and resistive to change, she embraced her new identity. As she crouched against the large oak tree, Estella caught sight of a man. As if from nowhere, the lone man trudged towards her. With teeth bared and a stiffened stance, Estella braced herself for attack. It was only as the man got close enough; she suddenly felt a little silly. He was elderly, dressed in oversized black rain boots. Also, he was human. He carried a large garden fork dressed in grubby overalls. He was clearly headed for the shrubs. With a nod of the head and a kind smile, the man strolled past and never looked back. Like vampires, Estella still had the gift of insight. He was at least seventy, a widower, and had no children. Though her desire for flesh intensified every day, Estella decided against killing him. To be fair, he hadn't much longer to live. In any case, she had always been a poor excuse of a vampire, and if she was honest with herself, she lacked an innate desire to kill and torture defenceless human beings. That being said Estella's interest in humans had spiked. Something inside had changed. Now, Estella saw them through predator eyes. Like animals, humans were seen as little more than cattle. Although Estella spiked her hunger had kicked in. Estella had plans to avenge her tormentors; a thought that had never left her mind. Today, she *would* kill. Today, justice would be served. Like most supernatural creatures, she was led by scent. Like a trained sniffer dog, Estella would find their whereabouts. Ruminating of the day it happened; she often smelt their rancid scents as if they had never gone.

Several feet away, the old man made quite a racket with his fork. He ploughed away noisily at the solid exterior, chopping harshly until a large chunk of wood crashed to the ground. With razor sharp eyes, Estella scrutinised the bustling market in the distance. She needed clean clothes and had no money. Even from here, she spotted a lovely red dress. Flowy and chic, it was unlike anything she had ever worn. Estella also eyed a pair of blue trousers. It had pristine white stitching along the hem. Deciding she would take them both, Estella geared herself up for a trip to the shops. The stall owner was a petite woman. Her unkempt mousy hair fell to the tops of her shoulders, with a worn pouch strapped across the front of her stomach. Estella reminded herself that she wasn't a thief but was doing what was necessary for the greater good of her child. With the baby secured tightly to her back, Estella teleported towards the market. The noise was excruciating. It was a mystery how humans lived amongst such mayhem. Like the vampire, daemons could shapeshift in various forms, rendering itself invisible by the untrained eye. With perspiring heaving bodies everywhere, the smell caused her hands to shake. The temptation to pounce on the first unsuspecting soul, proving hard to bear. Trying to ignore her natural instincts, Estella stood at the stall admiring the textures between her fingers, running her hand along the lines, enjoying the brightly coloured fabrics. Evidently the quality was far less superior than the tailor-made garments she had grown so accustomed to, but if it was good enough for the humans, it was good enough for her. It must be said, picking out her one's own attire, was a privilege she welcomed, and could certainly get used to. Reduced to nothing more than an undead housewife, Marc would often see to her entire clothing selection, making sure they were tailor made and nothing but perfection. No matter how hard she tried, the sound of beating hearts from the plethora of humans around her, made picking out clothing more difficult than it ought to be. Never had the sound of a well-functioning vein pumping blood through its body, caused her toes to curl. The stall owner was busy attending to a neatly dressed black woman who had a little girl by her side. With striking big brown eyes, the girl looked up at Estella and was immediately stunned. It appeared she was a gifted child and was able to see Estella for the monster she really was. The startled child held on tightly to her mother; her eyes filled with dread. Estella felt a pang of guilt. Scaring children wasn't part of the plan. Also, being caught red handed by a seven-year-old, definitely wasn't her intention. Nonetheless, Estella smiled wearily as she awkwardly crammed the red dress inside her shirt. She held her finger to her mouth, vowing the child to silence, of whom still had her eyes peeled to Estella like glue. Very soon afterwards, the girl begun to tug at her mother's sleeve, pointing at Estella. With young curious eyes upon her, Estella couldn't afford to tally for much longer. However, the infant needed clothes just as much as she did. Dressing her in dirty torn rags was hardly appropriate. Estella walked away from the child, scanning the crowds for something else. Then, she saw it. A small stall equipped for an infant. It sat right at the end of the market. Two women stood guard, as though they were selling gold. One of whom was burly and tall with wiry auburn hair, the other, short and plump with bleached hair and black roots, appearing to be in dire need of care. Estella slipped past the tall woman who was totally unaware. She curiously eyed the rows of pale pinks and soft blues, eventually settling on several pairs of various colours, bright yellow included. Ideally, Estella would have preferred her child to be dressed in black but was disappointed to find nothing other than a rainbow assortment instead. Estella crammed the entire lot down her top, making sure to take some larger pieces, too. After-all, this baby grew by the minute and would likely need bigger clothing a lot sooner than anticipated.

Within minutes Estella was back at her place against the tree, nestled cosily underneath the large overhanging leaves. She scattered the goods out on to the ground, inspecting each item meticulously. Feeling rather pleased with herself, Estella piled her new finds up into the brown bag, making sure each piece was folded with precision. Once this was done, Estella's torn soiled clothing was tossed aside, whilst she turned her attention back to the baby. Eyeing her as though she were a doll, Estella studied the infant as she made attempts to dress her in the garish colours, wondering why on earth any human would succumb their child to such monstrosity. Estella grimaced at the pink frilly dress with its matching frilly cardigan, fearing it to be the best of the lot. The poor child looked ridiculous. Fortunately, the baby seemed indifferent, still managing to gurgle happily each time Estella dangled another costume to her face.

'You look great'.

Estella smiled between gritted teeth. The baby kicked her legs about with a giggle. She must have approved. Estella's heart was stolen.

SEVEN

They say, the dead never sleeps. At least, this was certainly true for the undead. It had been weeks since Estella had any solid sleep at all. Catching an hour or two here and there had become the norm. Today, vengeance would be served. Warm blood would be shed, but her heart had grown cold. Estella, dressed conservatively all in black, had strapped the baby taut upon her back with a makeshift sling constructed from her old blouse. She took flight for the skies. Thankfully, teleportation hadn't disappeared. To be fair, Estella was not quite sure if daemons teleported at all. Only time would tell if, or when her luck ran out. For now, Estella would enjoy each day as if it were her last.

The skies were clear; the air was crisp. The stench of humans was stronger today. It was, indeed, a perfect day to teleport. Estella travelled eight miles through the skies. The scoundrels were easy to trace. Unaware and unassuming, they would have no idea of the plot against them. Minutes in, Estella landed quietly on the roof. Like a tiger hunting its prey, she keenly scanned the surroundings, covering every square inch within milliseconds. She spotted the back garden. There they were, chatting and laughing, completely unsuspecting.

Loud, bolshie, with beer cans in hand, one in particular was slurring his words whilst stuffing his face with barbequed burgers. Bizarre music blared in the background, to which one man stood and jerked his head back and forth while tapping his left foot. Oddly enough, their happiness was a massive turn on for Estella. The lewder the jokes, the more she wanted to tear their beating hearts out of their chests. *'Grotesque,'* she mumbled with glee. Never had she seen such despicable human beings before. She counted six of them. The other four, were unknown to Estella. But, as she knew, birds of a feather flocked together. They were likely just as repugnant as the other two beasts. They were shabbily dressed, with soiled trousers, and bellies which overhung beneath stained t-shirts. Most of the men had weird markings covering most of their arms, which appeared to be some sort of graffiti. One, even had piercings covering half his face. They were weak and vulgar, ghastly men. Estella decided to kill them all. Without hesitance, she jumped down, then pounced on the first culprit from behind. It all happened so fast she wasn't even sure the others had noticed. He was a big burly man. However, she picked him up as though he were a bag of sugar, then bit into his neck as blood splattered. Only at that point did he scream, wailing like a banshee on heat. His screams echoed through the air. With a severed artery, blood shed everywhere, littering the entire garden. The others made attempts to flee. They scattered, dropping their beers as they tried to escape. Their faces were pallor with fright.

'What the hell is that?' yelled one.

Terror and panic ensued. Estella slung the man's lifeless body to the ground as she spotted the second tormenter at the door. He tried to make a quick getaway, but Estella pursued him keenly. One of the other four men fell to the ground. He had tripped whilst trying to run, allowing Estella an easy kill. She jumped on his back, then struck her entire hand through his chest, plucking out his beating heart with her razor-sharp talons. Hot blood dripped through her fingers. Suddenly, she couldn't resist a bite. The urge for human flesh took over. She sniffed the beating organ whilst waves of pleasure rippled through her body. Estella bit into the firm flesh, tearing at it with teeth designed for a wild dog. Her body shook as she swallowed each bite. Working its way down her throat, thick firm flesh felt like lumps of jelly. Peculiar, but she liked it. Soon enough, Estella became consumed, losing focus of the men. Once she became satisfied, the heart was discarded to the floor. Estella scanned the wreckage. The other three brutes were already half-way up the road, two of which were on bikes. Estella spotted the lone man. He yelled and waved his hands frantically, begging the others to stop. His face beetroot red, radiating with fear. Estella pounced on his back. He fell to the floor.

'Argh. Someone, help!' he shrieked.

'Save your breath. Nobody cares.' She jeered. Estella bit into his neck. The splutter of bright red blood caused every nerve in her body to tingle. Little wonder the wolfs were so animalistic. Human flesh was definitely far nicer than Edgar's vile synthetic rubbish, which actually, bared no resemblance to real blood. Nor flesh. The man's screams fell to a deathly low pitch. Estella watched in awe as his life force was zapped from his body, which she discarded like an empty canvass. Estella licked his neck, then took another bite. Who would have known that such a vulgar man would taste so delicious? Estella latched onto his wound, then proceeded to drink his blood. She drank until his body was still. Estella stood up, wiping her mouth with the back of her hand. A woman approached from the other side of the street. Estella, with little time to waste, made a quick getaway from the gruesome carnage. As she sprinted after the others, the baby on her back could be heard gurgling with content. She felt relieved. In all the madness, she had not given a thought to the child at all. Estella became jerky while levitating. There was a stark decline in her ability to glide through the air smoothly. Her speed slowed as levitation became difficult. Nonetheless, she spotted the culprits on bikes. They were headed for a junction. It was manic. Traffic flowed in every direction. One of the men was the culprit in the alley. He became her focus. Estella gave chase. There was an oncoming lorry. The first bike narrowly missed it, by seconds. But the other, crashed headfirst into the lorry's side mirror, throwing the driver across the windscreen. There was a mighty crash as he collided with the vehicle. The bike spun into the air, crashing into an oncoming red car. Cars screeched abruptly. However, Estella didn't mind the chaos and continued her quest with little thought to the wreckage left behind. The culprit from the alley had escaped down a narrow road. It was quieter and had little traffic. Estella was slowing. She couldn't keep her pace as she used to. She levitated high and low, bouncing from building to building like a burnt-out kangaroo. And then, her luck came in. The bike came to a sudden stop. It was a blind alley; the end widened to a small cul-de-sac. The biker threw the bike down in frustration, then proceeded to run. Estella saw her opportunity. Hot on his heels, she literally jumped on his back, throwing him to the floor.

'You crazy bitch. Get off me.'

Estella grabbed him by the neck. She spun him around to face her. Her eyes studied his. He had to see the pain he had caused. The suffering in her eyes. The man nervously fiddled with his pockets. Estella had already spotted the knife and pulled it out for him. 'Looking for this?'

He was petrified. His face became white as though he had seen a ghost. Estella threw the knife to the floor. 'You won't be needing that. Do you remember me?' she smirked at him.

'I…I don't know you. I do not know you.' He stuttered.

'How convenient. Assaulting women must be a regular past time for you, then.'

'I've never seen you in my life. Leave me alone.' He screamed.

'I want you to beg. Go on, start pleading.' She hissed.

'Please. Don't kill me.' he begged.

Estella laughed at the man's pleas. He became incontinent. She laughed as urine trickled to the floor. His face reddened as he salivated at the mouth. Estella's eyes lit up. She enjoyed his suffering. 'Looks like someone needs a diaper. Look at you. You're truly pathetic.'

'Please don't kill me. I am sorry.' He squealed.

His pleas fell upon deaf ears. There was no one around. Just a lone bird who had begun to flap above Estella's head. Estella put her finger in his mouth. She pulled out his tongue. 'You talk too much,' she said. The man's eyes rolled back into his head as he attempted to scream. Estella studied the organ. She had never seen a tongue unattached. It was intriguing. She sniffed at it. Deciding it was far less appealing than the heart, she shoved it back into his bloodied mouth. She licked the blood from her fingers.

'Thankfully, I'm not hungry. Your tongue tastes like crap. However, I think you ought to eat up.' Estella shoved the tongue further down his throat as blood and bile poured from the sides of his mouth. His eyes wild with terror, he gagged as she forced the organ down his throat. Estella threw her head back with laughter. Another kind of evil had taken hold of her. Never, had she felt so good. It wasn't long before he chocked to a slow death. He had to feel a morsel of the pain she had felt that day in the alley. Severing his throat would have been far too easy. 'In death, you will never forget this face.' Estella whispered in his ear whilst licking the side of his face. She then bit his ear off and ate it all. That was her first real meal, and an introduction to what would become regular habit. Estella ate his other ear. She dropped his lifeless body to the floor in a heap. Estella felt justice had been done.

EIGHT

'How dare she abandon me? What has gotten into her?'

Marc spoke aloud. He had his back turned in the galley as he gazed up at the portrait of Vlad III. He had a glass of blood in his right hand. He took small delicate sips deep in thought.

'I think, you mean who.'

Marc turned to Edgar. Lately they were at loggerheads. Marc, convinced Edgar was deliberately trying to battle with him, became annoyed. 'What do you mean by that?' he yelled.

'I mean, she's been up to no good. Can you not smell her disloyalty?'

Marc's expression became stern. His eyes narrowed as he bared his fangs angrily. He flew into a rage and smashed the glass to the ground, shattering it to tiny pieces. He took several steps toward Edgar, pointing a finger sternly in his face. 'Don't try me. You have never liked Estella. She is not a pureblood, you said. She was never quite one of us in your eyes. Anyway, whatever the case is, I do not think Estella is an adulterer.'

'As usual, always first to her rescue. I am impressed. At least *you've* kept your loyalty. However, Marc, you know me too well. I will not be intimidated by your temper. Nor am I trying to go to war with you. I say what I see. Louisa has been disloyal. At first, I gave her the benefit of the doubt. But that smell cannot be anything other than a werewolf. At the back door on the grounds. Along the balcony also.' Said Edgar.

For a while Marc did not say a word. He stood there motionless, eyes piercing. His forehead crumpled as he tightly pursed his lips. His hands curled into a tight fist. The temptation to tear Edgar to shreds was dangerously tempting, but he was interrupted by the Stramus who had appeared at the door. He was tall and thin, and walked with the gait of an athlete.

'Edgar tells the truth. I have smelt the rancid scent of wolf, too. None of us want to cause any further distress to your mental wellbeing. But there has definitely been a hybrid wolf of some sort loitering around on these grounds, and frankly, I am most amused that it has gone by you unnoticed.' Said Stramus, in his deep pitched tone.

Marc's shoulders slumped. His defences lowered. At that moment, he couldn't allow his pride to get the better of him. 'So, was I too blinded by love? Either that or tell me, why the hell am I unable to smell her deceit. Is there something the matter with me?'

Stramus and Edgar eyed each other. Together they looked at Marc with empathy. Ever since Estella's departure, he was a broken man. Not a night had gone by without ruckus and sorrow erupting throughout the mansion walls, reminding them both just how unhappy and grieved he had become. On one particular tensed, bleak evening, at a quarter to eleven, Marc had pushed his entire fist through the drawing room wall, taking down part of the ceiling along with it. Despite words from the elders, the wall lay in a crumpled mess, no one bothering to fix it. Tormented with his soul, they watched quietly as Marc fell deeper, and deeper, into a dark depression.

Stramus sighed. 'Marc, I am afraid I don't have the answer. You're distressed, and not focusing. I suggest you take some time to recoup and recharge. At this rate, anxiety will become of you. I do detest seeing you in this state.'

'I just want answers. And for the life of me, none of you can provide any. So, this is it? Estella has supposedly run off into the sunset with some retched creature, and no one can do anything about it. I tell you what? I will not be accepting this.' Marc wagged his finger at the elders.

'Marc, I wouldn't waste time looking for her. She must have brilliant reason for her adultery. Quite frankly, I would leave her to it. Your time and energy are best spent elsewhere.' said Edgar. He raised a reassuring hand, to which Marc hastily brushed off.

'Do not touch me! You're a patronising old fool. I've given that woman everything you could possibly desire, and yet, I am to sit and just whittle away, accepting the pain and embarrassment she's caused me? I absolutely will not allow this to happen. For all I know, this entire farce could be a set-up, orchestrated by the pair of you. Neither of you really liked her, admit it. She was never truly accepted as a pure blood, was she? Perhaps you've both staked her through the heart and gotten rid of her. I find it hard to believe that she's gone off with some fornicating wolf, considering, I have not been privy to any of this. My senses have never let me down.'

'Marc?'

'Leave him be, Stramus.'

Marc sprinted out the galley. He flung himself up the stairs three at a time. Stramus followed in hot pursuit.

'Let him go Stramus. In any case, Estella is no longer one of us.' yelled Edgar.

Marc stopped in his tracks. He turned to the eldest of the vampires with burning rage in his eyes. 'What did you just say?' spat Marc, as he flew back down to the bottom of the stair. Infuriated, he gripped Edgar tightly by the collar. The vampires squared up, pushing each other with their chests. Stramus tried to intervene.

'Marc, you must calm down' he pleaded.

Edgar, unfazed as ever, reached for his cigar, to which Marc snatched from his hands, then threw to the floor. 'Tell me what you meant. What did you mean when you said, Estella is not one of us?'

Edgar eyed him as if he were a disillusioned schoolboy. He wasn't going to be threatened by a man who allowed a woman to weaken his spirit. Nevertheless, it would only do more harm hiding Estella's infliction. If Marc so wanted the truth, he'd have to man up and face the consequences of such bad news. 'Sorry to be the bearer of bad news but, Estella has changed. She's no longer one of us, and its little use me keeping it hidden from you. Simply put, she has fornicated and betrayed you with a werewolf. Not just any werewolf may I add. The monster is half daemon. We all know what happens when daemon's mate. Their DNA consumes the other. There was no easy way to tell you this.' Edgar's tone was dry. Sugar coating wasn't his style. Marc gawked at Stramus, who then shook his head in agreement.

'Marc, I am sorry. Edgar tells no lies. Indeed, it is a terrible reality, but you deserve to know the truth.'

Marc puffed angrily through his nose. His lips rigidly pursed taut. Blue veins bulged the top of his forehead. He honestly felt he may combust. The reality of Estella's betrayal was too much to comprehend. He shook with anger. Without another word, he was gone. He had disappeared upstairs faster than lightning. The elders exchanged weary glances. They knew Marc to well. He would hunt and kill her without question. It was pointless trying to stop him. His anger was so cold, the mansion turned black. The energy became bitter. The lovely plastic lilies sat in the framed portrait on the wall near the stair, turned a horrible rancid brown. Restless nights laid ahead. Heath Hall would never be the same again. Destruction laid in waiting. Finally, Edgar spoke.

'I will not be partaking in a manhunt. Not for that woman.'

With that, Edgar disappeared down the hallway towards the basement. Stramus, was left alone with his thoughts. He looked up to the top of the stairs. He came face to face with Marc. If anyone were to offer any comfort, it would be him. Within seconds, the vampires were in the drawing room. Without a word, Stramus poured Marc a generous glass of blood. He then sat cross-legged on a grand royal blue cushioned-back chair, waiting for Marc to sound off. However, Marc's thoughts were far away. He took the drink from Stramus, gulping it faster than he had done ever before. His blood shot eyes were intense. Dark thoughts plagued his mind. He wanted to rip Estella's heart out. Edgar's, too. Nothing could've prepared him for the grieve he felt. The embarrassment was more than enough to tip him over the edge. The last thing he wanted, was for this news to get to the other vamps. He would certainly be a laughingstock.

'Marc, what *is it* you suggest we do? I mean, you may not find her. Surely, she will hang herself with her own rope.' Said Stramus.

'We must find her. I cannot have her walking around out there. No one must hear of this.'

'Marc, you cannot blame yourself. I doubt anyone would blame you, either. She's the adulterous, not you. Pride must be left at the door.' Said Stramus bluntly.

'A vampire's morale is a vampire's pride. Therefore, right now, I have neither. I will soon to be a laughingstock amongst my peers. After all, I was the one who brought a human into our clan. I went against my better judgement. She was detested right from the start. My god, why didn't I ever listen to them. Love, they say. Love surely is blind. I have been a fool.'

Stramus took a long gulp from his glass. He wasn't sure who felt less at ease. It should have been Marc, but somehow, he too felt an uncomfortable ill-ease as the reality sunk in. Estella would be killed. Pity, he had grown rather fond. 'I will help you find her.'

NINE

Estella cradled the infant. It was bittersweet. Time was running out. Very soon, she would have the unfortunate task of facing Marc. Today, she would have to move again. The longer she lingered in one place, the sooner she would be found. After all, a vampire's scent was one of their best assets. Estella wrapped the infant in taut cloth. The baby was strapped across her back like a piece of luggage. Estella grabbed the weathered brown bag before levitating off towards the dewy sky. She flew six miles south. It was a miserable, bumpy ride. It should have taken half the time, but she fell to the ground, twice. It was a miracle she managed at all. Daemons certainly were not known for their levitating, that's for sure. Estella was backtracking in an attempt to throw them off her trial. Her mind wondered as she travelled through patches of strong winds. Her own mother would have been proud of her, that she was sure of. As an only child, her relationship with her mother was one she would cherish forever. Estella wondered about her mortality, and what if she had remained human. Perhaps she would've had several children, maybe a husband, too. A normal, humanly existence like everybody else, that's the life she should have led. No vampires, no werewolves, and certainly no retched daemons.

A sudden gust of wind caught Estella of guard. She wobbled with arms outstretched, trying to steady herself. Estella spotted a small mass of people. It was yet another little town full of unsuspecting villagers. Except for a rather large gas station attached to an adjoining restaurant, there was little else on offer. Estella had no idea where she was, sniffing the air for clues. Evidently, she had led a reclusive life. The last hundred years were spent behind the walls of Heath Hall, with little more than a handful of visitors every few months, or so. Estella felt like fish out of water being back out in the real world. A whiff of canine caught her nose. In fact, the stench of werewolf was strong, it hit her like a ton of brick as she tried not to retch. So, Estella was wrong. This was not a place inhabited by humans. Estella hid discreetly behind a stone wall. Just then, a lady brushed past from behind. She was an older woman, neatly dressed, carrying several plastic bags. She looked at Estella with narrowed hazel eyes and immediately behaved as though she had seen a ghost. She let out a squeal as she hurried on her heels. Estella rolled her eyes. It was the Daemon, apparently. The great mythical monster which had an even greater hold over the werewolf community. Estella remembered the young man at the motel. He had knelt as though greeting The Queen. Like a phantom goddess, she was coveted but also feared. Werewolves, with their big bad selves, showed little self-respect when faced with a real threat. This was partly why vampires dismissed them as inferior playthings. It was comical to gauge their reaction. Surely, vampires were too dignified to display such pathetic behaviour. Even when, faced with the Daemon. Estella walked a little then came to a row of shops. One in-particular stood out like a sore thumb. In big, bold lettering it read; "**Human bait here**". As she stared at the sign with intrigue, she was approached by two curious little girls tugging at her sleeves. 'Hello madam, our father says you look lost. We can help you find your way.' Estella looked at the adorable pair of girls. She smiled coyly.

'Where is your father?'

'Over there?'

The girls pointed to a tall, mysterious man. Dressed in head to toe black; he had piercing green eyes and a familiar face, though she couldn't quite place it. Estella stared open mouthed at the stranger. He too, gazed with intent. He knew exactly what she was and merely used the children to garner her attention. Was she being used as bait? Perhaps. The man walked toward her. Estella froze on the spot. He seemed benign, but a sudden dread crept from within. Paranoia took over and Estella fled.

'Wait,' he said.

Estella quickly scampered off. He behaved like he knew her. She could not shake off the familiarity. Unfortunately, she felt way too vulnerable to trust a soul. Ever since giving birth, she was in a permanent protective mode. Fearing that everyone was out to get her, she would trust no one. The infant gurgled something as though reminding her she was still intact. Estella was certain the infant already had the comprehension of a fifteen-year-old and always seemed to gurgle at just the right time, providing a source of comfort whenever the need arose.

'Thank you' Estella positioned her arms to give the child a gentle tap on the back. The baby gurgled again, kicking her legs happily as she did so. Estella looked over her shoulder. There in the distance, was the man. He was transfixed, staring at her with his arms rigidly by his side. could see the man staring her at her. He hadn't moved from the spot. Estella felt a shiver in her spine. The two little girls hung off either arm, beaming at her with their big curious eyes. Feeling rather spooked, Estella walked until she came to a well-lit store. The rising sun bounced off the glass door. Estella gently pushed the door, then stopped. "No vampires." Read the sign.

Deciding she was no longer a vampire; Estella was going to take her chances. Afterall, wasn't she now a daemon? In need of some sustenance, Estella went against her better judgement and pushed the door open. The door gave a peculiar chime as she walked in. Never had Estella been into a store, not within the last hundred and fifty years. She was greeted by rows upon rows of stuff. A large fridge stocked with cold beverages, was five-foot away over on the right behind a shelve of canned goods. Curiosity got the better of her. Estella walked towards the fridge, then yanked the door open. Quizzingly, she reached for a can. It was nice and cold as her hand gripped it tight. Beef flavoured soda, was inscribed on the side of the can. Estella took it along, eyeing it all the while. She walked towards the counter with no real means of paying for it but would have to use her powers of persuasion instead. The man behind the counter, beamed at her like a hawk. Rather surprisingly he didn't cower, nor did he seem bothered by her presence. He had friendly eyes, and a mop of dark hair.

'Tell me, am I seeing things? Are you for real?' he asked, glaring at her as though she were some sort of object.

Estella was taken aback. She couldn't work out if he was being rude, or just high-spirited. She eyed him suspiciously as his lips curled at the corners. Sensing he was no threat, she lowered her guard.

'Of course, I'm real.' she cheekily snapped back.

'I didn't know your type came around here. You're a Daemon, aren't you? The first I've seen since I was a six-year-old boy. I nearly got killed because of your people.'

His tone was casual with a playful demeanour. This being said, Estella didn't appreciate it. Being labelled a daemon was a disgrace. She felt awful but couldn't deny her infliction.

'What do you mean, my type? I am a vampire.'

The silence was deathly awkward. The man behind the counter raised a thick left brow. He looked a little confused, as did she. For a while the pair just stared quizzingly at each other, wondering what to say next. The man's face grew a little concerned. He rubbed his chin.

'Well, I used to bloody be.' Estella spoke beneath her breath. Her embarrassment was evident.

'Are you ok love? Do you need a seat? You look...'

'Awful? Yes, I am sure I do.' Said Estella, head lowered.

Estella looked up with tears in her eyes. There was something different about this stranger. His heart was pure. Unlike the others, there was no shred of hostility coming from him. In fact, Estella had never felt such warmth.

'Why aren't you scared of me?' she asked him.

'Should I be?'

That was a fair question. One in which, she couldn't fully answer. 'I don't know. Because everyone else seems to be.'

'Listen love, I'm a free thinker. Anyway, why don't you take a seat. Seems like you're lost.'

The man pointed to a brown wooden chair to the right of the counter. Rickety and small, appearing to be suitable for a young child. Nonetheless, Estella appreciated the gesture but knew she couldn't stay. It wouldn't be safe.

'Thank you, but I must go.'

Estella turned on her heels. The man saw the infant strapped to her back. 'You've got a baby. Is someone after you?' He sounded worried.

'A vampire.' She said, not bothering to turn back around.

The werewolf's eyes widened. 'A vampire? Why is a vampire after you?'

'It's a long story. I do not wish to bore you with it. I must go now.'

'You can hide out in here. I'm single. I've no wife or kids and could do with the company. I won't give you any trouble. Promise.'

Estella turned back to face the werewolf. She studied his face. Bizarrely, he seemed to genuinely care about her wellbeing. How could a stranger care as much as he did? Why did he care? However, Estella could see his thoughts as clear as day. He was an honest man, and nothing like the werewolves she had encountered. Perhaps he was a blessing in disguise. Estella looked around the little shop. She had nowhere else to go. Even for a supernatural being, she had grown restless. If she kept running, she would surely soon tire. Trusting her intuition, Estella reluctantly agreed.

TEN

The evening night was colder than usual. The bite in the air made for the perfect atmosphere. Tonight, the vampires were out in full force. Marc, with Stramus's reluctant aid, had managed to gather up two more men. Edgar had decided not to partake in the 'hunt'. Instead, Marc, Stramus, Ewin, and Adrian, would hunt her down fiercely through the night. Marc, driven by vengeance, and spurned on by humiliation, wouldn't allow another night to pass him by without seeking some recompense for his suffering. The four-strong clan had gathered at the mansion, keenly taking orders from Marc.

'We will travel from city to city, inspecting all human towns, and werewolf habitats alike. No ground must be uncovered.'

'You still haven't told us why we must look for her? Perhaps, she doesn't want to be found.' Said Adrian.

'I am afraid I cannot divulge such information. We must find her, then I, will deal with the matter.'

'Marc, she may be dangerous. She can be a threat to vampires.' Said Stramus.

Ewin wrinkled his brow. 'Dangerous? What do you mean? What exactly is going on here?' he demanded.

Marc pursed his lips with a deathly stare. They would surely find out sooner, or later. Truth was, such an infliction couldn't be hidden. After a long pause, his tone was deadpan. His head hung as he spoke. 'Estella has been tainted. She's not one of us. I will explain later. Just be careful, and make sure we keep her alive.' There were raised brows all around.

'Marc, I am sorry, but I need more than that. Tainted with what, exactly? I am not flying around the city for hours looking for some freak show. Plus, if she's a threat to vampires, I am seriously questioning your reasoning for putting us all at risk with no forewarning.' Adrian angrily curled his fists.

'Vampires do not morph themselves into another species.' declared Ewin loudly.

Ewin, tallest and most slender out the lot, had a sharp scar across his face. He was fearless and was known to kill on impulse. In fact, it was because of vampires like him, why the treaty came into position in the first place. There would be no humans left on earth if he had his way. Or werewolves for that matter. He was a proud vampire and tried to create a world with nothing but vampires.

'Is she…a werewolf?' His eyes looked eager. He was almost gearing himself up for a kill.

'Not in history has such a thing happened.' said Adrian.

Marc felt himself shaking. He became lightheaded and felt in need of blood. He had to steady himself on the banister.

'Can everyone shut up! That's enough. She's a whore. She's a god damned whore, and that's all you need to know.'

The room fell silent. The three vamps exchanged woeful glares. They knew Marc better than anyone. Her adultery was obvious, his usual joyful demeanour replaced by unrepentant anger and hostility, was unlike nothing they had witnessed in all his three hundred years they had known one another.

'Marc, you look rather pale. Even by vampire standards. You need a meal.' Urged Stramus.

'Thank you, Stramus, I'll keep note of that.'

'Very well, we best get going.' Said Stramus.

'So, are we to spare her? Werewolves have no place in our spaces.' Said Ewin.

'Of course, I want her alive.' snapped Marc. He gulped hard, doubting his own confidence. The thought of his beloved Estella out there was a blow too hard to fathom. As much as he toyed with the idea of ripping her throat out, he wasn't sure he could bring himself to do it. He wanted her back in the mansion, tied to the cellar, and punished if necessary. At exactly 12am, the vampires took flight. They headed for the nearest city, Aylesbury, of which was mostly inhabited by humans. Marc knew Estella would likely stray from other species, so this had to be the best bet.

The vampires flew five miles, south. The town was derelict, as one would expect at such an hour. Just on que, the humans were tucked away in bed, leaving stray animals to roam the streets. With little human distractions, 12am was indeed the best time for the supernatural to find one another. The four men scoured the town, searching any obvious hotspots high and low. They were led by scent, which was becoming steadily hard to track down considering she was no longer one of them. However, Marc was certain it wouldn't go unmissed. He knew her smell better than anyone. The hours rolled by.

'I want blood tonight. Real blood.' laughed Ewin.

'Not a single miserable human in sight. I can hardly believe it.'

'Not too fast Adrian. The night is young.' said Stramus.

'Stramus, you ought to know better. Killing humans is beneath us.' said Marc

'No one has time for the morality police, Marc. We want a kill tonight.'

Ewin's voice seemed to echo across the entire night sky as he spoke. His dark eyes were sinisterly wicked. Hours had rolled by, but the search wasn't over. The vampires allowed their senses to guide them, navigating through town to town. At 4am, Stramus decided enough was enough. They left the over-populated human town of Buckinghamshire behind and had instead flown West. They arrived at the last renowned vampire city, Killbraith. Hundreds of vampires filled the streets. The buzzing of chatter and noise was immense. Women, men, old and the young, they were all out in full force. Several synthetic blood banks were lined up sat side by side like candy floss machines, covered in red velvet cloth. Vampires queued to sample its delights. Apparently, it was the purest blood. That from a Tibetan monk. Said to give extra powers and heighten the senses. There was a charming man in a red suit waving at passers-by in an attempt to woo them with his blood machines.

'How interesting. Perhaps we should que.'

'We're not here to partake in some damned circus.' Snapped Marc.

'Well, I don't know about you, but I am rather ravished. We've hunted high and low for the best part of four hours. I will be damned if I do not get a meal. Either that, or I will gladly maul the first human being to cross my path.' Said Ewin.

Marc hissed angrily. Stramus gave him a gentle nod of reassurance. They had done their bit. A little indulgence wouldn't be such a bad thing. 'Marc, this blood is most intriguing. It wouldn't hurt to have a bit of fun.' He coaxed. Marc wasn't listening. Someone had caught his gaze. Someone far more interesting than what a Tibetan monk had to offer. Suddenly, he wandered off. 'Very well.' Stramus looked over to the line of eager vamps. Adrian had haply joined Ewin in line, who had already decided he wouldn't be leaving without a taste. Just then, Ewin, being the chauvinistic, flamboyant character he was, made an announcement. Adrian and Stramus eyed with suspicion.

'Ladies and gentlemen, boys and girls, can I have your attention please.'

Ewin's voice was deep and husky, causing a chill as he spoke. Suddenly, the chatter came to a still. Ewin had their attention. However, the man in the red suit became deeply irritated at Ewin's ploy to take over his show. Stramus was stunned. He looked on from the side lines, regretting his decision to ever participate. 'What would be greater than monk's blood? What if, we had an actual monk, here tonight. Wouldn't that be splendid?' The man looked horrified. He grew angry.

'You great buffoon. Who do you think you are?'

Ewin exchanged daring glances with the man in the suit. Adrian shook his head. He knew his cousin was an idiot, but this was a complete underestimation of his lunacy.

'Christ, can you not que like everybody else without making a scene?' he hissed

'Who am I? the question is, who are you? And why do these proud Vampires que like imbeciles for a taste of blood that supposedly originates from a Tibetan monk? Now, that's the real question.'

'I will pluck your heart out and feed you to the wolves. Are you deliberately trying to jeopardise my business?'

'I wouldn't do such a thing. I am just trying to get my people back. The real vampires. The ones who enjoy a good kill. There's nothing better than fresh blood. I am sick to my back teeth of all this synthetic rubbish. I am also 100% certain no actual monks were killed for its production. Isn't it about time we be gone with all this nonsense?'

Suddenly, the crowd cheered in agreement. Despite his reservations, Stramus mustered a sly smile. Truth be known, Ewin had a point. The vampire race had become weaker over the last fifty years. Definitely more docile. Nothing how they used to be. Taking away the opportunity to kill, had all but castrated them. Suddenly, Marc re-appeared amongst the crowds.

'He is right. Why do we subject ourselves to this nonsense? We aren't human beings, queuing meekly at a grocery store. We are vampires, for heaven sakes! And it's about time we start behaving as such. The treaty has a lot to answer for.'

'He is right. We should be killing again.'

'We are proud vampires.' yelled another.

Just then, the vampire in the slick red suit struck Ewin's throat. Distracted by the crowd, Ewin hadn't seen it coming. Blood spurted everywhere. But it wasn't over. Ewin grabbed the vampire by the throat, lifting him off the ground. He threw him several feet in the air, tossing him as though he were a bag of sugar. His throat had been cut. Fortunately, he healed faster than he bled. Ewin was mighty strong and would be a challenge for most. The crowd looked on with glee. For reasons unknown, vampires enjoyed a good brawl, more so amongst themselves. Ewin held his neck, moving it side to side as if readying himself for a boxing match.

'Those darn nails of yours.' he muttered

The man in the suit swiftly made his way back to the crowd. He wasn't the least bit impressed. 'I should have struck harder.' He seethed in anger.

'That is enough! Snap out of it, the pair of you. We ought to stick together, not fight each other.' said Stramus.

'Well, *I* have an announcement to make.' Everyone turned to Marc. He had their full attention.

'My beloved wife has mysteriously disappeared. Vanished without a trace. I desperately need your help. Tonight, we have searched high and low with little to show for it.' Just then, Marc removed a paper from his pocket. It was rather large. He took time to carefully unfold the edges. It was a portrait of Estella. Beautifully meticulous, just as she had been in better times. She looked immaculate. Marc held the paper high, allowing all to ogle his mate.

'We *must* find her. I want her unharmed. A reward awaits anyone who can bring her to me safely.'

'I want to help.' An older woman with neatly coifed mousy hair with lashings of red lipstick, piped up. As so did several others.

'Her appearance, may, or may not altered somewhat. But I am sure you are all wise enough to recognise a face if you see one. I reside in Heath Hall. That's where I will be. I am sure, every vampire will know where to find me,' said Marc.

'This is gate crashing, and I do not appreciate it.' Said the vampire in red.

'And for that, I apologise. We will be gone.' Said Marc.

Ewin squared up with the host. 'Aren't you going to offer us a hospitable drink?'

'No, I certainly will not.' Snapped the host in red.

Ewin and the host eyed each other with venom. Adrian tugged at Ewin's arm. Reluctantly, Ewin softened. The four vampires made their departure, leaving the lively town of Killbraith behind. The vampires of Killbraith vowed to help with Marc's quest. He had no doubts, they would. The journey back home was a heavy one for Marc to bear. Gravely disappointed, he hardly spoke a word. The air was bitterly sharp creating a frost around his ears. Perfect for the undead. Stramus levitated with finesse. Older than the others, he had a habit of disappearing into thin air, vanishing on the spot. It wasn't long before the men gathered at the mansion door of Heath Hall.

'Same time tomorrow night?' Adrian studied Marc's expression.

'If I end up with another severed neck, I'm suing.' Said Ewin.

'Perhaps, you won't be such a prat tomorrow night.' said Stramus.

'That's rather harsh. Ewin had some great points. We need our people back. We have become complicit puppets.'

Marc was on the side of the opposition. He felt strongly. They were no longer vampires. Instead, like sheep, they were programmed one after another, all complying to a dead man's quest. Tonight, was a wasted venture. However, Marc was not one to give up. He had pursued Estella keenly in hot pursuit until she caved into his manly charms. He was up for the challenge.

'Same time tomorrow night. I need you all on form.'

'Very well. I shall see you then.'

Adrian promptly disappeared from the mansion steps, levitating into the air at great speed.

'Merry men. Look for me at 1am.' said Ewin with a nod.

And with that, the men parted ways at the door. Marc and Stramus, headed inside. The pair were greeted by a gloating Edgar.

'Any luck?'

Marc took a swipe at him. 'One of these days, I promise to drive a stake through your heart.' he spat.

'Marc' Stramus became angry. Quite frankly, his tolerance for Marc's moody disposition was steadily wearing thin.

'Maybe, it's his fault she's gone. Look at him. I've never seen him so content with her disappearance.'

Edgar became rattled. He had put up with enough insults from Marc, and tonight he decided he had enough. Within seconds, he lifted Marc off the ground by the scruff of his collar, and threw him to the floor, crashing into one of the stately pillars adorning the marble staircase. Swiftly, Marc rose to his feet and shot in front of him. Edgar grabbed him by the throat.

'If you were not your father's son, you would be diminished.' Snapped Edgar.

'How considerate. Please don't let that stop you. I don't even care about the man.'

Edgar's usual cool demeanour had been stirred. He had little qualms about defeating Marc. If provoked enough, he would finish him without hesitation.

'Edgar that's enough. Let him be.' begged Stramus.

Marc struggled to free himself from Edgar's grip. He backed away whilst eyeing them both with vulgar. They had overstayed their welcome and he wanted them gone but needed their help.

'Very well. But stay away from me, do you hear me.' he hissed, pointing at Edgar with a keen finger.

Marc disappeared through the hall, and up to the landing. The two old vampires awkwardly glared at each other while Edgar straightened his collar. Edgar broke the awkward silence.

'Stramus, I have a confession to make. With all this ruckus going on, I fancy a kill tomorrow tonight. We have become accustomed to all this synthetic blood nonsense.'

Stramus eyed him oddly 'You do know we will be chastised if the board gets wind.'

Edgar brushed off any concerns with a wag of his finger.

'Stramus, there are ways old boy. Be wise and be weary, but not to the detriment of living. Truth be told, we haven't lived since the introduction of this blasted treaty. Anyway, daybreak is almost upon us. I'm off to sleep. If you're not too busy hunting down Estella, perhaps tomorrow night we could have a feast. A proper feast.'

Edgar walked off leaving Stramus bamboozled and open mouthed. He ran his left hand over his smooth bald head. He looked up at the twelve-foot-high ceiling with the huge bulbous chandelier centred to the middle. He despaired. He had already promised Marc his help. Once again, he was placed in a compromising situation created for Edgar's ego. However, he couldn't let marc down and would have to disappoint his cousin. Confined to a life of eternity with his warring cousin, was at times no easy feat. At times, Stramus felt his immortality was more curse than a blessing. Over the decades, he and Edgar had their sour moments, nearly severing his head on one gruesome occasion a hundred and- forty years prior. Quite frankly he was fed up of taking on the role of peacemaker in times of conflict. Stramus, had more pressing issues on his mind. Like the very reason they were called to Heath Hall in the first place. They had yet to find the predator prying on vampires, and now, his suspicions turned to the daemon. It was a feeling he couldn't quite shake off, and it made perfect sense. He would discuss his concerns with Marc tomorrow as perhaps; they were biting off more than they could chew. Maybe there were a whole herd of them, Estella included, just using Estella's disappearance as bait, waiting to be found. Vampires were strong and fast but daemons, were a whole other ballgame. A cold chill ran along his slender arms.

ELEVEN

Estella couldn't shake the rancid werewolf scent that lingered in the air today, more so than any other day in particular. Wrinkling her nose viciously only seemed to make it worse. However, it was an unfortunate reality, and one she was slowly becoming accustomed to, and could certainly tolerate it more than she used to. Estella got to know Stefan well. He was funny and humorous, nothing like she had expect a werewolf to be. Then again, what did she expect? Rarely had she frequented with them. Vampires spoke of them like a folklore character from a retched fairy-tale, so maybe her opinion was biased. Stefan lived in the cellar beneath the shop. It was the perfect secluded spot, free from preying eyes. Some days she ate flesh, others, she fancied blood. Sometimes, Estella would go days without any appetite at all. Perhaps this was the nature of a hybrid daemon. One night, she had followed Stefan to the human park. They killed a young man, feasting upon him like a bunch of wild dogs. Like a compulsive cannibal, Estella unashamedly ate the flesh and had enjoyed every limb. Marc would be disgusted, if only he knew. She was a complete anomaly, with no set routine or structure to adhere to.

Stefan said, there would be a full moon tonight. This was something Estella secretly feared.

'So, am I destined to become a damned wolf creature tonight?'

Estella surveyed his expression and immediately offered up an apology. Of course, she hadn't meant to offend him, but the fear of becoming a four-legged creature caused waves of anxiety churning itself around in her stomach. Frankly, she was petrified. Like a terrible nightmare, she feared herself and what she would become. Stefan, not one to take offence, smiled at her discomfort.

'I think not. But I guess you will have to wait and see'.

As usual, Stefan was cool, calm, and collected. That was all he said. Unfortunately, this done nothing to soothe Estella's fears. 'You're likely more daemon than werewolf, so I guess you will only half turn.' He teased. Stefan's laugh was infectious. He enjoyed joking around. A trait which Estella grew fond of.

'You are still part vampire, aren't you?' He winked at her playfully.

'I'm not certain I am. Not anymore. I was told my vampiric DNA would be diluted to such meagre portions; it wouldn't be worth mentioning. As far as I can tell. I certainly feel less vampire-like than I used to. I ate a man yesterday for heaven's sake!'

'Ah! And the humans think they got it bad!' He laughed. Stefan had a twinkling in his eyes. The infant was bouncing up and down on her mother's knee, chewing her finger, in fits of laughter.

'She's enjoying herself.' Quipped Stefan

'Look at the size of her. You would not believe she was born less than a month ago.'

Indeed, the infant was already the size of a six-month-old. Stefan looked surprised. 'Wow. that's some rapid growth spurt she had,' he said.

'Do werewolf babies grow this quickly as well?' asked Estella.

'No, not to my knowledge. I was a fat kid but that was down to my never-ending appetite.' He joked

'It does worry me, you know. Her growth spurt,' Estella's voice fell.

'It does?'

Just then, the door chimed loudly. Someone had walked in. Stefan gave Estella a quick glance. 'I'll be right back' he said, before darting off up the stair.

Estella heard the chatter of a woman's voice in a high-pitched irritable tone. She was debating on several cans of meat and couldn't seem to make her mind up.

'Wouldn't it be far tastier, and easier, if we could just kill on demand? I hate all of this 'keeping in line' nonsense. The humans serve little purpose. This canned meat, tastes like cardboard. Have you no livestock?'

'I am sorry mam, but we no longer stock human remains.' Said Stefan flatly.

'Another shop trying to be politically current. This fake meat is rubbish. It doesn't even taste like cattle.' She snorted.

'Well, it is real meat, I can assure you. Perhaps you should try the sheep. It's the tastiest out the lot.'

Stefan smiled stiffly through gritted teeth. This woman had been in once before, several months back. He vividly remembers the ruckus she had caused the first time around.

'Perhaps I ought to go to Aylesbury tonight. I fancy human.' The woman continued to whine.

'Well. I am sure you could, and that is entirely your choice. Eating humans should not be encouraged. But I am sure as an occasional treat, one human makes little difference, right?'

Stefan gave her a sly wink. His sarcasm was brilliant, but he couldn't help feeling like a hypocrite. After all, he had killed and eaten a man the night before, so felt wrong to patronise someone else on such a delicacy. Truth be known, he had not wanted to partake in it, but Estella was adamant she had to have a 'real meat' and swore she would do it with or without him. Truth be known, it was one of the best meals he had in a long time.

'So, are you admitting your food is crap?' she looked at him with her nose perched over her glasses like a disapproving school-teacher. Her voice was animated. It was obvious she was begging for an argument. Stefan's demeanour changed.

'No, I did not say that. I said the sheep is great, otherwise, do as you please. You want human flesh? Knock yourself out. I am sure you know exactly where to find them.'

Stefan's voice grew irritable. His playful tone was replaced by an icy sharp pitch. Estella had never heard Stefan like that. Stefan's arm was trying to usher the woman out of the shop. Reluctantly, the woman came to a decision.

'Ok. I'll have two cans of sheep.' She sighed loudly admitting defeat.

'Great. That's £32.'

The woman looked stunned at the price. She wanted to protest, but must've seen the annoyance on Stefan's face, and decided it better to keep quiet. The woman paid for the goods with a taut upper lip, then quickly left the shop. Hot sweat dripped from Stefan's brow. It was days like this he questioned whether he had chosen the right career. Farming was a childhood passion; one he never managed to achieve. After his father's death at fifteen, the family business had gone bust. The farm was taken away. Any plans to take over, had gone down the drain. Owning the shop was a lucky accident which had happened at the right time. However, Stefan was steadily growing tired of it and had recent contemplations of other pursuits. Without wife nor child, he was a roving bachelor and had led a lonely life. His first love decided she'd had enough of him two years in and had left him for an older more affluent wolf. If the truth be told, Stefan had never really gotten over that. Of course, charming werewolves had flung themselves at him on many occasions, but none of which Stefan took a shine to. He convinced himself it was better to be single, than risk another disappointment. Over the years, his sister had tried to 'pair' him up with many eligible women, but seemingly none were ever good enough to replace his Susannah. But something in him had changed since Estella's arrival. Stefan couldn't be sure exactly what his obsession was, but she drew him in like a moth to a flame. Suddenly, the idea of a ready-made family no longer filled him with dread. Unlike most women he had come across, Estella lacked that need to be desired. This was something he found very attractive. Despite having no intention to overstay her welcome, Stefan had practically begged Estella to stay a little longer. At the very least, in some warped way, he could pretend it was the family he never had. Though Estella was a species to be feared and wary of, this was no concern to Stefan in the slightest. In fact, it made him all the more intrigued. Stefan headed back down to the quaint little flat beneath the shop.

'So, any plans for today?' he asked with a smile.

Estella had placed the baby on a pile of cushions lying on the floor, and was walking from the bathroom with wet hair, towel in hand.

'I want to stay in.' she flashed him a wide grin.

Estella looked down at her hands. Thankfully, they were no longer curled over like a little old woman. Her rigid fingers were agile once again. Unfortunately, Estella knew the biggest change was yet to come. She felt like a freak and wanted to hide from the world. It was safer and not wanting to risk exposure of being seen by vampires.

'Ok, that's no problem,' he said.

Stefan sat on the sofa as she paced back and forth. With the exception of last night, Estella had not left the house since she had arrived. He knew nothing about her story. She said she was an unfortunate vampire who had endured a bite from a feral man and was now doomed to a life as a hybrid daemon. Estella had said little else, and Stefan didn't want to pry. But he smelt her fear. Like a bad perfume, she lingered in it. Today, his intrigued got the better of him. He took her hand in his.

'Estella, I must be honest. You radiate in fear. What really happened? What about the baby'

Stefan's tone was gentle. He asked with caution for fear of causing any unnecessary upset. Estella looked him square in the eye. She knew it would happen. Naturally, he would be curious of how she became to be, and she knew Stefan knew better. He wasn't convinced that she was bitten by some rouge feral daemon. After all, everyone knew vampires couldn't reproduce, so naturally he assumed the child was fathered by a daemon. Embarrassment and shame crept over her. How could she tell him her secret? How could she tell him she was an unscrupulous cheat, who had betrayed her partner of nearly three centuries? As if that wasn't bad enough, she then had an entire baby for someone else.

TWELVE

Back at the mansion despair and gloom echoed through the walls. Crows had taken to the roof in droves, seeping further blackness over the estate. Heath Hall had lost its great majestic appeal. Happiness had disappeared, and it showed. Marc hadn't eaten in several days. His eyes had sunken. His skin was pallor.

'You look ghastly. You must eat something. Not a single drop of blood has touched your lips for the past week.' said Stramus.

Marc stood like a fixture in the middle of the galley. He outstretched his arms. Long, thin, and covered in red veins. He fluttered his robe, which draped off him like a pair of badly fitting curtains. The candlelight reflected off his deathly pale skin. His eyes were sealed tight; wrinkles lined his forehead. Marc took little notice of Stramus. His anguish was driven by desperate thoughts of Estella, and no matter how hard he tried, he couldn't get her out of his head. He had begun hallucinating and was certain he had seen her in the bedroom this morning. He was literally, going insane. He spun around on his toes, exactly how he had done dancing with Estella. A sly smile erupted on his face as he continued to spin to the inaudible music that was playing in his head. Just then, Edgar strolled in the galley. Dressed in a silk black robe with a twinkle in his eye, he was determined to have a kill. He seemingly paid little attention to Marc.

'Stramus, are you accompanying me? hungry. I am ravenous,' he said.

Stramus frowned. He looked over at Marc. He continued to dance, locked within his own head, spinning around in a morbid state. Edgar raised a brow. 'Let's not worry about him. He is definitely old enough to fend for himself.' Edgar's tone was flat and unforgiving.

'I still worry.'

'Of course you do. You wouldn't be you, otherwise. You were never really cut out for this stuff, were you. After nearly five hundred years, you still haven't figured out how to control those emotions of yours, dear cousin. You really ought to toughen up. We are vampires, after all!'

Edgar grinned broadly. Practical and logical, he was often the voice of reason, albeit not a voice Marc resonated with. He pulled on his thick white eyebrows. 'We must remember why we are here. We must hunt the brute murdering our own. The culprit is still out there, and I am sure it is a daemon. Wolves are no challenge at all.'

After some hesitation, Stramus piped up. 'Ok, let's get some dinner.' He smiled broadly, but his eyes lacked their usual twinkle, suggesting he had allowed his concerns about Marc to get the better of him. Stramus looked down at his own robe. Nowhere as sophisticated and glamourous as Edgar's, but he wasn't one to make a fuss of things.

'Fabulous. This will be fun.' Quipped Edgar.

The duo left the galley. The old vampires teleported up the stairs as fast as lightning, then departed from the loft window. Within seconds, they were out through the roof. In true vampire superstition, they refused to take the door. Back In the galley, a disconsolate Marc spun a thousand times. His bellowing black robe danced along with him. His sorrow so black, every window in the galley shattered. A crow circled the ceiling. Sharp wind bellowed through the large room. In a hypnotic state, Marc and Estella danced hand in hand, two steps to the side, one step back. Her hands were as soft as soap. They used to dance all night. Estella's laugh was infectious. Marc smiled as he took in the serene waft of her perfume. Delicate and sinful hints of vanilla and jasmine could be smelt on her powdery silky skin. Like lovestruck teenagers, they could dance all night. Evidently, tonight, there was to be no hunt.

The Hampshire streets was lonely after hours. Except for a few stray cats, there was no one to be seen. For a Thursday night, you would assume it to be Monday. The night sky caused a lovely ambiance as the vampires travelled in a hazy mist like form, breezing through the cold autumn air. Edgar travelled with his eyes tightly shut. Aptly guided by his senses and had no need for sight. The night was perfect. It had been years since he had felt so free and was adamant to enjoy it. As usual, Stramus cruised several feet behind, never one to rush. The vampires had flown for twenty miles. Suddenly, something broke their concentration. A couple of teenage boys emerged from a park. They drank cans of alcohol and spoke loudly.

'She wanted it.'

A tall skinny boy with a mop of blonde hair, chuckled with fits of laughter as he teased the other.

'Fuck off. You're still a virgin.'

'Whatever, mate. You would know.'

The boys laughed and ribbed one another. The dark-haired boy threw his can to the ground. He dug his hands deep inside his trouser pockets, then spat twice upon the ground.

'Geez, it's getting cold man.' he said.

'Tell mummy to give you a jumper next time.' Said the other.

The blonde was elbowed to the ribs. 'Argh, Matthew. Why did you do that for?'

Unbeknown to the hapless pair, the eager vampires watched the teenagers like a hawk from above. Delight beamed in Edgar's eyes. This was a look Stramus knew too well, but one he hadn't seen in years.

'Time for dinner.'

'Edgar, they're only children.'

'No. They're a pair of rude, obnoxious little brats, and clearly old enough to be roaming the streets at such an hour.' He spat.

Stramus was reluctant. 'I refuse to kill children, no matter how insufferable they may be. I am afraid I'll have to sit this one out.'

Edgar rolled his eyes. Age had certainly mellowed his cousin. Several centuries ago, Stramus ran rampant. He was unstoppable, killing every other human in sight. Both young and old, Stramus had his turn. They were so gluttonous for fresh blood, not a single night went by without a blood bath. Other vampires got wind and wanted little to do with the uncivilised pair. Look at them now. How times had changed. With the introduction of the treaty, humanly rules had been put into place governing their every move. In fact, it had become hell on earth. Edgar longed for the good old days. The days where vampires were free again.

'Well, suit yourself. You're more than welcome to watch whilst I feed myself. This is a rare treat, and I'll be damned if I give in to that blasted machine tonight. My lips crave real human blood.'

'I don't have the heart for it. Not as I used to.'

'That, I do know.'

Stramus watched from the periphery as his cousin crept behind the boisterous teenagers. Totally unaware, they stopped in their tracks as Edgar appeared in their path from a mist of white smoke. 'Not so fast, boys.' He smiled.

'What the fuck.' yelled the blonde.

Their faces, pallor with fright. The blonde begun to back away. However, the red-head seemed traumatised to the spot. 'A vampire.'

'Well done. At least one of you was paying attention.' Said Edgar.

Edgar greeted them with a deathly stare. Arms outstretched, he opened up his robe to expose black trousers and shirt. Fangs bared his smile became chillingly sinister. The blonde attempted to run the other way. Edgar flew on his back, knocking him to the ground. His screams unsettled Stramus. It aroused a certain instinct he hadn't wished to awaken. The wet patch running along the sides of the other's boy's trousers, made Stramus all the more curious. As Edgar bit into his victim's neck, ravishing his flesh like a monstrous beast, blood trickled along the grey paving stones, turning it into a bloody battlefield. The redhead having somewhat recovered from his fears, made an ill-attempt to run. For a while, he scurried along under Stramus eagle-eyed glare. His shrill screams struggled to leave his mouth, panting with shallow breaths. Stramus eyes were transfixed. All his thoughts were on the frightened boy, desperately running for his life. His hands shook as he heard the swiftly beating heart a mile off. His adrenaline drew Stramus in like a moth to a flame. Very soon, Stramus vampiric instinct kicked in. His eyes bulged as he took flight after the running boy. His mouth opened wide as he prepared for a kill. Seconds in, he had caught up with the boy, landing on his back. He crashed to the ground in a heap. Stramus saw red. He gazed at the boy's neck as veins bulged to the surface. His blood smelt sweet. Sweeter than any he had smelt in years.

'Argh, don't kill me. Please.' The boy's pleas fell upon deaf ears. 'I'm only fifteen. I'm still a virgin. I didn't touch her, I promise.'

Stramus eyed him suspiciously. He knew better. Birds of a feather flocked together. This boy was as guilty as the other. Stramus had seen his misdoings. His molestation of that innocent girl was as clear as the images that flashed before his eyes. Like a high-definition computer screen, his heinous atrocities were played out despite his cries of the contrary. Any guilt Stramus may have had, dispersed quicker than the brutal bite he delivered to the neck of his victim.

'Quieten down little boy. It will be over before you know it.'

THIRTEEN

Estella had not the courage nor the gall to reveal what had happened. Claiming her mother was attacked by a daemon, was as best she could manage. She didn't want to be judged, and worried about Stefan's opinion if he knew the truth. How could she tell him temptation had led her astray? She'd be deemed immoral, a scandalous whore, and deserved everything she got. And where would she go if he kicked her out? What about the baby? She had settled into predictable routine at Stefan's and begun to oddly enjoy it. However, despite Stefan's chilled and goofy demeanour, Estella's insecurities intensified by the day. Truth be told, she was perturbed with anxiety. Quite often, she would question her own reasoning and wondered whether her fears were unfounded. She was concerned for her safety, and that of the child. She couldn't fathom the thought of becoming a functioning member of the gigantic daemon species, and what her life would become. Although the thick downy hair had disappeared from her hands, her fingers were almost an inch longer than they ought to be and were stiff and rigid in appearance. Three nights ago, Stefan pointed out the weird red lines running across the middle of her green eyes. The following day, the line had disappeared. It returned yesterday, though fainter than it had been. Stefan knew more than she did. 'The mark of the beast' he had said. A trait possessed only by the daemon. Akin to a name badge, only one in which she couldn't remove. Estella's embarrassment couldn't be hidden. She spent the day in tears; fearful she was going insane. Very soon, Estella would be unrecognisable, even to Marc, if ever their paths crossed again. She wore loose and unflattering clothes to hide the lumps on her back. They were ghastly and looked like something found on a prehistoric dinosaur. She wasn't sure when they arrived but was certain it had been a gradual development.

Life with Stefan had developed religious routine. They ate canned meat mostly but hunted fresh kill once a week. Usually, on a Sunday. The craving for blood had lessened. However, Estella's appetite for flesh was insatiable. Stefan ate four times a day. Estella on the other hand, could only manage one meal a day. Her stomach unfamiliar with food, it was a struggle to keep it down. Whilst Stefan was busy upstairs in the shop, Estella had taken to puzzles and problem solving. She would be clued to the puzzle book for hours on end, analysing sequences, geometry, and crosswords, as though her undead existence depended on it. Sometimes Estella would talk to the baby, telling her stories of her mortal life before the one she knew. Often times, the baby would look into her eyes as though she understood every word said. With a finger in her mouth, the child became contently snuggled within her mother's bosoms as she spoke. In the midst of it all, perhaps through boredom and overthinking, thoughts of Xavier and Marc took turns in Estella's headspace every other day. Ashamedly, at times Estella would become aroused thinking of Xavier. Thoughts of unscrupulous lusting as he licked her neck while semi-dressed, often incited great arousal. At times she became carried away and would touch herself pretending to be him. Once, Stefan awkwardly walked in whilst her hands were buried underneath her skirt. He seemed bemused, if not a little taken aback. She would feel his eyes lingering for a little longer than necessary. She knew she turned him on, but Stefan was far too polite to make it known. His awkward smile said it all. In contrast to this, a dark sadness crept over her when she thought of Marc. Many days she would become quiet and withdrawn and spoke very little. Stefan would tiptoe around, not wanting to upset her delicate emotional state. Estella had fleeting thoughts of turning herself in at the Heath Hall, allowing Marc to do to her as he pleased. She deserved it. However, she was a coward and couldn't do it for the baby's sake. Leaving the security of Stefan's home would be too much of a challenge. On worse days, Estella thought about begging Stefan to drive a stake through her heart and be done with it. It was the easier option. But, as soon as she looked at those marvellous brown eyes, her stomach sunk. She couldn't bring herself to do it. Becoming an orphan, would be a bitter fate to place upon an innocent child.

'What's her name then?' Stefan was perched on the end of the wide settee. He wrinkled his brow curiously.

'I haven't thought of one yet.'

'God. That must have been one hell of a shock. Finding out your pregnant whilst turning into a daemon. That really is a miracle. I guess the father doesn't know of this?'

'No, he doesn't. He didn't believe vampires could reproduce, so wanted nothing to do with it.'

'Vampires? Estella, that baby is a daemon.' Stefan eyed Estella sideways. A look he mastered when he was trying to figure something out. Estella remained tight lipped. She said too much and couldn't take It back.

'No, she isn't…' she muttered.

Stefan laughed nervously. He looked at the gurgling baby. 'Estella, is her father not a daemon? I won't assume a bite would have made this happen! Isn't it time you told the truth? Why are you so afraid?'

Estella's cold palms suddenly became clammy. She looked at Stefan as though he had spoken a foreign language. Who was she trying to fool? Everyone knew vampires couldn't reproduce. Weeks had gone by while Estella remained tight lipped, but the day had come to tell the truth. The baby was no more a vampire than she was. Stefan hadn't failed to notice her webbed feet, or the red lines that would occasionally display itself over her iris. Estella bit down on her bottom lip. She felt a hard lump well in the middle of her throat. She placed the baby on the brown settee as she got up, pacing back and forth with clenched fists. Stefan looked uncomfortable, but his smile was reassuring. She knew he had her back. After some hesitance, Estella spoke her truth.

'I was unfaithful.' she finally spat. 'There was never bitten. My infidelity has cost me my life, and now I pay the consequences. Whatever you think of me, you'll be right. I'm a terrible being and deserve no sympathy. Nor do I want any. I just need a place to stay as I've a bounty on my head.'

'My goodness. Does your partner know of the baby?' Stefan stuttered.

'No, not yet he doesn't. I'm not even sure that he knows I'm a daemon. But it's only a matter of time before the truth becomes unravelled. I just know it,' she said.

Stefan looked starstruck. 'That is one of the coolest things I'll ever know. I mean, you fornicated with a daemon, then conceived. Christ. Does that happen often? I'd beg to differ. That child is like... one in a million...she's a hybrid.' Stefan couldn't pierce his eyes away from the child, much to Estella's discomfort.

'Cool? That's my fucking life down the drain. How can you say such a thing?' Estella was incensed with Stefan's flippant remark. 'Do you think it's cool that she'll be hunted? The last hybrid daemon was over two thousand years ago.' Estella's tone was blunt. Stefan became remorseful. Instinctively, she bent and picked up the baby from the settee.

'Oh Estella, I am sorry. I didn't mean to upset you. Bad choice of words. But you've obviously been chosen to carry that child for a very good reason. My grandfather told me a story as a boy. Daemons were vermin, and vampires weren't any better in his eyes. Stay away from them all, he said. However, I'll never forget the story he told me about the ancient leader of the underworld. The one who rules us all. The one who governs our every move like some sort of Godlike entity. The chosen one, he said. His name was Ursk. Conceived between a vampire and a daemon, he was never supposed to happen. Until he did. Ursk lived over a thousand years but was eventually tricked to his death by a cunning vampire. No one knows if this story was really true, though my grandfather swore on it. He said, one day there will be another exactly like Ursk to correct the wrongs and punish those who disregard the laws of the land. However, this chosen one will be different than Ursk. Stronger, impossible to kill. And worst of all, be able to uphold such evil, that only darkness can fall upon the underground.' Stefan's voice trailed off as his eyes darted back to the baby in Estella's arms.

'Are you saying, my daughter is pure evil?'

'No, of course not. I'm saying, she could be. Or maybe not. But she'll have immense power over of all of us and can do with us as pleases.' Estella didn't fail to notice the melancholy in Stefan's usually upbeat voice.

'Her father is a hybrid. Shouldn't he have been the chosen one? I don't know what's so special about her.'

'Her father is half wolf, not vampire. That's where the difference lies. Half vampire, half daemon, literally never happens. The two species are so different. Reproduction is extremely rare. Werewolves, the dirty dogs, we've mated with daemons over the years many a time. Half werewolf-daemons, aren't as uncommon as you'd think. It's something about the vampire blood that seems to do the trick...' he said.

Estella looked nervous. She walked nearer the stairs. 'I think I've just compromised my safety. I should go.'

Stefan was stunned. His wondering eyes trying to work out what she meant. Was she afraid of him? That he would somehow try to kill the child. 'Estella. Where are you going? You and that baby, are safer in here.'

Estella looked into his brown eyes. The warm kindness still lingered. 'Are we safe with you? Because I'm suddenly not so sure now. Now that you know what she really is, you may gather your little wolf friends for a tea party.' She quipped.

'Gather my little wolf friends? Great. So now you don't trust me. Look at me. Do I look like some sort of crazed animal, pardon the pun. I've never had a family. I could love that child like my own. Listen to me, Estella. I don't care what she is. I have no fear. I just want you both safe, that's all. I know it was a hard push to confide in me. And thank you for trusting me in doing so. I will not betray you.'

Stefan took hold off Estella's free right hand. Cold tears fell to her cheeks as she struggled between duty, and love for her child. Could she really trust a werewolf with a hybrid baby? Her logical mind wanted to say, absolutely not. But something inside her said, yes. Stefan could be trusted. Even if her vampiric instincts were reduced, she still had pretty good innate intuition when not being clouded by hot lustful energy.

'Stefan, this baby is my life. If you harm her, I *will* be obliged to kill you.'

Stefan was stunned at the look in Estella's eyes. Dark and unforgiving. He knew she meant business. For a while, Estella just stood at the bottom of the stairs cradling her baby. She wept as her insecurities flooded through, like a house with a broken roof. After some coaxing, Stefan managed to regain her trust again. He placed an arm around her shoulders.

'I won't allow anyone to hurt you, or that baby. Not if I can help it. However, I must tell you one thing. It's a full moon tonight. Werewolves will undoubtedly be out on the prowl. I must go to the forest before dusk. I'll lock up. You will be safe in here.'

'It's a full moon? What happens to me? might I change, too?' Estella's eyes were wild.

'No, not to my knowledge. We're the only creatures inflicted by such damnation. You'll be fine,' he said.

Estella couldn't shake the unsettling feeling she had, despite Stefan's reassurance. What if several wolves broke in? They'd likely kill both her, and the baby. The elusive daemon was still a mystery, and Estella had no idea what to expect. 'What does a daemon look like?'

Stefan eyed her oddly. 'Like you and me. It's not evidently obvious.'

'No, silly. I mean, what does it look like in daemon form? I need to know what to expect if I ever start changing.'

Stefan gulped loudly. His eyes became shifty. 'Err, I've never seen an actual daemon in daemon form, except for stories my grandfather told me. Whatever the case is, we're all monsters, anyway.'

'Stefan, its ok. I'm a big girl and can handle the truth. Am I going to grow three heads?' Estella cringed as the last word rolled out of her tongue. It was like waiting for a bomb to go off.

'I honestly don't remember. But, whatever happens, just remember this. I turn into a seven-foot dog nearly every month, sometimes every two. In that respect, you can count yourself lucky. As far as I know, you'll only turn at will. I've no damned choice in the matter.'

Estella wanted to laugh but couldn't quite allow herself to relax. Stefan sat on the brown settee in preparing for the night ahead. 'Come on, have a seat.' He tapped at the cushioned seat beside him. Estella sat down with the gurgling infant, who then tried to stick a finger in Stefan's ear. 'I'm not sure you'll like what you find in there.' He quipped. 'She is awfully clever.'

Like a death sentence hanging over their heads, Estella and Stefan sat on the settee waiting for their time to come. Every tick tock of the wooden wall clock was like one step closer to dooms day. Stefan was anxious about leaving Estella alone. She was anxious about her own infliction, and what hideous creature she was destined to become. As the evening settled in, Estella became restless. She contemplated leaving the baby alone to join Stefan in the woods. Too fearful to take any chances, she didn't want to place the baby at risk. Estella rocked back and forth, humming a lullaby to the infant. Her eyes grew heavy. Finally, she allowed her anxieties to disperse long enough so she could truly relax.

It was ten o'clock when Estella opened her eyes. Three hours had already gone. The flat was quiet. The ticking of the clock became annoying. She peeped down at the baby in her arms, who slept with thumb in mouth. The basement flat was windowless, so Estella crept up to the shop. The night-sky crept through the shutters. Stefan had only put the grill on, allowing light to come through. There were no rampaging werewolves to be seen. Her thoughts turned to Stefan. Images of him prowling the forest on all fours made her grimace with gratitude. Just as she was about to turn away and head back down to the flat, a dark shadow went quickly past the window. Estella stopped in her tracks. Lights were off, but werewolves could easily see inside despite the grill. Estella felt uneasy. She ducked behind the shelf housing canned food. The shadow returned, but this time it lingered. Whatever it was, knew she was in there. For a while it just stood there in the darkness, like a knowingness. No growling, no werewolf outburst or howling. Estella could see the points of its ears, sharp and curious. Tuffs of hair could be seen sprouting out in the shadows, too. With no outward displays of aggression, Estella felt it best to attend back to the sleeping hybrid, despite her curiosity of the wolf. Creeping low with bended back, she slowly made her way back towards the stairs. And then, there was tapping at the window.

Loud, angry thuds threatening to break through the steel grill. Estella crouched on all fours, stopped in her tracks. Growling could be heard, its pitch getting deeper and louder by the second. Refusing to be intimidated by some common canine, Estella continued to venture downstairs, even if she was secretly preparing for battle.

By the time Estella got to the bottom of the stairs, there was rattling of the grill. This wolf wasn't just some silent observer. It was now obvious it wanted to get in. Estella looked over at the baby. She slept despite the noise coming from the shop. Estella's hands became clammy. She was anxious. She picked the baby up off the sofa and took her into Stefan's darkened bedroom. Estella wrapped the baby snugly beneath the sheets, then closed the door firmly behind her. Stefan possibly wouldn't be back until morning. What the hell was she to do until then? Estella was startled by the sound of metal clanging. The werewolf was on its way in, and there was little she could do about it. The sound of the grill being ripped apart and crashing to the ground outside, was horrendous. Estella's arms became rigid. The more the beast fought its way inside the shop, the more Estella begun to lose control of her body. With heightened anxiety and adrenaline flowing through her veins, something happened. Estella couldn't quite work out what was going on but became acutely aware something was happening to her body, of which she had no control. Her neck seemed to stretch twice as long as it should've been. Estella grabbed hold off her neck in an attempt to keep it under control but couldn't stop its growth. Panic was at full throttle. The growling and shattering of glass continued, whilst her arms became stiff and rigid. Her fingers turned to spindles, at least ten inches in length. Estella gawked as she literally morphed into something else. Seconds went by, but it seemed as though time stood still. Everything became more intense. Hazy, but dreamlike at the same time. By the time the Werewolf had made its way inside Stefan's home, the staircase had collapsed by the sheer weight of it.

What happened next, took Estella by surprise. Stefan's flat had a ceiling height of seven foot, but suddenly, Estella was the tallest creature in the room. The werewolf whimpered as she pounced on him. Estella stared down at the monster, not realising that she too, was a monster of sorts. The werewolf, no longer growling and snarling, was backing away towards the crumpled stairs. The next thing she knew, long green arms throttled the wolf. Her tongue ejected from her mouth, more than a foot long. Her tongue thrashed around, curling itself around the werewolf's throat. Like an out of body experience, Estella bared witness to her other self, the monster that fought the werewolf. After some grappling, she stood away from it all. The werewolf was slumped to the ground in a bloodied mess. Estella lifted her right arm. She gazed at the decapitated head held firmly within her grip. Green fingers like snakes, wrapped taut around it. As blood oozed from the decapitated corpse, everything became still.

When Estella came to, daylight beamed from upstairs through the dismantled staircase. The majority of the ceiling had fallen to the floor, where massive holes now took its place allowing you to see directly into the shop. Estella rolled on her back. She looked over at the clock. It had fallen to the floor but continued to tick tock all the same. It was 7.45 am. Estella, realising she had no clothes on, quickly stood to her feet, wondering what the hell just happened. She felt lightheaded. Woozy almost. Brain fog kicked in as she struggled to remember events from yesterday. She gasped as she ogled the carnage in the flat. Rubble fell around her feet, piles upon piles of it. Where the gorgeous oak-staircase had once stood, was now nothing but a crumpled mess. Fearing a house invasion of a grand scale, her mind turned to her baby. Unfortunately for Estella, by the time she turned on her heels to find her missing child, she got the shock off her life. There was a headless corpse lying amongst the rubble. She screamed aloud as she studied his bruised torso. He had a scar on his stomach, eerily similar to Stefan's. Just then, insidious panic caused Estella's hands to shake uncontrollably. Why there was a naked man in the lounge with a similar scar to Stefan? And where was Stefan? Truth be known, Estella already knew the answer but didn't want to face it.

What happened next, would haunt Estella for a lifetime. Within minutes she found her babbling child, who had been crawling around in the bedroom, with its door hanging off the hinge. Like a war-torn battlefield, navigating her way to the bedroom was a mission among the carnage. As she made her way back to what was left of the living room, child in hand, Estella nearly fell flat on her face as she buckled her toe against what appeared to be a piece of plaster. She managed to steady herself before falling on her backside but got the shock of her life. Laying there, eyes still open, was Stefan's decapitated head. In all her immortal life, never had she seen such horror. Estella retched green bile, emptying the contents of her stomach all over the floor. Shortly after her gruesome discovery, Estella made a swift entrance from the flat and didn't dare to think about it again. With no recollection of last night's events, she preferred to keep it that way fearing if she knew the truth about Stephan's death, it would be a burden too much to bear. With legs like jelly, Estella stood outside the shop with baby in hand. She couldn't shake off the morbid blackness that had now engulfed her every being. No matter how hard she tried to pretend everything was ok, Stefan's headless corpse told her otherwise. The town was eerily still, except for two men who were headed for the café on the other side of the road. One looked over at her, then nudged the other. Their faces fell pallor. Suddenly, they sprinted towards the café as though they couldn't get away fast enough. Even from here, Estella could see the worried faces peering out through the café window. She was so engrossed she hadn't noticed the mother and son duo who were headed for Stefan's shop. The boy held on tightly to his mother's hand, who however, had a face like thunder. It wasn't long before the woman made perilous eye contact with Estella. Immediately she stopped in her tracks, appearing to have seen a ghost. Just then, the woman grabbed hold off her son and attempted to drag him back the other way.

'Sorry William, we must go to another shop.' she demanded.

'Why? I'm thirsty.' he moaned.

'Don't question my decision.'

Estella pursed her lips angrily. She used to be admired, suddenly, she was a monster. Unfortunately, the boy became boisterous. He kicked up a fuss, attempting to wriggle his hand free from his mother's grasp. Ignoring his mother's pleas, he ran up to the shop door. Big doe-eyes looked up at Estella. With his dark hair and rosy cheeks, he couldn't be older than six. His striped, blue shirt was ruffled at the collar. He also reeked of meat which was evident of a fleshy breakfast moment before.

'Hello madam. Please, can I have some juice?'

'William, come back here at once.' She yelled mortified.

For a moment, Estella said nothing. Like her own child, she admired his innocence. His carefree unjudging disposition softened something inside of her. She forgot about his overbearing mother and gave him a gentle smile. However, truth be known, Estella's smile was tainted with sadness. She was sad because she almost wanted to tear his little head off. Her protective motherly nature was battling something far more sinister for even her to comprehend.

'I am sorry, but you must go. This shop is closed,' she said. Estella was stunned at the boy's persistence. He held his throat, saying how dry it was. Just some water, he said. Of course, Estella felt somewhat obligated to his demands. 'You cannot come in. Important refurbishment is taking place. Stay here, and I will fetch you some juice.' She promised.

The boy waited patiently for Estella's return. His mother, several feet behind him, stood with a stern face and pursed lips. Her hands-on hips further signified her annoyance. Moments in Estella returned. As promised, she gave the child a bottle of juice, and a bottle of water. He thanked her with beaming blue eyes. Estella watched as the woman grabbed her son by the scruff off his collar, then eventually marched off with him. Estella sunk to the floor trying to fight the overwhelming sadness she had kept at bay. She peered back into the shop, wondering what to do next. With Stefan dead she ought to lock up the shop, fearing it to be a target for thieves. She owed him that much. For a while Estella sat there too scared to venture back inside. She needed Stefan's keys for the shutters but would struggle to face his headless body once again. She looked at the baby for reassurance. The child's eyes were deep and questioning. She stared at her mother, for far longer than Estella felt comfortable. The baby wasn't babbling, nor gurgling. Her brown eyes simply consumed her mother's. Estella was stunned. The baby *was* trying to reassure her; she was certain of it. The exchange was intense, filled with love and strength. The baby, although too young to talk, her knowing eye contact was all the communication Estella needed. Guilt arose, but for her child's sake, Estella couldn't give up. The underworld was a fierce one. The baby wouldn't stand a chance. Estella's love for her was immense. This was all the courage Estella needed. She stood up, baby in hand, and turned to the shop door. As Estella pushed it open, the atmosphere changed. Stefan, although deceased, Estella was certain she could feel him. His presence was overbearing. She asked outload for his forgiveness. Cold tears fell hard as she leaped to the bottom of the flat, narrowly avoiding sharp points of broken wood from the dismantled stair. The baby touched her cheek as Estella looked around the carnage. And there they were. On the wall shelve nearest to the bathroom, strangely still intact. However, Estella didn't dare look down. She hadn't the strength. She could hardly digest the fact that she could have killed her best friend, the kindest werewolf she had ever met. Like a bad dream, she hoped tomorrow would be brighter.

Estella made her way to the other side of the road. The infant could be heard chomping away at her own hands. Minutes later, Estella arrived at an intimate eatery. She looked up at the neon emblazoned sign splattered across the door. It was a werewolf establishment and packed full of them. Evidently, Estella would be made to feel like a freak. Demoralized, Estella carried on further along the town trying to find somewhere quieter, and perhaps less intimidating. The sun was steadily going down. Her feet began to pound. Estella had no idea how long she had been on pacing this town, but several hours had passed. The infant had fallen asleep. Estella's stomach growled for a meal. Just as her thoughts were about to consume her, yet again, Estella came to an abrupt stop. A murder of crows gathered outside a small diner. Two dozen of them at least. As if awaiting her arrival, the crows gave way as Estella headed for the door. They formed a neat line, slightly endearing, if not a little bizarre. As Estella entered the diner, she noticed it was empty. Well almost. Except for a little old man sitting at another table, puffing away on a fat cigar. There was also a curly-haired teenager behind the counter. A noisy television blared in the background. It was perched high up on the counter, in which the old man was studying diligently.

'It's got to be those blasted vampires. We would have eaten the entire carcass. What a waste of meat,' he said.

'If we get blamed, they'll be trouble again.' Said the teenager.

'I should have driven a stake through their hearts when I had the chance.'

Estella loudly cleared her throat. The teenager turned to her. Surprisingly, he showed no fear and behaved rather normal. The old man was still engaged with the news report and ignored her presence. He seemed mesmerized by the killings.

'Hello. What can I get you?'

The boy had a heavily freckled face. His smile was wide, also genuine. He had beautiful straight white teeth, one of the best Estella had seen. But his lack of fear was most intriguing. Perhaps he hadn't heard the bedtime stories. Fearing to be uncovered and kicked out, Estella's nerves gave rise again.

'Hello. I'll have some meat please. And a glass of water.'

'On today's menu, we have cow, rabbit, and lamb. Oh, and human.'

The boy laughed with a wink. Estella tried to smile but instead mustered a stiff grin. 'I'll have some human brain, please.' Although her face was deadpan, the boy's humour didn't go over her head. Estella's eyes beamed at the boy. They shared the same dark humour. And then, the old man turned his attention to her. His face felt white as his cigar fell from his mouth.

'What's your kind doing here? You must leave at once.' He demanded.

'I don't mean you any harm. I only want to feed my baby.'

The old man quickly became frazzled. He scrutinised her as his eyes cast their gaze up and down. He turned his attention back to the young man behind the counter. 'Billy, you cannot serve this woman. We don't deal with vampires, or the devil incarnate.'

Estella eyed the old man. Being likened to the devil definitely wasn't complementary, but his rancid tongue was even worse. He spat his words out with such venom; her body could've caught a light from his wrath. Anger brewed within as Estella struggled to keep a hold of her emotions. She looked down at her baby. She too stared at the old man; her big brown eyes didn't even blink.

'Sorry Gramps. I thought she was one of us.'

'One of us? Jesus Billy, are you silly or something? Don't you recognise your own kind? She's a daemon, the worst of the bunch. I'd quicker suffer a vampire.' He snared.

Estella was stunned at his unprovoked outburst. 'How dare you talk to me like that?' she said.

The old man scrambled from his chair and was now thrusting his index finger towards Estella's face. His yellow eyes set in. The hair on his face had now steadily increased. Estella was certain he was about to morph into a four-legged dog demanding a fight. Billy haplessly tried to calm his grandfather down, to no avail. As the old man continued to rant, something miraculous happened. It was the infant. Within seconds, she had managed to free herself from Estella's arms, then leaped towards the old man with a single jump. She latched herself onto his face as Billy's eyes bulged with shock. Never had he seen a baby do such a thing. Nor had Estella, whose face was amused. It all happened so fast. Estella knew not what to make of it. Whilst the old man tussled with the baby, she began biting small chunks of flesh from his face. Though she had no teeth, her gums were razor sharp. The old man was unable to shapeshift as he had too much energy poured into defence mode from the baby. Blood ran from his left cheek. He was hollering to his grandson for assistance, but whom had already been warned off from Estella for any intervention. Estella covered her mouth, partially hiding her laughter. She pondered whether to get a hold off her child but decided to leave her to her own devices. After all, the old wolf had it coming.

Nearly ten minutes into the attack, Estella decided enough was enough. Clearly, this was no ordinary child and was obviously one not to mess with. The old wolf had partially morphed, his tail wagged viciously side to side. Chunks of blood, hair, and slime covered the floor. Estella tried to work out if the bright green slime was oozing from her daughter, but it was impossible to tell.

'Ok, little madam, that is enough.'

Estella yanked the infant away from the wolf. With Estella's touch, the baby became limp and passive again. She flopped into her mother's arms like a ragdoll. As if butter wouldn't melt, soft eyes peeped beneath a face full of blood and coarse grey hair. She looked up at her mother with a discerning eye. She was a baby, but her soul could've been a hundred years old already. Estella felt a subtle chill run the length of her spine. At merely months old, her own child was literally a killing machine.

'Gosh, look at you.' Estella's eyes beamed with pride as she frantically begun wiping bits of hair from her daughter's face. She chuckled. In angelic fashion, those big brown eyes starred back at her with adorning innocence.

'Take that thing out of here. You're not welcome.' The old man grumbled.

He limped and whimpered, then ran behind the counter to the back of the diner, disappearing with his tail between his legs. Billy became awkward, shifting his eyes to the floor.

'I am sorry, but I think you best go,' he said.

"*Two more headless human bodies discovered this morning. It's a rampage.*" The blaring TV distracted both their attention. It wasn't clear whether these deaths were caused by werewolves, or her own kind. However, Estella was certain the same culprits were behind the spate of earlier deaths, in particular the headless corpse they'd found upon the grounds of Heath Hall. As a precaution, the treaty had been called upon. The werewolves would likely rally round and put their own measures in place, with either species blaming the other. Humans had been quarantined with 7pm curfews.

'Sorry madam, you have to leave.'

Estella turned her attention back to the boy. She had already caused enough trouble. She smiled stiffly at the young man before heading for the door. As before, the murder of crows gathered at the door. Like before, with much conviction, the crows formed a neat little line allowing Estella to pass freely. One crow in particular caught the baby's attention. She stuck her tongue out teasingly. The crow cackled, then took flight. Estella felt proud. This baby was a warrior.

FOURTEEN

'He's playing shy. Kiss me.'

Hearty giggles erupted throughout the grand bathroom. The slinky blonde pushed her naked breasts up against Marc's bony chest. Not that he cared. Marc had his head back in a comatose state.

'Mmm, such a handsome devil.'

'Perhaps he will loosen up if we give him some blood.'

The busty redhead held her head back with laughter. She ran her tongue over his chest, licking his translucent skin like flavoured ice-cream. Just then, the door burst open. Polished footsteps tapped loudly on the floor, click clacking towards the middle of the room where the bath sat.

'That's enough, girls. It is only 12am. Give him another hour. He will soon be good to go. Edgar calls for your company.'

Stramus held out a pair of snow-white towels, to which the blonde grabbed one from his thin long hand. She rolled her eyes. Reluctantly she wrapped it around her taut body.

'What a waste. He ignored me the entire time. I could be out doing better things, you know.' She spat.

The blonde bared her fangs angrily at Stramus. She eloquently stepped out of the massive round tub, toes pointing to the floor. The redhead, relentless and more stubborn than her sister, sat amidst the bubbles fawning over Marc. She ran her hands through his thick dark hair, trying to arouse his attention. Giggling in his ear as her red curls bounced along the water's edge. Despite this, Marc was in a world of his own. Eyes closed tight; his head gently swayed with the rhythm of the water.

'Bernadette, can you stop faffing around like a child. I told Edgar this would be a complete waste of time.'

'Lighten up old man. I am after all still nineteen, and forever a child at heart.'

'Yes, nineteen plus two centuries.' The blonde laughed at her own humour. She animatedly threw her head back as she done so. She was perched upon a crushed velvet chair metres from the bath.

'Just hurry. Don't keep him waiting.'

Stramus's tone was irritable. Bernadette hissed angrily at him. She stood up in a strop. She cheekily flashed him her bottom, throwing the towel to the marbled floor. Stramus was stunned. His eyes were transfixed. Never had he seen such perfectly pert buttocks. It was at least a century since he had even been intimate with a woman. And that ended in disaster. The blonde giggled at his obvious embarrassment.

'What's the matter, old man? Cat got your tongue?'

The fiery sisters roared with laughter. As they disappeared, a watery mist was left behind. They made their way to the grand foyer where Edgar sat in waiting.

'Marc, you are skin and bone. If you do not have a proper meal soon, you will surely perish.' Stramus knew Marc well enough. He knew how stubborn he could be, and absolutely nobody would be able to convince him otherwise. He also knew that Marc was willing to die for his missing bride. Estella had become his obsession. She meant the world to him. And no amount of naked supple flesh was going to change that. Marc's deathly pale body cast a shadow in the water. The dark circles underneath his eye sockets left frightful shadows over his face.

'Ok, suit yourself.'

The old vampire vanished from the spot. Alone with his thoughts, Marc opened his eyes. His entire existence was a blur. As if it were playing out from a television screen, a thousand lifetimes flash before his eyes. Marc saw his nine-year-old self, tugging at his mother's hemmed skirt. She was a widower. He knew nothing of his father. It was 1625, a leap year. The year, he was killed. They say it was an abduction. Shortly afterwards, Marc came to learn of his mother's death, by hanging. They said she was found swinging from a tree, with bite marks circling her neck. Marc lived within a big farming close knit community. The day of his abduction was all a blur. Why he was chosen to return from the dead, he had no idea. Until this day, his assailant was a mystery. Some say it was his own father, though this hadn't been proven. At that time, vampires were unheard of. Fearing humans and what he had become, young Marc hopped onto the back of the neighbour's tractor one dreary Friday morning and had never returned to the village. They say, once you are bitten by a vampire, old age will never come upon you. Well, that was only partly true in Marc's case. Year after year, he matured into a spectacular young man. Until suddenly, in May 1679 at the ripe age of forty-five, he aged no more. It seems, Marc was a peculiar case. His DNA was rather resilient to the fresh vampire venom running through his veins.

Marc studied the enormous bathroom. He slowly rose to his feet. His pale slender body was emaciated, his veins crimson red. Marc's sense of smell was incredible, and he couldn't deny the powder fresh scents of the two young women. It appeared he must have blacked out, but their unfamiliar dewy odour was enough to rouse his interest.

It was certainly different to Estella's. Hers, sharp and musky, tinged with jasmine. If this was Edgar's cheap attempt of erasing Estella from his memory, he had wasted his time. Indeed, the girls were young and beautiful, but Marc had little interest. Tonight, he was going to create havoc. He would feed off the innocent and kill at leisure. He cared no more about the treaty, or what may come of it. his soul was already in turmoil. He cared little about repercussion. Marc's strength had dwindled. He glanced around for his robe, but it had disappeared. Filled with frustration, Marc called for Stramus, who within seconds, the old vampire was back in the bathroom carrying a sleek black robe.

'Most kind.' He spoke in a whisper.

'The pleasure is mine. You are going to kill tonight, aren't you?'

Marc turned to Stramus. His blood red eyes beamed at him, his face searching. He outstretched his thin pale arms. Ignoring the question, Marc fired a question of his own.

'You and Edgar killed those boys, didn't you? How was it? It must have been somewhat of an epiphany.' Marc held a supercilious gaze through half-lidded eyes. He wasn't about to be patronised by Stramus, nor Edgar. It wasn't one rule for them, and another for him. Stramus awkwardly cleared his throat. He held his nose in the air to assert himself. Marc never failed to catch him out, and it would be little use denying it. Stramus hesitated before he spoke.

'Um, they were delicious, thank you. But it was just the once. Marc, please don't go on a rampage.'

'Would I do such a thing?' A sinister smile crept over Marc's face. Who was he kidding?

'Right now, I think you would do a lot of things. Some less savoury than others.'

'Stramus, I bet you reluctantly enjoyed every sip of that poor young boy's blood. Just think about that for a moment before trying to lecture me in morality.'

Marc's hands trembled like a leaf as he fastened his robe around his slender waist. 'Now, where are those girls?'

'They're with Edgar in the galley. Care to join?'

'Yes, I would.'

Like shadows on the floor, the vampires left the bathroom. Seconds in, Marc arrived at the gally. Its sliding door slowly slid open. Although his silhouette had become rather fragile, Marc's piercing eyes gave him the confidence of the seasoned vampire he once was. He strode in without a care in the world. Edgar, with a stout cigar in his mouth, had reclined back into the old high-backed mahogany chair. He greeted Marc with his eyes, then carried on puffing lightly watching the show. The hapless girls caressed each other several feet away on the floor. The blonde had her hand taut over the other's breast while licking it playfully. Edgar was the epitome of a dirty old man and had a fondness for young flesh. He studied them with intent. His face curious yet satisfied. He grinned slyly. Marc stood silently still. He observed from afar. This was a regular past time for Edgar, one in which Marc never cared to indulge. Estella had a distaste for it, but the elders were doing their part in helping to keep Heath Hall safe, so Marc kept his nose out of Edgar's business for the most part. However, today was different. Despite his fragile emotional state, and his initial lack of interest, Marc succumbed to temptation. His heart pined for Estella, but his hunger was intense. Somewhere deep inside, he knew Estella had gone and would unlikely return. No longer at the restraints of monogamy, he was going to have his delights. Like a moth to a flame, Marc's eyes transfixed on the redhead. What a beauty she was. Her translucent skin was blemish free, glistening like silk under the candlelight. Her lustrous red hair like a beacon of light, she looked at him with huge brown eyes and licked her tongue playfully. Marc threw his robe to the floor. He had become so weak, his knees threatened to buckle beneath him.

'I'll be excusing myself.'

Not one to indulge, Stramus left the galley. Far too old and dignified for such behaviours, he thought Edgar ought to know better. He knew of Edgar's sordid lust for Estella, proving he was a hungry philanderer with little dignity. For all Edgar's fine points, he behaved with little morale where women were concerned and enjoyed nothing better than 'conquering' fresh meat on an almost weekly basis.

'I wish Stramus wouldn't take himself quite so seriously. After all, we could be here for an eternity. We may as well find pleasurable ways to occupy oneself.'

Marc wasn't listening. He was on bended knees; his thin arms draped around the young women. The blonde was relentlessly licking his chest; however, his sights were set on the other. He ignored the blonde's attention and reached over to tenderly kiss the redhead. He gazed into her eyes and felt alive again. For a moment, Marc allowed himself to forget the pain of the loss of his spouse.

'Gosh, you're so beautiful.'

He passionately held her chin, then stuck his tongue down hungrily her throat. The rejected blonde was annoyed. She turned to Edgar in the chair, lips pursed angrily. 'Why does she always get the men?'

Edgar didn't respond. His eyes were fixed firmly on the kissing pair. Marc, so consumed with passion, he hardly noticed the tantrum. The redhead took centre stage as Marc firmly caressed her neck, before lowering his mouth to her breasts. Voluptuous and enticing, he was again reminded of Estella. He suckled them like a hungry baby. Seemingly all jealously had been forgotten as the blonde became aroused. There she was open mouthed, touching herself, then began fondling her own breasts. The redhead encouraged Marc to suck harder. With a sturdy hand on her chest, and the other lowered towards her crotch; fangs bared, she held her head back as waves of passion echoed through her body. Marc was excited. He quickly turned her over on bended knees. He grabbed her hair, then applied hard smacks to her buttocks. He lightly ran his nails against her supple skin. His eager thrusts were spurred on by loud enticing moans of ecstasy. It wasn't long before he came to climax. Unbothered by the audience in the room, he showcased his manhood. Once he had finished, Bernadette turned to him, offering her neck. She smiled.

'Drink. You need it.' She demanded.

Marc didn't need much convincing. He bared his fangs then quickly latched on to her slender neck. The pair embraced tight. Bernadette had her eyes closed as he drank. Her curly red hair tumbled against her bottom, brushing lightly against her hip bone. Her sister focused intently on the twosome. She panted and moaned, touching herself to ecstasy. As Marc drank, his body was slowly replenished. He sucked vigorously whilst his body jerked with rhythm. Sure enough, it wasn't long before the blood-stained ring around his eyes slowly disappeared. His sallow cheeks became firm. He was nourished once more. Though he was undead, he suddenly felt quite alive.

A Sudden rapping at the window got everyone's attention. A huge bat flapped loudly against the pane. The wind blew harshly against the rustling trees. The vampires looked up for the intruder. The noise was distracting and horrendous. The bat flapped its wings with sheer determination until the window gave in. The window shattered loudly with a crash. Lilith, the blonde, quickly cowered behind the master piano. She knew who it was. Bernadette recognized the caller but stood her ground. It was *her.* Swiftly, she motioned the towel from the floor and flung it snugly around her torso barely covering her modesty. Marc looked over at the tall mahogany chair. It rocked back and forth, empty. Edgar had long disappeared from the galley, perhaps bored of his antics. Marc's face became suspicious. What was she doing here? The bat broke the window and flew into the galley. It circled the ten-foot-high ceiling several times, then came to an abrupt stop right under the black rimmed chandeliers. Marc stood up, reaching for his robe. In the blink of an eye, the bat became a woman. Her long raven hair brushed against her tailbone. She wore a black and red gown, and sky-high black shoes. Her eyes were emerald, green, adorned with thick black makeup. She flew to the floor in smooth fashion, feet pointing like a poised ballerina. The woman took centre stage in the middle of the galley.

'Achllys. What brings you here?' Marc was stunned.

'Marc, that's no way to greet your aunt.'

Marc's expression became stern 'You are no aunt of mine. It has been two centuries, and still, you play this game. You will also be paying for the broken window.' He hissed.

'Play nicely.' she grinned.

Marc eyed the woman, as she him. After an awkward silence, the vampires took slow confident strides towards one another. The precision sound of tapping shoes echoed along the marbled floor. The girls eyed each other from across the room, filled with apprehension. They prepared for a mighty brawl between the powerful duo. Bernadette frowned. Although she came to enjoy her immoral life, she hadn't yet forgiven Achylls for turning them into nightwalkers, and probably never would. 'Who does she think she is?' Bernadette muttered beneath her breath. She came out of hiding, strutting confidently along the floor to comfort her sister. This fiery nature was in high contrast to that of her timid sibling. Achylls side eyed her sourly. In all honestly, Achylls hated cowards and admired her gall.

'They're about to fight. Do you want us both killed?' Lilith was angrily. Her face was riddled with anxiety. Bernadette was perplexed. She lowered herself beside her worrisome sibling.

'Why do you panic so much?'

'I don't.'

'Yes, you do! She's just a woman, like me and you. I won't submit to her. Never.'

Lilith was visibly shaken by Achylls presence. Bernadette rolled her eyes. In life, her sister was always a worrier, and since becoming a vampire, hadn't changed. A human trait in which Bernadette felt should have been left behind.

'That's why she will never respect us. You cower every time you catch a scent. She thinks we are fools. You need to toughen up, Lilith. Remember, you're a vampire now.'

Lilith looked defeated. Her sister was right. But hard habits die hard. Achylls was strong and powerful, and Lilith felt like a mere mortal when she was around. Just then, the elders entered the galley. Edgar had a cigar dangling from the right side of his mouth. The old vampires had seen her coming and knew there would be trouble. Their presence was a well needed source of comfort to Lilith.

'Achylls!' Stramus was surprised. He turned to Edgar, who in turn raised his left brow.

'How nice of you to drop by.' Edgar spoke with suspicion. His brows raised with curiosity.

'Do not get too excited. I bare news, some, rather unpleasant.' She said. Piercing green eyes scanned the men with vigour. Her sharp voice echoed around the room like a bellowing wind as she spoke. White mist erupted beneath her feet. Her skinny fingers were adorned with silver rings of varying variety. Long black nails completed the look.

'Orpheus is dead. His severed head found hanging from a tree.'

Shocked gasps echoed. How was this possible? Orpheus was Edgar's senior cousin, one of the members of the board. He was most feared and respected by many. But who would dare to challenge him?

'How did this happen?' asked Edgar.

'We have ruled out the werewolves. They're not quite as cunning. But there have been sightings of something else. A species only spoken of as folklore, and one we know very little about. A Daemon.'

Edgar glanced at Starmus. This wasn't news to them. Achylls directed her gaze to the elders as she spoke. 'We are under attack.

This tragic incident has put the whole community on high alert. We vampires must put our differences aside and band together.'

Edgar pulled the cigar from his mouth. 'We were expecting this. No less than six deaths have been reported locally. Including two headless corpses found on our very grounds.'

'What! Six deaths, and not one of you thought to tell me or the board?'

'We didn't feel it was absolutely necessary to alert the board. These were rogue vampires, most newly turned. In fact, I recognised not one. They certainly were not thorough bloods. Not like us. However, nevertheless, precautions were made. We've been on keen watch ever since'.

'We feel the perpetrator resides close by. It was a warning.' quipped Stramus

Achylls sniffed the air like a hungry dog. Her gaze fell upon Marc. He could hardly believe news of Orpheus's death. Distraught, he fell to his knees on the cold smooth floor. Orpheus had been a great mentor, and a great friend. Orpheus had stood by Marc in his darkest times and had enjoyed some of his best. Marc reminisced over the last three hundred years with bittersweet memories.

'How is it that daemons are upon us? The last time I set eyes on one of those creatures, I was a mere boy.' Marc seemed shocked; his anger was evident. His fingers curled as he spoke.

'That, we do not know. But I *will* find out.'

Achylls mustered a sly grin. She turned to Lilith. Blonde tufts could be seen poking out behind the grand piano. 'Oh Lilith, poor sweet girl. Come here at once.' She demanded.

Achylls beckoned with a sharp index finger. Like a deer in headlights, Lilith's eyes lit up for all the wrong reasons. Like a naughty schoolgirl about to get a scolding, she sheepishly scuttled towards the woman in black. All eyes were on her. Bernadette grimaced.

'Calm down girl, I only want a taste of your blood. I can smell it from here. Young and fresh, so fresh, so fresh. You and that sister of yours, the memory of your fate still like yesterday. Oh, what a joy it was seeing you scream your little lungs out. Anyway, worry not. You're in good hands.' Bernadette shivered as Achylls spoke. She was responsible for turning them both, and every so often, liked to sample them as if they were her very own cattle. It had been two years but seemed like yesterday that they were plucked from obscurity and thrust into the dark under world.

'You were always ridiculously flamboyant.' Edgar rolled his eyes with irritation.

'I certainly do not miss you at the castle! In fact, it lovely not having to contend with you, or your misery, Edgar. Perhaps, you would care to join me.' smirked Achylls.

Marc looked on in silence. His mind was far. Truth be told, Estella was never far from it. News of Orpheus death only heightened his longing for his mate. Lilith stood before Achylls then knelt at her feet. Achylls was eccentric and demanding, but indeed, she owed her undead life to her. Having the worry of disease and death eradicated from her existence, was perhaps enough to be grateful for. Any hatred she had for this woman, was too heavily steeped in fear. So much so, Lilith had little choice but to succumb to her wears. At the very least she would stay young and beautiful forever, a thought that bought great joy. Lilith slowly looked up at her mistress. A meek submissive smile slowly formed across her face. She exposed her bare neck and positioned herself ready for the taking. Bernadette was mortified. It was only a matter of time before she too was next on the menu. Very soon, Achylls would be fed up of Lilith's blood, and would be craving hers instead. They were merely spawns in a game, helping to satisfy her craving for new immortal blood and power. Without hesitance, Achylls lowered herself then latched onto Lilith's neck. Bright red blood dripped along the sides of her mouth. Lilith winced. This was a regular occurrence but felt no easier than the first. Achylls drank and drank. Tonight, it seemed she had quite an appetite. Before long, Lilith's body jerked uncontrollably as the blood flowed out through her veins. Bernadette gasped! hands cupped to her mouth. Seconds later, Achylls stopped feeding. She stood and wiped her mouth with the back of her hand, licking her lips like a well-fed puppy. Like a floppy ragdoll, she casually tossed Lilith's weakened body to the floor.

'For heaven's sake. Wipe that pitiful look of your face. She's a vampire, not dead.'

Achylls scowled at Bernadette, who quickly turned to avoid her gaze. Seconds in, she watched her sister slowly regain her composure whilst Achylls straightened her gown.

'I feel somewhat refreshed. Now, where were we. Ah yes! Unfortunately, we have another issue. The treaty has been broken.'

Marc's eyes widened at the news. 'What do you mean?'

'I mean, someone has been extremely careless. Or perhaps they've grown so comfortable with their own inflated sense of self, they think they're immune to repercussion.'

Edgar awkwardly cleared his throat. It was as clear as day what this visit was really about. Achylls believing to be of higher importance than everyone else, took it upon herself to assert control over the others ever since Cerberus had been laid to his century long hibernation. How wrong was she. He was the most powerful, and wouldn't be dictated to by a woman, and certainly not by Achllys. Ever since Edgar had retired, Achylls had appointed herself role of peacekeeper and authoritarian forming close allies to many Edgar deemed disloyal. Achylls often took it upon herself to punish those who didn't adhere to its ancient laws and regulations, rejoicing in the proverbial pat on the back. She was rewarded, whilst others grew weary.

'Say what you mean, and mean what you say, Achylls.' Edgar's voice was loud and stern. He had seen these pesky threats time and time again, and quite frankly, he'd had enough of her power-hungry quest for control.

'Have I hit a nerve?'

'Oh, I wish you'd hit a nerve in my ear to drown out your whining. If vampires are being hunted, slaying a few pesky humans is the least of our worries.' He spat.

'Always armed with bags of sarcasm, you've not lost your edge. Anyway, Edgar, I think the treaty would love to hear from you. As I am sure you are all aware, there are rules in place, to which we must obey. We need to keep the order. If we slaughter every human within a five-mile radius, we can forget about ever drinking human blood again. We will be slurping plastic blood for life. Look what happened Kayne and Damascus, of whom were mysteriously wiped out after a monthly binge on human. It is a food chain. The humans are a crucial part to our very existence. We simply cannot slaughter them. Well, not all of them.' she said.

'Quite frankly, I am sick of this synthetic rubbish. We benefit from the blood bank only twice a year, and you expect gratitude? This may be rather presumptuous, but I am pretty sure you lot sat up at the castle aren't suffering to plastic blood every night.' Said Edgar angrily.

Marc finally chimed in. 'Edgar's right. This synthetic stuff tastes like crap. Kidnapping and selling a single human to the vamps up in the East is only to the benefit of the board. They reproduce like rats anyway. We could never kill them quick enough. So, their supposed extinction is the last thing we ought to worry about.'

Achylls eyed him with intent. With pursed lips, her eyes grew curious. She looked up to the high marbled ceiling and around the galley walls before turning her attention back to him. 'Hmmm, it's a little quiet around here. I don't suppose Estella has better things to do.'

The elders looked at one another. Marc looked at them, as they he. He became edgy, his shoulders stiffened. One wrong word about Estella, he thought he may explode.

'And that's absolutely of no concern to you, is it.' He snapped.

'Marc, you're so…tense. Even at your most intense, I've never witnessed you this defensive. If I didn't know any better, I would think Estella isn't even here. Has she up and gone? I can't smell that cheap perfume she so often enjoys dousing herself in.'

'How dare you speak of her like that.' Marc flew into hot rage. With bulging eyes and baring teeth, he clenched his jaw tightly. It was a mean feat trying his hardest not to rip Achylls head from her body. She never failed to anger him. 'Leave this house at once.' he ordered her off with a wave of the hand. Marc's face was twisted with anger.

The smirk which had adorned Achylls face, was now replaced with astonishment. Her eyes widened. She too became defensive and bared her fangs. Her pride wouldn't allow Marc to address her as though she were a child. Certainly not in the presence of the girls. Stramus looked over at Edgar, who had already flown over to the warring pair with his pipe dangling from his mouth. He stood in the middle of the galley. Long arms outstretched. A fierce rage contorted his face.

'That's enough. I promise to sever both your heads.'

Marc knew Edgar well enough to take him at least partially seriously. For all the battles they fought, Marc had never seen him quite like this. His extra-long thin fingers, almost ten inches with nails ejected, transforming them into weapons of destruction. Edgar waved them around like long white pickets attached to his hand. Edgar being one of the oldest vampires, had an air of snobbery about him. Between he and Achylls, it was a power battel. Like Achylls, he too demanded upmost respect, though seemingly gave very little to anyone else.

'Achylls, go. You've served your purpose here. I want to hear nothing more of this matter. With the humans. Tell the board we have a real threat on our hands and must prepare ourselves. We do not know what we are dealing with,' he said. And you ought to mind yourself out there. It's a blood moon tonight.' he continued. Edgar's sarcasm was like no other. He knew how much she hated it and revelled in his own provoking mannerism.

'You need to put a sock in it.' she snapped.

'If you don't tally, I may very well be tempted to put a certain something in you.' Edgar smiled wryly. His upper lip curled over, inciting insidious smirks from the other men.

'You repulsive old fool. Not if your undead body depended on it.' She spat back.

'Ok, tally on then. Safe travels.'

Achylls eyed Edgar sourly. She detested him, but it was pointless creating enemies with her own people. They had enough of those already. News of Estella's disappearance would come as a surprise to the board. But she had a satisfying sense of smugness at Marc's expense. Words were unspoken, but it didn't take a fool to see Estella had gone. With the speed of a fly, Achylls flew towards the smashed window and swiftly disappeared. A thin string of black lace was left behind as she made her exist. Marc caught sight of the lace. Becoming mesmerised, he studied the rogue piece of lace as it slow danced through the air before hitting the ground. Like a child, Lilith scuttled towards the thin piece of fabric. She picked it up off the floor, twirling it around her left hand. She admired its delicate edges between her fingers. After several minutes of adoring admiration, Lilith wound the lace several times around a thick bunch of hair, positioning it into a delicately placed ponytail at the top of her head. Bernadette smiled in admiration at her hapless sister. Marc fell back to his knees. Bernadette was a mere distraction, but his heart was empty. He longed for Estella. With his masculinity at question, the pain was evident for all to see. With reddened eyes and an anguished soul, he turned to the elders.

'Tonight, I am going to scale every corner of this earth. I will leave no stone unturned. I must find her.'

Stramus gulped uncomfortably. He knew it would be nothing more than a wild goose chase. Edgar didn't respond. He sucked on his pipe with a still confidence only he mastered so well. He ushered the girls away from the galley. 'Be gone the pair of you.' he ordered. The semi clad girls scurried across the galley floor, promptly disappeared in a vanishing mist. Edgar turned to Marc. His expression was indifferent.

'Marc, I am sure you don't care for my opinion, but it must be said. I know your anguish runs deep at this delicate time. However, with news of Orpheus death, we must prepare for attack. I am fearful you will allow yourself to wallow in self-pity, allowing your grief to consume you like a bad smell. You could very well become another statistic. We must travel back to Castle Dravenheard. Staying here could put us all at risk. The threat of daemons, aren't to be taken lightly.'

Marc quickly grappled for his throat. Edgar struck him back as quick as lightning. With flame red eyes, Edgar meant business. The men fought as though their undead lives depended on it. Marc exploded in hot fury. After several minutes of dodging, ducking, and throwing each other towards the ceiling like puppets, Marc threw Edgar towards the galley window. He crashed into it at lightning speed, shattering the polished glass to a million pieces. With Marc's strength fuelled by anguish, Edgar struggled to overpower him. Stramus stood and observed. He decided not to intervene. This had to be resolved, once and for all. He could no longer bear the constant bickering between the pair, nor the immense tension that filled the air since Estella's disappearance. Tonight, they would either kill each other or come to their senses. Marc marched towards the old vampire with clenched fists.

'I will finish you off, once and for all.' He yelled.

Edgar raised his hands in defeat. Dread and despair filled his eyes. Marc's strength was immense. Twice he had tried to overpower him but had failed miserably. His defeat would prove a huge blow.

However, he was man enough to accept it. Maybe, he had pushed him too far. Undeterred, Marc triumphantly charged towards Edgar. Like a demon on a rampage, his eyes blackened, filled with sinister intent. Stramus became alarmed. For all his cousin's faults, his demise was the last thing he wanted. Unfortunately, Marc had already slashed his throat with keen precision. Within seconds the old vampire fell to the floor gripping his throat tightly. Marc positioned himself for the kill, but Stramus jumped intervened before he could muster the final blow.

'Marc, let him live. Please. I am pleading with you.'

Marc stopped in his tracks. He exchanged weary glances with Stramus, of whom mercy was written across his face. His benevolent spirit must have touched Marc in more ways than one. Quite suddenly, his black eyes disappeared, returning to a light sea blue. Without a word, Marc disappeared from the galley.

'Stramus, I am bleeding out. I do not know if I can heal fast enough.' Edgar's hoarse voice was shallow and weak.

Stramus gulped at the stream of bright red blood that now seeped across the galley floor. He knelt beside his cousin. To lessen the bleeding, he helped to manoeuvre him on his back. This would also aid his healing. 'You're very fortunate. It's not an entirely deep wound. Marc merely grazed you. I guess you can take heed, that if he really wanted to finish you off, he would have decapitated you quite nicely.'

'I meant no harm. I thought I was doing the right thing.' Said Edgar.

'I know. However, Marc is ruled by despair right now. He's hardly himself. Better we head up to the board and leave him to it. I have no doubt he will join us when he's ready.'

Edgar was already healing. The cut had partially begun to close itself up. However, it would be some time before he regained his full strength. 'Agreed. Give me an hour. I should've regained some strength by then.'

FIFTEEN

Eager eyes watched in the dark. They shone brightly under the blood moon, lying in wait like a predator. Marc became transfixed on his own immortality. With the anticipation of a kill, he clenched his fists and stiffened his stance. The smell of despair was inescapable. News of Orpheus death had been the final blow, and now, he was headed for destruction. Although news of the daemon was still freshly etched in his mind, tonight, he had no fear. Tonight, there would be bloodshed. Hearts would shatter. He had loyalty to no one. Marc travelled through the air with the agility of a butterfly. He flew smooth and fast, looking down at the sleeping towns. Nothing mattered anymore. Suddenly, he was distracted by the chatter of a human voice. Gazing into the darkness, there stood the silhouette of a tall man carrying a bottle in his right hand. He appeared intoxicated and walked with an unsteady gate. He spoke loudly, making very little sense at all. It appeared he had gone out on the town and had himself a very good night. Marc's eyes studied his every move. He observed the redness of his face, to the scuff on his shoes. This was far too easy. He would have almost preferred if the man was sober and pleading for his life. It was over quick and fast.

Marc carried the body upon his back for several feet before deciding to suck him dry. It was almost fifty years since Marc had savoured the taste of a fresh blood meal. His body jerked as the blood filled his stomach. His veins bulged as he became stronger, nourishing his body back to its natural state. Once Marc had his fill, he meticulously ripped the lifeless corpse to pieces. He mimicked the cunning wolf. He clawed across his chest, making sure to rip out chunks of flesh. Minutes into his quest, Marc stood to his feet. He felt refreshed. He almost felt himself again. The weakness and pallor had long left his body. His deathly pale complexion became dewy once again. Gosh, the difference was remarkable. Suddenly, there was an energy coming towards him. It was swift and fast, most definitely another vampire. She stopped and eyed him with glee. It was the daughter of Orpheus.

'Elena! What brings you out here. You're awfully far from home.' Marc studied the face he hadn't seen in years. For the most part, she hadn't changed.

'Marc, what a surprise! I was headed to Heath Hall. I thought you could do with some company. News of Estella's disappearance has travelled fast,' she said.

'Doesn't it just. I don't know why I didn't kill that whore when I had the chance. And I don't mean Estella. That Achylls has no right spreading news based on presumption. Anyway, forgive my manners. Please accept my condolences for your father. He was one of the last greats.'

The vampires embraced. Elena still as beautiful as ever with her sparkly eyes and perfect smile. She smelt good. Although Marc appreciated the gesture, it was a blood moon. The night when werewolves and supposedly daemons, go crazy. He didn't want Elena at risk. Marc gulped awkwardly. 'Elena, it's dangerous tonight. There is something out there, more vicious than our own kind. You should not have come alone. I can't protect you.'

'Marc. I can protect myself. I just want to find the bastard responsible for my father's death.'

A rustling nearby caught their attention. It was an unfamiliar energy. On high alert, the vampires scanned the darkened street. Superior eyesight allowing them superb night vision. And then suddenly, there was a high-pitched wail of a cat in distress. Seconds in, a decapitated cat head was flung across the ground, landing inches away from where they stood. 'I think they're trying to make a point.' Said Marc

'Those bloody hounds.' Elena hadn't lost her sarcastic wit.

'No. It is not a werewolf. I would have smelt it a mile off. Nothing beats the rancid scent of wet dog.'

Marc spoke in a whisper. He bared his fangs. Elena scanned the surroundings. He was right. The werewolf scent was overly familiar. This was sharp. Musty. The vampires were on edge. Bracing himself for a brawl, 'Show yourself.' he demanded. Marc was up for the challenge. He felt he had little to lose. With so much grieve running through his veins, there was no time to be fearful. 'Keep close to me.' he said. Marc turned to Elena. She had disappeared from the spot. He stood for a moment in limbo, pondering whether Elena would be the latest statistic, and what he was going to do about it. And then, in the blink of an eye, her svelte physique steadily appeared as if from nowhere. Elena was smiling and giggling with a tall, robed figure. It was Apollyon. How had he gone unnoticed?

'Apollyon! what are you doing here?'

'He masked his scent with sage. No wonder we were thrown off.' Laughed Elena. She beamed at Marc over her shoulder. Marc was as surprised as she. He hadn't seen Apollyon in a decade. Elena became smug. If he hadn't known any better, he would think she was being frivolous.

'Marc, what a pleasant surprise. I was trailing Elena, successfully undetected. She was so adamant to avenger her father's death, she refused to be accompanied. I figured we couldn't afford to lose another member of the board.'

'You know I am as stubborn as an ox. And I certainly didn't want the entire board following me down here.'

'So, you dowse yourself in sage? Genius. An old but effective trick.' Marc eyed the tall figure before him. 'I guess killing that cat and throwing me his head was some kind of game of yours?'

'Killing a cat? Why would I exert precious energy on a feral cat? I am flattered you'd think I'd be that creative, but I have no idea what you're talking about.' Apollyon's tone was flat.

'We're being watched.' Marc pursed his lips tightly. His fists were also clenched. Elena heard his teeth grind harshly against each other. She placed a reassuring hand on his arm.

'It is, ok. I am sure we will find the culprit.' She quipped.

Apollyon's tall svelte figure towered over Marc's modest six-foot statue. His bright yellow hair shimmered under the moon light. His cool calm manner remained unchanged. Marc's anguish couldn't be hidden, however, there was no easy way of disclosing Estella's infliction, nor did he feel any obligation to. The biggest challenge they currently faced was the cunning daemon who was making light work of their community. They already had reduced numbers and couldn't afford to lose anyone else. 'Listen, we are up against something much more sinister. If daemons are behind this, we need to band together. It would be wise to head back to Castle Dravenherd where we have strength in numbers.'

Marc looked at him. 'Are we really up against daemons, or is this some sort of fantasy? I mean, come on. Daemons haven't been seen in decades. Last I heard, they were a thing of the past. Are we sure we this isn't just a pack of cunning rouge feral wolves trying to give us the run around? Maybe a pack of them. Perhaps they have mutated.'

'Marc, I do wish that statement had some actual truth to it. Unfortunately, feral werewolves are the last of our problem. It would have taken an entire pack to defeat the great Orpheus. Or any other vampire for that matter. Werewolves' biggest strength is in numbers. They're messy and unsophisticated. Not even a trace of hair was left behind.' Said Apollyon.

'That is why I suspect it's a pack. Maybe they're trying to make a stand. After all, they're an outcast within the community.'

Marc was met with astounding silence. It was evident, neither Apollyon nor Elena felt the same way. Always the diplomat, maybe he had over-simplified everything. Just then, laughter and giggles to be heard within the distance. The vampires turned to the voices. It was a well-dressed couple strolling hand in hand. They were werewolves. On approach, the twosome stopped in their tracks. They exchanged careful glances with the vampires. Although Marc was close to home, they were boarding on a werewolf community. Two miles further, they would be venturing into the well-known town of Glides. The werewolves became angry, in particular the woman.

'What are you all doing here?' she spat.

As her irritation grew, the man-made attempts to keep her calm. Unfortunately, the presence of vampires incited anger. The vampires eyed each other. They shared the same thoughts. It was clear, the werewolf wouldn't backdown without a fight, and for sure, they would happily oblige. Under the blood moon werewolves had enhanced strength, but this done little to deter the group. They were pure blooded vampires and displayed the confidence of a pride of lions.

'We are still on vampire territory and have as much right to be here as you do. We are being hunted.'

Elena's inexperience was obvious. She was quickly hushed by Marc before she could say anymore. Elena was a product of a privileged upbringing and had lived a fairly sheltered existence as far as vampires go. Truth be known, she knew nothing about the town or its borders, and they were indeed venturing onto wolf territory.

Marc's vampiric pride was extreme. The last thing he wanted was to show any vulnerabilities or expose any shortcomings within the group. If the werewolves felt their numbers were compromised, they could possibly raid Killbraith, and the castle, too.

… 'I think what Elena meant to say was that we are hunting. Looking for any pesky humans to quench our thirst.'

Marc's lies went over their heads. The werewolves were already on to them and refused to back down. 'I hope whatever hunts you, kills the lot of you. One of your kind killed my son. I promised to avenge his death, if I ever laid eyes on one of you again. It has been twenty years, but my grief is as fresh as it was on that fateful day. A day I will never forget.'

The werewolf was seething. Just then, the werewolf begun to growl. She collapsed to her knees. She wriggled around on the floor whilst her head jerked in a back-and-forth motion. It wasn't long before her clothes tore at the seams. The man she accompanied looked uncomfortable. He was obviously the peacemaker and seemed to want to avoid a confrontation. Elena was fascinated. She had only seen a werewolf shapeshift once before. It was as interesting now, as it had been then.

'Gloria, please control yourself. This is not the way to go about it.'

Gloria's husband must have had brilliant insight. Any brawl between the fivesome, was bound to end in at least one casualty. Unfortunately, unlike his wife, his hunch told him this was not a battle they would likely win. Unfortunately for him, Gloria was already in wolf mode and now stood upon hind legs. Standing well over six foot, she became a monster. The vampires braced themselves. It had been years since Marc fought a werewolf. In fact, centuries. 'I am afraid, we will have to kill your wife. She continues to obstruct our journey and leaves us little option.' Apollyon was matter of fact. His voice echoed as he spoke. It was a standoff. Within seconds of his statement, the pleading man fell to the floor. He too begun to shapeshift to a four-legged creature.

'Hmm, well, as one would expect. Of course, he has to protect his wife. Better to die trying, than not to try at all.' Said Marc. He admired the man's dignity. Willing to risk his life for his wife, he was honourable. Marc felt a familiar resonance. He too, would kill for Estella. He was courageous, and for that, Marc rather admired him. But unfortunately, due to his wife's indignant mood, they would both likely die a miserable death. Marc's evening took a surprising turn. He had been driven to violence with hopes of spilling human blood but hadn't seen a brawl with wolves on the cards. Suddenly, the wolves charged at them. Ferocious and snarling, like the beast they had become. The vampires were ready and waiting. Baring fangs and blood red eyes, a sign they too were ready to battle. The female wolf stood shoulder to shoulder with her male counterpart. Intense yellow, red eyes peeped beneath thick black fur which covered the length of their bodies. The wolves sprinted towards the vamps. Their ferocious teeth only marginally more intimidating than their aggressive growl. As a trio, the vampires were impressive. Levitating through the air with great agility and precision, they took their positions. Marc made a swift swipe at one of the wolfs. Faster, and with greater technique than Elena, he jumped upon the wolf's back. Admittedly, it wasn't as easy as he had initially assumed. These wolves had a reason to be angry. Their love for their son fuelled their passion for revenge. Marc grappled with the male wolf, doing his best to take it down. However, the werewolves were big creatures, and it took brute strength to conquer them. Elena, she was light and swift. However, she had been tackled by the she-wolf, and together they rolled upon the ground, each one trying to over-power the other. Elena delivered a bite to the wolf's neck. It howled but refused to give up. Though she had suffered at the hands of the wolf's claws, a vampire healed fast. A few scratches wouldn't deter her. Apollyon had enough of the spectacle. He was the only vampire who had managed to hold back. Like the rest of his clan, he thought little of the werewolves and didn't think it would be too hard a task to put them down. But now, he had enough of the spectacle and had to put an end to it. Whilst Elena delivered bite upon bite to the wolf's neck, Apollyon grappled with the beast from her underside, plunging his fists to her stomach. He dug his teeth into her chest cavity, while digging razor sharp nails deep into its sides. But it was Elena who delivered the final blow. A fatal swipe to the chest, plucking out the heart. There was a feeling of smug satisfaction as she pulled out its beating heart. Immediately, Apollyon took the heart from Elena's hand, and bit into half of it. His face became animated as hot blood dripped from the sides of his mouth.

'You eat flesh now?' she was surprised.

'I am tempted on occasion, one being now.' Apollyon wiped his blood-stained mouth as he spoke between small bites. Elena winced, baring her teeth.

Elena dragged herself from off the ground. Her dress was torn and tarnished and covered in blood. She looked like an orphan, lost, on its way to a village. Red streaks adorned her blonde hair. Claw marks covered her chest and back but were healing already. She looked back at the carcass. It was a gruesome sight. The werewolf had lost its entire chest cavity. Together they watched as the defeated beast slowly morphed back into human form. With one wolf down, their attentions turned to Marc. The battle was being won. With a lethal combination of skill and speed, Marc managed to outwit the wolf. Landing on its back, he dug his entire arm into its neck, before giving him the kiss of death. He bit down forcefully, grinding his teeth through the thick, dense flesh. His nails patterned punctures along the sides of the wolf's stomach. Soon enough, the wolf grew disorientated. Clawed arms desperately tried to reach for the vampire, as Marc bounced around its head like a tennis ball. For the wolf, the fight was over. His strength had dwindled. Throwing the vampire off his neck became mission impossible. It wasn't long before the wolf fell to his knees. He howled and hollered at his demise. The vampires had to get going. Very soon, there would be a hoard. Marc jumped off the creature. He sprinted over to the others. His crisp white shirt had been ripped to shreds. He simply pulled it off, then tossed it to the floor. The black overcoat was merely enough. Marc wiped his mouth off wolve residue. Chunks of hair fell to the floor.

Elena smiled teasingly. 'What's the matter, Marc? Do you not fancy seasoned wolf?' Apollyon sniggered with a glint in his eye.

SIXTEEN

That night, the trio flew a hundred miles. The air was brisk, and the mood sombre. In fact, it was perfect for a vampire. Decades of immortality conjured up in one night. Crows could be heard in the dead of night. They cawed continuously, an irritant to the sensitive vampire ear. They crow's cawed in sync, communicating with the coldblooded threesome as though their lives depended on it. Before long, the vampires reached their destination. That night, there was a bloodbath. Nine humans were slaughtered, possibly ten. It wasn't all entirely planned. Several had merely been unlucky. However, Elena and Apollyon had proven weak under Marc's influence. It didn't take much persuasion to give into the temptation of human blood. Marc went on a rampage, and they had done little to stop him. Treaty rules had been broken, but he was willing to put his soul on the line. Only upon sunrise would the extent of the damage be known. Mauled bodies had been slashed from ear to ear. The vampires wanted to place the blame squarely at the feet of the wolves, but it was impossible to entirely mimic to such effect. Unfortunately for them, several of the bodies were drained dry. Their cover would be blown. Ultimately, someone would have to pay the price for their indiscretion. Upon the mountains, the fog was thick and dense. Even with razor-sharp eyesight, the vampires struggled to see clearly. Castle Dravenherd, with its sheer size, stood out despite the dense fog. The journey to the top was arduous. Designed like a medieval playground, creating a fortress almost impregnable to its enemies. Elena, thin and nimble, was the first to reach the expanding doors. Almost spontaneously, the massive doors crept open, recognised her on sight.

'Come on you two, keep up.' yelled Elena over her shoulder. She stepped inside. Runa was at the door to greet her. With fanged teeth, she smiled sweetly.

'Thank goodness you're back. Where is Apollyon?' Runa's face became worried.

'He's coming. And, he has company.' Elena Smiled.

Just then, the door swung open. A gust of cold air bellowed through the hallway. Apollyon strolled in. His heavy black boots had blood stained to the front. Seconds later, Marc entered the hallway. He appeared dishevelled, weary also. Runa was stunned. She hadn't seen Marc for over a hundred years. He had chosen to leave the security of the castle for a new life with Estella and never looked back. After proclaiming his love, he had refused to be involved with the treaty and wanted no part of it. He disagreed with many of their principles and often clashed with the others for his opposing opinions. Most of the originals were governed relentlessly by Cerberus. He was the catalyst to the board. The pinnacle of their being. One of the first vampires to walk the earth. His body laid bound, buried under a solid aluminium coffin. Kept within the castle walls, but few knew of its whereabouts. The elders took turns to 'feed' him blood. Like a sacrificial ritual, they allowed themselves to be dictated to as though he were still alive. Maybe, he was alive. However, Marc, found the whole thing quite ridiculous. He was often knocked back with the suggestion of creating their own destiny or implanting new rules. To be frank, any thought of individuality, wasn't taken kindly. Runa was his first cousin. Their mothers were sisters. Born human, Runa's mother was inflicted by the bite. She attacked her only child, then stalked her own heart. Barely five feet tall, she was seldom taken seriously. Having to prove herself, she eventually won the respect she deserved. Though she was the smallest vampire known, she proceeded strength like no other. With cropped raven black hair and deep brown eyes, she bore an exotic kind of beauty. Marc was prepared. Estella's whereabouts would be met with growing curiosity.

'Marc! What a pleasant surprise.' Runa greeted her cousin warmly at the door. With arms outstretched, she wrapped them snugly around his torso as she beamed up at him, dwarfed by his six-foot stature. Marc felt rather awkward. He grinned, then returned the affection to his cousin with a warm embrace. Although it was over a century since they had last met, it seemed like only yesterday. 'What brings you here? I thought I may never see you again.' She searched his eyes for answers.

'Estella.'

'Estella? Has something happened? Is she dead?' Runa became animatedly flustered.

'Runa, I don't care to discuss this now. Certainly, I will explain later. Right now, we need to worry about banding together and hunting those responsible for Orpheous death. He was like a father to me.' said Marc.

'The castle has been on tenterhooks.' She said, squeezing his arm for comfort. She felt his pain. Orpheous was like a father to her, too. She was still mourning his death and had deliberately starved for five days after the news. Elena, meanwhile, was robust and rather resilient, and took a more diplomatic approach to news of her father's death. She was on a mission to seek vengeance and allowed it to destruct her every thought. The vampires headed for the Great Hall. The castle was dark, lit only by large wick candles.

Footsteps echoed along the marbled floor as the vampires stomped like soldier's marching on a quest. Marc looked towards the ceiling. Grand and exuberant, Heath Hall felt tiny in comparison. As though he were a stranger in new surroundings, he barely recognised the place. A hundred years had gone so fast. Nevertheless, he had no regrets for his decision to leave the castle. He and Estella lived in pleasant solitude away from the vampire community. And, truth be known, it was a decision that bore no regrets. Marc was hesitant to go before the board. Sour reminders came rushing back. Trying to remain as chilled as possible, he turned to Apollyon, who too, seemed deep in thought. Apollyon had been conflicted for some time. He was tempted to tell Marc the truth about Estella but had decided against it. Once they all got wind, she would be hunted like a rabbit with no way out. He sensed the longing in Marc's heart and knew it would destroy him. Apollyon felt it was news best coming from another source. For all her wrongdoings, Estella had been a firm friend. Apollyon held her loyalty over everything else. After all, it was better to hold on to a dream, than be crushed by the reality.

'You're miles away. I thought I was the only one with reason enough to appear so downtrodden' said Marc with a nudge. Apollyon glared at his peer. The two strolled at a slow steady pace alongside each other.

'This must be quite an awakening. With you being here.' Apollyon replied.

'Well, I am definitely awake, that's for sure. I'm not even sure why I agreed to this. We know nothing of our excursion tonight. My guilt is yours too. Anyway, I must make my mark, or I suspect I will be looked on as an outsider.' Marc's voice was blunt and matter a fact.

'Never. You are family. The board will be thrilled to have you here.'

Marc didn't miss the sarcasm in Apollyon's voice that fell to a whisper as they reached the hall. On que, the door opened immediately. Big black doors nearly seven feet tall. Elena and Runa entered first. Like everywhere else in the castle, the hall was dimly lit, filled with rows upon rows of candle chandeliers. At nearly thirty feet high, the gold rimmed venetian ceiling had an immense presence. Marc had forgotten just how vast the hall was. It was three times as long, as it was wide. To the left, there was a huge fireplace. On the wall above, sat several coloured portraits of Cerberus. His eyes were stern and enticing, you could almost taste his venomous desires. The walls, they were lined with canvas portraits of times past, and people great. The vampires walked to the other end of the hall in still silence, headed towards the top table. Even from a distance, stern expressions could be seen upon chalk-white faces. Four-sets of eyes, studied them like hawks to its prey. Acheron took a sip from a silver beaker, then proceeded to lick his lips.

'We have a visitor.' Elena smiled stiffly at the board. She remembered the state she was in, then felt a little sheepish. 'I best be gone.'

There was silence all around. They studied her like a puzzle, and then, shared curious glances with one another.

'Not so fast. Do you care to enlighten us as to why you appear so utterly dishevelled?' Acheron's voice was distinctive. Deep and authoritative, yet, velvety and dry.

'We were attacked by wolves.' She said, her eyes shifting to the smooth marble floor.

Acheron turned to Apollyon. He was trying to figure out his reasoning for joining Elena on her quest. It seemed rather ridiculous.

'I followed her out. We've lost enough men.' Said Apollyon.

'It is a blood moon. What do you expect? There will be a lot more than a pack of rabid dogs hunting the streets tonight. Anyway, by the state of you both, I take it they were defeated. Good.'

'Yes, they were. Acheron, can I be excused. I must go and change.' Elena turned on her heels. As quick as lightening, she headed back down the hall.

At last, Acheron addressed the elephant in the room. He turned to Marc. With an expression-less face, Acheron rose out of the tall, backed chair. He gathered his robe across his chest. Each and every finger was adorned with chunky gold rings, further highlighting his eccentricity. 'So, isn't this a surprise. What brings you back here? Have you come to seek sympathy for your missing spouse?'

Marc scanned the boardroom faces. He had a rich history with Acheron, fraught with indignation and opposition. Already, he became indignant. How dare he be spoken to like that. What gave him the authority? Marc fought against his urge to rip his heart from his chest. He willed himself to remain calm. The last thing he wanted was to create a scene and allow Acheron the satisfaction of his displeasure. 'No, I've come to seek peace. Orpheus was like a father to me. There have been a dozen deaths thus far. This is a sign for us all to band together. For the sake of our kind.'

Acheron cleared his throat. He remained stony-faced and stern. He turned to his left. He eyed Lucas, whom in turn, eyed him in agreement. 'Your selflessness disturbs me. I didn't know you had it in you.'

'Forgive me, Acheron. But your provocation is wasted energy. I've come in peace, not war.' Declared Marc.

'Give him a chance.' Said Apollyon.

Acheron turned to Apollyon in angst. He looked surprised. 'Apollyon, are you dictating to me? I am quite capable of making my own decision.' Snapped Acheron.

'No. I am simply saying to one vampire from another, let him be. We need Marc as much as he needs us right now. Plus, in case you forgot to notice, he is one of our best fighters.'

Just then, Achylls stood up. She could hardly move in the skin-tight dress that seemingly stuck to her entire torso. She eyed Marc squarely. Her green eyes were more intense than before. They stood out like flashlights beneath heavy black rimmed liner. The corners of her mouth curled as she spoke. 'Marc. Firstly, welcome back. I think we could certainly do with another pair of quick nimble eyes. After all, you are family.'

Acheron admired Achylls. He allowed her the floor. She satisfied his every need, at least, enough to keep him in agreeable alignment. He didn't agree, but keeping his mistress happy, was paramount. Reluctantly, he nodded, before lowering himself back into his seat. Lucas and Lorcan eyed each other. Their matching bald heads studied the other. As Cerberous younger brothers, they were quiet and unassuming. Nevertheless, vital members of the board. Absolutely everything discussed by the board, had to be supported by the twins. Lorcan was a solid confidante to Marc. Before Marc's departure, he was one of the few vampires who truly understood him. In contrast to his brother, Lorcan was fair and fluid, not ridged and structured like the others. Along with Marc, he wanted to implement many changes but was fraught with resistance from the others. Lorcan stood up. His broad stature robust and strong. He held a silver beaker in his left hand. His eyes twinkled warmly.

'Welcome, Marc. What a pleasure to have your back. Still a handsome devil, as always.' Lorcan gestured to Marc with his right hand, then took several sips from the other. Fresh blood gathered along the rim of the cup. 'You were always a true friend, and your presence will be a cherished addition to the castle.' Lorcan returned to his seat as Lucas eyed his brother sourly. It was evident he felt differently and thought his brother to be a fool. 'Try not to be quite so enthusiastic.' Lucas spoke in a whisper, ceasing any eye contact with his brother at all. This came as no surprise to Marc. Lucas envied the bond he shared with his brother. He was in opposition to everything, listening only to Acheron and Achylls. Many a time he would disregard the views of his brother, only to agree if reiterated by a senior member of the board. Quite often, foul-mouthed profanities were exchanged between the twosomes. Nevertheless, the twins shared a special bond and would inevitably reunite shortly after an argument. Lucas glared at Marc. His venom couldn't be hidden. Marc remained cool. Lucas was the least of his worries. 'I don't suppose you have finally scared that woman away, have you? Or have you simply had a change of heart?' Lucas's voice was shrill and dark. It echoed around the hallow room as though booming through a megaphone. Though they were twins, Lucas and Lorcan were strikingly different. Lucas was thinner. His chiselled face less forgiving. The fact Achylls had told the entire board of Estella's disappearance, was of lesser concern than the fact that Lucas actually thought he gave a damn. Marc said nothing. He returned his vitriol with dignified silence. His fists stiffened, the lines across his forehead became prominent.

'Lucas, thank you for your inquisition. However, I do not honestly think you expect me to justify that with an answer.' Marc was stern. He certainly wouldn't be intimidated by a vampire who got caught red-handed exploiting underaged human girls for his seedy pleasure.

'Marc, come and take a seat. We have lots to discuss.' Acheron motioned with his hand. There were two empty seats beside Achylls, to which Apollyon and Marc reluctantly sat. Acheron offered glasses of blood. It was fresh. Despite the treaty, it smelt suspiciously human. Marc was intrigued. He refused, but looked on as Apollyon took his fill, twice over.

'Forgive my ignorance. But am I right in thinking that is human blood?' Marc's nose twitched as he spoke. He already knew the answer. There they were slaughtering humans in the castle and supplying synthetic rubbish to everyone else. Achylls became uncomfortable at Marc's intrigue. She fidgeted awkwardly. Acheron cleared his throat. It was little use hiding the obvious from a vampire. The stench of human remains was far too strong to dismiss. The atmosphere became tense.

'Yes, it is. But please do not make any rash conclusions. We feast upon that plastic stuff daily. But the occasional treat every now and again, shouldn't be condemned.' Acheron's eyes were shifty. His hypocrisy couldn't be hidden. Marc eyed him with contempt. Once again, his intelligence was undermined. He was immediately reminded why he left the confines of the castle in the first place.

'Marc don't be so uptight. This is a rare treat.' Achylls smiled sheepishly, as if, to soften the blow. Marc was less than impressed.

'So, you reprimand others for the very rules, in which you partake?' he said.

Acheron became stony-faced and wolfish. He outstretched his arms across the table. Marc was already proving to be a challenge. A reminder of times old and days past. The tension was so stiff, you could slice the atmosphere with a knife. 'Marc, for goodness sakes. Can you not be so combative? No one is being punished for slaughtering a human, or two. I have already seen the likes of Edgar and Stramus. And you, too. And perhaps, a dozen more this month. We've seen it all. Under the circumstance, we have relaxed some of the rules. Vampires are being hunted. Maybe drinking human blood will give us the extra spark we need to keep us alert, and as fit as possible. I can't help but wonder, has that synthetic blood turned us into sheep?'

Lucas piped up in agreement. 'We have pondered this for weeks. For now, we may have to return to nature. At least, until we know what we are up against. In fact, we will be actively encouraging all vampires to hunt again. Acheron will send out the memo to Killbraith, today.'

Marc was stunned. This had obviously been going on for a while. But it was no point being hypersensitive. Indeed, he had already slaughtered a fair few tonight.

'Anyway. Marc, I don't imagine you're thirsty after all that blood you've just consumed.' Acheron smiled, though his eyes were serious.

Marc smirked. Truth be known, he had never felt better and was certain human blood had played a part in his renewed strength and rejuvenation.

'Rightly so, Acheron. Rightly so,' he said.

'Well, let's raise a toast. To Marc's return!' Lorcan interjected the sour mood. He stood up, raised glass in hand. He looked around the oblong table, vying the others to follow suit. In turn, Apollyon stood. So did Achylls. After much deliberation, Acheron rose to his feet.

SEVENTEEN

Although Estella had gained an increase in strength, the transformation had been difficult on her body. Although some vampires were known to shapeshift, it wasn't an ability she had been gifted with. But now, her body had a life of its own. Three days ago, her entire hand took the form of something ghastly and otherworldly. Green in appearance. She was trying to work out if it resembled a lizard, or something else. It took several hours for the offending hand to revert back to human and proved to be an extremely difficult inconvenience while it lasted.

Tonight, was a night like any other. Estella had jumped from building to building, levitating at super high speeds. Teleportation was yet to happen. Apparently, it was the daemon's go to mode of transportation, and the most efficient. Estella had travelled far and wide, eyeing the view discreetly from afar. She avoided vampire towns like the plague. In particular, Killbraith. Now their archenemy, the last thing she wanted was a trail of vampires on her backside. More importantly, it had been two nights since her last meal. Estella was hungry and had now begun to gaze at humans. It was a different sort of gazing. She would lust at them, wanting to tear their delicate insides away from the rest of their bodies. This hunger had plagued her for weeks. Yesterday, she nearly killed a lone human. A young woman out and about, wondering the streets after curfew. Estella followed her for ages, just watching and waiting, pondering whether to strike, or not. She nearly pounced for the kill, but decided against it after the baby began babbling, more so than ever. It was as if the child knew something she didn't. Or perhaps she disapproved of her mother's newfound lust for flesh. Fearing the guilt, Estella had taken to considering birds, or other large animals. Trouble is, they were not particularly easy to come by. Farmers went to great lengths to conceal their livestock, particularly with the threat of the supernatural. Finding a lone cow, was gold dust. However, time was running out. Soon enough, she would have to make a kill. With nowhere to go, and an increasingly empty stomach, Estella had few choices left. At nearly midnight, Estella felt at her peak. Home tonight was on the roof of a large building. Estella spotted a rusty signpost in the distance. Placed next to a meagre tree, it read; Creaker, three miles south. Creaker, was a mystery. Unheard of and unfamiliar. Estella pursed her lips. She screwed up her eyes, scrutinising the sign. That was it. The que she needed. With the baby strapped taut to her back, Estella set off in pursuit of the bizarrely named town. Within minutes, Estella arrived at her destination. Or at least she thought she had. Creaker, was a thick mass of trees and open space. The natural light of the moon gleamed down, casting shadows along the dark streets. There were no shops, nor houses. Just vast acres of land, and roads. In fact, Creaker was a place like no other. It wasn't immediately obvious who inhabited a place like this, but the obvious lack of human scent told her the residents were likely supernatural creatures as much as she was. Estella sniffed the air. The baby gurgled. The air was sweet, yet weirdly sickly. Stuffy almost. The lack of meat shops on display was also a good indicator that werewolves wasn't around. Brash and obtuse, they were a species who lacked any discretion. Displaying human limbs for all to see, was like some sort of coveted glory. Estella suddenly felt hopeful. Perhaps this was a place inhabited by daemons. A species she knew absolutely nothing about, and yet, here she was. The baby begun chewing at her own fingers. She slurped them loudly, much to Estella's annoyance. A pang of guilt tugged at her stomach. She hadn't fed the child in days and had now taken to eating her own fingers.

'Worry not, little one. You will soon be fed.' That was all Estella could muster, hoping to soothe the hungry infant on her back. Much to her surprise there was a sizeable white house sat in the distance, practically in the middle of nowhere. Obscured by picket fence, complimented by a huge, paved driveway, there was a rusty old car parked up. The house was unfashionable. Its roof flattened. The gutter stuck out and looked in need of repair. One thing was obvious; whomever habited the home, were a keen gardener. There were vegetable gardens along the front lawn. All of which were thriving a sprightly assortment of coloured veg. There were flowers, too. All different sorts. Many unknown to Estella. She admired the colours, so many of them. Her nose wrinkled as the smell of fresh flowers wafted up her nostrils. But why was such a house alone in the middle of nowhere? Estella sniffed the air for clues. The familiar scent of tender human flesh was missing. It was a home inhabited by the supernatural. Fearing it could be vampires, her senses shot up. However, despite the obvious risks, Estella was drawn to the house like bees to honey. As she studied the rustic sash windows with its chipped paint and rotting wood, she felt herself being sucked into its charm. This house was like no other. Enticing and inviting, she was being sucked in by its web like a stranglehold tarantula. Estella could hardly help herself as she crept toward the gate. With feet barely touching the ground, she was gliding. Effortless, even with a baby strapped taut to her back. Estella cautiously lifted the hinge on the gate. The walk towards the door, was like walking to her death.

With every step she took, the reality of being confronted by an angry supernatural who could kill the baby, became a real one. The door was there, black and curious. Though slightly dilapidated, its gold numbering was bold and intense. It was number 13, strange, as it was the only house around. With anxious trepidation, Estella stood looking at it, deciding whether knocking was worth the risk. The baby suddenly gurgled, which Estella took as a positive sign. Estella lifted the solid iron knocker positioned underneath the number. With two quick knocks, she chewed on her bottom lip anxiously waiting. After a minute had gone by, Estella knocked one more time. The wait quickly became tedious. Deciding no one was in, Estella sat down with her back against the door. With all the will in the world to leave, something kept telling her to stay. As if the house knew more than she did, Estella took up residence on the doorstep waiting for the return of its occupant. There was a bitter frost in the night air. The blood moon was nearly over. Thankfully, nothing out the ordinary had happened. Feeling grateful to not having turned into a four-legged canine, nor was there a repeat of the monster which had showed its head back at Stefan's place. This was all very reassuring. Perhaps Stefan had been wrong. Maybe she **did** have some control over it. Though with the death of her friend, that was little too late. Estella's thoughts were interrupted as a crow appeared from nowhere. It made a beeline for her as it hobbled up towards the path. It stopped and looked her square in the eye, as if it knew her secret. Estella eyed it with intrigue. And then it happened. The bird spoke.

'Embrace it till your death.' It spoke.

Estella was stunned. It was obvious the crow was a messenger. It had been sent as a warning. But from whom? How did it know her whereabouts? She was literally off the grid. Estella angrily shooed the bird away. 'Thanks for the message, now get the hell out of here.' She spat. Estella gave an icy stare. Suddenly, the crow backed away then took flight. Its wings fluttered in a flurry. A single feather fell to the floor. Estella eyed it as it landed at her feet. She picked it up off the ground, then held it to her nose. It smelt like raw meat. But she liked it. Estella shoved the feather in her dishevelled hair. Just then, the door squeaked open. Caught completely unaware, Estella became flustered as she tried to pull herself together. She quickly stood up and turned to the door. A slender, elderly, woman stared back at her. She was scruffily dressed and looked unkempt. She wore a long tattered black skirt covered in stains. Lastly, there was a red cloth wrapped around her head like a bandage. Estella greeted her with kind eyes. 'Hello. Sorry to bother you. I just need a place to stay, for a day or two. I have a baby.'

There was a long pause. The woman studied Estella like a map. Her face deadpan, expressionless. Every hair on her body was met with scrutiny. Estella didn't allow her discomfort to show. Keep it together, she reminded herself. Strangely enough, Estella couldn't ascertain if this woman was a werewolf, or a vampire. She had an entirely different energy, unfamiliar to anything else. She was tempted to place her bets on the werewolf, but still, couldn't be sure. The baby sucked her finger loudly. This caught the old woman's attention. Suddenly, the stranger's interest was ignited. She became animated, whilst ignoring Estella entirely. The old woman stepped out of the house to see the baby on Estella's back. Estella watched in disbelief as she smiled broadly at the baby, waving at her with a stiff hand. Estella thought she was strange, certainly eccentric. Just then, as if she had heard her thoughts, the old woman shot Estella a disapproving look.

'Not as strange as you dear!' she said.

Estella was stunned. She wrinkled her brow trying to figure out the mysterious woman. Her arrogance was astounding. The child could be heard gurgling happily at the woman with a twinkle in her eye. Feeling like a third wheel, Estella abruptly cleared her throat as she tried to regain the old woman's attention. The old woman shot her an irritable stare. 'What is the matter?' she asked in vexation. 'What *are* you?' asked Estella, who was met with silence. The woman wrinkled her brow, as if trying to figure out the question. The old woman placed her hands along her hips; her mouth formed into a frown.

'I am, what you have become.' She said. Estella's mouth fell open. With the exception of Xavier, she had never met another Daemon. No wonder she couldn't detect her by scent. The daemons were master deceivers. Unlike the other species, their scent could be mimicked for something else. Estella studied the old woman. She surveyed every embedded line etched upon her face. *So, this was what daemons looked like-* she thought. The thing is, there was nothing remotely different about this woman. She looked, normal, albeit very eccentric.

'And how do you know what I have become?' asked Estella, feeling slightly violated.

'I know all about you. You used to be a proud vampire. Perhaps, slightly conceited if I may say so.' she exclaimed loudly.

'Conceited? Excuse me?'

Estella was left open mouthed by her claims. But that didn't stop the old woman carrying on with her vitriol. 'For what it's worth, you still are. But that won't last long. You've had to humble yourself immensely. Don't worry, your change is almost complete. Don't get too complacent, however. You'll always be viciously hunted by the vampires, just as I am. And before you ask. Yes, you've a lot to learn.' A bizarre smile erupted across the old woman's face. Her hazel eyes twinkled under the nightlight. Strangely enough, Estella felt enamoured. Though she barely knew her, there was a weird sense of security. At last Estella didn't feel so alone. She fought back the lump welling in her throat. 'Well, do you want to come in, or not'?

'I appreciate your hospitality.' Said Estella as the old woman quickly ushered her in. There was a pungent smell of garlic. It was overwhelming. So much so, Estella gagged. Within seconds she broke out in a cold sweat. The baby looked up at her mother. Clearly the child was unbothered by the stench. 'Gosh, that is…strong.'

'It has to be. It's the only thing to keep those vampires at bay. You still have trace amounts left in your blood.'

'Do I? Are you trying to kill me?'

'There are far better ways to kill you dear. You will live. You do not have enough vampire DNA in your blood for it to destroy you. In fact, it's merely remnants at this stage.'

The kitchen was cluttered. Aluminium was plastered to the ceiling walls. As like the walls, table and chairs. In fact, the entire house looked like a science project. There were steel pots stacked on top of each other in a corner. All of which were neatly lined up in order of size. There were no windows. Just an empty space where it should have been, positioned above the sink. 'Do take a seat. That poor mite must be hungry. She needs blood, not flesh.'

Estella stiffened her lip 'Really?'

'She is a Daemon offspring. Flesh is terrible for her delicate digestive system so early in life. Vampires aren't the only blood drinking species, you know.'

'I've been feeding her birds, mostly…my own craving for meat is through the roof.'

The old woman rolled her eyes. 'Well, that's because your body is a mess. Quite frankly, it doesn't know what's hit it. You were a vampire, who fornicated with a daemon, and now it doesn't know what it is! You are literally one in a million. Such a thing has never happened before, not in my lifetime, anyway. Now, you listen to me young lady. If you want to keep that baby alive, you best do as I say' Estella's mouth fell open. Was that a threat? She was spoken to like a child. Her brain went on autopilot, envisioning the many ways to kill the old hag. Stake by heart or, the severing of her throat, both seemed fitting. Louisa snarled, eyes piercing. The old woman was unbothered. In fact, she looked bemused, egging her on to take a swipe. 'What is the matter? Are you not going to bite me to death? Before you get ahead of yourself, you ought to remember that I am the legitimate daemon, not you. You're simply a hybrid accident. You will never be accepted as pure blood.'

'Are you threatening me? And exactly how do you know all of this?' Estella's voice grew irritable. The old woman's cocky demeanour wasn't taken to kindly. Despite this, Estella felt her back against the wall. Warring with the old daemon would render a useless waste of energy. She had better things to do and decided she was best tolerated through gritted teeth.

'No. I'm not threatening you. I am stating a fact. Why do you think vampires hunt my kind by the dozen? It takes an army of them, for one of us. We are faster, stronger, ten times as big. We are the chosen ones.'

'You seem to know a lot about my life. I'm guessing clairvoyance is one of your strengths, too.'

'Oh yes. Us daemon's see and know everything. I can see it all in your eyes. It's ok, I won't judge. I feel your plight. He knows about the baby you know.'

'Marc?'

'No, of course not. I mean, the baby's father.' Spat the old hag. Estella snarled stiffly. How the hell did *she* know who the father was? Any talk of Xavier stirred up unpleasant feelings. It was bad enough he had disappeared. But how could he neglect his own child if he knew? Estella pulled out one of the aluminium chairs. Her legs felt like jelly. 'Don't worry dear. The baby will be fine. She *will* be just fine.' The old woman continued nattering to herself. Estella had already zoned out and was thinking of ways to kill Xavier if ever she saw him again. The baby starred at the old woman. Her eyes sparkled. She was babbling something and smiling with a wide gummy grin. The old woman fiddled about with her own fingers in an attempt to make the baby laugh.

'So, am I to assume it is you hunting the vampires? There were several recent deaths before I left. Things had gotten tense.' Estella's question cut the air. The old woman seemed startled. She looked at Estella quizzingly.

'No, of course not dear. I may have a disinterest for vampires, but they are definitely not worth my precious time. I, have better things to do.'

'Really. Like what?' Estella raised a brow. This old woman had absolutely nothing better to do, and she was sure of it. Estella was compelled to play devil's advocate. But she quickly bore regret. Suddenly, the old woman charged at her with bulging red eyes. Estella swiftly disappeared out of her reach, cheekily appearing from behind. The old woman growled viciously. It was deep and demonic-like. In fact, it made the werewolf sound like a mere kitten. *Gosh. I pray to never sound like a demon on steroids.* Estella's thoughts were interrupted by the old woman. She spun around as quick as a whippet. Her face contorted, bending and twisting out of shape. To be honest, it was an horrific shapeshifting episode.

'Ok, ok. I apologise. No need to bring the daemon out of its cage' Estella held her hands up in defeat. The last thing she wanted was to piss of the daemon then be thrown back out on the streets. Suddenly she wished she had kept her mouth shut. The baby gurgled something. On impulse, the old woman became civil again. Like Jekyll and hyde, her personality appeared split, her face returned to normal. She smiled sweetly at the baby. Estella's discomfort grew at the strange woman's erratic behaviour. She seemed to coo over this baby more than necessary, all the while treating her like a second-rate citizen.

'If you are to stay here, you must abide by my rules. Do I make myself clear?' The old woman turned to Estella, her eyes narrowed and intense. If looks could kill, Estella ought to be buried six feet deep.

'Crystal clear.' Estella bit her lip uncomfortably. She pondered whether this really was the right thing to do. The house obviously wanted her here; however, the old woman's confrontational nature and fiery attitude was a little too much to handle. Estella knew it was only a matter of time before things potentially got out of hand. But, for the baby's sake, she had to bite her tongue and carry on. Another daemon was the only family she had right now. 'Come this way. Let me show you to your room. The entire house is vampire proof. You will be perfectly safe here.' Estella followed the woman out through the kitchen, and out onto the dark hallway. It seemed the entire house was layered with aluminium. Every wall, and the entire ceiling was covered in that weird metal wrapping. Estella was stunned.

'Are these sheets proofed with silver?' Estella was bemused.

'Yes, of course.' Snapped the old woman.

After a short walk, they arrived the end of the long hallway and was met with a dimly lit landing. An odd, shaped table was sat by the side of the wall, with a silver framed photograph placed on top of it. It was a young couple. They were smiling and happy, arms wrapped around each other. For a moment, Estella's heart sank. Would she ever find that happiness again? 'That was my Gilbert. Back in the good old days. The days when we could walk freely without fear, or whisper. Approximately a thousand and ten years ago. Before most of our kind were hunted.' Estella couldn't believe it. This woman was nearly eight hundred years older than she was. That was some achievement.

'So, how did your husband die?'

'Vampires.' The woman's tone was easy and casual. It was clear she had come to terms with her husband's passing. Suddenly, the seriousness of Estella's own situation hit hard. There was nothing she could say but nod her condolences and pray the same would never happen to her. There were two doors on the landing side by side. As before, they were both covered in thin aluminium wrapping. The old woman stood in front the doors, eyeing them with suspicion. She appeared confused. She kept pointing her finger at each door as though deciding which one to enter. After a moment of indecision, she opened the door to the second room. The smell of mould was undeniable. The pungent scent wafted out the room the moment the door was opened. Estella coughed trying to ease the scratch at the back of her throat. The room was larger than expected. At least twelve feet either side. With exception to the windows, it was painted all white. Two large candle wick holders were mounted either side off the walls. Each filled with a large white candle. A sizeable bed was laid out in the centre of the room, with two large wooden wardrobes sat on either side. The little wooden chair sat opposite the bed looked wobbly and had part of the back missing. Bits of chipped wood flaked from the exterior. Finally, there was a shaggy brown rug laid across the floor.

'So, why isn't this room plastered in metal sheets?' Estella turned to the woman, who in turn, looked at her as if she had spoken a foreign language. Her face bore little expression.

'The windows are enough. I haven't the patience for it anymore. Covering my scent in sage, which seems to do the trick also. If they find me, they will have to kill me. I am tired of hiding. I tell you what though, I will not go down easy. They will have hell on their hands.' The old woman pursed her lips. Her eyes were sad.

Of course, it was the sage-said the voice in Estella's head. It was a centuries old trick, used by vampires mostly, but evidently worked on other species too. Estella sensed the pain written across the old daemon's face. Every line and wrinkle told a story. Estella felt a knot in the pit of her stomach. Would she have to live in hiding like some weird recluse? It was hard to comprehend. Being a vampire, was coveted. It was glamorous and prideful. Most of which lived a life of exuberant luxury Once a human girl pleaded with her, begging to be turned. She wanted a better life but was bitterly disappointed when Estella refused to give her the bite. However, it was unlikely anyone would envy the daemon. 'What ***is*** it the vampires fear so damned much about your species?' Estella's voice fell to a whisper. Secretly, she was scared. She feared for her child and her safety. Her life was now an uncomfortable reality. To think she would be slaughtered by the vampires if ever given the chance, sent a horrifying ripple down her spine. Estella wanted to learn more about the daemon, and what she had become. She felt like it was a disease that needed a cure. Hopes of ever becoming a vampire again, looked increasingly slim.

'Like everything in this world, you fear what you don't know. We are the only species able to challenge and kill a vampire. For the most part, the werewolves are seen as easy feat. The vampires are strong fearless creatures. However, the daemon has magnificent strength and could destroy a couple vampires easily. There aren't many of us left. They would have killed me too, if given a chance. I slaughtered six, and several escaped. Unfortunately, Gilbert had an injury and was unable to fight off the army that had come down on him.' Her face fell as she recounted Gilbert's last days. Suddenly she turned to the child in Estella's arms. The twinkle in her eye returned as she changed the topic of conversation. 'This child is a gift. She will have men kneeling before her, and women taking her lead. She will be a ruler of her own accord. Indeed, this baby is a hybrid like no other, and incredibly powerful. However, she must be vigilant. The vampires won't hesitate to cut her precious little heart out.' Estella looked horrified. She gripped the baby tightly as she old woman made attempts to prise the child out of her arms. The old woman scowled in an attempt to hold the child.

'Do you mind.' Snapped Estella. The woman became defensive. She shot Estella a disapproving glare.

'She doesn't belong to you. She is a product of Lazurus, our greatest warrior.

You were just a carrier. You know as well as I do that vampires cannot reproduce. This, was no accident.' She said. The baby whimpered at the constant tugging. This was the first Estella had seen her so visibly upset. Hot rage rosed to the surface. Clearly this woman was delirious. Estella could no longer tolerate her bad manners. Suddenly she snapped. 'I think I have outstayed my welcome. We won't be staying after all. You've got shit for manners, and I am restraining my better instinct to rip your old throat out.' The old woman looked appalled at Estella's outburst. Before she had a chance to protest, Estella headed for the bedroom door and quickly disappeared down the dark landing. Just as she reached the front door, the old woman could be heard shouting down the corridor.

'You won't get very far out there. They will hunt you in droves. You will be finished. This is the safest place for you, and the baby.'

'I will take my chances. You're way too combative. I suggest you find some other undead unfortunate to spew your vulgar attitude at.' With that, Estella headed outside and slammed the door shut. Seconds in the old daemon was standing in the doorway with her hands by her sides. Red-faced and angry, she lowered her gaze to the floor.

'Please do not leave. I'm so lonely. My tongue gets carried away with me. I would really love it if you stayed.' She pleaded.

Estella looked over her shoulder. She was stunned at the sudden softening of her hardened demeanour. Truth be known, she was exasperated, and no longer in the mood for small talk. However, the baby was weary, and hungry. Estella decided really had had enough of jumping over high buildings for one day. After some more grovelling on the old woman's part, reluctantly Estella agreed to stay a little longer. The old woman became rather friendly and hugged Estella as she arrived back on the doorstep. Back inside the house, it was a different atmosphere the second time around. The old woman was warm and kind, offering her warm beverages. The baby was given a drink of blood and settled to sleep. That night, Estella learnt a lot. The woman told stories of her kind, whilst preparing Estella for the worst. Estella was well versed on the strange creature and was shown ways in which she could keep it at bay. It was possible for her to live a life in human form, never having to change at all. She had to resist sleeping under the blood moon for three days in a row. To do this, she must sleep with an apple seed planted firmly underneath the tongue. Apparently, this, kept the daemon in its box. She could bathe in sage to keep the vampires at bay. This would also prevent being tracked or traced. If she were discovered, the sage would leave no clue of her identity. If no sage was present, the daemon could mimic scent of any other being, even a human if they chose to. However, the old woman warned against this as often time, anything mimicked was still a potential snack to a vampire. Sage was far safer, she said. Estella spoke about events back at Stefan's shop. Her remorse and anger came flooding back. She spent most of the evening in floods of tears, hoping desperately not to look like a babbling fool. Surprisingly, the old woman was empathetic. Estella was told not to burden herself with blame, for she had little control over herself. Apparently, that was her first 'show'. Sleeping with an apple seed would avoid that happening again. The daemon urge was a strong one, especially for an inexperienced newbie. If all else failed, drinking a drop of one's own blood, every ten days often done the trick. Unfortunately, despite all efforts, sometimes the daemon had to be let out the box. It was a viciously strong being, and even this daily ritual wasn't enough to stop shapeshifting it was the daemon's will. For the most part, at least the rancid werewolf had control over their change. This was the most horrific part of it all. Her craving for meat would lessen over time, only IF she followed the rules.

'Can you help me track her father?' Estella looked hopeful, but the woman became cold. 'I am sorry. But you are better off forgetting about him. It's for the best.' She said.

'Why would he do this to me? Why didn't he warn me this would happen?'

The old woman stood in front of the open fireplace with her hands to her hips. Despite her earlier promises, she became angry again. 'No one encouraged you to fornicate with a daemon. You made that decision all by yourself. You better leave that man alone. It's for your own good.' Estella was taken aback. She curled her lips angrily, but to be honest, the old daemon had a point. It was the hard cold truth, undressed and exposed. The woman glared at her like a bull ready to charge. Suddenly, the room became tense. That was the que Estella needed, deciding she ought to head to bed. As Estella levitated up the stairs in one swift jump, there was an odd sense of relief as she slammed the bedroom door firmly behind her. Evidently, the old woman was best tolerated in small increments. As Estella hopped atop the hard cold bed, her mind recalled the evening's events. The thought of sleeping with an apple seed underneath the tongue, was bizarre. It would be almost comical if it wasn't her reality. Estella turned to the baby. Wrapped taut in a white sheet, who would have known this innocent child was the most powerful creature to walk the earth? The thought sparked an uneasy tingle down Estella's spine.

EIGHTEEN

Thuds to the door woke Estella out of sleep. She stirred uncomfortably. The pounding continued. The voice of the old woman could be heard shouting, demanding to be let in. 'Open that door at once, otherwise I'll knock it down. Do you realise what time it is?' Estella bolted upright. She turned to the baby, who was already up smiling and eyeing her with glee. Like always, she seemed undisturbed by the constant chaos around her.

'Gosh, you're resistant. You're like a little ball of steel.' The baby laughed at her mother. Estella swore she understood every word of it. She was sucking her fingers, probably demanding more blood. The old woman gave her a jug full yesterday evening. Estella was in awe when the baby finished and then cried for more. Her cheeks glowed rosy, red, and her eyes seemed to sparkle more. The woman had been right. Blood had done the trick. The banging on the door got louder. 'I'm coming!' Estella screamed in anger, banging her fists against the wall. The baby side eyed her mother. Estella surprised herself. That anger had come from nowhere. Estella reasoned with herself in order to survive, she had to ignore the old hag and learn the essence of keeping calm. Surprisingly, the knocking stopped. Faint footsteps could be heard walking back down the hallway. Estella wasted little time. She was up and dressed in a flash, baby in tow. Although her hair looked as though she had been dragged through a hedge backwards, Estella felt refreshingly ok about it. As she entered the dimly lit kitchen, the old woman had her back to her, stirring something on the stove. Whatever It was, smelt of death.

'Good morning. You're late. You must be down by 7am. It's now, twenty minutes past.' Estella refrained from rolling her eyes or making any other obvious impolite gestures with her face. Instead, she replied with understanding. 'I'll make sure of it tomorrow.' 'You may not be around for very long, so you ought to make the most of your time with that baby.' Here she was again, making unpleasant statements just to make her feel uncomfortable. Estella was almost certain she got a kick out of it. 'Why do I have to be reminded of such a thing?' Estella felt her shoulders stiffen in defence. She hated how easy she allowed herself to be triggered.

'Because it's the truth. Start getting her into a routine to do without you.' surprisingly the old woman's voice was light and airy, almost tediously so. Estella bit her lip through gritted her teeth. It was no use getting upset. Clearly this was a ploy to see how quick she would fly off the handle. 'Listen dear, I don't want to upset you, but I need to show you something. First, you must have some breakfast.'

'I'm ok. I really don't fancy anything this morning.' Estella replied.

The old woman continued stirring the pot. She lowered her nose, sniffing wildly at the contents. 'I think it's ready.' she said with a smile, ignoring what Estella had said. Estella watched in disbelief as the old woman opened the nearest cupboard to the stove and eagerly brought out two green bowls. In fact, it was the same colour as the stew she stirred. Estella thought she might gag. She was grinding on her back teeth in a desperate bid not to. All she really craved, was flesh. Preferably human. 'Do you have any meat? I don't mind, human or cattle.' The old woman stopped abruptly in her tracks. She turned to Estella with her mouth hung open in disapproval as she quickly placed the bowls down along the aluminium wrapped table.

'No dear, we do not eat meat. You **cannot** eat meat. That will poison your mind.'

'Poison my mind? What exactly do you mean by that?'

The woman became rattled at Estella's naivety. 'Don't question me dear. If you want to stay alive, DO NOT eat meat. The minute you start craving flesh, you will become a killing machine, and will lose all control over yourself, or any decisions you make.'

Estella couldn't believe her ears. She didn't know what was worse. Turning into a manic human slaying beast or being told she couldn't eat the one thing she craved the most.

'Wipe the shock off your face. How do you think I remain under the radar for so long? When you drink this, it will take all those naughty meat cravings away. It helps to keep you safe, and out of trouble.' The daemon's smug face irritated Estella. Her stay was steadily turning into a nightmare. She felt like a child again, unable to make her own decisions. Her mind cast back to her father. Even he wasn't this patronising. And that was saying something. Just then, the old woman rushed over and prised the baby out of her arms. This time Estella didn't resist. It felt like her life had been taken over. She felt powerless and watched helplessly from afar as the old woman sat around the table and began feeding the baby a small cup of blood. There she was, playing the doting grandmother role, dipping her fingers in and out of it, then shoving them awkwardly inside the baby's mouth. She also poured herself some of the green stuff and took small sips from a large wooden spoon. Suddenly Estella felt her limbs weaken. Her mind was boggled. She felt odd and then there was darkness. When Estella came to, she was face to face with the old woman. They were seated in the backyard amongst thick shrubs and a burning fire. The baby was nestled on the old woman's lap contentedly playing with a loose thread from her skirt. The sun had disappeared, evening had set in.

'Welcome back dear. How are you feeling?' The old woman had her face an inch away from hers. Her breath was rancid, her eyes curious. She observed Estella as though she were a delicate doll. Estella placed a hand to the top of her head. She pulled a leaf from her hair as she tried to muster a smile.

'I feel fine. Did I pass out? Is that normal for your species?'

The woman smiled broadly. 'You'll be happy to know there is no trace of vampiric DNA left in your body. Even your fangs have gone. But you must eat.'

Estella clenched her jaw. She was horrified at the thought of becoming a fully-fledged daemon, despite the old woman's pride as though it were some sort of achievement. Estella had no words. She just sat there feeling empty and confused. In the space of a few weeks, she had managed to swap her entire species. Unheard of, and yet, here she was the poster child of the impossible. Estella placed her finger to her mouth. She nearly jumped out of her skin. Her fangs had disappeared. A grave horror rippled through her entire body. This was the grand finale. And all because of her retched yearning for some enticing stranger who managed to worm his way in. 'Don't look so disheartened, dear. We are far more superior than any vampire could ever be.'

'I am starving.' Estella clutched her stomach, in hopes of changing the conversation for something less daunting.

'Here you go. Drink it all until you feel better.' The old woman handed her a bowl of the green stuff, which seemed to be conveniently sitting on the ground at her feet. Estella didn't refuse. She eagerly grabbed the bowl and held it to her nose. It looked like slime and smelt like filth. Nonetheless, Estella tipped her head back and gulped it all. 'It wasn't too bad, was it? If you keep drinking this, you will have little to worry about.' promised the woman. Estella thought she was mad. She had *everything* to worry about, especially her baby. In fact, it would be nice not to worry. 'I must tell you something. You need to know what is really going on. You were chosen to have this baby, and actually very lucky. Lazarus doesn't choose freely. He thought you were special.'

'Who is this Lazarus you speak of? The baby's father, his name is Xavier.' Estella's tone became matter of fact. Actually, slightly condescending. The old woman didn't respond. Instead, she raised her brows quizzingly, as though she knew something Estella didn't. Her face became sheepish. Estella was intrigued. She eyed the old woman like a hawk as she brushed her wrinkled hands against the baby's webbed feet. 'You seem to have a habit of avoidance. Why don't you answer the question?' Estella probed further. Suddenly the old woman put her head up. Her eyes glazed over as she spoke.

'He wanted a daemon hybrid spawn and chose you for the vessel. It was no accident. You gave your temple to the Daemon warrior. He has killed many and fought many wars. It was written in the 'Esoteric Fortress', orchestrated over a thousand years ago. This baby, she is the next messiah.'

Estella grew irritable at the constant mumbo jumbo. She wanted answers about Xaviar, and yet, was offered none. A numbness brewed within. 'Who the hell is Lazarus. Tell me at once. I take it, Xaviar is not his name, is it? Anyway, I was told about that book. Many years ago.' This statement piqued the old woman's interest. Her eyes became alive. She starred at Estella as though waiting for more.

'You know about the book?' asked the old daemon.

'Oh. So now you want to talk to me?' Estella frowned. It was obvious this woman wanted a hold off the baby, at any cost. Estella wasn't well versed but remembered being told about the book. It was fleeting, but the message was clear. Only a few would seek out its existence, and fewer could comprehend. A vampire named Cyril had introduced her to it when she first turned. She demanded Estella read it and said her life as an undead would take on greater meaning. Marc didn't allow her the privilege, and labelled Cyril a lunatic. That was the last time Estella saw Cyril, and any mention of the book since. 'Well, I guess I should say I am flattered I was chosen. But boy oh boy, I should have at least had a choice in the matter, don't you think? Well, you can tell your precious Lazarus that, if I see him again, I shall pluck his heart out. The old woman gulped loudly. It was obvious she didn't approve of Estella's intentions.

'Don't go looking for trouble. You will certainly get more than you bargained for.' Said the old woman. Estella suddenly got up. She needed some space to breathe, to think. Turning back to the house, the old woman watched Estella's every move with eager eyes. She scowled, then turned her attention back to the baby. Once inside, Estella hurried to the bedroom. A hollow darkness had taken over. What happened next, Estella hadn't prepared for. Nevertheless, Estella was on autopilot to get out as fast as possible. With a dead-pan expression, she begun to gather her belongings. However, the baby's stuff was deliberately left behind. If Lazarus and the old hag craved the baby that much, they ought to look after her. Once Estella had finished packing, she made her way to the front door. Within minutes she had already disappeared down the path. She wanted to stop herself for being an idiot and return for her baby. But she couldn't. As though she were a puppet being craftly manipulated by a puppeteer, Estella had nor the inclination or the will to turn back. Estella had gone, never to return.

NINETEEN

Castle Dravenherd

Icy stares and curled upper lips, the eight sets of eyes studied each other with intent. Runa walked in with a large beaker of blood. She laid it out on the table centre with a smile. Suddenly, the mood lightened, and everybody relaxed. Edgar puffed eloquently on a cigar. He was egging Lorcan to follow suit. For the first time in centuries, all of the vampires had come together. Like a covenant of witches, nothing else mattered at a time like this. 'So, gentlemen, how was the journey back? I have never seen Stramus so dishevelled.' Marc smiled stiffly. There was laughter all around. Stramus however, became frosty. 'I care not for your opinion. One's appearance is of no concern to any of you.'

'Chill out, old boy. No need to bite our heads off.' said Apollyon. Achylls studied Marc across the table. She was contemplating. He knew her extremely well, and she had something to say.

'So, Marc, what exactly has happened to your…erm…Estella?' The chatter died down. Acheron's icy gaze was intense. He glared at Marc, waiting for an answer.

'If you really want to know, she has fled the mansion. It had been three weeks, and I'm no closer to her whereabouts than the day she left.' He quipped, no longer giving a damn about anyone's ill-conceived opinions. Edgar awkwardly cleared his throat. Stramus eyed him suspiciously. He hoped Edgar refrained from this conversation and didn't get involved. There was already enough chaos between him and Marc back at the mansion.

'Oh really? I am intrigued. Please carry on.' The prominent lines between Acheron's brow stiffened. The visible cords in his neck pulsed. Lucas wrinkled his nose before joining in the conversation. 'Isn't this a surprise. I wondered what it took for you to come crawling back.' He spat.

Marc tensed his jaw with clenched fists. His eyes bulged with steady rage. He looked over at his cousin Runa for support. She was concerned. He wanted to rip Lucas in half, but for her sake, he had to remain calm. Runa sensed his frustration and offered a gentle smile. Marc remembered what Edgar had told him. If it was somehow true that Estella was no longer a vampire, a claim as ridiculous as the man himself, Marc definitely didn't want the entire board knowing about it.

'Well, I am sure she will soon tire and return once she has had enough of gallivanting around town.' Marc's face remained solemn as he spoke, eyeing the curious vampires in hopes they wouldn't somehow figure out what was really going on. 'Of which is none of our business.' said Lorcan eyeing his friend sympathetically. Acheron locked his gaze on Lorcan. He was Marc's friend, always quick to his defence. Secretly, this quietly riled Acheron, who became cold and frosty at his statement. His clenched jaw and narrowing of the lips became pronounced as he eyed Lorcan with contempt. 'Anyway, let's cut the bullshit. I am sure Achylls has wasted no time in briefing you all on my love life. If you don't mind, I would rather discuss other things.' Marc looked around the table. His unreserved tone did not sit well with some of the other vampires. Fangs baring, he was met with silence. Then Runa piped up.

'Marc, I want to help you find Estella.' she said with a smile.

Lucas raised an eyebrow. He looked at Acheron, who in turn eyed him cautiously, then shook his head sideways. Lorcan side eyed his brother. He wanted to help Marc but felt best he stay quiet on this one. He already knew he had ruffled Lucas's feathers and didn't want to cause unnecessary conflict. Although he was placed in a difficult position, ultimately, his loyalty remained with his brother.

'May I excuse myself.' Suddenly, Apollyon got up from the table. His mind was troubled by Estella, his eyes wandering. As the only vampire who actually knew what was going on with Estella, it had become a burden too heavy to carry. Of course, he feared for her safety but was also gravely conflicted by loyalty and duty. Estella was a daemon and they, were a great threat to vampires. Just then, Achylls stood up also. Her green eyes scanned the table.

'I am sorry Marc. I will not be helping in this quest. Estella is an adult, not a lost puppy in need of a search party. Our main focus, should be avenging Orpheus death, and nothing else.' With that, she too headed for the door. Her pointed heels tapped against the smooth stone floor. Marc turned to watch her to the door. There she was, swaying her hips sideways. Her dark hair trailed the length of her back. There was no denying, Achylls was an attractive woman. Albeit a cold-hearted corrupt one. Marc saw the look in her eyes. It was obvious she hated his guts merely because of Estella. She might have been his deceased uncle's wife, but her lust for him was obvious. Marc had lost count of all the times she had cunningly propositioned him. Acheron cleared his throat angrily.

'I see you still have quite the roving eye.' he declared loudly. Marc turned his attention back to the table. He ran his left hand through his thick dark hair. He was mentally exhausted and had little fight left. It had been three days since his arrival, and already he had grown weary. It was almost daybreak.

'I am heading to bed.' Marc abruptly stood.

He left the five men around the table. He marched to the door and slammed it behind him. The walk down the corridor was a lonely place. Big and vast, it was a three-minute walk to his room. The longest three minutes he had in a long time. His journey took him past the pantry where a sombre woman sat. She was one of the maids. A human slave kept hostage to run their errands. In fact, the castle had three human maids, all of which had a task in keeping up the appearance of the castle. They were treated with contempt, merely kept alive for the vampire's own selfish reasons. The forlorn maid looked up at Marc. Her eyes were empty. Like his. She waved at him wearily. He simply nodded and carried on to his room. Pushing back thoughts of Estella, Marc was optimistic to be back in his own territory soon enough. Staying at the castle was a punishment too much to bear. Small talk was becoming increasingly difficult. He wondered if Estella was behind the recent deaths. Had she become a vampire slaying beast, determine to take them all out? Perhaps there were a few of them, plotting and waiting. It was a crazy reality, but one he was having to slowly come to terms with. As Marc stepped into the darkened room, he noticed the bed was bare. A wooden coffin sat feet away, an open invitation to get in. Yesterday, he had slept cocooned in layers of Egyptian cotton sheets. Evidently the maids were instructed to replace them with coffins instead. Marc stripped himself bare before jumping in. Sunrise was on its way.

'I was attacked; I tell you. Someone knocked me to the floor, flat out. It was quick and fast, and I couldn't detect the scent.'

'But you're a god damn vampire. Are we all turning to mush?'

'Acheron, isn't it obvious? Whatever it is, this creature is stronger and faster than any of us. Clearly, we don't know what we are up against.' Elena's blonde hair fell wildly upon her shoulders. She pinched her lips in vexation.

'Well, we cannot remain locked away in this castle. From now on, we travel in pairs.' said Acheron. Lucas was visibly annoyed. He was arrogantly proud. In fact, he was astonished that something was stronger than he. With his nose in the air, he turned to his brother.

'Lorcan will travel with me.' he said.

Lorcan said nothing. He raised the beaker to his mouth, taking huge gulps. Traces of blood dripped down the sides of his mouth, which he gently wiped with his index finger. Just then, Marc walked through the great hall doors. He looked miserable. More so than the night before.

'Good night, Marc. Nice to see you looking so upbeat. How did you sleep?' asked Elena, her words coated in dry sarcasm. Marc said little. He approached the table and pulled out a seat. There was a large beaker of blood laid out in front of him, to which, he knocked back quickly. With a full stomach, he finally acknowledged the many faces starring at him. He turned to Elena.

'I am sleep deprived. Nevertheless, here I am, ready for another night.' He forced a half smile.

'Are you up for some fencing?' Runa beckoned to her cousin.

'What. Now?' Marc was surprised.

'We practice combat every other night. I, will be joining you in the armoury shortly, Runa.' Interjected Achylls.

Runa turned to Achylls, nodding her acknowledgment. The vampires discussed politics. Treaty procedure, ways in which to preserve the vampire species. Marc's eyes glazed over. He found the conversation dull, engulfed in topics he had no real care for. The chatter went on for a while. Minutes, but likely a lot longer. It wasn't long before Marc realised that he was the last one left around the table. Alone with his thoughts, he could barely function without a picture of her floating through his mind. Runa was worried but played down her fear. He could see the sadness in her eyes and knew he had to pull himself together. Wondering whether Estella was dead or alive was doing him no good. He gave her everything. But, somehow still failed. He felt used, and unappreciated. With his mind working overtime, he suddenly became angry. Marc threw the beaker down on the table. Slumped over, he buried his head in his hands. Killing, had only been a temporary band aid. Needing to clear his thoughts, Marc got up and headed for the armoury. The armoury was at the other side of the castle, a journey that featured winding corridors and twirling staircases. Suddenly, something flickered from the corner of his eyes. He stopped in his tracks. He hid behind a pillar as the shadow came into focus. It was Apollyon. He appeared to be coming from Acheron's room. He was hooded and held his gaze downwards. Wondering what he was up to, Marc followed his shadow. Apollyon was headed in the opposite direction. Marc's curiosity got the better of him. Before he knew it, he was trailing his every move. Apollyon was headed to the courtyard. Marc watched his shadowed silhouette from afar. Apollyon was alone and appeared distraught. Truth be known, he looked anguished whilst whispering under his breath. He seemed to be begging for forgiveness. This piqued Marc's interest all the more. It certainly beat sparring in the armoury. Apollyon paced back and forth, head lowered, hands behind his back. With little else to see, Marc headed back inside the castle.

TWENTY

Down in the armoury was a clashing of swords. The vampires of Castle Dravenherd fought superbly, fencing with meticulous precision. Adorned in face masks and white suits, the vampires left no stone unturned. Indeed, combat was taken very seriously. Marc watched intently from the side. A quiet smile grew across his face. Stramus was magnificent. He had never seen the old vampire so fierce. He was a wonder with the sword, and tackled Lucas like a pro. Lucas struck his sword to the stomach. Stramus saw it coming and managed to duck out of the way with immense speed. His skill was remarkable. Marc couldn't take his eyes off the warring pair, and felt inclined to join in. Without warning, Achylls came blazing towards him. She sparred with Elena and appeared to be backing away as if her undead life depended on it. Elena, however, was a beast. Swift and eloquent, she moved the blade as though it were a work of art. Eyes seriously intense. Perhaps, a bit too much. She clanged away viciously, all the while, aiming for Achylls head. Marc was charmed. His eyes followed her around the armoury with new respect. He was rather old fashioned and certainly did not think a woman had the guts nor ability to put up such a fight. Elena fought like a beast. Strong, confident, and precise. Marc thought she was a killing machine. Unfortunately for him, his thoughts didn't go unheard. Elena's vampire intuition heard every word. She turned to him. With her attention on Marc, Achylls had the upper hand. Elena tackled her to the floor.

'Argh. Damn it!' she screamed. Elena got up off the floor. She angrily pulled of the protective headgear then threw it to the ground. Within a millisecond she had sprinted over to Marc. She grabbed him by the throat, angry to have lost. Achylls pulled off her own headgear. She stood open mouthed, bemused by the spectacle. 'What the hell is the matter with you? You distracted me! Would you rather I be in some kitchen fetching you buckets of blood?' she hissed. Marc was shocked. He couldn't understand why she were so angry. He backed away, hands in the air, pleading with her to calm down. Elena's eyelids were raised, eyes glaring. She bared her teeth in vexation. 'You sexist bastard.'

'Listen. I was giving you a compliment. Anyway, it is not my blasted fault you read my mind. Blame yourself for being a damn vampire.' Marc really didn't want a scene. Now, he felt backed into a corner. Elena turned around and marched out of the armoury. 'I've had enough of this' she spat. Runa, who had been sparring with Edgar, sprinted over to her cousin.

'What was that all about?' she asked.

'She has evidently had a bad day. I wouldn't worry about it,' he said. Runa looked puzzled but did not probe further. She shrugged her shoulders, then sauntered back over to Edgar, who in turn looked comically amused. Marc wasn't surprised by this. Edgar took pleasure in Marc's discomfort. There he was, literally gloating at Marc's humiliation. Deciding not to allow Elena to dampen his mood, Marc approached Lucas. The defeated vampire couldn't hide his apparent displeasure at being beaten by one of the ancients. His pride wouldn't allow it. 'Can I have the pleasure?' Marc outstretched his hand.

Lucas looked at it as though his hand was covered in filth, then wrinkled his nose sourly. He looked at Marc, who raised a curious brow.

'I admire your confidence. Just remember, Stramus is an accomplished fighter.' said Lucas, obviously rattled.

'So, he is. But that has nothing to do with me. You sound rather defensive.' Teased Marc.

There was little room for two gigantic egos in the castle, and if anything, this statement rubbed Lucas up the wrong way. That was enough for Lucas to agree. If only to prove Marc wrong, who he felt was trying to belittle him. Lucas reluctantly placed his mask over his head frothing at the mouth. The two vampires squared up. At this point, Marc became aware that everyone else had ceased practicing and was eagerly gathering up to watch he and Lucas battle it out. Lorcan, who had been busy practicing solo with a gleaming gold nunchuck at the other end of the twenty-foot-wide armoury stepped forward. He looked tense. He knew his brother well enough. And he knew Marc. Headstrong the pair of them. Their venom for each other was no secret. They were old enemies, and this, made all the difference. What should have been sparring, could potentially be the spilling of blood and guts.

'I think you will be needing this.'

Edgar eagerly handed Marc his headgear. He had a glint in his eye. Marc snatched it and fastened it over his head. The vampires practiced fencing differently than tradition. The swords used, were neither Epee or Saber, but samurai swords with the sharpest points, and capable of decapitating a head with one swoop. Lucas and Edgar exchanged wonderous glares. It was obvious. They wanted Marc dead, and what better way to do it. Accidental death didn't have the same tone as murder. Lucas was cautious and careful. He hovered about a lot. He was slow and steady on his feet, and it was tricky to ascertain his next move. Marc was swift and fast. He put on quite a show. He dodged the sword diligently, proving to be nimble on his feet.

'You should have never come back. I shall behead you in front of your cousin's very eyes.'

Marc didn't care for Lucas's threats, though Runa looked startled. Marc was unaroused, he struck his sword to the shoulder, to which Lucas narrowly missed. Marc held his blade even, a perfect undaunted horizon. Blades flashed as the vampires struck in sync. Lucas swiped to the head with keen persistence and missed every time. Marc proved to be a natural. The sound of clashing swords intensified. And then, it happened. Marc didn't see it coming, or perhaps he was distracted. Truth be known, he wasn't sure how it occurred so fast. The slice to his chest was painful. Though, not as painful as one would expect for a vampire. The bright red wound gleamed in contrast to the black shirt he wore. Adrenalin raged through his veins like a bubble waiting to burst. Marc knew, this was just the beginning. Although the vampires wore masks, the hint of smug in Lucas's eyes was evident. He had made the first strike. And thus, his ego was propelled sky high. Marc hovered back. Just then, a figure entered the armoury. It was Acheron. Marc ducked swiftly, narrowly missing his left ear. Again, he had lost focus. He thought himself to be frivolous. He became angry. Marc's piercing eyes became vigilant. A silent rage took over his body. With frustration and provoked indignation, he struck his sword harshly towards Lucas's torso. Without hesitance, he struck twice more, swiftly and keenly. Lucas managed to avoid Marc's wrath, but Marc's unwavering insistence was evident. With raw intent to harm, he struck his sword several times, aiming for Lucas's head. And then, he done it. Marc struck Lucas to the throat. Thankfully, the wound wasn't deep enough to cause any real bodily harm, but large enough to send a message.

'Please, Marc.'

Lorcan stepped forward with pleading eyes. Marc held his hands steadily in position. His blade glistened under the candlelight, resting centimetres away from Lucas's jawbone. 'The temptation to sever your head has never been so strong. You are incredibly fortunate, for your brother has saved you. Take this as a warning. The next time, you may not be so lucky.' Said Marc. Marc dropped his weapon. He looked at the others whilst Lucas hung his head in defeat. With his ego shattered, Lucas became uneasy and awkward, and could barely make eye contact with his brother, nor anyone else. In fact, one would say Lucas appeared tremulous. He headed towards the arched door. Just then, Acheron walked over. He seemed pleased. Uncharacteristically, he patted Marc across the shoulder.

'Your skill is impressive. I want to show you something.' Acheron's distinctive voice was gravelly and hoarse. Marc wasn't impressed with his flattery and eyed him with caution. 'Marc don't be so abrasive. You are one of the best fighters we have. I would like for you to remain with us.' Marc looked sheepish. Suddenly he became spaced out and felt the urge to get out of there. He turned to Acheron.

'You know where to find me.' he said before sprinting out of the armoury.

Lorcan turned to Acheron. He became angry, dropping the nunchucks to the floor. 'I shall assume the smile you wear, is as fake as the one you present to my brother. I suppose you would be applauding if Lucas's head were on a stick.' He said. Acheron became defensive and vague.

'I don't care for your accusations.'

'Well, I'll be damned.' spat Lorcan.

That night was a misery of sorts. Lucas had been reduced to a mere shadow of a vampire and had lost the respect he had so carefully earned. For a few, the mood was bittersweet. New parameters had been set. It was unspoken, but the message was clear. Acheron wanted Lucas demoted from the board and replaced by Marc. Loyalty meant little amongst the heads. Likewise, power, meant everything.

TWENTY-ONE

Marc pulled the door open with bloodshot eyes. He was hungry, and in need of a meal. He hadn't allowed a morsel of blood to touch his lips since yesterday evening and had ceased communication with most of the castle's residents all night. He had taken no notice of Runa, nor Achylls. They had knocked at least twice, pleading with him to drink. Marc was surprised to see Acheron at the door. 'What is it you want?' he asked.

'I want to show you something.' said Acheron.

Marc's temperament was wavering. Yesterday, despite his win, his tolerance had become low. All he thought about, was Estella. Anyway, tonight was a new day. He tightened his robe, then hesitantly followed Acheron as he led the way. The vampire's walked the castle in cold silence. Lined upon the walls, were centuries old portraits of vampire's past and present. Marc's keen eye spotted his own portrait. He looked prideful with his arms wrapped around Elena. The year was 1801, two years before he met the love of his life. That night, the mood at the castle was explosive and exciting. It was the annual ball. A night where vampires paraded their wealth and power. They feasted upon the finest humans they could find.

Young, fresh, and virginal, the adolescents were the best meal. Their blood was always sweeter. The men walked along the cobbled steps down to the Undercroft. It was the biggest of the two cellars, the other being at the opposite side of the castle. There were not many candles along the hard stone cellar walls, and for the most part, it was in stark darkness. On arrival, the rattling of heavy chains could be heard. Marc sensed the energy. This was a place of malevolent activity. A cellar used to store humans, caged like animals. That was before the treaty came into place. Nevertheless, Marc didn't expect to see what he saw next. There were five young woman, none older than eighteen. Chained by their necks, they had their hands tied behind their backs. Their hair fell over their faces, partially covering their eyes. Probably too frightened to scream, as not one of them made a peep.

'How long has this been going on for? How many years have you been taking us all for fools? feeding us that damned manufactured blood whilst you dine on virgins.'

'We haven't. These girls were brought to the castle a fortnight ago. Ever since Orpheus death, we decided things have to change. Its ok. The vampires at Killbraith know the position. They too are free to hunt. Just as nature intended. We do not know what we are up against and must get back to our real brute strength and agility. That synthetic blood, has certainly let us down.' Said Acheron.

'How can we be certain human blood will make a vast difference if we are up against the unknown. This thing could be highly skilled and have brute strength we can't even fathom.'

'Marc, I do wonder about you. We are vampires for goodness' sake. We shouldn't allow any other creature to rattle us. Seems we are all lacking in confidence. Stop being the pessimist and have a meal.'

Marc didn't take much persuading. Truth be told, he was ravenous. With his vampiric instinct's engaged, he could hardly resist the smell of fresh human blood. He fell to his knees then slowly crawled over to the chained girls. Despite his better judgement, his natural instinct to drain each of them dry, overpowered the voice in his head which told him not to. For several weeks, he had slaughtered unworthy humans. Mostly criminals, or those he deemed no credit to society. However, these girls were innocent. They didn't deserve to die such a barbarous death. Marc promised to make it quick and easy. She would feel no pain at all. One of the girls eyed him discreetly. Her dark long hair was straggly and unkempt, concealing most of her face. Unlike the others, Marc saw fire in her eyes. She wasn't afraid. Not of him, or any other vampire. She was a fighter. Marc admired her courage. He looked over at the second girl. Fair-haired and slim, she had a nervous energy. She kept her head lowered, refusing any eye contact at all. She was radiating in fear. Like a moth to a flame, her fear enticed Marc. He crept closer. She screamed at his presence. He rubbed his left hand along her slender innocent face. He took pity upon her. Poor young thing. Scared and pleading. Marc forcefully broke the chain around her neck. He held her close. Her fragile body flopped into his arms. She shook like a leaf as he smelt her hair. He closed his eyes preparing for the bite.

'I promise, you won't feel a thing,' Marc whispered in her ear.

Marc kissed her neck tenderly, then it was over quick and fast. He latched onto her neck, sinking his teeth within a carotid artery. Her screams echoed around the cold stone cellar. It was traumatic, even for him. But he was a vampire. Killing was a part of his genetic coding, and it felt good. Her blood was exquisite. He had a good drink. The others watched eager-eyed, fearful they were next. Marc handled the body with care. Meticulously and delicately, he laid the corpse upon the ground. She looked peaceful. Sprawled out in a bloodied white vest and dark denim, he could have given her the 'gift', but decided she would only become another distraction, obscuring his mind further from Estella. He stroked her hair, then ran his index finger along her plump pink lips. She wore a thin gold chain around her neck. It had a pendant attached to it, half of which appeared broken. Marc studied the picture. She was with an older woman, probably her mother. They looked happy. Marc felt a familiar stir of emotions rising in his stomach. He stood to his knees. Acheron, who had observed the entire thing, seemed pleased with himself.

'Give her a good burial. She deserves some respect.' Said Marc.

Acheron was stunned. Marc's empathy for the human made him uncomfortable. He thought of Marc as a pathetic fool, driven by his emotions. Of which should be devoid. Marc brushed past, then disappeared from the cellar.

'You sicken me. You, ungrateful inbred.' Acheron grew angry.

Marc disappeared before he could make a scene. Acheron studied the body on the floor. He clenched his fist, then roared with anger. His dark heart was like stone. Unsympathetic and black, he expected everyone else to follow lead from his examples. There was no room for kindness. He stomped his foot, then picked the body from off the floor. He carried it further along the darkness until out of sight. There was a pit in the ground. Mostly used to collect drainage water and other fluids for disposal. Acheron dropped the body in the deep hole. The stench of decomposed flesh wafted up from the pit. Acheron turned on his heels. With heavy stomps in buckled boots, he headed back upstairs.

TWENTY-TWO

I have loved, but the love I have for you, is incomparable to anything I have ever known. I've lived a hundred lifetimes, though, still as ignorant as the first. I still seek knowledge, and wisdom. Sometimes the burden of loving you is too much to bear. Dear Daughter, you were a miracle that wasn't supposed to happen. And yet, you are the best thing that has ever happened. If I shall have the misfortune of never seeing you again, please take comfort in the knowledge that, I would have killed an entire army for you.

The last 24 hours were a blur. Estella couldn't be sure how she ended up back at Stefan's, but somehow, she had. A young werewolf named Jasper found his way in. Just like Stefan. He too was kind and accommodating. He said he had been sneaking around for cans of meat when he came across Estella's near lifeless body with a badly scribbled note in hand. Apparently, she had passed out. Jasper ran her a bath, then fed her cans of meat until she felt better. Jasper was 21, not much older than she had been before she left home. Stefan's decomposed body was a horror. The shock must have been too much for her to handle. However, Jasper knew Stefan rather well. He was a regular customer for several years and thought of Stefan as a big brother. With Jasper's help, they took charge of Stefan's corpse, burying him five miles at the local cemetery. After some probing, Estella broke down. She owned up to Stefan's death. She also spoke of her daughter. Regardless of her shortcomings, Jasper seemed kind and non-judgemental. Like Stefan, Jasper was unafraid of the daemon. In fact, he wanted to help.

'Why are you so nice to me? I don't deserve it.' Estella was suspicious, thinking it too good to be true.

'You were nearly set upon by a group of werewolves. My cousins. I talked a good talk, so they left you alone,' he said.

'What have I done to deserve your remorse?'

'Nothing. There is something about you. I really don't know. Mostly, I go with my gut.' He replied with a shrug.

'That is very kind of you. How can I ever repay you?'

'No need for monetary payments. I need you to help me kill someone.' He said.

Estella's eyes widened at the revelation. Of course, there had to be something in it for him. How could she be so naïve. She clammed up, becoming more serious.

'Please do not look so shocked. My uncle deserves everything coming to him. He is killing innocent humans, youngsters mostly. Every day, I plead with him to eat canned meat instead. He says I'm an idiot. I cannot possibly be a real wolf. Yesterday he killed a local girl named, Kaitlyn. I actually loved her. Can you imagine it. A werewolf and a human. It was like chalk and cheese, but it felt right. Truth be known, I am absolutely distraught. I hate what I am, and what I am capable of,' he said.

Estella sat up right. Suddenly, she took notice. Jasper's story wasn't too dissimilar to herself. They had both fallen for the wrong species, and thus, paid a detrimental price. She smiled at Jasper softly. He was crying, cross legged, with tears streaming the sides of his face. Estella gave him a light hug.

'It's ok, I can help. I was in love with a daemon, now I am one.'

Jasper looked stunned. 'What do you mean?' he asked.

'I was a vampire once. For many years, actually. But I was a frivolous fool. Who would have known the handsome stranger I fell for was actually a Daemon. He told me he was a Werewolf. We had a short dalliance, and I, fell pregnant. And then, it happened. I began to change. It was so subtle at first. I hardly noticed it, assumed I was going mad. But then, my infliction couldn't be hidden. It became evident that something was desperately wrong with me, so I left my home. I left my husband. I concealed my pregnancy for a long time. Unfortunately, I was followed by one of the vampires who taught me the truth of what I had become. My pregnancy was a literal miracle. Now here I am. Counting down the days. I know they'll find me sooner, or later.'

Jasper was stunned. Intrigue was written all over his face. How was it possible. 'So, where is your baby?' he asked.

'I left her behind. She's with an old daemon. Someplace called Creaker.'

'You left your baby? That child is going to become the leader of the entire underworld. You must get her.' He demanded.

Estella eyed him, curious by his insistence. 'What does it matter? She can look after her, better than I ever will. Plus, she is safe. I have no permanent abode.'

'We can stay here together. I will help.' Said Jasper.

Estella's expression became cold. 'I am not getting that baby. She is better off without me.'

'Ok, whatever you want.' Said Jasper.

Suddenly, a stampede came charging through the shop. The shatter of glass was piercing. Voices could be heard. Jasper looked worried. Estella tensed up.

'Jasper are you here?' asked one.

Jasper remained schtum. It was his aunt, Jane. His uncle's wife. She must have been with at least three other werewolves.

'I am sure the little shit is in here. How dare he protect a creature like that,' she said.

'He said he would take care of it. I can't help but think that he lied to us all. He wants to protect her.' Said another voice.

Estella and Jasper exchanged weary glances. The werewolves were headed downstairs. With the staircase collapsed, an open space sat in its place, easy to jump from the shop floor to the flat. Suddenly, three werewolves leaped down. All three in human form, though one had begun to shapeshift.

'Surprise, surprise. Here's the prissy little shit, couped up with some vampire.' said one.

Estella was offended. At the very least, get it right. Clearly, they had no idea what she was. A vampire being the likeliest option.

'What are you doing here? I don't answer to any of you.' said Jasper.

Estella looked on at the herd. They were going to attack, and she, had to defend. Jasper wouldn't stand a chance against three of them. She was his only defence. A young man piped up. 'Can't you talk? Wolf got your tongue?' he mocked.

'Actually, I am trying to decipher who to kill first.' Estella's tone was calm and collected, despite the pending threat. The werewolves roared with laughter. Just then, all three of them begun to shapeshift. As growls commenced, their sheer weight made dents in the cast iron floor. Estella turned to Jasper. He was visibly upset; his hands shook with anger. 'You best run out of the back window in the bathroom. Its small about enough for a human to wriggle out from. As long as you don't turn!'

'I can't leave you. They will likely tear you to shreds.' He quipped.

'Let me, worry about that. Now run.' She demanded.

Jasper quickly scurried behind her. The wolves were almost in full werewolf mode. They growled angrily, determined to rip her apart. Estella braced herself. She didn't actually know If there would be a repeat of what happened back here all those weeks ago with Stefan, but thus far, she was still in human form, stood there with her sweater sleeves rolled up to her elbows. Willing her daemon to come out, Estella begun to back away. The werewolves stomped towards her, baring equal sets of menacing teeth. Fearing she may never morph, Estella backed away towards the bathroom, then made a quick run for the window. The beasts lunged after her. They were too large to enter the door, so crashed into the entire frame. Thankfully, this slowed them down. Estella managed to wriggle her way out of the window before the stampede came charging through the wood and plaster. Unfortunately, Estella landed in the arms of a mighty werewolf who had been waiting there all along. He grabbed hold off her, then proceeded to run off. Estella screamed and shouted, willing the daemon to make an appearance. Unfortunately for her that day, the daemon never did show up. The werewolf ran about three miles, leaping in huge strides. Suddenly, Estella realised what was going on. The werewolf was trying to protect her. The creature bounded into the nearby graveyard, before slumping on the sides. Estella was dropped to the ground. She rolled along several tombstones which had broken her fall. She grimaced at the knock to her head as she collided with a huge tomb. In a flustered state, Estella got up and tried to put herself together. Then she noticed the werewolf sat several feet away. It was on bended knees and appeared to be morphing back to human form. Indeed, it was Jasper. Dishevelled and worse for wear, he was in a dire state. As was she. Though she was grateful, Estella grew angry.

'I told you to run. What were you playing at?' she asked, while taking bits of rubble from her hair.

Jasper dragged himself from off the floor, attempting to conceal his modesty with his hands aptly placed over his crotch. He seemed frazzled. 'I…I couldn't leave you there. They would have killed you.' he stammered.

'I said I would be fine. I can handle myself.' Estella was frustrated. More so because she was still trying to figure out why she hadn't changed. She screwed her face, biting down on her bottom lip. 'I am sorry. Of course, I appreciate what you've done. But I can take care of myself.'

'You look angry.' Jasper's words were cautious. He sensed Estella was upset.

'I didn't change. And I don't know why.' She admitted.

'Maybe you're stressed. Does it happen on que?' he asked.

'Well, it did. The blasted beast reared its ugly head all those weeks ago, resulting in Stefan's death. But now, it acts coy when a group of bloody vigilantes tries to murder me. Argh!!' Estella's frustrated scream could be heard a mile off. Jasper reminded her they were not in the clear. Those werewolves were still out there.

'You know, being a supernatural being, we do not often have control over these things. Yes, I know. Werewolves can turn on que, not only on a full moon. However, I have been known to 'turn', many times when I really didn't want to. Like the time I turned at my grandmother's burial in front of the entire grieving family. My embarrassment was evidently through the roof! Sometimes it takes a while to harness the monster,' he said. 'I really wouldn't worry about it.' But Estella was very worried about it. Had she lost her powers? Was she reverting to human? Why had it happened when she didn't want it to? Her questions danced about in her head. As she made her way back over to Jasper, cold tears fell against her cheeks. Stefan's death had hit hard. The reality of it came flooding back when she eyed the spot they had dug days earlier. Without a proper headstone, he was a nobody. Stefan deserved a little more respect.

'Perhaps I ought to seek out a headstone. So, people know he actually exits.' She whispered.

Jasper looked over the hole in the ground. She had a point. 'Ok, my cousin sells them. I can get it sorted.' He promised.

'You might want to walk behind to spare yourself the embarrassment' she smiled.

'Agreed.' Said Jasper.

The pair walked towards the entrance. Jasper called her back. 'We cannot return to the shop. We must seek out an alternative,' he said. Estella spun on her heels. A frown emerged. Weary, she sunk to the ground.

'I have absolutely nowhere else to go' she said.

'I know a place. There is an old, abandoned church in the human town. It has been locked up for years. We could at least spend a few days there. Just long enough to find somewhere else a little more… safe.' Said Jasper. With few options, Estella reluctantly agreed. First, they would have to lay low at the cemetery until night fall. Estella thought that was a bad idea. They were more likely to be seen at night. Jasper thought otherwise. Apparently, his family were a bunch of cowards. They preferred to kill during the day, to lessen the competition at night. 'They stay in most evenings. My cousin is in dispute with a neighbouring wolf family. The Johnsons. A ferocious family, they take demand respect from the rest of us. My cousin Benjamin stole from them. They own the streets at night and promised to shred my family to bits if seen again. Now, seldom do they venture out during peak werewolf hours.'

'But will they not attack us?' asked Estella, eyes glaring.

'No. I am pretty friendly with them. Another reason my family hate my guts. Trouble them, and they come for you. Otherwise, they are pretty easy going. Just don't steal!' he laughed.

'Fair enough. Gosh, this will be a long day. And I wish you would put some clothes on.'

The pair laughed. They found a corner to the back of the cemetery where they sat for hours, talking, telling jokes, together they shared each other's highs and lows. For a long time, Estella felt she could truly relax. The last time she felt this way, had been at Stefan's several all those weeks ago. Jasper's hazel eyes twinkled as she spoke. Still recovering from the death of his girlfriend, they were bonded by grief. As evening fell, the night air was brisk.

'I still can't believe that baby is the next leader. A literal God. That is…amazing.' He said.

'It is…frightening. I ask myself all the time. Why me? what did I do so great, or so wrong, that I was given such a responsibility.'

Estella and Jasper looked at each other. He seemed somewhat fearful. She became cautious. Had she said too much? Would he want to hurt the baby? Fears brewed to the surface. Jasper squeezed her hand reassuringly. 'It's ok, Estella. I am here for you. I've not met anyone quite like you. And please do not think for one minute that I could hurt that child. I don't expect you to trust me, but you can. As if I care being governed by a woman.' He smiled.

Estella studied his face for any indications of false truths. Somehow, he seemed genuine. Estella. Anyway, if he betrayed her, she would have to kill him. Feeling rather fragile, Estella changed the topic of conversation.

'You may as well wear my top. Wrap it around yourself. At least I have on denim.' Said Estella.

'No way. It is far too cold, and I don't wish to deprive you. I can manage for a few more hours.' Said Jasper calmly, clearing shivering.

'I am not taking no for an answer.' Estella pulled her top over her head, exposing her white underwear. She plonked it on Jasper's lap. His eyes were peeled. Estella became coy. There she was. Bra exposed. Jasper couldn't take his eyes of her. It happened so fast. Before she knew it, he had taken her head into his hands and now kissed her tenderly on the lips. Jasper ran his hands over her breasts, but Estella didn't stop him. With his sandy brown hair and perfect white teeth, he was boyishly good looking. Soon enough, the pair were making out beneath a large tree among old tombs. Jasper's excitement was evident. Estella hadn't failed to notice how well equipped he was. He removed her bra and suckled like a hungry baby. Estella's arousal was intense. She ran her hand through his hair, demanding that he suck harder.

'Your beauty is astounding.' He exclaimed.

Minutes later, the pair sat contentedly nestling into each other's arms. Their naked bodies intertwined. Jasper had his strong arms wrapped around her torso. His body smelt of jasmine. For a moment, Estella got carried away with flights of fantasy. She could dream of being human again. Having a life less complicated than the one she currently had. Jasper was attentive and caring, he would make a great partner. Plus, sex with him was amazing. They kissed again. This time, sticking tongues down each other's throats. The night dew bounced along her shoulders.

'I think we best head off to that church.' Said Estella.

Jasper seemed far too comfortable despite the bitter cold. He shrugged his shoulders, eyes smiling. 'Maybe we can rest here for the night.' He said, stroking her back with his fingers.

'I am not sleeping in here! No way. We must leave.' Estella demanded. 'Have you no way of getting any clothes?' she asked.

'If I go home, but we both know that is not an option. Do you not like my naked backside? What about my incredible bare chest?' he teased.

'I guess, tomorrow we can take care of that. By the way, I love your naked backside.' She smiled. Together the pair made the way out of the cemetery. The journey to the church was rather uneventful. Due to the recent killings, the humans were on curfew. Eager werewolves were all over the place, some searching for their next meal. Estella's true being was recognised by some though many thoughts of her as a nothing more than a vampire. Whatever the case, with Jasper by her side, they left her well alone. Until one particular werewolf barged past, deliberately shoving her out of the way.

'Oh, sorry. I didn't see you there.' He smirked. 'What's your kind doing here anyway?'

'My kind? What about your kind? Only humans are supposed to inhabit a town like this.' Yelled Estella.

'Yes, humans. So, unless you are here to eat, I guess you fuck off back to vampire land, or Killbraith, whatever you call it.' Snarled the man.

'I am a daemon. And no, I won't be fucking off anywhere.' Estella's eyes begun to flicker. Before she knew it, she grew three times her size whilst her clothing ripped at the seams. The werewolf made headway as Estella's change took hold. Jasper watched in awe as the daemon reared its head. In less than a minute, Estella was nowhere to be seen. In her place, was a beast so ferocious, it made the werewolves look like kittens. At nearly seven-foot tall, the hairy monster-type creature peeped out beneath hooded eyes. She leaped after the werewolf. The ground shook like an earthquake with every step she took. Speed was the daemon's strength. It wasn't long before she caught up with the werewolf. He had already shapeshifted, nevertheless, he was no match for Estella's monster. Estella grabbed the werewolf by the throat, tightening her grip on its neck. As the wolf growled in agony to be released, the daemon shoved its hand through the chest, pulling out its guts. As intestines and gore fell to the ground, other werewolves were hollering for one of their own. But it didn't end there. Riled by the eager-eyed werewolves that had now gathered, Estella roared her displeasure. She was set upon by two wolves, who swiftly came to regret their decision. Estella pounced on them both. Showcasing her superb strength, she lifted the werewolves off the ground, one held in each hand. As they thrashed around, attempting to wriggle themselves free, another pounced, knocking her to the ground. Very soon, quite a few angry wolves took keen bites from the daemon's hairy exterior. As black blood oozed to the ground, the daemon stood to its feet. She managed to fling the werewolf off her back, of whom bit her severely on the neck. Though Estella had strangled two, one had survived. And then, she disappeared. The surprised pack were left looking at each other, wondering how their victim had escaped. Jasper, who hadn't left his spot several yards away, looked distraught fearing the worst. Jasper eyed the narrow street. The wolves had dispersed their separate ways, leaving several bodies spewed across the ground. With Estella's top wrapped around his lower half, Jasper's naked torso shivered as the rain began. With no humans around to feast upon, the streets were soon empty.

'Estella?' he called.

Jasper decided to search the graveyard. Perhaps she had returned to escape the mob. As his feet shuffled on the grainy ground, bits of pebbled gravel gathered between his toes. The rain fell harder. Once he arrived at the cemetery, it was obvious that Estella wasn't around. The spot where they had been seated, now lay empty.

TWENTY-THREE

The bolt around the church doors were stiffened and tough. It took brute strength even for a werewolf to open it. As the door slowly creaked open, a huge bolder fell to the floor with a thud. Fearing he would be found, Jasper made every effort to close the door, which proved equally as difficult as it were to open. As he cautiously stepped inside, his black footprints tried to avoid the shattered stain glass remnants which was dispersed around the entrance door. Pleased to be out of the rain, Jasper tugged at the soaking wet cloth as he tore it from his body. The darkness was still. Cobwebs hung low and high as he pushed his way through the arched doors. With a thud, it fell to the floor. A splinter caught his hand. The rotting wood was merely stronger than plyboard. With sharp eyes in the dark, Jasper caught sight of a pew. In fact, there were several. He plonked himself down, wondering how old this church was. As far as he knew, it had been locked up for nearly a five hundred years. A yet, its foundations remained strong. The old pillars, despite some surface cracks, still stood just as strong. And then he heard it. Someone was calling him. The voice was familiar. He turned around expecting to see Estella, but this voice was different. Thinking he were going mad, Jasper shrugged it off as tiredness. However, the voices didn't stop.

'Jasper, it is me.' said the voice.

'Who are you? I see no one.' He replied, brow raised with intrigue.

Suddenly, a hazy apparition took hold before him. It was Bea. His human girlfriend, who had been brutally killed by his uncle. She was smiling, seemingly happy to see him. Not one to believe in ghosts, Jasper was stunned.

'It's ok, you will be alright. The daemon will return.' She said.

'You're not real. You died. You cannot be real.' He said, wiping his eyes.

The apparition disappeared as quick as it came. Convinced he was sleep deprived and hallucinating, Jasper forced his eyes shut. The next time he opened his eyes, morning had already set in. Sunspots were already beaming through the dusty church windows. Jasper gasped in shock. Right there on the floor, feet away from the pew, was Estella. Blackened and blue, she was sprawled out like a rag doll, head down and snoring. Jasper stood in shock. He turned to the door. She had managed to let herself in. Unfortunately, she also left it pretty much wide open. Jasper hurriedly sprinted over to the door, pushing it shut tight. As he approached Estella, she stirred.

'Thank goodness, you are alive. How did you find the church?' he peered down with a smile on his face. She was as naked as he. Her bruises began to fade before his eyes. Estella slowly opened her eyes as she sun beamed across her face. She carefully lifted her head.

'Hi. I don't know how I got here. I must have blacked out.' She said softly.

'You are a fighter. I'll give you that. I'm just pleased you are alive. I feared you were dead.' He said.

'I'll be damned if I allow them the pleasure. I have my baby to tend to,' she said.

Jasper smiled as he helped her to her feet. The pair embraced, then sat along the nearest pew. 'So, aren't you going to tell me your trick?' he asked.

'What trick?' she quipped.

'How did you disappear like that. I wish werewolves had that ability.'

'I don't know. I literally lose all control as the daemon takes over. I guess, it must be some protection thing. You were right, it seems to have a mind of its own. I didn't plan on turning for just one silly werewolf. Clearly, there are two of us in this body' she chirped with laughter. 'As for that disappearing stint, I guess it is as random as the sky is blue. Estella studied her arms. Despite being bitten, she had already heeled.

'Well, whatever the case maybe, it is a pretty impressive skill.' Said Jasper. 'Anyway, we ought to get some clothes on before we get done with breach of decency by the werewolf brigade. And then, let's go and find that baby of yours.'

Estella smiled at him. Though she hadn't known him more than a few days, already he proved to be a valuable friend. He grabbed her face, she grabbed his, too. Estella straddled him as they rode the waves of passion. As ripples of ecstasy ran through her body, she was taken back to her sordid affair with Xavier. Jasper pulled her in closer. The pew fell to the ground, colliding with others behind. However, nothing could stop the rambunctious pair. Jasper let out a mighty groan. Estella moaned as she too came to climax. His eyes studied hers with intent.

'You mean a lot to me.' he said. 'I realise we've just met. But already, I like you far more than I should.'

This revelation shocked Estella more than she expected it would. She became withdrawn and coy, nor did she acknowledge Jasper's statement. The last time a man fell for her, her world fell upside down. She was a cheat and couldn't be trusted. The last thing she wanted, was another man declaring his unrequited love. It wasn't that she couldn't love. But love, if used wrongly, proved to be a dangerous tool. Marc, despite her infidelity, had been her first true love. And to some extent, he still was. Jasper was warm, lovely, and enticing, but she could never love another quite how she loved Marc. Estella wasn't even convinced she was deserving of love. She would only ruin it, and he would end up hating her guts. Estella became tensed as she got up from his lap. Her face remained dead-pan. 'We best find some clothes.' She replied. She could tell by the look on Jasper's face he was disappointed at her response, however, getting her daughter back was the only worry on Estella's mind right now. Estella felt she made a grave mistake by giving her to the old daemon, and now, desperately wanted her back. At any costs. Feeling an awkwardness arrive between the pair, Estella tried to soften the blow.

'Jasper, you're such a joy. But come on, we barely know each other!' she smiled stiffly. Without words, the twosome left the old church. Jasper remained schtum on the subject. But, whenever Estella attempted eye contact, his eyes would shift to the floor. Grabbing him by the arm, Estella looked him dead in the eye. 'No need to feel awkward. We are friends, right?'

Jasper nodded awkwardly 'You are totally right. I feel a fool. We have known each other for a total of 48 hours!' he exclaimed. Just then a man strolled by. A human dressed in denim and a blue shirt. The two glanced at each other. That was their master plan. Jasper lunged at the unsuspecting human, dragging him back by the arm. 'Do not scream, or I will kill you.' he said. 'Now, take your clothes off.' He demanded. The human made protests but soon complied when he met with a display of Jasper's razor-sharp teeth.

'P…Please don't kill me.' he stuttered. 'I'll undress.'

Within minutes the human was sent on his way, as naked as the day he was born. Jasper, stood admiring his new garments, noticed the denim swung far too high up on his ankles. A disadvantage of being quite a bit taller.

'It definitely looked better on him' jeered Estella. Jasper shrugged. It certainly beat walking around with is pale backside on show. 'Is someone else ever going to stroll by? I don't imagine many come round here often. I mean, look at it. An abandoned old church, and little else.' Moaned Estella.

'Be patient! Someone will come along.' Jasper reassured, placing an arm around Estella's bare shoulder.

'I mean, we could always venture back to Stefan's. My own clothing would obviously be preferable.'

Jasper eyed her as though she were mad. 'We are not going back there. They will likely be expecting you to return, and will no doubt be waiting for it. Just be patient.' He kissed her on the cheek, rubbing her back. And then out of nowhere, two teenaged boys strolled by. With hands in pockets, they spoke to each other at the tops of their voices. Dressed warmly in sweaters, denim, jackets and trainers, it wasn't the most glamourous get up Estella had imagined but was certainly better than nothing.

'Hey boys.' She called. The pair turned to her. Their eyes popped out of their heads at the sight of Estella's bare breasts on display. They turned to each other laughing. It didn't take long for one of the boys to step forward, though his friend seemed more hesitant. 'I want to show you something.' She continued. Jasper couldn't hide his embarrassment. He had turned his head, refusing to be any part of it. Estella twirled to showcase her figure, twirling her hair with her right index finger. Showing a pearly set of teeth, slowly, the eager teenager walked towards her. His eyes transfixed; he couldn't hide his apparent excitement. Estella grabbed him by the collar; she lunged her mouth against his. His friend looked on in bewilderment. 'Now, take your clothes off.' She ordered. The teenager became coy. His stance stiffened at her request. 'Go on, do it. You wouldn't want to upset my friend here, would you? We all know how dangerous those werewolves can be.' She threatened. The boy begun to shiver. Fear radiated in his eyes. With nervous shaky hands, the teenager slowly pulled off his clothing, much to the horror of his friend. 'I won't be needing your jacket. The sweater and denim will do.'

It had taken a hell of a while to find the house. Estella had lost her bearings, and most of the journey, had been trial and error. In order to avoid Jasper's crazy family, they had spent most of the day in the old cemetery, exactly as they had done the day before. Sex was no longer on the cards in fear of Jasper becoming too attached, so most of the time was spent talking, and sleeping. Also, keeping an eye out for other supernatural's. Now, evening had set in. Here they were like thieves in the night, crawling on bended knee as they headed down the familiar drive. Perhaps it would all end in disaster, but Estella wasn't prepared not to try. Yes, she was taking her baby back. Unfortunately, a full moon was out. Jasper tried his hardest to control the beast but finally caved in just before they arrived at the house. Probably it was for the best. She would have to go in alone. As Jasper begun to growl, it wasn't long before his shapeshifting was complete. So, there he was. Looking out through peeping yellow eyes, concealed within dark brown fur. Estella feared he would wake up the old daemon with all that moaning and growling. Jasper, not being able to fully control his own urges under the moon light, escaped to the nearby woods, leaving Estella solo. If she had a beating heart, it would have been pounding. The back windows plastered in aluminium, was a sort of silver lining. The old daemon done a bad job at the dining room window, in which it hadn't been properly sealed. A small bit of aluminium stuck out an inch long, just long enough for Estella to manipulate it a little. With a bit of probing, the old draughty window rattled somewhat, then finally it caved in. Slowly, a little at a time, Estella prised it open. The constant creaking was startling as she squeezed her way through. As she viciously tore through the silver sheets, Estella was convinced the daemon heard every sound of it. She landed headfirst on the dining floor. The familiar garlic stink, more pungent than before, made its way back up her nose. Estella crept on all fours, bypassing the hideous floral carpets and colourful cushioned-back chairs. As she took to the stairs, visions of the old daemon stood at the top waiting for her arrival, sent a ripple of fear down her spine. The last thing she wanted, was a showdown with a woman three times her age. And possibly, three times as strong? The wind could be heard bellowing from outside. The trees rustled, swaying back and forth. An old clock ticked loudly on the wall at the top of the landing, which made Estella squirm. Her knees ached as she reached the top. Estella was dumbfounded, eyeing six identical doors laid out either side of the narrow landing. Further along, she spotted the two doors at the very end-one of which had been her room. This could take a while. Jasper would likely be well on his by the time she ventured back out. The landing was pitch black, the old-fashioned lampshade swayed from the ceiling as though it knew she was there. Estella was hesitant to push the first door. For a while she sat there, looking up at it, feeling like a naughty child about to get scowled. Willing herself to grow a pair and stop being a sissy, Estella finally gave the handle a little push. The lock was noisy as the door clicked open. Like a rabbit in headlights, Estella froze on the spot. She pushed the door just wide enough to see inside. There was nothing but a neatly made bed and an old bedside table sat alongside it. Feeling somewhat relieved, Estella crept back out. She had to start the process all over again, feeling even more tensed as she entered the second room. Estella knew the old daemon wouldn't hand over her child without a fight. In fact, she had firmly set her claws on the child the minute they arrived. Just like the first, the second room was empty. Another neatly made bed with a single drawer placed to the left. The wall had a massive portrait, however. A man with intense eyes and a white collar, glared at her from its depths. Feeling very creeped out, Estella quickly backed out the room, taking care to close the door firmly behind. Unfortunately, that's the last she remembered. Estella was wacked around the head with an iron bar, then dragged to one of the bedrooms. When she came to, daylight beamed through the window. Gagged and bound, she was sat on the bed freaking out. The old daemon entered the room with her daughter in hand. As though Estella didn't exist, there she was gloating, laughing while cuddling the child. The baby caught sight of her mother on the bed. Suddenly, her eyes were wild. The baby begun to wriggle her way free from the old woman, who then tightened her grip even more. Estella knew her daughter well enough by now. Recalling events back at the werewolf diner, Estella felt a tinge of relief that something would be done. Of course, she could break out the daemon to release herself from the shackles which had been placed upon her, but that had to be the last choice. Fearing the daemon may lose control and harm the child, Estella didn't want to turn unless absolutely necessary.

'Stop looking at her. I, am your mother now, and I, am all you will ever need.' Said the old woman to the child, who was desperately trying to get another glimpse of her mother.

Estella moaned through gagged mouth. She tried to wriggle free but was tied with barbed wire which cut against her wrists. Just then, the baby babbled. Suddenly, she bit the old daemon on the arm, somehow hard enough to cause a bleed. The old woman shrieked. Estella looked on, as things looked up. 'You are a naughty little blighter. How dare you bite me? I should wring your little neck.' She yelled. The baby begun to moan. She babbled something else, then bit the old daemon again. Suddenly, the baby managed to fly out of her arms. Unfortunately, the old daemon grabbed hold off her, scowling as she grabbed her by the arm. Estella's eyes widened in shock. Annoyed and feeling disrespected, the old woman squeezed the baby by the arm causing her to let out an almighty wail. Estella's anger grew at the sight of her crying child. A red-hot rage erupted. The old daemon shot Estella a look of death. 'Don't you dare move, or I will kill this child.' She yelled. Just then, the baby clawed the old woman across the face. She lunged at her, taking a small chunk out of her right cheek. The old woman hollered. Then it happened. The child went wild. Just as she had done back at the diner, the baby lunged herself back towards the old woman's face, latching onto her left cheek for dear life. As though she were a leech, the child became transfixed. Estella's anger turned to joy as the old woman begun to scream, making ill attempts to remove the child from her face. So around, and around they went. The baby was glued to her face. She spun in circles trying to remove her. It would have been comical if the situation hadn't been serious. With her pride down the window, the old woman begun to shapeshift. This was what Estella feared. She had to do the same, otherwise, neither her nor the child would stand a chance. The old woman jerked rapidly as the daemon took hold off her body. Thick black hairs could be seen on her arms as her clothing fell to the floor. Estella froze in fear. The baby was still glued to her face. In sheer panic, Estella willed her own daemon to make an appearance. With legs bound, she was unable to get off the bed in any ordinary fashion. The thought of her child being brutally killed by another daemon, was enough to start her change. Suddenly, Estella's body jerked uncontrollably as the daemon reared its head. The appearance of dense black hair was another sign the monster was on its way out. However, the old daemon was out of its box faster than she.

At well over seven foot, the old daemon's head crashed through the top of the ceiling as the rubble collapsed to the floor. Dust and plaster wood scattered everywhere. The daemon's roar was insidious. With added strength, she was able to pluck the baby from her cheek, throwing the child to the floor. Horrified, Estella's face was pallor as she watched her child land on the floor with a thud. Thankfully, the baby landed on her back. Luckily, nor was she human so was tougher than most. Despite this, the baby let out a frightful shriek. To her mother's surprise, she then managed to sit herself up, then turned to her mother with big brown eyes. After some gurling and tries at conversation with her mother, the baby crawled towards the bed, then buried underneath the six-inch gap. Proving to be buckets more advanced for her age, the baby's comprehension of danger was spot on. She hid safely away until her mother dealt with the obvious threat, and only then, would she venture back out. The old daemon stomped towards Estella, grabbing her by the throat. The wire's edge ripped through her wrists. Estella roared in agony, as did the daemon. Within minutes, the pair were equally as large, and equally as fearless. It was a clash of monsters. The beasts squared up. They crashed through the bedroom wall, landing outside at the other end of the garden. As the house collapsed around the warring beasts, their rage for each other intensified. The old daemon grabbed Estella by the neck. She managed to place her in some kind of choke hold. Estella clawed at the daemon's back in a desperate bid to loosen her grip. The old daemon; highly skilled and more experienced, was able to restrict Estella's airway, rendering her to a near comatose state. She flung Estella to the ground in rage. As Estella gasped for breath, the old daemon stomped angrily towards her. Deciding it was better to play dead, Estella remained still. Unfortunately, the old daemon was not finished with her just yet. Estella was suddenly dragged to her feet, then punched to the face. Estella fell face down in fertilizer and weeds. Estella had two choices, continue this brawl, and possibly be killed. Or think about the safety of her child and accept defeat. Suddenly, it felt like a three-ton truck weight had been dropped to her back. Estella heaved at the force. She was being kicked like a piece of rubbish on a shoe. With her life in the balance, something snapped. Perhaps it was adrenaline. Or perhaps it was being so close to death that caused the surge in determination to survive, but whatever it was, a raging hot flame brewed within. Estella regained her strength. Somehow, she managed to roll off her back, then grabbed the old daemon by the ankles. Red eyes glaring with an intent to kill, Estella yanked the daemon off her feet. She tripped as she landed to the floor, breaking an ankle in the process. Now with the upper hand, Estella jumped on top of the daemon, delivering sets of furious blows to her face. Estella saw red. As the daemon tried to tussle arms flailing, Estella grabbed her by the throat. She roared loudly as her grip tightened. Much to Estella's surprise, the daemon suddenly displayed open psalms. A sign of surrender. For a moment, Estella carried on choking the daemon to death, ignoring her plea for mercy. And then, as though a switch had been turned off, the passion to kill the beast beneath her became less intense. All Estella really wanted, was her baby. As the daemon bowed in submission, Estella stood to her feet. Exhausted and weary, Estella watched as the daemon returned to human form. Defeated, the old woman lay motionless on the ground. Without a word, Estella ran back into the demolished house. The bed had overturned, but the baby remained intact. She had wisely curled up in a ball, shielded by the corner of the bed. It was a moment of triumph as Estella left Creaker with her baby in hand. She never looked back

TWENTY-FOUR

This was the fifth night since Marc had killed that innocent girl in the cellar. His conscience wrestled with it often. He hadn't been back down since, despite prompting from Acheron, who now eyed him with contempt. Marc had taken to sparring with himself, an hour after everyone else had left the armoury. Nor was he talking as much, becoming very antisocial and rather elusive. The only other vampire more elusive than Marc, was Apollyon. Like a thief in the night, he had his own routines, not adhering to structures set within the castle.

'Oh my god. It's a vampire!' The woman's shrieks could be heard a mile away. She had managed to drop her leather bag and was unable to keep up with the others. She had tripped over herself, fallen head-first upon the concrete. Her friends scattered. Two ran off towards the traffic lights, and another in the other direction. It was her thirtieth birthday celebration. She wore a brightly coloured sash draped over her right shoulder, parading her big day for all to see. Her neatly coiled hair had turned to a puffy humid frizz but still had a couple of stray ringlets neatly positioned to the sides of her head. As one would expect, she had had a few drinks but was far from drunk. 'Please, don't leave me.' Desperately fearing for their own lives, she watched as her friends disappeared out of sight. The streets were lonely, except a little blue car that drove speedily past. The driver appeared to slow down but suddenly picked up speed and was off like a rocket, leaving a trail of dusty fumes behind. The vampire's eyes were gleeful. Radiating off her fear, he's eyes flickered from green to red, then he gazed at her with piercing intensity. The hapless woman froze with fear. Twice she tried to get up, but her feet buckled with each attempt. The vampire, dressed all in black, stomped towards her with heavy black boots adorned with silver buckles and thick black laces. Apollyon stared at the woman on the floor. He knelt beside her whilst baring his teeth. His hands muffled her screams. He held her neck in prime position. He bit down hard and fast, then sucked until her body became limp. He drank his stomach full, then picked up the body. He slung it over his left shoulder, then disappeared as fast as he came. Unusually, Apollyon hadn't drained her dry. The taste of his victim was so sweet to his lips, he wanted the others to try it.

Back at Castle Dravenherd, Marc was deep in thought examining the blood-stained letter he had written minutes earlier. He had re-written it several times in hopes of giving it to Estella, if ever they met again. '*What is a man. Troubled, pain riddled with covetous longing for someone who cares little about anything but themselves. For I, am nothing but dust. My soulless existence has been indescribable since you left. Your perfect face, the tone of your voice still echoes strongly in my mind, no matter how hard I try to forget you. Destruction has set in. My darkest days are my deepest fears. Like a shadow of my former self, I am a changed man. Broken, anguished and hopeless. I would surrender myself to the darkness, to see your face again, just one last time.*'

Marc was so engrossed he hadn't heard Runa enter the drawing room. He sipped on a large glass of blood, his feet propped up upon a grand footstool dressed in the finest gold and red velvet. Runa wore a long flattering navy gown. She appeared ready for the evening's escapades. 'You need to stop torturing yourself. She will return when she is ready. And even if she doesn't, there are many others just as worthy.' Marc remained quiet but took another sip of blood. He was staring intently at the portrait on the wall in front of hm. It was Acheron, taken at least a couple of centuries previous. As usual, he looked bold and fearless, though there was a certain discretion in his eyes. Many secrets were hidden in those eyes, some of which Marc knew to be true. Runa sat on one of the golden trimmed armchairs alongside her cousin. She was cross-legged, then pulled a knife out from her chest. It was about eight inches long but had been concealed within her bra. Like most of the weapons kept at the castle, the handle was delicately crafted from the finest wood. Runa beamed at it like a new toy at Christmas. Suddenly, Marc turned to his cousin.

'Tell me. Do you trust Acheron? I cannot quite put my finger on it, but there is something rather dubious about him. Perhaps I'm just an old cynic, but he is not fit to lead this board.'

Runa glared at Marc, confused by his statement. She screwed up her eyes. 'I trust no one. Not even my own cousin, whom I care for.'

Marc smiled. He seemed satisfied with such an answer. He then took another sip, before placing the glass to the polished wooden floor. 'I must ask you something. This may seem foolish, but I plague myself with the possibility of such a thing and need an answer. Is it even remotely possible for a vampire to somehow, change?' Marc's voice fell. He felt ridiculous. Runa frowned. She bit her lips, becoming animated. She held the knife rigid.

'Whatever do you mean? Change into *what* exactly?'

'Never mind. It is a silly question.'

Runa sensed his apprehension. She placed the knife on her lap, curious about his question. She knew her cousin well enough to know that he hadn't been the same ever since he stepped foot in the castle. 'Marc, I know something has been bothering you the minute I laid eye on you. Or are you going to continue treating me like a fool? Has something happened to Estella?'

'I am in the dark about her wellbeing and have not seen or heard from her since she left. I am just exploring all possibilities, that's all.' Marc almost confessed what Edgar had told him but had doubts upon the theory. Vampires didn't, nor could they change. Somehow, Runa's reaction eased his fears. Of course, it was a foolish theory. Marc felt Edgar was merely trying to stir up unnecessary trouble.

'Well, I will certainly give you a great big chest of gold if vampires suddenly start changing. You may as well ask if pigs' fly. Marc, you must curb that imagination of yours. The only thing Estella has changed, is her heart. Unfortunately for you, that is a greater change like no other, and I wish I could make the pain go away, dear cousin.' said Runa.

'I am a train wreck waiting to happen.' Marc smiled, but only one side of his lips curled up. Runa nodded at his statement. Just then, Stramus entered the drawing room. His black robe was lined with the deepest blue. Made from the finest silk, it was exquisite. There were remnants of blood stained along the corner of his lip, evidence he had just had a meal.

'You could cut the air with that fine knife of yours, Runa. This castle, is like trekking through Death Valley.'

'We cannot all be as jovial as you, sir.' Runa smiled through worried eyes.

'A pity. You've both missed out on a delicious meal.' Said Stramus as he pulled a bright white hankie from the inside pocket of his robe. Marc studied the elder like fine art. He looked on as he delicately wiped the corners of his mouth. He took extra care outlining the curve of his lips.

'Was that blood laced with gold? Or fine scotch, perhaps?'

Runa giggled at Marc's sarcasm. Stramus winked cheekily. It was certainly the best meal he had in a while and questioned whether

Marc's statement held any truth. He pulled out a chair two seats away from the others, then with arms outstretched on the upholstered rest. 'Perhaps not gold, nor alcohol, unfortunately. However, the girl is remarkably unfamiliar to anything I have tasted. And I've tasted an awful lot of humans in my time. The boy done good.' He quipped.

'Boy? And whom may that be?' Marc piped up with a raised brow.

'Apollyon.' said Stramus casually.

'Apollyon? How thoughtful,' said Runa.

'Thoughtful? This kind gesture is certainly odd.'

'Marc don't be so dubious. I think it is very kind of him to think of us. Especially at a time like this.' Runa sprung out of her seat. In the blink of an eye, she had vanished. Marc turned to the empty chair.

'Someone's hungry,' he said.

'Go and try it. She's delicious.' smiled Stramus.

Marc became serious. Apollyon had been out of character for some time, but Marc was too consumed with his own grief to scrutinise someone else's behaviour. 'What is he hiding? I cannot have a decent conversation with the man. Suddenly, he avoids me like the plague. And now, he brings back a body for all to share?'

Stramus eyed him. 'How peculiar. I am dumbfounded.'

'That, makes two of us.' said Marc

TWENTY-FIVE

The body emitted a stench that repugnantly filled the air. Runa, Acheron, Achylls and Elena, were tucking in as if they had never been fed. Runa knelt on bended knees. She held an arm with both hands, sucking from it forcefully. Blood dripped down the sides of her mouth. Runa was so entrenched with the meal that she took no notice of Marc when he entered the garden. Apollyon, already full and satisfied, watched his peers from afar. He stood with arms crossed behind his back but turned away when Marc arrived. This prompted Marc's curiosity. Despite his reluctance, Marc approached Apollyon. 'Is she a witch? What makes her blood so sweet? In all of my centuries in this retched existence, never have I seen such excitement.' Exclaimed Marc. Apollyon slowly turned to face him. His bright blonde hair glistened under the night sky. His red eyes flickered back to green.

'She's a rare one. I call it angel blood.' Apollyon's voice was sharp and abrupt.

'I see. Maybe I ought to join in.' said Marc, side eyeing the suspicious vampire.

'That is entirely up to you. But, if you don't mind, I am trying to gaze' replied Apollyon. It was clear Apollyon had no time for small talk. Certainly not with Marc. He seemed offended. For what, Marc didn't know. Apollyon's eyes were shifty when he spoke. He appeared to be looking everywhere, but at Marc.

'Pardon my inquisition, Apollyon. But what are you gazing at?' Marc was intrigued.

'Life. The vampires at Killbraith have caused quite a ruckus. With no treaty in place, they have literally gone mad. There won't be any humans left at this rate.'

'Unlikely. Human's breed like rabbits. Doubtful their existence is at any risk of extinction, any time soon.' Marc shot back.

Apollyon turned his back to Marc. This was a sign of disrespect, to which Marc didn't take kindly. 'Have I offended you?' Marc's voice rose in anger.

Acheron strolled over to calm the frostiness which was steadily brewing between the pair. 'Is there a problem here?' Acheron's voice cut the air. It was deep and authoritative. You definitely took notice when he spoke. The vampires turned to him.

'That is a good question. I am merely trying to have civil conversation with a fellow vampire.' Said Marc.

'And? What's the problem?' probed Acheron as though he were a school headmaster. Apollyon simply looked on with nothing much to say.

'Actually, your tone of voice is beginning to be a problem.' Spat Marc.

Marc didn't take kindly to being treated like a child. His serious eyes studied the pair of them. Feeling frustrated, Marc vanished from the garden. He felt he may combust in rage; he couldn't stand the pretence any longer. Like a dirty secret, he felt everyone was in on it, except for him. Either that, or he was going completely insane. One, or the other. Apollyon was hiding something. Judging by his behaviour, Marc was certain it had everything to do with him and was determined to find out. Back outside in the garden, the two vampires conversed in private conversation between themselves. They spoke in a whisper, making sure not to be heard from the others.

'He is becoming a problem.' whispered Acheron.

'Intolerable. He has taken to spying on me every night. He knows something.' said Apollyon.

'Poor man. It cannot be easy on him. Imagine being cheated on with a…a monster. Then left with no explanation.' Whispered Acheron. He peered over his shoulder as he spoke, eyeing the corpse fifteen feet away on the lawn. The other vampires had full stomachs. Most had already headed back to their own private quarters, with the exception of Runa. She was sat on a bench at the other side of the garden, head up, watching the night sky. Her presence made Acheron slightly uneasy.

'I keep thinking about it. That hybrid baby, is one of its kind.' Replied Apollyon.

'Apollyon do not allow your conscience to eat away at you. You are a good vampire. You have done the right thing. We simply cannot allow our species to be under threat from a hybrid, who may become our worst enemy.'

Apollyon remained silent. He looked up at the twinkling sky. The rain was coming. Just then, rumbling thunder roared through the skies. Strikes of lightning flashed from above. Runa's squeal could be heard as she scurried back inside. Apollyon and Acheron turned to each other.

'Have you spoken to Edgar?'

'Oh yes. Oh yes.' replied Acheron.

Back inside the castle, the atmosphere was somewhat lighter. 'Marc, do come and dance with me.' Achylls voice boomed from the drawing room. The door was wide open. She spun on her heels, waltzing underneath the high chandeliered ceiling. Marc was bemused. He looked on in a daze, impressed with her dancing skills. Ever since his stay at the castle, Achylls done her upmost to befriend him. Marc was untrusting of her charms, and had managed to resist, but was slowly warming. The music was tantric, mesmerizing to the soul. He leant against the door frame. Edgar was sat on one of the plush armchairs, adorned in deep red velvet. Actually, every room in the castle had matching coloured chairs, dressed in the finest materials. As expected, Edgar puffed away on his pipe, eyes glazed over. If there was anything Edgar loved the most, it was women. He found nothing more pleasurable than spending his days lusting over the opposite sex, usually semi-clad and dancing.

'Marc, do come in.' he said.

Marc cautiously stepped inside the large room. He made a task of trying his best not to ogle Achylls too much. She was such a tease. Her hips swayed with the beat, sashaying side to side. Achylls knew all eyes were on her and played up to it. Whilst licking her lips and playing with her hair, she stepped towards Marc. She lured him in with her neatly manicured index finger, making it very clear how she really felt. It was no secret that she wanted him. It was half the reason she was behaved like a total bitch. So, there she was, hips swaying, bosom revealing inches from his face. The dance was seductive, allowing Marc to forget his troubles, at least for a moment. Marc tried to hide his excitement, but it was rather obvious. Achylls kissed him softly on the lips. Suddenly, he kissed her back. It was slow and tender but quickly became more passionate and intense. Achylls placed his hands to her bottom. She danced whilst he wrapped his arms around her. Edgar paused. He was enjoying it far too much. He watched open-mouthed whilst undoing his own trouser. He too, wanted her as much as Marc did. Marc glanced over at the old immoral vampire. He should call the man uncle, as Edgar was his absent father's brother, apparently. Not that any of it made much sense. Marc assumed his parents to be human. But rumour had it, his father was a vampire, who had charmingly seduced his mother, then killed her when she refused to bare him another son. They say, it was his own father who had turned him out of frustration. Marc was born human with little vampiric traits at all. If this were true, he should have been a hybrid. Unfortunately, Marc remembered very little. He was abducted and found it hard to recall what exactly had happened, or how he became to be. The entire story was recounted by Edgar, whom wasn't an entirely plausible source.

'Look at me, god damn it.' Achylls held Marc's chin firmly in her hand.

'You have my undivided attention, unfortunately.' Grinned Marc.

Just then Achylls dropped her underwear to the ground. She slipped the delicate strap of her black dress over her shoulder, exposing her bare breasts. She gyrated harder and faster, manipulating Marc's hands to grab hold off them. Marc closed his eyes, squeezing the soft flesh between his fingers. Just then, they were rudely interrupted. It was Elena. She charged into the room like a bull on heat. She was flustered.

'Cerberus has woken.' she yelled.

The room became deathly quiet. The music was abruptly cut. The pleasure drained from Edgar's face. Achylls quickly pulled herself together. 'When did this happen?' she asked, her voice panicked.

'I cannot be sure. I was disturbed from my room and told to share the news.' Replied Elena.

'By whom?' asked Edgar.

'Apollyon.'

Achylls pulled a face. 'Gather In the hall.' Said Elena before dashing away. Marc watched her svelte silhouette in her baby blue dress waltz down the hallway. Edgar awkwardly stood up. He fastened his trouser zip back in place, though still appeared scruffy and not quite put together. He remained silent, seeming to be deep in thought. Then, without a word to the others, he sprinted out onto the hallway. He travelled fast and sharp with his black robe flowing precariously behind him, being extra vigilant to avoid knocking portraits from the walls. Achylls and Marc exchanged weird glances.

'This is remarkably odd. Something *very* important must be happening.' said Achylls with suspicion.

Marc raised an eyebrow. He looked quizzical. 'intriguing' was all he said.

'Cerberus does not wake for nothing, Marc. He must have good reason too. If I am entirely honest, there is bad news.' She said. Achylls had her chest pressed into him. Her cold breath misted across his face as she spoke. She carefully smoothed out the corners of his robe, rubbing her hand several times over the fabric. Marc admired with masked eyes. He did not fully trust her, and honestly never could. But she certainly aroused his sexual appetite in many ways.

'We must go.' Marc lifted her hands away from him. His thoughts returned to Estella. There was an uneasiness in the pit of his stomach. He was not particularly overjoyed at the news of Cerberus awakening, nonetheless, he quietly and calmly made his way towards the Great Hall. Seconds in, he was joined by Achylls. She was levitating, then lowered herself to her feet.

'Where are your manners? I expected you to wait for me.'

Marc turned to her. He shook his head. 'Well, I am hardly levitating. I knew you would catch up.'

Achylls rolled her eyes. She hated and craved him in equal amounts. Mostly, she hated herself for her beguiling desire, which was largely unreciprocated.

The line up in the great hall was impeccable. All the vampires wore their very best dress, with the exception of Edgar, and Marc, of whom didn't think it worthy enough for the effort. Acheron and Apollyon wore coloured masks on their faces. Their golden robes stood out in a mass of colour. Marc was surprised to see Ewin and Adrian. They were visitors to the castle, although Adrian would often spend ample time at the castle when he chose fit. He was unattached, but a hit with the women. He often had another young vampire on his arm. Ewin, lived at Lodge Green. A smaller, more conservative vampire town, within close enough proximity to the castle. Unlike Killbraith, the vampires at Lodge Green were exceptionally wealthy. Amongst them were noble aristocrats, and some previous board members. Ewin preferred life away from the castle. He was somewhat a recluse and was often seen alone. Marc smirked to himself. Runa's outfit had to be the most exquisite thing he had seen in a long while. She was dressed as though waiting for the Queen. Like a red Indian, a dozen black and red feathers showcased her head in a circular fashion, adjoined to a black band cleverly disguised against her Jet-black hair. The Red dress she wore, was akin to a second skin. Rubber and lace clung to places he didn't necessarily care to see. He felt vaguely incestuous watching the tight fabric stretch against her ample bottom and felt ashamed that twice his eyes had darted down wards, when he had desperately been trying to look at the solid silver coffin housing the head vampire.

'Good night, to each and every one of you. As you all know, our head has woken. This is not a call for celebration, but one for deliberation. Important things are to be discussed.'

Acheron's low gruff voice echoed around the large room. He stood over the coffin, which had risen from the ground. It was housed in a large glass tomb, which had been buried within a mechanical sliding floor concealed within the hall. It was almost an hour since he had made Acheron had made a shocking discovery and had immediately called upon Apollyon to usher the others. 'Our head will grow stronger over the next few hours. We expect he will rise before daybreak. Whatever the case, we must prepare ourselves for what lies ahead.'

'What has awoken our master?' Elena asked, genuinely intrigued.

'War.' said Acheron without hesitance.

'War? Is it the blood?' asked Adrian, straight-faced and serious.

'No, unlikely. Drinking human blood is for our better good. I am sure that even Cerberus would give it the seal of approval. Listen, it is not my place to divulge, nor speculate. That would have to be revealed by Cerberus. For only he knows what has disturbed his sleep.' Said Acheron.

'It must be good. He has been comatose for more than a century.' Snapped Achylls. She looked at Marc. He was gazing. She elbowed him. 'Snap out of it.' she hissed. Marc gave an icy stare. Suddenly he disappeared from her side and reappeared at the front of the gathering.

'I have the answer.' he exclaimed.

The vampires turned to Marc. Runa looked as if she had seen a ghost, hoping her cousin not to make a fool of himself. Their curiosity spiked. He felt the penetrative glares of Acheron and Apollyon, burning through him like hot coal on scorched skin. The tension on their faces could shatter a glass. He had his suspicions. Call it vampire intuition, but he knew Estella had *everything* to do with this. However, he had to play the fool to catch the fool. 'This, is about Killbraith.' He exclaimed. Relieved gasps were heard all round. News of Killbraith wasn't half as exciting as some unknown mission, prompting the head out of his coffin. However, Marc would ultimately play ignorant until he found more answers and was able to get to the bottom of it.

'Killbraith?' Apollyon's face relaxed slightly. His bottom lip formed a curl.

'Ever since Orpheus's death, demolishing the treaty has us rampant. I have seen it. Every night, the streets are a slaughter. The humans are evacuating. They have called in the Army. They are placing blame at the werewolves. However, a large portion of those deaths are vampire killings. Cerberus wouldn't want us behaving like animals. This, has stirred him in his coffin.' Said Marc.

'Well, we are being targeted. We cannot continue drinking synthetic rubbish. It has weakened our senses. Since I have resumed feasting upon humans, I have never felt better.'

'Elena, you speak truth. But I believe the head has risen because we have gotten out of control.'

'Thank you for your commentary, Marc. However, this needs to be addressed by Cerberus. Only he can decide what the next steps are to be.' said Acheron scanning the chalk-white faces.

TWENTY-SIX

Like a discontented spirit, Estella paced back and forth. She had been like this for hours, becoming steadily more agitated and distressed.

'Can you stop that.' snapped Jasper.

Estella bit her nails. She glared at him wild eyed. 'No, I can't. I am starving. I have to kill' her voice was shaky. Estella hated killing senselessly, but her hunger had grown tremendously. Jasper seemed unbothered. He was curled up against one of the fallen pews, dressed in a checked black and red shirt with brown scruffy trousers. Apparently, after he had left Creaker, Jasper had returned to the church. But not before killing an innocent man. Clearly, he had a full stomach after last night's meal.

'You could have left me a morsel. That would have been… thoughtful' Estella was irritated.

'Do you honestly think I have that kind of comprehension on a full moon? My only instinct is to kill…and kill. I didn't deliberately eat every ounce of that poor man out of spite! You try reasoning with a werewolf and see how far that gets you.' he replied. The baby babbled. She eyed Jasper with those big brown eyes. A pang of guilt stirred within him. He sighed heavily, placing his hands on his head. 'You stay here with the baby. I promise to find some food,' he said.

Estella looked weary. 'Will it be human? I am not sure I can handle any more of that canned rubbish.'

'I cannot promise. Estella, we can't keep killing humans every day. They have already called in the Army. Soon, there will be push-back.' It was true. The senseless killings had sparked a huge outcry with the human government. Army officials had already made an appearance on the streets. Not that a bullet would do the supernatural any real harm. But it wasn't about that. The human's made a stand. Estella shrugged. She begun to perspire. Black liquid dribbled along her forehead. Feeling slightly unsteady, she shoved her daughter in Jasper's arms. He looked at her as though she were mad.

'Estella?' he looked concerned.

'Look after her for an hour. I'll be back. I really don't feel too good. My craving for meat, is far too intense,' she said.

'It is not safe out there. The streets run rampant. I was nearly attacked last night. By vampires,' he said.

Estella seemed unbothered. She was determined, and nothing he said would make any difference. 'I can look after myself better than you can. I am, a daemon after all. I really cannot sit back and allow you to get yourself in any trouble, just because my stomach wants to be fed.' She smiled stiffly, running her hand along his right jaw. 'Plus, you are a natural. She loves you.' Estella looked at her offspring, who seemed preoccupied with Jasper's small sandy-coloured goatee. 'I told you she loves you.' Jasper didn't know what to say but found himself meekly agreeing. Before he could insist, Estella had already gone. He was left with the baby, eyeing her as though she were a toy, or some sort of alien.

Estella knew she was playing with fire. But the chances of meeting a vampire, was unlikely. At seven in the evening, it wasn't late enough for the bloodsuckers to venture out. As for the werewolves, they didn't pose quite the same level of threat. Stupid, clumsy feral dogs, she didn't think they were intelligent enough to even care. All she needed one was human. One uncivilised, disgraceful human who served little purpose being alive. That way, Estella would feel less guilty. Plus, a fully grown human would last her a week, child included. Unfortunately, the moment Estella left the church, the ruckus began. A group of young werewolves gathered across the church. Thought to be teenagers, they were arguing amongst themselves. One spotted Estella, alerting the others. Suddenly, all eyes were on her. They watched her like a hawk as she headed for the opposite direction.

'Oi. No vampires allowed.' Yelled one.

Estella kept walking. Evidently, they were too stupid to even recognise she was not from the fanged toothed community. Just then, a thud landed upon her shoulders. It was abrupt. Estella turned to face the culprit. The spotty faced teenager was grinning. He waved towards the others, enticing them to join in. Estella saw red. She grabbed him by the throat, eyes blazing. 'Do I look like a fucking vampire?' she yelled. The youngster trembled. Estella flickered her eyes, showcasing the red colouring. 'Now, go and tell your little mates to go home. If I come back and find you scoundrels on these streets, I will cut their hearts out.' Estella released her grip on the boy. He scurried off in a haste. He kept looking over his shoulder, fearing she may pounce. Estella watched the spectacle.

'She's a daemon. We best get out of here.' She heard him say. Their faces white like chalk. Estella smiled. The werewolves were a nuisance, if nothing else. Preoccupied with her thoughts, Estella bumped into a man. She gasped as she came face to face with the vampire.

'Excuse me.' he said.

Estella was dumbstruck. There was something about her former species that held such great power, she was actually petrified. The vampire community wasn't large enough to be completely rogue. Someone was bound to recognise you. Even the vampires of Killbraith knew most of the others. Estella tried to avert her gaze. She stiffened her stance, her shoulders tensed. The vampire eyed her meticulously. Her fear aroused his interests. She wondered what he was doing out at this hour. Though the sun had gone down, it wasn't dark enough to be wandering the streets. Or perhaps she was wrong. Maybe it was totally dark enough to wander the streets. Truth be known, Estella was so detached from her former self, she couldn't be sure what was what anymore. The vampire stood in front of her. His arms crossed over the other.

'What are you?' his tone was quiet, but suspicious.

'I am a werewolf. I must get going. Sorry to bump into you like…'

'Why must you lie? What are you hiding?' The vampire grabbed hold off Estella's arm as her anxiety went through the roof.

Estella looked him dead in the eye. It was no use lying. She had a child to protect and had to be strong. For her sake. His brown hair was neatly coiled. His grey eyes were tainted with deceit. He was dishonest, a rebel. Estella didn't want any trouble, but suspected trouble would eventually seek her out. 'Let go off my arm, now.' She spoke firmly, disguising any hint of fear. All she wanted, was a bloody meal. To her surprise, he released her arm. It must have been the fire in her eyes. Vampires were drawn to fear like a moth to light. However, they feared the brave. Their fragile egos couldn't handle it. Estella walked away feeling rather lucky. If the vampires got wind of the child, there would be no telling what they wouldn't do. Estella felt his eyes piercing through the back of her head. She had aroused his suspicions, and was now, on his radar.

The human town was a ghost town, with the exceptions of Army officials and police officers. They had been cautioned to stay indoors. Rightly so. Estella's appetite was rife. She had become a killing machine, with little control. She walked slow, attempting to mimic the human gait. Slow strides appear forlorn and weary, she told herself. It wasn't long before she was spotted by a policeman. His black and white uniform looked ridiculous. Clearly, he took his job very seriously judging by the disgruntled look on his face.

'Excuse me, madam. It's after seven. You should be indoors.' He strolled over to her, overlooked by a colleague who stood several feet behind him. Estella carried on, determined not to stop. This was the third unnecessary encounter since leaving the shop. Her patience grew thin. She tried to ignore the man, but he persisted to talk.

'Madam do not walk away. Can you stop please,' he said.

'I had to get food.' She shouted over her shoulder. 'I am headed home.'

The police officer became rattled at Estella's disobedience. He was the law, and she, had to obey him. Or so he thought. Suddenly, he ran after her, tugging her by the arm. 'Madam, I do not appreciate you ignoring me. You can be arrested.' Estella was bemused. She fought the urge to laugh out loud but must have looked fairly smug as the officer became annoyed. 'Ok, because you think this is some kind of joke, I am placing you under arrest.' He said sternly.

Estella froze. She eyed the silly human and his silly suit. 'I will only ask once. If you do not release my arm, you shall surely regret it.' She said.

The officer was stunned. 'Are you threatening an officer? That, is a chargeable offence.'

'Yes, it is a threat. And one you should take very seriously.' She spat.

Just then, the officer attempted to shackle her with handcuffs. Estella saw red. She roared loudly, citing the attention of the other self-obsessed humans. Her eyes flickered red; the penny dropped. The officer appeared to have seen a ghost. 'Surprise!' she said. Estella grabbed his arm, twisting it tightly behind his back. The officer screamed. 'You have no authority over me, officer. You humans, with your entitled warped reality. You are little more than scum on my shoe. Who do you think you are? Bossing people around, thinking you are more important than everyone else. We are at the top of the food chain. Remember that.' Estella took a bite out of his neck. She shoved her hand in his mouth in an attempt to choke him to death. Aware a monster was in their midst, the Army officials begun to fire shots. Estella used the body as a shield, ducking as they sprayed him with bullets. She ran fast, dragging the body along with her. The shots ceased. The humans knew as well as she did, that bullets were useless against the undead. At the very least, the body was large enough to serve her a while. Estella laid in waiting at nearby parkland. She had to go back past the officers in order to return to the church, but was so hungry, she decided it best to full her stomach to keep up her strength. The park was quiet. Wind swayed between trees causing them to rustle. As she crouched to ravish her meal, Estella spotted a body amongst the bush. Drained dry, slashed ear to ear, it wasn't obvious who had caused her death. The body had already begun to rot. Her naked body had already turned a shade of blue. Estella ate as though she hadn't eaten in months. Every bite was better than the last. Blood smeared the corners of her mouth as she crammed chunks of flesh into it. She stumbled upon a gun in his back pocket. Estella pulled it out, eyeing the odd object. It was rather heavy. She pitied him. Actually, she pitied all of them. The human race was a lost species. So lost, they needed men dressed up in suits to keep them all in line. What a silly concept, she thought. Why not just appoint one leader to rule them all? She also thought ditching the coordinating suits would be a good idea, too. Rustling in the trees caught her attention. Estella sniffed the air wildly. Vampires were nearby. And then she noticed a small gathering of eight. They were about twenty feet away, backs turned, all appearing to be in some sort of semi-circle. Estella eyed them keenly from the bush. She munched on the officer, looking on with intrigue. They were eating. As they passed around pieces of ample flesh, Estella noticed the body on the floor. Suddenly, they turned to her. Estella forgot just how keen the vampire senses were. She ducked back but thought it was little too late.

Within seconds, the group had gathered around her as though they had morphed on the spot. She recognised one of them. It was the same vampire who had grabbed hold off her arm less than half an hour earlier. Estella was certain they were from Killbraith. Before she knew it, she was grabbed by the neck, while another dug her through the chest. It wasn't deep enough nor serious enough to do any real damage, but it was enough trauma to get the daemon out of its box. Something that Estella didn't really want to happen. She found shapeshifting to be quite painful and would always end up feeing rather bruised when she finally returned to human form. Anyway, it was about to happen all over again.

'You're the wanted girl from Heath Hall.' Said one.

'Well, she's not one of us now. I couldn't dig deep enough. Her chest cavity must be steel' Said the other.

'We were not supposed to harm her. He wants her alive.' Said one, dark haired, stout in stature.

'Are you sure that's the missing vampire? She certainly looks different from the picture.' Said another.

While the vampires discussed amongst themselves, Estella had begun to change. They looked dumbstruck as she morphed, her clothes tearing at the seams. Daemons didn't frequent the area. With exception of a small handful, many vampires had no real clue what they were.

'What the hell is that?' asked one.

The stunned vampires watched the daemon grow three times its size, appearing to be some sort of creature. Surprisingly they didn't run. One piped up 'I think that's a daemon.'

'A daemon? Do they still exist?'

Estella roared loudly. At this point, most of the vampires were already delivering blows to her seven-foot exterior. Being too large and too heavy to feel any real impact, Estella struggled to throw one off her back.

'We must kill her. If she is a daemon, we cannot allow these creatures to threaten our food supply. We already have those blasted dogs to contend with.'

Estella grabbed one of the vampires who had bitten her legs. After some grabbling, she picked him up, then chewed his head off cleanly off his neck. That was one the moment the vampires backed off. Fearing how dangerous she could be, they vanished. Estella knew the trouble had only just begun. It was clear they knew who she was and had likely been instructed to seek her out by Marc.

TWENTY-SEVEN

The old woman nursed her wounds on bended knee. She cried in angst on the wooden living room floor; her hands were wobbly as she drank sips of green broth. How could she allow that woman to defeat her? In her eyes, Estella wasn't even a Daemon. Not a proper one, anyway. Worst of all, the baby had gone. The one thing she was supposed to keep hold off, had slipped away so easily.

'I am a terrible daemon and deserve the worst death imaginable' she muttered.

'Don't be so harsh on yourself, mother. She overpowered you. Unfortunately, this means you will not be seeing the child again. You had your chance and blow it.' said the voice.

'That is my grandchild. You cannot keep her away from me.' she yelled.

The old woman looked up at her son. He stood at her feet with all his 6'2 stature. He looked disgusted. His mother grabbed hold off his leg. 'Do not touch me.' he spat.

'I always loved you, son. But I didn't know just how powerful you would become. I had no clue that, you would father the chosen one. I know I haven't been a perfect mother, but don't you think it is time you treated me like your mother, instead of a pawn in some game. You let that girl think I was a werewolf!'

'I can say as I like. You're no mother to me.' he replied flatly.

'All I want, is to see my grandchild.' She pleaded.

'You forfeited any rights you had as a mother, and a grandmother, when my father died. You left him to die.'

'No. You know, that is not true. I loved your father very much, but the vampires would have killed us both. I had to protect you. You were merely a boy. Lazarus, please I am begging you. Forgive me.'

'You're forgiven mother. But you promised to bring my child to me and failed. There is little more I can do.'

'I can try again. I will summon her back here.' Said the old woman.

'And how do you think you'll do that? I placed a spell on this house to draw her in. A very powerful spell, one I cannot conjure twice in short succession. She is unlikely to venture here again,' he said.

The old woman became angry 'And why must you call yourself Xaviar? Do you now like the name I gave you?

Lazarus was stunned. He bent and grabbed his mother by the hair. 'How dare you? I call myself whatever the hell I please. You were meant to bring me my child.'

'Let go, Lazarus. You are hurting me.' she yelled.

Lazarus released his taut grip. He walked towards the dismantled living room wall, turning his back to his mother. The old woman clutched at her hair. Like a rat, she scurried across the room, crouching behind a chair. Tears fell against her cheeks as her son disappeared from the room. Like that, he was gone. She knew her son well enough to know she was unlikely to ever see him again. A thought she couldn't bear, only second to the pain of not seeing her own grandchild. Suddenly, a deathly quiet set in. She bawled with frustration. She felt angry that she had allowed him to use her, yet again. Lazarus done nothing, for nothing. The old woman got up, then walked to the back of the house. She entered the backyard, then sat along the shrubby bushes. The old daemon chewed on her bottom lip, ruminating on the past. In despair, she struggled to hide her fleeting emotions. Bizarre thoughts of kidnap came to mind. The child was worth millions, dead or alive. She had ploys to use the baby as a bargaining tool for a better life. The old daemon envisioned a life of luxury, and not having to live in this squalid house of misery and raw painful memories.

Almost a century ago, years before her husband's demise, her husband was a master of sorts. He worked with many powerful figures; many of whom were never revealed. He was a fiercely private man and rarely let his wife into his business life. He was strict in his affairs, keeping his personal and working life neatly compartmentalized. Her husband owned many homes. As a family, they often took long holidays to the small daemon island of Shin. They had servants, and were treated like royalty, waited on hand and foot. They were the richest daemon family in the town of Creaker. Lazarus was a spoilt child. He was privately educated within the small daemon community. An only child, his childhood was one of luxury and wanting for nothing. Her firstborn died days after birth. It was a common feature with the daemon. Infant mortality was morbidly high, usually accidental. They're suckled by their mothers. However, the daemon's milk can be so acidic, the young daemon's undeveloped immune system sees it as a threat, rendering the milk poisonous. Thus, feeding daemon infants a diet of meat was preferred.

At age four, Lazarus was sent to an alchemist, upon his father's insistence. He wanted his son to be greater than the average daemon and was taught a great deal. Every Sunday, Lazarus's father would travel with him by car, ten miles to the only daemon island, Shin. He would drop his son off at seven in the morning and would be back by approximately six in the evening. To this day, the old woman knew nothing of his tutor, and Lazarus was told to keep this information to himself only. He became advanced in his knowledge and conversed mostly with his father. Everything was a game of hide and seek, and often, she was the last to know anything. She felt her husband treated her as an afterthought and began to secretly resent the boy. For reasons unknown, Lazarus ceased from going to the alchemist upon his tenth birthday. Her husband said he had 'outgrown' his passion, but she felt differently. With little else to do, Lazarus would sit in his room for hours, seemingly staring at the blank wall. Around this time, her marriage suffered. Her resentment towards her son continued and was made worse by the fact he barely spoke a word to her. Lazarus couldn't shut up when is father was around, which was seldom infrequently with his ever-increasing business meeting and trips away. As a result, she struggled to raise her son.

One evening when Lazarus was aged eleven, something remarkably strange happened within the town of Creaker. She was woken up to a blazing fire. But the fire wasn't inside of the home. It was the entire town! Every house, shop, and land were set ablaze. It was a nightmare, panic ensued. Luckily, the family were miraculously able to escape the town. But there was one thing that still puzzled her to this day. The disappearance of the town. The moment they got to safety outside, it seemed the entire town had disappeared. Not even a single pile of burnt rubble was to be seen. Like an odd parallel universe, they suddenly found themselves in the middle of a werewolf town, a town they had never seen before. The daemons had to conceal themselves for weeks, seeking out a secluded spot three miles from the hustle and bustle. Eventually they settled out farther, to a mysterious uninhabited place named Creaker. With the exception of her son, the old daemon was the last of her kind to be seen again. Up until this day, she was *still* the only habitant of Creaker. Nothing was spoken of the incidence, and any inclination of conversation was pushed away by her husband who would clam up and refuse to discuss it. The same happened with Shin. The joyful island of daemon haven also mysteriously disappeared off the radar, ten years after Creaker. The old woman suspected her son played a part, as bizarre a thought that may seem. Truth be known, Lazarus was an odd child and grew to be just as weird as an adult. At sixteen, he had asked to be addressed as Xaviar, a name she detested and refused to use. He decided he hated being a daemon, and would fantasize becoming a werewolf, or the occasional vampire. She found it odd, but didn't think much of it, dismissing it as a childhood affliction, or wanting to fit in with the locals. One thing that struck her, was his innate ability to manipulate magic. Daemons had their own power. However, Lazarus demonstrated remarkable ability, almost god-like in nature. He could dictate the weather, and would manipulate people's thoughts, often hers, better than any vampire ever could. Burning entire cities and bringing destruction to others, seemed to be his most spectacular power.

A fierce bolt of lightning shot through the sky. The daemon's thoughts were broken. She looked up with a frown. She took it as a warning from her son. He knew her intentions and, was making it known. She gulped uncomfortably, trying to shift the lump which had formed in her throat. She wasn't an inherently evil daemon and certainly didn't mean her grandchild any harm. But she was unhappy and hated being alone. The old daemon scowled herself for being silly. How could she think such a thing? It would never happen anyway. The competition for the baby, was fierce. The vampires were already on the hunt. The werewolves would kill the child if they got wind. Any chance of capturing her granddaughter, was as just as unlikely as her Gilbert returning from the dead. Just then, the daemon started to bawl. She buried her head into her weathered and worn slender hands.

'I just want my Gilbert back. I can't bear to be alone.' She said aloud, looking up to the skies.

'He is gone mother. You ought to get over it by now, as you're the one who killed him'.

Lazarus's voice came from nowhere. She frustratingly roared in anger. How dare he taunt her from afar.

'Why don't you just kill me and be done with it.' She yelled.

TWENTY-EIGHT

'Lilith, what brings you up here?'

Runa was surprised. Lilith, nor Bernadette were frequent visitors to the castle. They were newly turned and were not considered one of the originals. Lastly, they were also Achylls playthings, and for the most part, were not given the same credence as the pure bloods. Actually, Achylls demanded they not visit the castle. Nevertheless, Runa welcomed Lilith inside. There was a thundering storm; the rain was beating heavily. Lilith's hair clung to her head like a second skin.

'Thank you, Runa.' She smiled. 'I have news. I've seen Marc's lady. The missing one.'

'Really?' Luna's eyes widened.

'Yes. In the werewolf town, a hundred miles South from here.'

'What were you doing there? What is she doing there?' The questions came hard and fast as Runa tried to make sense of it all.

'I was seeking food. I haven't fed or caught a human in days. Not even a stray cat. Our synthetic supplies have dried up. We no longer get deliveries.'

Runa looked shocked. 'You don't want to be eating stray animals. You will soon turn feral'.

'Feral? What's that?' Lilith wrinkled her brow.

Runa studied the poor girl. She shook her head. Like a two-year-old exploring the world at hand, innocence was written all over her face. Lilith had lots to learn and was still very young in her outlook. Runa offered a sympathetic smile. 'Don't worry about that. Let's get you something to eat. Come with me.' she said.

Lilith became worried. She looked down the large hall with a fretful look on her face. 'She will scold me.'

'Don't worry about Achylls, I'll have a word. Come this way' demanded Runa.

Runa beckoned to Lilith, who meekly followed suit down the hall. They arrived at the maid quarters, then made the journey to the kitchen. It took the vampires less than five seconds to arrive at the pantry. Coming from a middle-class family, she was used to a reasonably large house, but this was one of the biggest pantries Lilith had seen. The room was as large as any other in the castle and housed some of the biggest cupboards. There was row upon rows of foods, groceries and other provisions, including silverware and dishes. There were large sacks of rice and potatoes clearly labelled for the chef. Lilith frowned. She tucked a blond curl behind her ear, then glared at the food in awe. It had been a while, but Lilith still remembered the taste of real food. Like her mother, she had a penchant for steak, rare.

'Who is eating all this food?'

Runa smiled. 'We feed the humans.

'Humans?

'Well, we have in-house maids and cleaners. Plus, we need to keep the captures alive for blood resources later.'

'You have human maids? Are you not ever tempted?'

'No, not mostly. Despite what you hear, we are not entire monsters. We respect those humans and treat them like our own,' said Luna looking pleased with herself.

'I have something else to tell you.' said Lilith cutting the air.

'Go on.'

'She wasn't a vampire'.

Runa's eyes widened in horror. What did she possibly mean by that? Her face became curious. 'What do you mean. Of course, she's a vampire.'

'No. She was something else.'

'Like what?' Runa probed.

'I cannot be sure. Not human, not a werewolf either.' Said Lilith.

Runa had heard this before. Marc had said the same. Edgar had given him the news, but he was doubtful. She screwed her eyes up, trying to rack her brain for some explanation. None could be given. She made Lilith promise not to mention a thing to anyone else, then said nothing more on the matter. Runa walked over to a small ash brown cupboard in the far corner of the kitchen, then pulled the door open. There were at least two dozen bottles of blood. Some smaller, others as large as five litres. Runa grabbed of the smaller bottles, then tossed it over to Lilith. Runa, dressed in black leather, with lashings of black liner rimming her eyes, looked like a vampire ready for action. Her dark hair was gelled to her head, like a bond girl escaping from the sea. 'Feed quickly. It is human blood and will do you a world of good.'

Lilith finished within seconds, then demanded more. Runa gasped at her appetite. Sympathetically, she handed Lilith another bottle, then told her to be on her way.

'You best go' said Runa, concerned.

The vampires vanished from the kitchen. Seconds later, they had materialized at the front of the castle door. Just then, Achylls appeared from nowhere. She raised her brow suspiciously. To Lilith's surprise, Achylls wasn't hostile. In fact, she greeted Lilith in a manner she had never done before. 'Lilith. What brings you here' She asked, eyeing the bottle of blood.

'Ah, um'

'She was hungry, so I kindly offered her a bottle. She's just about to go.' interrupted Runa.

'I see. How hospitable of you, Runa. Lilith, perhaps you would like to stay a little longer. After all, your sister is being well acquainted to the castle.' Said Achylls with a sly smile.

Both Runa and Lilith were surprised. Neither had no idea Bernadette was in the castle.

'My sister is here?' Lilith was stunned.

Achylls laughed. 'Do not look so surprised. Your sister is a fine young woman and has her pick of fine young vampires waiting at her fingertips. We have given her a room'.

'Oh. Really. This isn't a castle. More like a brothel. Charming.' Said Runa, unimpressed.

Achylls gave Runa a humorous grin. She candidly shrugged her shoulders. Runa shook her head disapprovingly.

'Forgive my judgement Lilith. She is your sister, after all. I forget quite how big this castle is. No wonder we haven't met'. Said Runa.

'Well. She has hardly been here 48 hours. I am sure this evening, she will have a wonder.' Achylls grinned.

'I am sure she will' replied Runa.

Lilith frowned. The news of her sister's stay in the castle, shouldn't really come as a surprise. Men adored her wherever she went. Like a prize wrapped in gold tint, she was adored as a human, and that hadn't changed one bit as a vampire. She was spoilt and always had been. Bernadette had left her sister two days ago in search of food, and here she was, at Castle Dravenherd. Lilith was annoyed. She felt hideous, like the ugly sister that no one wanted. Not even ugly old vampires like Edgar. She felt undeserving of love and resented her sister. Just then, her eyes shone the brightest green. This happened when she was jealous, or sad. In fact, Lilith's eyes had the extraordinary ability to change various colours, mood dependant. Achylls noticed the glow.

'No need for jealously. We all have our strengths. It just happens that, your sister's biggest strength, is her beauty. She may arouse the nether regions of men, but nothing beats intelligence. Or charisma. Both of which, aren't very high on her list, may I add. You, my dear, are special. Your innocence is wonderful. You **will,** get your turn'.

Achylls placed an arm around Lilith's waist. She ushered her back down the hall. A stunned Runa walked off in the other direction, not wishing to get involved with Achyll's past time, mostly consisting of sexual escapades of some sort, or torturous blood bonding sessions.

'Lilith, I will be in my room if you need me.' Runa called over her shoulder.

Truth be known, Runa's thoughts were on news of Estella. She knew the hysteria that such reports would bring and held back from sharing it with Achylls. Runa decided to disclose matters only with Marc.

As they paced the second hallway, Lilith became worried about being left alone with Achylls. The thought made the hairs on the back of her neck stand up. Lilith didn't trust Achylls. Despite her kind gesture, she couldn't quite relax. She feared she was probably waiting to pounce on her neck and drain her dry, as she did ever so often. Lilith gulped uncomfortably. Suddenly, she wished she had never come to the castle. Achylls turned to her.

'Lilith, you won't be needing Runa for the rest of your stay. You will be having way too much fun' she winked.

Achylls held her hand as though Lilith were a young child, then pushed the door open. It was a very large room, well lit, with two exceptionally large beds. Lilith gasped. Right there on the second bed, she was greeted with Adrian's naked chalk-white bottom, thrusting vigorously on top of her sister, whom had her legs spread wide in a quarter past nine fashions. Bernadette was moaning and groaning, and neither seemed to mind the intrusion. Adrian continued. He began to thrust harder. Achylls smiled and stepped inside. She watched them like a hawk, eyes wide, joyfully licking her lips. She was so consumed, Achylls did not notice Lilith's disinterest.

'I must go' said Lilith wincing.

Just then, Adrian stopped mid-action. He turned to the two women. His face became serious. 'Take her out of here. I do not want an audience'.

'We have been here an entire ten minutes. Surely you don't mind.' teased Achylls.

'I do mind. This is her sister!'

Bernadette looked up from the pillows. She studied her sister's glum expression, then hurried pulled herself together, demanding Adrian get off her.

'Lilith. What brings you here?' she asked, seemingly shocked.

'She came for food but will be staying a few days. I think, it is time we found Lilith a man.' said Achylls.

'I wish you luck, but can you excuse us, Achylls. That girl is far too innocent. And, with a face like that, I wouldn't count on it.' snapped Adrian.

Lilith froze with shock. She expected such a comment would earn him a firm backhand from her sister. However, to her surprise, Bernadette chuckled with laughter. She beamed at her sister smugly. Achylls rolled her eyes. She grabbed Lilith by the arm, then quickly escorted her out, as though shielding her from anymore insults.

'Adrian, I will speak to you later' she hissed before slamming the door shut.

Back out onto the hallway, Lilith was already distraught. Cold tears rolled fast against her cheeks. Achylls pitied her. She scrutinized her face as though examining a puzzle, then gently wiped her cheek. Just then, Lucas and Ewin walked by. The two men made a menacing pair. Neither of them was the friendliest vampires but seemed to be enjoying each other's company. Both carried glasses of blood, immersed in hearty dialogue. Since the order of the treaty had been lifted, Ewin had been back at the castle, righting his wrongs. With synthetic blood ceased, and the humans under curfew, blood was scarce. The only place with the best resources, was castle Dravenherd. Very soon, the vampires from Killbraith would come knocking.

'Good evening' the men nodded their manners.

'Hello gentlemen' replied Achylls flatly.

'And whom may this be?' asked Lucas, eyeing Lilith oddly.

'Ah, this is Bernadette's sister. Lilith'

The men looked astonished. Like a revelation out the blue, she sensed the scrutiny on their faces as they tried to make sense of it. Lilith felt judged and lowered her gaze. She knew what they were thinking. Making lewd comparisons to her sister, wondering how something so perfect, could possibly be related to someone so hideous. Ewin eyed her for some time but didn't offer a greeting. To her surprise, Lucas beamed broadly.

'It is my pleasure to welcome another beauty to the castle.' He smirked.

He took her right hand, then kissed it tenderly with a smile. Lilith was too embarrassed to blush. With red eyes and rain drenched hair doing little to ease her insecurities, she remained solemn and tight lipped. She struggled to muster a smile. However, Achylls beamed and walked off in a hurry.

'How lovely. Can I leave Lilith in your capable hands? You can give her a grand tour of the castle. I must address business' she smiled stiffly.

Lucas was stunned. He looked over at Ewin, who remained reticent and unforthcoming. He simply took another sip of blood, then seemingly admired the frosting on the glass. Achylls was glaring at Lucas, willing him to say yes. Lucas eyed Lilith, then smiled in agreement.

'Ok, sure. Ewin, you will have to excuse me.' he said.

Ewin seemed unbothered. He walked off back down the corridor and headed for the main hall. Achylls promised to catch up with Lilith that evening, then quickly disappeared before Lucas had a change of heart. She had Acheron to tend to and knew she had kept him waiting longer than necessary.

'Runa, we must find her to get to the bottom of this. I have searched my head for three whole months and still cannot figure it out.'

'Marc, you must lower your voice.'

'I fear, it is too late for that. Apollyon and Acheron are on to something. Perhaps Edgar, too. We must act with caution.' He replied

'You have my word' promised Luna.

'I say we go out tonight and have a wander.'

'Well, I am ready when you are.'

Runa held her arms up animatedly. Marc looked impressed with her all-black leather ensemble. He too, was dressed head to toe in black. He grabbed a black leather jacket from the wooden chair nearest the bed, then promptly put it on, complementing his crisp black shirt. The vampire's opened Marc's bedroom window. It was a peaceful night. The moon was out. Werewolves howled in the distance. Marc climbed out first, then beckoned to his cousin. The vampires teleported through the brisk night sky with hopes of not being seen.

Back inside the castle, Ewin, Edgar, Stramus and Apollyon, were engrossed in chatter, drinking jugs of human blood, laughing amongst themselves. Despite earlier announcements, Cerberus hadn't fully woken, but was gradually becoming less corpse-like, and had begun taking small sips of blood. The residents of the castle had been on standby for an entire day, with little to show for it.

'So, is anyone going to tell me what has really awoken Cerberus?'

Ewin sat cross-legged. He looked around at the men for an answer, all of which becoming shtum. Apollyon and Edgar exchanged cunning glances, whilst Stramus awkwardly cleared his throat.

'I wish, I had the answer to that myself.' Said Stramus awkwardly. He took a massive gulp, then lowered his glass upon the gold rimmed table. Appearing deep in thought, he slowly ran his left hand over his bald head.

'It just seems a little strange. After all this time. It ***must*** be something highly significant' continued Ewin.

Apollyon's eyes flickered red. He scanned the men. His face stern. No longer could he bear the burden of his deceit. He wanted the 'secret' out for public knowledge, and for the vampires to all be on board. He wished Acheron was present to divulge the news. Being delivered from someone else's mouth, would ease his guilt. The three vampires turned to him. Ears sharpened, intrigued and waiting. Stramus glared at Edgar. This was about Estella. Like a cunning game of Chinese whispers, he suspected Edgar was at the root of it.

'I visited Estella three months ago. She was holed up in a human motel, South Harmand Cole Street,' said Apollyon.

'Harmand Cole Street? The heart of riot central. What on earth was she doing there?' asked Stramus keenly.

'Stramus, can you allow him to finish?' Edgar took his pipe from his mouth. He side-eyed his cousin with a curled upper lip.

'Duly noted. Please carry on.' Quipped Stramus.

'I traced her scent. On hindsight, I should have left her be. But what I discovered, was shocking to say the least'.

All eyes were on him, while Apollyon directed his gaze to the floor. He became remorseful. The other vamps were on tenterhooks, waiting for the big reveal. Apollyon clammed up. He appeared tense.

'Apollyon?' Ewin was concerned.

'Estella, she is no longer one of us. Her fornication with another specie has turned her into a monster. I suppose, she can only blame herself. Her DNA has mutated into something sinister. And another thing. She was with child.'

Apollyon was met with deafening silence. Ewin almost choked on the remnants of blood he had left in his mouth. Edgar didn't flinch. He had been privy to this information far longer than Ewin or Stramus had. However, Stramus was stunned. Never would he have guessed that Estella could be with child.

'What do you mean with child?' asked Ewin, trying to fathom how such a thing could be possible.

Apollyon looked at him blankly. 'Ewin, which is exactly what I mean. She was with child. Estella is a Daemon. Poor Marc, I do not have the nerve to tell him.'

'Christ! This, is preposterous.' Said Ewin. 'That is the most ridiculous thing I have ever heard, in all my centuries walking this earth.'

Ewin stood up angrily, his eyes glaring in disbelief. He refuted the idea and deemed Apollyon a trickster. Or worse, insane.

'You believe me, or you don't. It's that simple. You wanted to know why Cerberus has woken, and there you have it. That child is no vampire. It is a hybrid daemon, highly dangerous to our wellbeing.' Continued Apollyon.

The three vampires studied each other. Edgar puffed quickly on his pipe, squinting his eyes shut. Ewin gazed at Apollyon. His face fell pallor. The realisation that Apollyon was serious became discernible, and he promptly sat back down. The word 'daemon' brought with it a rippling terror within the room. To be frank, the vampires were alarmed.

'Daemon? How can that be?'

'It took me weeks to get my head around such an idea, so I understand the surprise, Ewin. Estella, betrayed Marc. At first, I thought I was going mad, but I couldn't get the retched scent out of my mind'.

'So, the child is a hybrid?' Stramus appeared to be mumbling to himself, still trying to figure it out.

'More than a hybrid. We suspect the child, is the next undead messiah. Acheron and I has spent an entire month educating ourselves and studying its history. I know little about the father. From what we gather, everything suggests the child's birth was written in the Book of Dead, a bleak prophecy for the underworld. Can you imagine being governed and ruled by some other greater force? Having to answer to someone other than ourselves?'

'Well, I will be damned. The next messiah? Not if I can help it.'

Ewin's eyes became hostile. There was no way he wanted a Daemon Prophet dictating to them all, trying to rule over their entire empire. The vampires would be finished. They would be left to the wayside, whilst the Daemon's thrived and took over. Stramus had his mouth tightly pressed together. He was deep in thought, mostly thinking about Marc. Edgar's eyes flicked from yellow to green, then back again. The news was paramount and would change everything. Everything they'd ever known, would be wiped out in a flash. They would become, what the humans were to them. The enslaved race. Apollyon's revelation had whetted their appetites. Now, the child was prey.

TWENTY-NINE

The atmosphere in the master bedroom three floors up, was entirely different to what had taken place downstairs. Acheron and Achylls were lying on a grand Queen-sized bed, hungrily kissing each other like starved animals. Acheron had positioned himself behind her and was passionately kissing her neck with every thrust. With a hand on her hip, he smacked her thigh, grinding his crotch against hers. With every moan, she demanded he smack her thigh that much harder. Suddenly, he stopped. He turned to something on the floor.

'Come and join us.'

Acheron waved his hand to the fearful girl, who was forced to watch their explicit displays of affection in the corner of the room. He had admired her bravery down in the dungeon and thought she would be better suited as a sex slave, catering to his every need. Her long straggly dark hair fell hastily over her face. She was dirty and unkempt, and in need of a good bath. Partially dressed in rags, soiled and torn, Achylls objected to Acheron's demands.

'You must be out of your mind. Look at her. Like a rotten animal. She needs to bathe before coming anywhere near me, or this bed.'

Acheron pulled an unsavoury frown. Achylls was right. Indeed, the girl was in dire need to be cleaned from head to toe and realised he had behaved in haste.

'Are you so desperate for young flesh?' enquired Achllys.

'No. Not at all. I suppose my brain hadn't engaged the fact she was so filthy. You know the effect you have on me, Achylls.'

With that, he held her hand then planted a kiss in the middle of it. Achylls gritted her teeth. With bare breasts and buttocks exposed, she got up from the bed then beckoned to the girl to follow her towards the en-suite bathroom.

'Come on. Let's get you cleaned up.' she demanded.

Achylls tone was patronising. The girl stayed put. With deep eyes, she sat rigid. She turned away, not wishing to see Achylls naked flesh on display. This, enraged Achylls. Not one to be disobeyed, she strolled over to the girl, then dragged her up by the arm.

'You are a firecracker, aren't you? A stubborn little madam. Come here at once.'

'Argh, you're hurting me.'

'Well, I wouldn't have to pull you if you had listened to me the first time.'

The girl was dragged into the bathroom. The soiled rags adorning her body was quickly discarded to the floor. Achylls shoved her into the shower. The girl squealed like an animal whilst Achylls hosed her down with the golden rimmed shower head. The water was freezing cold. The girl cried and whimpered, then asked for the temperature to be adjusted. Achylls admired her gall. She was certainly the feistiest human she had ever met. Impressed by her bold nature, Achylls reluctantly balanced the temperature. Achylls decided on the girl's fate. She would see to it she became one of them. Her bold confidence was invaluable. Lilith had been a mistake. She was far too emotionally charged, and certainly not the most physically appealing. Besides her youth, Achylls felt that Lilith held little value, and was only chosen due to her sister. There were considerations to stake her heart and be done with it.

Acheron's eyes almost popped out of its sockets while admiring the young beauty who stepped out of the bathroom. Freshly washed, hair neatly brushed, she looked to be a completely different person. Achylls beamed like a proud mother, or a child with a new toy. Acheron admired her bare breasts. She was particularly big chested, more so than Achylls. Acheron was practically drooling, arousing a certain jealousy within Achylls, one he hadn't seen before. She eyed him venomously. He grinned to soften the blow. Achylls mouth eventually curled to a wry smile. He had her blessing. The girl's brown eyes darted to the floor. She was encouraged to walk over to Acheron and join him in bed. She was hesitant but took slow strides towards him. Just before she reached the bed, he grabbed her arm, insisting she crawl in.

'You are stunning. I am awfully sorry that I nearly got you killed. What a waste that would have been.'

'I shall be leaving you both. Do come and join us later in the main hall. And whatever you do, do not turn her. She, is mine.' Achylls didn't mince her words. She pulled herself together, then glided through the bedroom door as though she were a ghost. Acheron barely noticed she had gone. The girl tensed. She didn't want to become a vampire and protested against it.

'It will be ok.' he soothed.

'No, please don't allow her to turn me to a vampire.' she said.

'I cannot promise, but I do promise that you will have a new lease of life.' He hissed, smiling insidiously. Acheron grabbed her close, then kissed her forcefully on the mouth. The girl winced through gritted teeth. She couldn't bare it but had little power to interject. Little did he know Achylls hadn't moved from the other side of the door. She had her ear pressed against it and took pleasure in Acheron's unscrupulous behaviour. She smiled wryly to herself before disappearing down the hallway.

'Marc, this is no use. She isn't here.'

'It has only been a couple of hours. We can scale the entire city in another hour.'

'She probably knows you are looking for her and won't wait around. If what Lilith said is true, she may even be a werewolf and definitely won't give you an opportunity to find her'. Said Runa.

'Estella is not no damned werewolf. They have all gone mad. Vampires don't suddenly become something else. I refuse to entertain that ludicrousness.' He replied.

It was nearly morning before Marc was satisfied with his search. He and Runa had searched the entire werewolf town. All three of them. Meanwhile, the human cities and towns had become desolate. Every tree, every corner, even every rubbish skip was overturned. Most shops were locked and protected with metal sheets, though others were ransacked and broken into. But the vampires had made a crucial mistake. Assuming no vampire could enter such a building, nor would they want to, the old, abandoned church had been overlooked. Marc was flustered and fed up. Runa was only half bothered. Disheartened, the vampires arrived back at Castle Dravenherd mere minutes before sunrise. It had been a futile search, and Marc, had lost all hope. Runa waved goodnight, then wandered off in the other direction of the hall, levitating quickly up the twirling stairs. Marc had a mini portrait of Estella propped up against his bedside table. He clutched it close to his chest, holding it tight, as he had held her for so many years. He sunk himself deep within the thick, ample duvet, then fell into a deep state of sleep.

THIRTY

Estella's world had collapsed. On return to the church, she learned her daughter had been kidnapped. Jasper says he had been sleeping and knew nothing what had happened. The last thing he knew he had woken, and the baby had gone. It had been two days since her daughter was taken, and Estella had not moved an inch from the corner of the church where she had chosen to huddle like a ball. As if that was not bad enough, her cover was blown. The vampires were onto her. A worried Jasper tried to soothe her fears, but nothing he said made any real difference. Knowing she was potentially on borrowed time and may never see her daughter again, Estella had become a ball of anxiety.

'Estella, please say something. You have not uttered a word since yesterday. We will, find your daughter. As for that officer, …he is just a human.' Jasper hoped to rouse Estella out of her sombre mood. She eyed him as though he were mad.

'You think this is about a human? Wow.' she replied snarky.

'Estella, you know I did not mean it like that. I would appreciate it if you stopped ignoring me, it is not helping the matter. I didn't deliberately fall asleep putting your daughter at risk. I was exhausted.

I was cradling her on my lap; I assumed her to be safe. I promise, to find your daughter.'

Estella's red eyes blared at him. 'You do not know the hell my life has become. I killed a friend. He was the first werewolf to show me any kindness at all. He was a good man and didn't deserve to die such a brutal death. That plagues me every day, and I only have myself to blame. And now, the one thing that means the world to me, has gone. How can I go on?'

Jasper frowned with his eyes. He wanted to console her but did not know how. 'Everything will be ok, and I am sure your friend is at peace. He… forgives you.' he gulped, hoping he had said the right thing.

'Does he? I am a monster of the worst kind. I do not deserve forgiveness.' She snapped, fearing Jasper to be incredibly tone deaf in the wake of her daughter's disappearance.

Jasper sat along one of the pews. He put his head in his hands, an indication he was just as fed up as she was. Estella noticed his body language. Suddenly, she softened.

'There were vampires at the park. An entire gang of them. I was attacked. They knew who I was, Marc has obviously put the word out. Although I managed to scare them off, I am on borrowed time. I don't have a clue how I will ever get her back.' Her voice fell to a whisper.

Jasper put his head up. He glared at Estella.

'Evidently, they know where we are. It is only a matter of time before they come looking for me.'

'You're assuming she was taken by vampires.' Said Jasper

'Well, who else would have taken her?! Of course, it was vampires.' She yelled.

Jasper was stunned at Estella's outburst. He felt guilty and awkward, shuffling about in his seat. Just then, they were interrupted by a knock to the door. Estella froze. Jasper was on high alert. All eyes were on the door. This time, the knock was louder. Estella glared at

Jasper. Her mouth quivered. And then, the door crept open. A tall man dressed all in black with a tweed cap, took slow strides towards the pews. It was only when he entered the space behind a fallen pillar, did Estella recognise his eyes. It was the same man she had met with those two little girls several weeks back. He wasn't a vampire, and certainly not a werewolf. Nor did she think he was human. Jasper said nothing, he eyed the stranger ever suspiciously. The mysterious man said nothing, he just stood there watching Estella like a hawk.

'What are you doing here?' she said, shouting across the church.

The man took off his cap. 'Are you Estella Vincent?' he asked.

'Who wants to know? She replied. "Who are you? and what do you want?'

'Excuse my manners. My name, is Rory.'

Estella became fearful. Her shoulders stiffened as she prepared for attack. Noticing her discomfort, Rory said 'Please do not be alarmed. I am the same as you.' he said.

Estella's eyes widened at the revelation. It was totally unexpected. 'You're a… daemon?'

'Yes, I am.'

Estella fiddled with her fingers. She didn't expect to see another daemon for miles. As far as she knew, there were not many of them left. Not in England, anyway.

'So, what do you want?'

'To help.' he replied.

'Listen, I appreciate it, I really do. But I don't need any help, thank you very much.' Estella was too proud to back down now. And she certainly didn't think some random stranger could offer much in the way of help, considering the entire underworld would soon be on her back.

'Your daughter is under initiation. By aged three, she will already be a master of her craft, ready to rule an entire nation. She, will help our people thrive once again.'

Estella looked puzzled. 'How long have you been following me? and how do you know all of this about my.'

Rory interjected. 'Forgive me for my intrusion. But, ever since the day I laid my eyes on you, my curiosity piqued. With the exception of Lazarus and his mother, you are the first female daemon I've had the pleasure of laying my eyes upon in years. I couldn't stop wondering about you.'

'Where are your daughters? The two little girls?' Estella was curious.

'My daughters? The girls are adopted. I found them as babies, vulnerable, wrapped up on my doorstep covered in blood. God knows how they found me. I practically live in the middle of nowhere. Anyway, the girls are human.'

'Human?'

'I suspect, their father was killed by a werewolf. Their mother gave them up. Why she chose me to this day, is still a mystery. With the underworld thrown into chaos, I have had to send them off to a nice human woman, who has promised to look after them. I nearly killed them both a week ago. My instincts became uncontrollable. I fear, I have become a danger to them.' said Rory.

'So, where Is my daughter?'

'In a town, three hundred and fifty-three miles north of here.'

Estella was stunned to say the least. She couldn't quite believe how much distance there was between herself and her child. Jasper cleared his throat. Rory looked at him, his eyes widened, his face suspicious.

'What do you want with this woman? You, allowed them to take that child.' Said Rory, his mouth hung open.

Estella thought she had misheard. Jasper's eyes became shifty. An uncomfortable feeling brewed within her stomach. With all eyes on him, Jasper became defensive.

'How dare you accuse me of such a thing.' he snapped

Rory studied the young werewolf. He stepped closer to Jasper's tensed face. 'I am a daemon. You may have fooled Estella, but you cannot fool me. This was a set up. You are a traitor.'

Estella couldn't believe her ears. Goose bumps pricked her skin realising she may have been a fool. She gave Jasper a sinister stare. Had her emotions clouded her judgement? Jasper begun to back away from the pew. He kept shaking his head. 'Estella, he is lying' he exclaimed.

Suddenly, much to Estella's surprise, Rory gave chase. "You sneaky little dog. Tell her the truth. You were commissioned by Lazarus.'

'That, is a lie.' Yelled Jasper.

Rory made a dash towards Jasper, who backed away until he was trapped in a corner. Suddenly, Jasper jumped straight towards an old window. Estella, who was now on her feet, watched from afar, still trying to fathom how she could have been so stupid. Glass shattered as Jasper broke the seven-foot-tall window, then subsequently, jumped out of it. Rory studied the shattered stained glass which fell around his feet. He turned to Estella.

'We must go,' he said. 'Hurry.'

Estella hesitated. Could she trust yet another stranger, pretending to care? She was divided. He seemed to know a lot about her daughter, but this could all be a ploy to get her where he wanted, then would kill her. Rory grew impatient.

'Listen, you do not have to trust me. But if you love your daughter, you must hurry. I am not vying for your trust. This, is about the child.' He looked serious.

Estella, fearing she had little to lose at this point, reluctantly followed suit. She was reminded that with every minute wasted there was a potential to never seeing the child again. Before she knew it, she and Rory had left the church, hot on the heels of Jasper.

As the pair left the church, Jasper was nowhere to be seen. Estella was frazzled. She felt responsible. Her face was solemn as she scanned the streets, humans were everywhere. Rory scratched his head, then peered at her.

'I see the sadness in your aura. I lost my own daughter many hundreds of years ago. I know the pain. Lazarus was a friend. But his unscrupulous nature caused a massive divide between us. We have not spoken in half a century. Perhaps I am biased, but your little girl is better suited with you, than she is with him. You actually care.'

Estella was stunned. Why would he say such a thing? He barely knew her. Seeped in paranoia and heightened suspicion, Estella wrinkled her brow at him. She couldn't work him out, one way or the other. Then she said 'Oh I see. This is simply to have the upper hand over him, isn't it?

'What? no, no, no. I didn't mean it as literal as you have taken it.' He quipped.

Estella studied Rory. It all made sense why he was so keen to help. This wasn't about helping her. It was to spite Lazarus. Nevertheless, Estella longed for her child, and was glad for his help, no matter his intensions.

'I appreciate your help.' She mumbled 'So, how do we get there.'

'We teleport. There is, no faster means of travel. And that is our biggest strength.' He said.

Estella was tense. Teleporting oneself hundreds of miles away, was arduous work. 'Can we not just levitate?

Rory looked at her as though she were mad. 'Levitate three hundred miles? Are you insane? It would take days to get there.'

Estella shuffled her feet. 'So…what about Jasper? I cannot allow him to get away with this.'

Rory's expression was deadpan. The lines on his forehead wrinkled. 'Jasper? You mean the werewolf? You're best placing your attention elsewhere. Focus, on getting your child back. You can deal with him later.'

You're right. I'm just being emotional. I can't help wanting to strangle him with his own intestine.' Estella's voice trailed off.

'That is a…imaginative thought. I have no doubts he will be dealt with. Anyway, are you Ready? follow me.' Said Rory.

And just like that, Rory was off. Estella, not wanting to be left behind, had little time to brace herself. Rory was fast and furious, Estella struggled to keep up. For a while, they travelled as a white mist, weaving through time. Suddenly, Estella came to an abrupt stop. She fell headfirst onto a rocky hill, almost breaking her back. The force sent her flying. Rory must have noticed. Suddenly he was stood over her, shaking his head in disbelief.

'You really must try harder. You're a daemon for heaven's sake.'

Feeling annoyed and irritated, Estella snapped. 'Can you just shut u….'

Rory interjected. 'Don't be mad at me because you're not capable of doing something that should come naturally.' He spat. 'Anyway, I don't imagine your back feels too good. Not on those rocks.'

Estella sighed through gritted teeth. She dragged herself to her feet whilst giving Rory dirty looks. 'My back feels just fine. Anyway, how do I know this isn't another elaborate plan to get me where you want me? Look at me, chasing after some stranger. I don't even know if I can trust you.'

'Considering you've already laid your trust in some unscrupulous werewolf I think you ought to.'

'How dare you?' snapped Estella.

'Listen, I can go home right now and be done with it. The only reason I'm even doing this, is for the betterment of my own kind. There aren't many of us left,' he said.

Estella stuck out her lips. She hated to admit it, but perhaps he had a point. She should have known better than to trust a werewolf.

After all, it would be unlikely there were many as genuine as Stefan walking around. She felt a fool, and Rory made it worse by eyeing her as though she were an absolute imbecile. After a moment of awkwardness, the twosome carried on with their journey.

Teleporting was like a cold tornado, only one in which you were stuck in. Like a vacuum sucking you in with every twist and turn, Estella felt nauseous by time they abruptly arrived, with Rory exclaiming. 'Seventeen minutes, and twenty-two seconds…could be worse…'

Suddenly, Rory took a slap to the head. His shocked face scanned Estella's in disbelief. If she were a man, he would have returned the slap across the head, however, Rory didn't hit women, but believed that they too, should not hit a man.

'Don't, do that again,' he snarled, eyes serious.

'I will not. But do not patronize me either.'

Those were Estela's last words before she retched green bile. Rory grimaced as Estella projectile vomited the entire contents of her stomach along the gravel ground. Estella shook as her nails scratched the surface of her palms, so hard, she drew blood. Rory became concerned.

'I take it, you've not teleported often?'

Estella was angry with herself. She felt inferior and inadequate next to Rory. What kind of a daemon was she? It didn't help that he reminded her of her shortcomings every half an hour. Estella drew heavy breaths, allowing the brisk air to fill her lungs until she felt better.

'No, I haven't.' she snapped. 'Long story.'

Estella looked up at the derelict building. It was abandoned, adorned with graffiti. The stench of urine lingered in the air. It was a ghost town. Not even wildlife habited such a place. There were no birds, and definitely no humans. The trees were dead, just a collection of barren snags with crocked branches. It was eerie, even for the undead.

'Where are we?' Estella peered cautiously over her shoulder for any signs of life.

'The town is unnamed, and still pretty much a mystery. No other species have made the journey and gotten out alive. Or so they say. Many don't even know of its existence. His house, is the only one here.'

'Really? well, for the sake of my child, let's hope we do,' said Estella. 'Anyway, how do you know of such a place?'

'That story, is for another day.' Said Rory.

'So, is this it? It looks demolished.'

'No. We must stay quiet. The house, is right over there.'

Rory pointed in the far distance. A hundred feet away from the abandoned building, was a large house surrounded by black and gold gates. Estella looked up to the skies. The orange sun had begun to cast its shadow. She had never seen it like that, the colour was almost red. Rory said, the orange sun was a sign from Lazarus. Apparently, the skies here were never blue. His energy feeds off it, Rory said. Estella stood in awe at the incredibly bizarre surroundings, wondering whether to believe the folklore. She still could not fathom how she had allowed herself to submit to the monster. Speaking of Lazarus as though he were some sort of sorcerer, ran shivers down her spine.

The walk towards the house was unpleasant. Estella's un-beating heart was in her mouth. Rory sensed her fear but kept reassuring her they would be ok. Her legs felt like jelly; her mind was frazzled. Lest of all, Lazarus lived in a mansion evidently larger than Heath Hall, but had given the impression he was averagely poor, and had very little. As they trudged through tall grass, Estella turned to Rory.

'I have to tell you something,' she said.

Rory raised a brow, encouraging her to proceed. Estella's hands shook like a leaf. 'I…I was a vampire.'

'And you fornicated with Lazarus, thus, you're one of us now. I know.' His tone was casual and unsurprised. Estella wondered how the hell he knew all about her, yet he seldom explained how.

'How do you know…'

'I have read the book. All clues point to you; it wasn't that hard to decipher. Book of the Dead, I suggest you read it. Although the scriptures are hidden, there are ways to uncover it.' He quipped.

'Book of the Dead? Interesting. Clearly, I have a lot to learn.' Said Estella, feeling like an unsophisticated newbie. Seconds in, the daemon's stood in front of the house, looking up at the twenty-feet high gates. The house was surrounded by large white pillars, and ornate gargoyle statues that gazed at her as though they were alive. One in particular, winged, with a menacing smirk, overshadowed the other. The black door appeared to be iron, or at least, steel. The daemon's exchanged weary glances, wondering how the hell they would get in. Teleporting wasn't an option. He would see them anyway.

'I'll be decoy, while you try to find a way in.' said Estella, deciding she could use her charms as a distraction. Rory appeared visibly shaken. Suddenly, he jumped the gates, prompting Estella to do the same.

'I'm going to see if I can find a way in around the back. Maybe a window, or something.'

'Great, I'll stay here. Perhaps I'll wiggle about, do a little sway. Hopefully, he'll see me.' said Estella, sounding more confident than she felt.

Seconds in, Rory had disappeared to the back of the house. Estella eyed the gargoyles, as they her. A lone tree, its limbs full and thick, took a backseat behind the statues at the far end of the enormous drive. The house, entirely black, with a hint of white around the windows, had an energy of death. Destruction lingered in the air. The smell of flesh was unmistakable. The more Estella sniffed, the stronger it became. She smelt fear, too. Many tortured souls had departed from such a place. Goosebumps pricked her skin, just as Rory returned.

'You look as though you've seen a ghost.' She exclaimed.

'No ghost, but I've seen your daughter.'

Apparently, Lazarus had company of a woman, whom Rory deemed to be a maid. A werewolf. They were seated around an extremely large table, eating equally large pieces of meat, most of which was definitely human. The baby was seated on her father's lap, seemingly sharing in the delights. The werewolf maid was under instruction and did not look particularly happy. It was obvious she wanted little to do with Lazarus or the baby and was held against her will.

'He is distracted. Now, is the perfect time to sneak in. I have seen a way in through a high window to the back. Its open.' Said Rory 'follow me.'

The daemon's crept behind the mansion like thieves in the night. There was a huge back porch, with large sliding glass doors. Rory felt it best they avoid such an entry, fearing it to be too close to Lazarus's dining room. Instead, they took the route of a window ajar, thirty feet away from the sliding doors, and three floors up. As the daemons shot up the wall like spiders, Rory gently tugged at the window. After little probing, it slid open wide enough for the two to crawl through. They landed in a very large bedroom, laid out with chequered marble floors and a four-poster bed with surrounding net curtains.

'I mean, this looks more like a museum, than a bedroom. What's with the huge fireplace and bizarre mannequins?' Estella gawked.

'Never one to do anything by halves.' Whispered Rory.

As the daemon's made their way out of the room, they arrived at a hallway. There were a dozen doors on either side, dark mahogany and polished to a shine. Estella eyed the butterfly staircase in the middle, littered with various portraits along the walls. Stern faces in period dress, historical figures from another era. There were other portraits of people undressed, doing all manner of things. Estella caught sight of a couple making out, whilst a monster suckled her bosoms.

'Good grief, these pictures are vile.' She spoke beneath her breath.

Frankly, Heath Hall was a pussy cat in comparison. Lazarus's home was a lion. Fierce suits of armour stood in guard on either side of the stairs, swords in hand. Evidently Lazarus had a great deal of wealth and had turned his home into a medieval fortress. Estella and Rory peered at each other. They agreed to take either side of the stairs. They had to tag team in order to defeat Lazarus, but they needed his guard down.

'While he's distracted with you, I'll take the child.'

'Ok.' Estella was unsure. She wanted her child and did not really like the idea of anyone else taking her. Nonetheless, it was likely to be the only way around it.

'You will have to go ahead. Tease him, declare your love. Just make him want you.' said Rory.

'Do you really think this is going to work? I have a horrible feeling. One I can't shake off.' Estella was hesitant.

'Well, unless you've got another plan, we better get a move on.' Rory's voice was unsympathetic.

THIRTY-ONE

I had lost everything, including hope. If you had told me that my undead existence would never be the same again, I would have ridiculed you with shameless mockery. I had everything and wanted for nothing. I never knew what it meant to be taken for granted, until I took it for granted. The vampire life was the best life. We ruled the world. Our ignorance served a sense of entitlement, I, **was** *the superior race. I had no fear, and no limitations were made against me. Now, I live in hiding. Like a circus freak, I'm ostracized by society. Very few of my kind are left. And not all are for me or my plight. Power is everything, and, right now, I am powerless. Like a pauper, no one wants much to do with me. Their only incentive, being my daughter. I would do it all again for my daughter. She is about the only thing that keeps me going. But sometimes I am not sure if that's even enough.*

Marc, you were my first true love. I am regretfully repentant, guilt-ridden, and have rightly been served my just deserts. If I shall die here, please know that I had never stopped loving you. I simply couldn't love enough, not the way in which you deserved. I failed us both. Marc, if you can even vaguely hear my thoughts, I am at an unknown location, in an excessively big mansion, owned by a daemon. I believe I am three hundred miles north from the biggest werewolf town. Please, save my child.

Estella felt a fool reaching out for Marc. As she scribbled her thoughts upon her bloodied psalms, she knew, it was hopeless. Telepathy between distinct species was unheard of, and, unlikely. Still, she had nothing to lose by trying. It had been four days since that fateful visit to Lazarus's mansion. Events had taken an horrendous turn for the worse. Lazarus was too powerful. Rory was knocked unconscious. Estella put up a good fight but was ultimately struck down. The next thing she knew, she was trapped in this cellar of a prison, hungry and dehydrated. Her feet bound with iron wire of the strongest kind; Estella had cut her feet to set herself free. She wasn't entirely sure why she had not healed, but, for the last two days, she sat soothing her wounds, grimacing at the bright red cut covering both feet. Despite trying to turn, the daemon wouldn't come out to play. She suspected Lazarus had conjured dark magic, or some other sorcery to render her powers useless. Estella had bouts of sleep to preserve her energy, as she hoped for her release. Estella knew if she didn't find her way out of Lazarus dungeon soon enough, she could die.

Estella angrily banged her fists against the hard stone floor. She kicked her legs about like a disobedient child as dust and gravel stuck between her toes.

'Let me go, you son of a bitch.' She yelled, as her voice echoed back.

'Stop resisting Estella. You will have to eat your hand.'

Estella froze. She looked out into the darkness, wondering where the voice was coming from. The jingle of keys could be heard. A bright light shone brightly from nowhere. It was Lazarus. His footsteps were slow and strong. She tensed as he approached.

'You're so stubborn. It would be easier if you just accept defeat.' He snarled, staring down at her through cold eyes.

'Fuck off, you bastard.' Estella screamed as adrenaline pumped through her body.

'I have been called worse. I take little offence.'

Lazarus was squirming. Estella growled, willing the daemon to make an appearance. He laughed heartily at her anguish.

'No wonder you are so screwed up. With a mother like yours, I would be too.'

Those words cut Lazarus like a knife. He marched up to her, knelt down, then slapped her hard across the face. Memories of his childhood and his strained relationship with his mother, was a sore talking point. Estella smirked, knowing she had hit him where it hurt. He grabbed her by the hair, yanking it until she slumped back onto the wall. Estella was far too weak to react, but what happened next, took her by surprise. Lazarus sunk back into the wall inches from where she sat. He begun to weep like a broken man. He turned to her, seemingly remorseful.

'I never mean to hurt you. Estella, please believe me when I tell you that was never my intention. I have been on this quest longer than you could imagine. Along my journey, I have met many vampires, both good and bad, and everything else in-between. Most of them cunning, I can't begin to tell you how many times I have had to dodge my own death. None were suitable for my offspring. But you were different from the others. Like a beacon of light, you were refreshing. Challenging, but not overbearingly so. I nearly wished we had never met as I couldn't bear the thought of inflicting pain on you. It probably means absolutely nothing to you now, but I actually liked you-very much'.

Estella stirred. Her eyes hurt. It was easier and less painful to keep them closed. Her body ached all over. Her head had taken so many blows, it felt like she had been wrestled by ten daemons in a headlock. The last thing she cared about was anything coming out of Lazarus's mouth, but strangely enough, it brought a bizarre sense of comfort.

'I am very hungry. I need to eat.' She whispered.

'I have no problem feeding you, Estella. But you're not taking the child' he warned.

'She is my child. And you have no right to take her away from me.'

'Actually, she is our child. This could be so easy. We could be one happy bloody family, but you're too damned resistant. Bawling about your old vampire life, instead of embracing the new one given to you.'

Estella turned to him in horror. He actually felt he had done her a favour. His ignorance was shocking. Oh, how she wanted to rip her claws through him, if only she had the energy. She lowered her head, weeping with frustration.

'I've little enthusiasm or energy to entertain your argument. All I ask for, is something to eat. Please Lazarus, I'm dying.' She begged.

Estella was met with quietude. For a while, Lazarus said nothing. The only sound to be heard was the faint gasps of their breath. Lazarus had his head lowered, buried in his hands. Then he said. 'She is better protected here with me. You cannot defend her against the other species. Nor are you as powerful or experienced as I am.' With that, Lazarus got up and headed back out the door. The heavy cast iron door slammed with a thud. It was an hour before Lazarus returned. Estella was curled upon the floor, using the back of her arm as a cushion.

'Here'

Lazarus chucked a piece of flesh in front of her as though she were a dog. It was a human arm. Skinny and spindly, Estella doubted it would do much good. Still, she was grateful. Estella quickly bit a massive chunk out of it. Lazarus watched as she gorged upon the flesh, hardly stopping for air. Finally, Estella looked up, her mouth dripping with blood.

'Thank you.' she said, with a mouth full.

'I'll be going now.' said Lazarus, turning to the door.

Estella put her head up. He was leaving her here, holding her captive like a prisoner. She panicked.

'Wait. You can't leave me here forever.'

'Yes, I can. Estella, I cannot let you go. You will only challenge me, then, I'd have to kill you.'

Estella studied the man without a heart. He was a totally different person to the vision she had in her head. Her hate for him flourished. She wanted him dead. However, she went full on survival mode, then said,

'No, I love you. Please Lazarus, we can be a family.'

Lazarus stopped in his tracks. He turned to her. 'I can smell the lies rolling off your tongue. You don't expect me to believe that do you?'

'I'm not trying to convince you. Lazarus, I am telling the truth. All I think about, is you. Every night before I go to sleep, you are the last thing on my mind. I wish, things could be the same.'

Estella pleaded through wet tears, hoping to soften his heart and change his mind. She reached out to him with arms outstretched. He glared at her with his piercing green eyes, evidently trying to work her out. As he pondered whether or not Estella was telling the truth, Lazarus stepped closer. Estella's eyes widened as he knelt beside her, then held her face between his hands. Unexpectedly, he begun to stroke her cheeks, studying her face as though he were scrutinising every line. Estella froze.

'Ok.' he said.

Within seconds, Lazarus had his lips pressed against hers. Open mouthed and eager, Estella returned his passionate kisses. Soon enough, there was an exchange of hot wet kisses. Lazarus grabbed hold off her shirt, ripping it from her back. He planted kisses upon her chest, then yanked her trousers off, guided by her hands. Estella was excited, although knew she shouldn't be. It was all a game. However, she was a great player and vowed to play until the end.

'Turn around' he said, protesting she got on all fours.

Estella cringed. She felt terrible. Her mind relayed back to all those months ago when they had their first encounter. This had been her undoing. Yet, here she was, doing it all over again. He penetrated her with great force. With her knickers hung halfway around her thighs, she jerked back forcefully with every thrust. Estella bit her lips through gritted teeth, as the beast had her yet again. It went on for at least an hour. Her knees rubbed sorely against the hard gravelled floor. She moaned, she groaned, yet nothing brought it to an end any sooner. Her patience wore thin. She silently rejoiced when it came to an end. Lazarus spanked her hard on the bottom, before pulling himself together. Feeling even worse than she had felt before, Estella turned to him.

'That was great.' she lied.

Lazarus looked proud. He beamed at her with a wink 'Maybe we'll do it again sometime.'

Estella was stunned. He hadn't been fooled. Lazarus got up to leave, demanding she stay put. He headed to the door. Horror crept over her face as she struggled to contain her displeasure. Then, it all came out.

'How fucking dare, you, you bastard. You have ruined my life. I will kill you.'

Lazarus smirked 'I would like to see you try. Be grateful I don't leave you here to rot.' He spat, turning for the door.

And those were the words that propelled Estella into action. She wasn't sure where she mustered the energy from but couldn't seem to stop herself. Suddenly, she sprung up and pounced at him as he walked away. It was unexpected, Lazarus didn't see it coming. The brawl begun. The daemons fought like wolves. Lazarus, stronger and bigger, knocked her to the ground twice, but each time Estella rose to her feet prepared for the challenge. She wrestled him with vigour. He held her into a tight lock, tightening her head between the crease of his arms. Just then, the iron gate opened. Lazarus had left it unlocked. Estella was surprised to see Rory sauntering in. He was horrified.

'What on earth.' his mouth hung open.

Estella was choking, but her eyes cried out to Rory for help. Lazarus had his back to the door and seemed more consumed with killing her than anything else. His grip tightened. Rory looked on in disbelief. Estella seemed to be barely conscious; eyes semi-closed, drool hung from the sides of her mouth. Rory growled. He begun to change. Lazarus heard, then swiftly spun to the door. He was shocked at Rory's presence, then decided not to bother with Estella. Lazarus released his grip, dropping her motionless body to the floor like a ragdoll. He, and Rory were going to battle it out. Rory growled, so did he.

The daemons fought hard. Standing over seven feet tall, they were a fearsome pair. They grappled and wrestled with fierce agility and swiftness. Lazarus, the stronger of the two, had the upper hand. He flung Rory through the dungeon-sending him crashing into the cast iron walls with a thud. Lazarus stomped towards him baring his teeth, fists clenched. Rory staggered back to his feet, ready for battle. He ran towards him, then swiped Lazarus on the stomach with four-inch nails. Lazarus hadn't seen it coming. Rory took joy watching blood ooze from his wounds. This made Lazarus angry. He roared loudly, eyes red. Lazarus, despite his injury, was still mighty strong. He made a lung for Rory, then managed to grab hold of him by the scruff of his neck. Sensing Lazarus was weakened by his wounds, Rory swiped Lazarus to the face, managing to poke out his eye. Lazarus released his grip. Rory ran to the other side of the dungeon, prompting Lazarus to follow suit. Unbeknown to them both, Estella had woken. She laid still, waiting for the crucial moment. She watched as Lazarus pounced towards Rory, sending the pair of them crashing to the ground. Lazarus had the upper hand. Rory was pinned beneath him. Estella crept towards the warring daemons, her head bobbing like a pigeon. Suddenly, she lunged herself at Lazarus's back, shoving her entire hand straight through his firm flesh. Lazarus hollered in pain as she pulled out his heart. He made attempts to stand up, but was kicked to the back by Estella, before subsequently falling to the ground. Rory rolled free. They looked upon Lazarus's lifeless body. He was face down, the gaping hole in his back oozed black blood. Estella couldn't quite believe it. She shot Rory a look of disbelief. He smiled wearily, shrugging his shoulders.

'He had it coming.' He spoke.

'For sure.' smiled Estella.

'He almost killed me, and I thought he had killed you. I was left for dead, tied up against a tree.' Said Rory.

Estella studied Rory's face. He looked grateful to be alive. She owed him her life. 'I thought you were dead. Rory, I cannot thank you enough. Anyway, where is the baby?' Estella became worried.

Rory became remorseful. 'I think the werewolf has taken her. I searched each and every room before I arrived upon this…dungeon. But she was nowhere to be seen. But please do not worry. We will, get her back.' He promised.

Cold tears ran against Estella's cheeks. She nodded, too grieved to say anything else. Rory placed his arm around her shoulders. The daemons left the dungeon. The door hung off the hinge. It swung lose, toing and froing. The shock of Lazarus death, was still a lot to take in.

THIRTY-TWO

'Shh, we can't let them see us.' Rory pushed Estella back with his arm. He had poked his head around the door, watching and waiting.

'They're going to kill her' she whispered, visibly shaken.

The daemon's stumbled upon Jasper and his family. Lazarus's maid wolf, was there, too. Rory was stumped. He had checked every room, all of them were empty. Perhaps they had left and returned, whatever the case was, an entire congregation of werewolves now gathered in the drawing room. They stood in a circle, laughing and jeering. On close inspection, the maid wolf was being held hostage. She was seated to the corner, her mouth gagged. A woman, Jasper's aunt, was stood in the middle, roaring with laughter, holding the baby up for all to see. And there, was Jasper. His face appeared distraught.

'Look at her. Such a precious little thing. I wonder how she feels about another squeeze to her little hand.' She snarled.

Just then, cries could be heard. The infant was being harassed. She appeared to have been attacked for attempting to claw the werewolf's face off.

'Do that again, and you'll have another thing coming.' She yelled.

'Burn the child, burn the child.' A man's voice boomed out.

Estella tightened her grip onto Rory's arm. She felt as though she might pass out and had to steady herself from the shock.

'We can take on a few, but we must distract them. Take them down one by one, as they're stronger in numbers.' Whispered Rory, peering behind the kitchen door.

The kitchen sat directly opposite the drawing room. Estella was beside herself, so Rory had to think alone. While she riled herself up, pacing back and forth, Rory took a large wooden cup from one of the units, then hurled it towards the floor.

'That, should do the trick.' He spoke.

Back in the drawing room, the werewolves were alerted by the noise. There were whispers amongst them. Suddenly, Jasper's aunt said. 'Harry, go and check on that.' Rory eyed Estella. She became rigid, eyes intense. Her lips pursed tightly as though she were ready to pounce. They waited behind the door. Footsteps were heard heading their way. Minutes in, a young man with mousy hair entered the kitchen. Casually dressed in a black hooded top and denim jeans, his hands were tucked into his pockets. Rory grabbed hold off him. Estella cuffed her hands over his mouth, whilst Rory placed him in a strangle hold. The kill was quick and easy. The werewolf struggled a little but was no match for the two. Seconds later, they dropped his lifeless body to the kitchen floor. His neck had been severed.

'There are at least eight of them left.' Estella whispered, back at their positions behind the door.

'They may send a couple in to check on their inbred.' Said Rory coyly.

'Do you really think we're going to sit back and allow you to grow up? We won't stand a chance.' Said another female voice coming from the drawing room, loud and threatening.

The daemon's exchanged cautious glances. Then a voice said, 'Harry, hurry the hell up, will you. We want to kill the little brat already.'

'Oh no you won't' whispered Estella, her adrenaline through the roof.

It wasn't long before several footsteps could be heard going up the stairs. The daemon's waited, hoping to strike. The werewolves searched the rooms upstairs. They pottered about, doors slamming and opening. After a while, footsteps we heard bounded back down to the ground floor. Suddenly, Jasper entered the kitchen. Estella froze. Rory lunged at him, snuffing him in the face. Jasper's muffled screams went unheard. Estella kneed him where it hurt. Rory wanted to snap his head off, but Estella preferred him to suffer.

'Not yet.' She whispered. 'I want him to see me. I need him to realise what he has done.'

Estella knelt beside Jasper on the kitchen floor. Rory had his arms wrapped around his neck, his face reddened, eyes shocked. Estella demanded he look her in the eye.

'How could you do this to me? I foolishly trusted you.'

Jasper spluttered. His shameful eyes bore regrets. He put his hand up in forgiveness. Estella, spat in his face. 'That is how I feel about traitors.' she snapped. Estella stood to her feet. Rory took care of the rest. Jasper put up a struggle, but his windpipe was compromised. He struggled for breath, whilst Rory tightened his grip. It was over by the time the others grew suspicious.

With the discovery of Jasper and Harry's deaths, the werewolves were beside themselves with fear, wondering who was responsible. The daemons had snuck out through the large kitchen window and were now on the other side of the house, peering through the drawing room from the outside. The werewolves had scattered. The baby had been left with Jasper's aunt, whilst the others checked the mansion.

'How are we going to get back in there, unseen?' Estella said beneath her breath.

Just then, a voice was heard behind them. 'You slimy little snakes.'

The daemon's turned to an older man. Estella recognised the face. It was, Jasper's uncle. He leered and snarled, showcasing his teeth. Seconds in, he began to turn. Rory glared at Estella. They had to do something quick.

'Not so fast.' Rory pounced on the werewolf, knocking him to the ground. The two men tussled for a while. Estella looked on, then decided to get involved. With eyes blaring red, she stormed up to the werewolf, dragging him off the floor. Together, they broke his arm, then dislocated his jaw. The werewolf was dragged across the back garden. Estella took a bite from his neck. Rory joined in. They chewed at his limbs. Surprisingly, the werewolf was sweet. His flesh was better than most. This was unusual. Estella got carried away. She wanted to carry on eating, but was stopped by Rory, who reminded her they had a job to do. Estella wiped her blood-stained mouth with the back of her hand as they crept back towards the drawing room window.

'We can take those three down.' She Estella, pushing her head up against the glass.

'Where are they? Perhaps, they're still searching.' Said Rory, pulling a hankie from his jacket pocket.

'Fuck it, I'm going in.' Estella shot off towards the door, with Rory not far behind.

As the daemons crept through the front door, one of the men were headed down the stairs. It was too late. The daemons were seen. He yelled for the other three, who then made a great big fuss. The daemon's ran back outside. They hid at the back of the mansion. Rory had a shovel in hand; they braced themselves for a brawl. Voices could be heard as the werewolves searched the front of the house. Footsteps ran along the gravel. Estella's shoulders stiffened.

'Argh'

A werewolf came speeding towards the garden wall. He was then knocked out by Rory with the shovel to the head. Rory ploughed at him, striking the werewolf repeatedly until his body grew limp. Blood pooled his head; his face was crushed. Estella had seen it all, but none quite as bad as this. She squirmed, hoping not to projectile vomit her distaste. Whilst Estella's attentions were preoccupied, she was jumped on by an older man, who had snuck up on them from the other side. He dragged her to the ground, taking a bite from her shoulder. Rory became panicked. He made attempts to drag the werewolf off Estella's back, but the werewolf had Estella in the grasp off his hands. He was bigger than the others, and seemingly stronger. Estella tried to fling him off her back but was bitten several times. She winced as the beast clawed her viciously. Rory struck the werewolf to the back of the head. He wrapped his arms around his neck, but was bitten so badly, he had to release his grip. Rory had to command the daemon. That was the only way to deter this wolf, who had pinned Estella to the ground, and appeared to be biting her to death. Rory begun to shapeshift. His growls intensified as the monster took over. Estella made attempts to change, too, but was too weak. Within minutes, Rory's daemon took over his body. The beast rose to his feet, a staggering seven and a half feet tall. He took a massive swipe at the werewolf's back, plunging his claws into his neck. The werewolf hollered as Rory delivered a devastating blow. Rory had plunged his hand into the werewolf's stomach, pulling out his vital organ. The werewolf released his hold on Estella, then was kicked in the back by Rory, who sent him flying in the air, landing in a heap at the other side of Lazarus's huge garden. Rory staggered. Estella was motionless. She needed blood, fast. Rory sunk to the floor, jerking as his body became human again. He cut his wrist, then rolled Estella on her back, demanding she drink. Estella was badly injured but slowly opened her eyes. She struggled for breath. Rory dripped his wound over her mouth, making sure she ingested his blood. Seconds in, Estella coughed and spluttered. Her eyes sparkled again. Rory looked relieved.

'Count yourself lucky that you aren't a vampire. Only daemons, can survive wounds as deep as yours. You should be dead already.' Said Rory, matter of fact.

'I guess your blood has nothing to do with it.' Estella smiled. Her sarcasm went unnoticed.

'Indeed, it has a lot to do with it. You've replenished faster,' he said.

'I owe you, my life.' She said, as Rory pulled her to her feet.

'You owe me nothing. I look after my people. This is what we do. With the exception of Lazarus of course, who was just hell bent on power.' Smiled Rory.

'You can say that again.' Said Estella with a twinkle in her eye.

'I take it we have killed the lot, except the woman. One of us can distract her.' Said Rory.

The daemon's crept back towards the house, eyeing through the drawing room window. The daemon and child had disappeared. Lazarus's maid had been killed. She was slaughtered in the chair, her head hung as blood dripped to the floor. Her hands still bound behind her back.

'Shit. She's taken my baby.' Wailed Estella, her voice increasing in volume.

'You must remain quiet. She could still be inside. Follow me.'

Estella followed Rory back inside the house. They searched the bottom quarter but came upon nothing. Each time they entered a room, Estella held her breath, hoping to find her baby. The daemon's crept up the stairs, one either side, then met up at the top of the landing.

'I'll search rooms on the right, you the left.' Said Rory.

Just then, the daemon's stopped in their tracks. It was the werewolf. She was whispering to the baby. The sound of water could be heard. Estella's eyes widened with shock. Rory peered cautiously over her shoulder. The werewolf was in the bathroom, three doors to the left off the hallway.

'Come on,' he said.

The daemon's crept the length towards the bathroom door. They listened in at the sound of splashing water. The child was distressed, and whimpering. The werewolf appeared to be trying to soothe it, singing some lullaby song. Estella grimaced. 'Crazy bitch.' She mouthed.

Rory motioned with his eyes. They geared up to burst in unannounced. On the count of three, Rory pushed the door open. The werewolf gasped. The child's deep brown eyes perked up with the arrival of her mother.

'All your men are dead. We've wiped out your entire family. Give us the child, and you will live.' Said Rory, taking cautious steps towards the bath.

The werewolf was perched on the outside, while the child sat in the tub partially dressed. The woman quivered. Her eyes were wild. With a trembling lip, she reached for the child. However, before she had a chance, Estella pounced on her, grabbing her neck into a choke hold. The werewolf gasped for breath.

'Touch her, and you're dead.' Said Estella.

Rory walked over, then took the soaking wet child out of the bath. Her cotton trousers miserably clung to her wet body, causing some distress to the child, who began to cry. Estella's heart was heavy. The werewolf pleaded to be sparred, but Estella saw red. She sunk her teeth into her neck, blood splattered along the porcelain tub, and the mirror, too. The werewolf grabbed her arm, but Estella was adamant to strangle her to death. She squeezed her grip around her neck until the werewolf struggled for breath. Rory looked on as Estella finished off the werewolf with one single blow to the head, banging her skull harshly along the bath. Her skull cracked open, as blood pooled the floor. Estella released her lifeless body.

'We best get out of here.' Said Rory.

Estella agreed. She took her child from Rory's arms, fearing her feet may buckle. Exhaustion wasn't foreign for the undead, Estella felt she had run a marathon. Icy tears fell along her cheeks as she embraced her child again. Despite Rory's pleas to leave Lazarus's mansion, Estella was too engrossed with her child to care. The baby babbled at her mother; Estella kissed her tenderly on the cheek.

THIRTY-THREE

The atmosphere buzzing around the table of the great hall, was delightfully different. Cerberus had woken. At nearly three thousand years old, his deathly white skin took on an illuminous glow. He was smartly dressed; his shimmery black robe sparkled under the candle wick lights. For a man who had spent the best part of several centuries buried in a chrome casket, he looked remarkably well. Cerberus demanded all residents of the castle wear their best attire. It was midnight, the vampire's peak hour. Lorcan was already seated. He had his arms wrapped around a mystery woman. She was tall and willowy, with a rather long neck. She was stunningly beautiful, resembling an Egyptian goddess, with her raven black hair and bronzed skin. Lorcan kissed her hand several times, evidently, he couldn't resist her charms. Marc sat directly in front of the couple. He caught Lorcan's eye once or twice and would nod his approval with a glint in his eye. He had never seen Lorcan happier. Within minutes, Achylls, Elena, and Stramus, entered the hall. It was quite a spectacle. As usual, Achylls was sexily dressed in sheer black lace which clung to every curve. Elena looked like a fairy princess. Her white Cinderella style dress was incredibly bouffant and seemed more fitting for a five-year-old. Stramus, with his tall wiry stature, looked superbly polished with his deep blue robe draped over his bony shoulders.

'Is this…everyone?' Cerberus's voice was metallic and nasally. His red eyes scanned the table.

'No, we have more to come.' Said Elena, her voice higher than most.

Shortly thereafter, Runa came bounding in. She seemed flustered but gave her apologies for being fashionably late. Cerberus seemed unimpressed. He eyed her callously, priming his lips taut like a disapproving parent. Runa pulled out a chair beside her cousin Marc, greeting him warmly with a smile. Marc admired his cousin's keen sense of fashion. As usual, she was stylishly dressed. Her navy-coloured velvet dress, fitted like a glove. She even wore a matching hat.

'I think I should address you as, Your Royal Highness.' he smirked, squeezing her arm playfully.

'It wasn't intentional, I promise.' she smiled.

'Your style, is like no other.'

'Now, who else are we waiting for? I must remind you all, punctuality is of upmost importance. This, is ridiculous.' Cerberus was irritable.

Just then, the door swung open. Two couples strutted in, followed by Ewin and Edgar. Acheron strolled hand in hand with his new young thing under Achylls watchful eye. She had already given her approval, and tonight, they had both enjoyed their new delight. The girl looked incredible. Marc struggled to recognise the girl from the dungeon. He couldn't believe how different she looked. But there was something else different about her, and not just her appearance. She had been bitten. Gone was her humanly innocence. The vampire influence was written all over her. She wore a crisp white dress, an odd combination of silk and lace, with a gaping hole exposing her lower back. Her long dark hair hung over her breasts. Achylls smiled as they took seats beside her. The next couple to sit at the table was Bernadette, the beautiful redhead. She hung off Adrian's arm like a new accessory. Ewin and Edgar, with his pipe rooted firmly on the side of his mouth, looked like real gentlemen. Both dressed in white shirts and black robes; they had small bowties hooked tightly under their necks. Runa smirked. Cerberus was angry. It was fifteen minutes past midnight.

'This is outrageous.' he slammed his fists on the table.

'Beg us pardon, sir, Cerberus.' said Achylls.

'And where the bloody hell is Lucas?' he asked, scanning chalk white faces around the table.

No one knew where Lucas was, not even his brother, Lorcan. Achylls knew he had been with Lilith and figured they must have had quite the session. However, she kept this to herself. Suddenly, the door flung open as though it had been propelled by a great wind.

'I am ever so sorry. Time ran away with me.'

All eyes were on Lucas. He appeared sheepish and seemed to have dressed in a hurry. He pulled out a chair next to Edgar, who in turn, wrinkled his nose curiously. Lucas, smelt rotten. Achylls looked around for Lilith. The timid blonde was nowhere to be seen. Cerberus snarled with disgust. He was a stickler for time keeping and felt he had been disrespected.

'Can we begin?' he snarled, his teeth on show.

All eyes focused on their master. Now, was time for the serious part. Most of the vampires already knew what was going on, but some had no idea, including Marc.

'I am sure by now, some of you know why I have woken. Truth be known, I couldn't sleep in peace. I am disgusted. I cannot fathom events which have taken place, right under our very noses. We have a new child among us. A hybrid daemon, and a threat to us all.'

'What?' Runa screwed her eyes up, trying to make sense of Cerberus's revelation. She turned to Marc. His expression was frozen; his shoulders became tense. Cerberus turned to Runa

'Runa, is there a problem? What is it you don't understand, dear girl?'

'Who is the child? She asked.

'I suggest you ask your cousin, Marc. The child, belongs to Estella.'

The gasps in the hall could be heard a mile off. Everyone glared at Marc, as if he were the child himself. Mouths fell open, eyes bulged as though ready to pounce.

'Christ.' exclaimed Elena.

'We thought you woke for the killings, to avenge Orpheus death!' said Ewin, with his dark sense of humour.

'My brother's death will be avenged in due time. My suspicions fall upon a particular daemon. That will be dealt with after Estella's capture. And the child.' Said Cerberus.

'I heard this vile rumour but still don't believe such a thing. Explain to me, how is it that Estella, a vampire, has given birth?' Adrian was yelling.

'Not anymore. She fornicated under the watchful eye of Marc, who foolishly had no clue she was exchanging bodily fluids with a daemon.'

Marc thought he might lose consciousness at the sound of Cerberus's voice. The table was spinning. Everything became a blur, voices was inaudible. He shook so violently, the vampires around the table shrieked in horror. They had never seen this reaction in a vampire before. Runa became hysterical.

'What is happening to him.' She cried.

Within seconds Marc had collapsed. He fell off his chair, landing headfirst on the smooth marbled floor. He was unresponsive. Apollyon felt a sense of guilt. He was the first to attempt Marc's revival. He leaped off his seat to attend to the poorly vamp.

'He's gone into shock. There is nothing we can do until he comes round again.' he said.

'Give him a sip of blood. That might do the trick.' yelled Lorcan.

Cerberus rolled his eyes in annoyance. 'Leave him alone. What is the matter with you all? You're all behaving like humans. It is shock, nothing else. What do you expect, having a wife for a whore.'

As soon as the last words had rolled off Cerberus's tongue, Marc roused. He opened his eyes and was shocked to see the residents of Castle Dravenherd peering down at him as if he were some sort of exotic animal. He sprung to his feet, then casually brushed himself down. He turned to Cerberus, pointing at him with his index finger.

'Don't you dare touch her.' he yelled.

A shadowed silence filled the air. Everyone eyed each other vigilantly. Words were unspoken, but the vampires all thought the same. The search for Estella and the child, was imminent. Marc turned around and walked away. His echoey footsteps paced fast and furiously as he strutted through the hall doors. A great silence followed his departure. Runa left her seat, then scurried after her cousin. Minutes in, she was at his bedroom door.

'Marc. Can I come in?'

'Runa. I am in no mood for banter. I must leave this castle at once.'

Despite her cousin's protest, Runa pushed the door open. She was worried about his wellbeing. She felt if anyone could talk him round; it would be her. As she peered her head around the door, Marc was sat at the old wooden desk, his head in his hands. He had written a letter, then swiftly tucked it away in his pockets. Runa stepped inside.

'Marc, I only want to help. Please don't push me away.'

'I am not discussing this.' He said.

'Please hear me out. If, this is in anyway true, that baby will destroy us. We will be under duress, forced to live on synthetic blood or other means for an eternity. The daemon's hate us. We'll become a slave nation again.'

Marc turned on his chair. His eyes were red. 'Runa, I, will deal with this myself. I want Estella alive.'

Runa shook her head. 'Dear cousin, Estella was involved with another man. How could you be so weak?'

Marc was stunned. 'Damn you. I will show you who's weak.'

Marc pushed over the desk in a deadly rage, shattering a nearby window. He turned to Runa. The veins in his forehead pulsed with anger. Marc flew at her, grabbing her by the throat. Runa wrestled him. She swiped at his face, then kicked him to the shin. The vampires flung each other around on every wall, crashing into it as bits of plaster crumbled around them. The vampires tussled relentlessly, neither really trying to cause serious harm to the other. Suddenly Achylls marched in.

'Stop that at once, the pair of you.'

Marc released his grip on his fiery cousin. The warring vampires turned to Achylls. Fangs bared with venom. Marc hissed loudly like a snake, then brushed past the women, slamming the door behind him. Runa brushed herself down. Her dress was torn, her hat missing.

'Runa, it is little use wasting energy on your pathetic excuse of a cousin. Estella is a dead woman walking. And that baby, is ours.' She hissed.

Within hours of Cerberus's fateful meeting, the twelve strong vampire clan had left Castle Dravenherd in search of Estella and the child. Marc's whereabouts was unknown. Their first stop was Killbraith. Cerberus was confident Estella would be found within 24 hours, and demanded posters be put up around the town. A rally was chaired, igniting waves of hatred by the other vamps. The hunt for Estella, was on. An uncomfortable fear settled in the pit of Runa's stomach.

She feared Marc would be killed in protest. Since the revelation, Apollyon was a changed man. He was determined and seemed willing to do anything for Estella's capture. Killing Marc would be a viable option. He made this clear in conversation with Acheron.

'Is the child a hybrid?' yelled a woman with mousy brown hair and neon yellow eyes.

'Yes. The child is a hybrid daemon monstrosity, and very dangerous to our species. We need to eliminate it before this thing grows and dictates our existence.' said Cerberus.

'We need to enlist the help of the werewolves. They too, will be under instruction from the child.'

'The wolves, have their own agenda.' said a tall thin man.

'It's imperative. We need all the help we can get. Estella has the strength of two of us, we can't allow daemons to roam around with us on these streets.'

It was an hour before the gathering ceased. Cerberus led the way, inflicting terror and torment on any unsuspecting soul to cross their paths. The humans were curfewed, but that didn't stop some random soul disobeying the regulation. The vampires ripped apart a young man. He looked about twenty. He was coerced by Elena, the beautiful blonde, then jumped upon by the others. It was carnage. This went against everything Runa believed in.

'Runa don't look so darned miserable. Your cousin is an idiot.' snapped Bernadette.

'You're a mere girl. What do you know about idiots?'

'Be quiet the pair of you. We have a long mission ahead of us tonight, so you may as well get on.' said Cerberus firmly.

The streets were quiet. The nightlights served little purpose to the town, it was dark and hard to see. The vampires decided to venture to Glides to spread news of the child. With the arrival of vampires on their territory, the risk of war was likely, but Cerberus thought it a risk worth taking. The vampires travelled fifteen miles.

Most teleported, others levitated. It wasn't long before they reached their destination. Like thugs at a football match, the vampires took to the streets, parading strong and proud. The town was asleep, not a soul could be seen. On Cerberus's order, the vampires mimicked the call of the wolf. Ten minutes later, most of the werewolves had taken to the streets. The weary curious eyed wolfs, congregated in small packs, wondering what the hell was going on. Cerberus stood amongst his men, centred, with arms outstretched. Some of the other vampires, were dubious of such a plan.

'I'm not so sure this was the best idea,' admitted Ewin with a frown.

'It's little too late now.' Spat Acheron.

Evidently, the werewolves didn't take well to the presence of the vampires. They walked with staggering gate. Some more sceptical wolves had already begun their change. Cerberus waved his hands in protest, exclaiming he didn't come to war.

'I come not to war, but to call a truce. My fellow species, we have come with a revelation.' he shouted.

Cerberus's pleas fell upon deaf ears. Some of the werewolves became angry begun throwing stones at the clan.

'Get out of our town.' one shouted.

'We will kill you all,' said another.

'We come in peace' said Apollyon, trying to settle the herd.

It took a while for emotions to settle. Nonetheless, with enough reassurance, the werewolves had calmed down and agreed to hear them out. Cerberus offered a generous reward for Estella's kidnap. The werewolves were not sold on the idea of such a reward, fearing Estella meant little to them than she meant to the vampires. They were angry over blood and wanted a trade-off for humans. But this meant the vampires would have to take a backseat and feed off synthetic blood for another century.

'No way is that a fair trade. We need to eat, too,' shouted Acheron.

'That plastic blood is killing our species.' moaned Achylls.

'That is not our problem. We eat meat. And the humans are the tastiest meat there is.' said a werewolf with dark hair and piercing eyes.

'We will only help if you stop taking our food. It's that simple. Otherwise, that child belongs to us if we find it first.'

'The child belongs to no one. Do you think you will be free to roam killing those humans as you please? Of course not. You will be forced to eat grass like the rest of us. The child, will feed you rations.' Said Cerberus.

'How do you expect a daemon hybrid to live off rations. I'm sure it needs to eat, too' yelled a werewolf man, dressed all in black.

'It's the bloody messiah. It probably doesn't need to eat' shouted Adrian from the back.

'Look, we can bicker out here all night. It will not change the fact that some hybrid child is roaming our streets waiting to dictate and control us, and we, will have little say in the matter. The hybrid is a powerful entity. Stronger than us all. It was prophesied over a century ago. The time, has now come to pass.' Said Acheron, standing shoulder to shoulder with Cerberus.

'How do we even know you vampires speak the truth? How can we trust you?'

Cerberus rolled his eyes. He had little time to waste and had lost his patience. He erupted. 'Why are you ghastly dogs so bloody resistive? Do you think, you will all be spared? This, is pathetic'

'Who the hell do you think you are talking to, like that?' A big, tall burly man with curly hair stepped to the front, coming face to face with the vampire leader. With clenched fists, he pushed out his chest. 'I think it's time you Vampires flew back to your den.' he snarled.

'And who the hell are you?' Cerberus refused to be spoken to like that and immediately bared his fangs. His green eyes flickered red, a warning he was angry.

Just then, Runa's voice projected amongst the tension. 'Please. We come in peace, not war.'

She pushed her way to the front, then stood in between the warring pair who were about to rip each other's heads off. With arms outstretched, she tried talking sense into them, but it was little too late. Tensions were high, plus, Cerberus had a reputation to withhold.

'Get out of the way. This is not over.'

Cerberus shoved Runa aside, then struck the burly wolf to the throat. Blood splattered. The other werewolves displayed their anger. They howled and growled; the change was quick and fast. Suddenly, things got serious. The vampires braced themselves for a brawl. Runa was so annoyed, she didn't want to be a part of it, so teleported in search of Marc. Within seconds of her departure, the war had begun. The battle was fierce. Elena was flung to the ground and struck to the back. She quickly leaped to her feet in retaliation. She grappled with the werewolf, managing to jump on its back. It thrashed around angrily as she bit into its throat. Acheron and Apollyon fought two. It was brutal, bloodied mess. The vampire's best trick was jumping on the werewolf's backs. This caused disorientation, allowing easy access to its throat. Some werewolves knew this ploy and begun striking out. Acheron tried but was flung to the floor. Apollyon, the deadly swordsman, was a skilled fighter. He fought with precision, taking keen swipes at the wolf, slashing its stomach to shreds. He was then jumped upon by two, who managed to pin him to the floor. The creature bit into his shoulder. His screams could be heard by all. Cerberus was having the deadliest fight with the biggest wolf. Both had been injured but were still battling on. The wolf had more leverage. Cerberus bled from the leg, but the wolf had a bleed to the head. Cerberus had narrowly missed his throat.

'Argh, you beast.' Yelled Achylls

Achylls hated a defeat but wouldn't give up easily. She leaped onto the wolf, digging her teeth into its chest. The wolf clawed back viciously, attempting to ravage her insides. Achylls was angry. She dug her incredibly long claws into the wolf's stomach and had the pleasure in watching it holler in pain. She bit into its chest, delivering a last fatal blow. The monster fell to the floor, allowing Achylls the perfect opportunity to attack its head. Unfortunately for her, she was outsmarted by the wolf, who had played dead. The werewolf lunged at Achylls, grabbing her tight with both hands. With her body held between the wolf's grasp, he crushed her ribs together until it crumpled. Acheron saw the horror unfold. His wife's limp body fell to the floor in a heap. He was grieved. Unfortunately, with his guard down, he was set upon, becoming easy prey for an unsuspecting wolf who grabbed him from behind. Luckily for him, Ewin was inches away. He jumped on the wolfs back, sinking his teeth into his throat. Acheron was dropped to the ground, whilst trying to shake off the vampire from its back.

It was a soothing night to levitate through the trees, jumping higher than many buildings around. Marc enjoyed the air blowing on his face. It was cool and refreshing, enticing him to close his eyes in a state of calm. For some reason, he had a strong inclination to head South. He knew nothing about daemons and merely went on instinct, but he couldn't resist the unfamiliar pull, drawing him close like a bee to honey. The streets were bare. With the implantation of the curfew, scavenging for a decent meal was hard. An hour ago, he had seen the entire town of Glides deployed, making strides to meet the clan. He shook his head, muttering obscenities beneath his breath, wishing to have no part of it. Marc, lost track of time. He allowed his senses to lead the way. He levitated mid-air, feet gliding along an invisible line, then something caught his attention. It was an unfamiliar town. He kept his pace while admiring the town's rustic charms. There were few shops, but all with their shutters up. The streets were insanely clean, as though they had never been walked upon, and the trees were almost too green to be real. Within minutes Marc caught site of a big white house, sat in the middle of nowhere. His curiosity piqued. Marc lowered himself to the ground, then crept towards the mysterious house. For a while, he crept around outside trying to have a look in but proved difficult. Almost every window was covered up by some sort of silver paper. He scratched his head in despair. He was about to ring the solid metal knocker when the door opened.

'What are you doing on my door?'

Marc came face to face with Lazarus's mother. She seemed sourly angry and thoroughly bitter, and demanded he go away. Marc realised she was a daemon. He felt he was on the right track. Where there was one, there must be others.

'I am looking for someone' he said warmly.

'If it's the girl, I have no idea of her whereabouts.' Spat the old daemon.

'Do you know her?'

'Yes. And I assume you are the one that got away. Count yourself lucky. She's messed up. Now, if you'll excuse me. I don't entertain small talk with your kind.'

The old daemon slammed the door shut, leaving Marc with a barrage of unanswered questions and brewing frustration. He wanted to wring her neck, detesting against her attitude. Against his better judgement, and fearing she was his only hope, Marc knocked abruptly on the knocker, one, twice, then three times. The daemon refused to open the door. Marc wasn't about to give up easily. He yelled through the narrow letter box.

'I will pay you handsomely. Please. I need your help.' He called.

After hovering around for ten minutes, Marc reluctantly gave up. He begrudgingly made his way back down the cobbled path, eyeing the disjointed flower bed that had seemingly been trampled on. Just then, the door squeaked open. Marc stopped in his tracks, turning his attention to the daemon at the door. She appeared upset. Her palms were open. Suddenly, the daemon fell at her doorstep, bawling her eyes out.

'My son is dead. And that wretched girl is responsible.'

Marc looked on, dumbfounded. After a moment's silence, he eventually said 'I am sorry for your loss. If you do not mind my enquiry, who is your son?'

The daemon looked up at Marc as though he had asked the obvious. 'The father of the child! You best get that baby before she kills it, too.' she pleaded.

'Do you know her whereabouts? I have tried and have come up with nothing'.

'Look around. You're a vampire for goodness' sake, use your imagination. I can still smell her rancid stench. She cannot be far.'

Despite further prompting from Marc, was all the daemons said. Refusing to say anymore, she slammed the door shut. Marc felt he was armed with enough information to lead the way. He turned on his heels, then levitated back through the air. He thought about what the daemon had said. Estella could be nearby, and that was all he needed. He would search every corner of this town if it killed him. He *had* to find Estella and the child before the clan did. Marc wandered the streets with a lump of determination in his stomach. Thus far, Marc's search had been fruitless. However, something inside indicated he was close to a breakthrough. He came upon a narrow lane as he flew through the air like a villain on a mission. A flutter of crows fluttered past him in the other direction. There was a steep hill at the end of the lane. Marc flew swiftly; his black robe bellowed in the wind. His dark hair blew against the cold night air. Nothing more but wild grassland and dead shrubs, was all that could be seen. Crickets chirped loudly. He was several hours in and fought against the urge to give up. Even for a vampire, it was tiring.

Miles in, Marc spotted a little house in the distance at the top of yet another hilly space. It was significantly smaller than the white house, and appearing to be unkempt, with bits of timber wood hung loosely to the frame. Marc full circled the windowless house. He wasn't hopeful but had little to lose. After some hesitation, Marc trudged towards the little house. He had knocked twice already, and was still waiting several minutes in. It wasn't long before Marc became weary. He knocked again and waited, deciding this would be the final curtain call. They say, a vampire must be invited in, but Marc was willing to break the rules. Against his better judgement, he gently grabbed hold off the chipping doorknob. To his surprise, it rattled a little, then slowly clicked open. Marc was cautious. He placed a foot inside the house, his senses on guard. He called out to its inhabitants but was met with silence.

'Who are you?'

Marc nearly jumped out of his skin. He turned to the familiar voice. And that, is the moment everything came crashing down. What happened next, was surreal. Events played out like a movie on the big screen. Marc thought he was dreaming. With shaking hands and a paper white face, he was stunned. Estella looked equally surprised with a quivering mouth. She must have realised the state she was in, and made hasty attempts to neaten her hair, knowing that her usual grooming habits had ceased since becoming a daemon. Dressed in dark trousers and a stained denim top, this had become her reality. Marc couldn't peel his eyes away. He was so shocked to see his former companion, he had hardly noticed the child she carried in her arms. Rory approached the door.

'Marc? What are you doing here?' she stuttered.

'You're being hunted. My people and the werewolves are out for you tonight. Give me the child, or she will be killed.'

Estella's stomach sank. She turned to Rory, who seemed equally distraught. Her eyes darted to the floor as the frightful revelation set in. She hoped this time would never come, but now, it had. Estella swayed unsteadily. Her legs felt like jelly. Marc couldn't quite believe the reality of the situation. He kept glaring at Estella, then back to the child, trying to fathom what sort of sorcery was responsible. In all honesty, Marc fought the urge to tear Estella's head off her neck, but seeing the innocence she had created, softened his heart. It took a while for Marc to gather his bearings, all three appeared as stunned as the other. Marc became unsettled. He could sense the clans drawing near.

'Estella, you must run away tonight. Grab your passport and get out of here' he ordered.

Rory's worried face done little to soothe her fears. 'Estella, listen to him. We cannot stay here'.

'I can't give you, my baby. She is all I have.'

'You don't have much time left. Cerberus has woken. And he means business.'

'Cerberus?' Estella gawked. The situation was more serious than she imagined.

Marc furrowed his brow. His jaw clenched as the truth unfolded. Estella saw the anguish in his eyes. His pain was evident. She sobbed, begging for his forgiveness. Marc was solemn. Undeniably he still loved her very much but felt she couldn't be forgiven. The pain was too raw. He grabbed her face, prising it between his hands. He grimaced at the voice in his head telling him to crush her face as hard as he could and be done with it. But Marc, was weak. His love for her, too strong. He felt a fool but couldn't deny the strength of their bond was the only thing that kept him going. He wiped the tears from her eyes. Estella made an admission. She felt suffocated and smothered and was forced for intimacy. To please him, she would do so through gritted teeth. If she refused, Marc would punish her with silence, becoming cold and unbearable to be around. Marc had never laid a finger on her, but the mental torture was bad enough.

Over time Estella's heart hardened, resentment grew. They made love at night, but Estella was unsatisfied for years, becoming a prisoner to her emotions. It wasn't mere lust she craved. She wanted a loving relationship but felt dictated to all the while.

'I am so sorry you felt this way.' Marc buried his head into his hands.

'Don't be. I've never wanted for nothing. I allowed temptation to get the better of me'.

'I didn't see it at the time. But perhaps I was a little over-zealous with my emotions overbearing.'

'None of us are perfect' she whispered. The baby gurgled trying to free herself from her mother's grasp.

'Estella, I have never stopped loving you. And no matter what happens, I never will.'

Estella was chocked. She was undeserving of Marc's loyalty and wished he would have struck her instead. As the sound of chirping crickets rippled through the air, Estella knew this was it, but at least she had closure. The resentment she had bottled up for so long, began to slip away. Her fateful companion for more than two centuries, she would unlikely form such a close bond with another man again. Time had stopped, but reality came pouring back when Rory's voice could be heard saying,

'Estella, the wolves are drawing close. I can smell them.'

Marc and Estella looked at the daemon by the door. Rory's deep-set eyes were hollow and lonesome, echoing a shadowed sadness Estella hadn't seen before. Rory decided to travel with Estella, they would go into hiding until things settled down. He also felt it was best to give Marc the baby as the child would surely slow them down them down.

'Estella, she is safer with Marc. At least for now.' Rory reassured.

Estella was fraught, her lips quivered at the thought of handing over her baby, with no guarantees of a safe return. Her fearful face gawked at Rory's idea, hoping she had misheard. Rory gave a gentle nod, encouraging her to hand over the child. Truth be known, Rory had a grave fear for Estella's safety and couldn't discount the gruesome premonition he had encountered days earlier. He had seen her death play out right before his eyes but hoped it had all been a bad trick of the mind.

'We must go now' he demanded voice shaken.

Estella tearfully handed Marc her precious child. His shoulders tensed, his face was fearful, wondering if he was really up to scratch to protect something so delicate. Rory left his position on the doorstep. He approached Marc. The men exchanged hopeful glances. It took seconds to size each other up. Rory knew, Marc was not like the others. He had a heart. Rory agreed with Marc, their plans to meet days later. They were to return to Heath Hall once things had settled, where Marc would be waiting. Marc made promises to take care of the child until they meet again.

'She is beautiful, just like her mother.' Marc spoke in a whisper, while dodging a poke in the eye by the rumbunctious infant.

Rory nodded his goodbyes. The lump in Estella's throat hardened like a rock. She clammed up, unable to talk. The most she managed, was woeful eye contact with the man she once loved, who held her child in strong protective arms. With plans in place, Marc vanished as quick as he came. Estella was inconsolable. She buried her head in his shoulders. Rory placed a protective arm around her, although, nothing he done could take the ease the pain.

'We must, get going' he said, with a stroke of the arm.

Estella looked up. She had red eyes, and a jaundiced complexion. 'I cannot run anymore. I'm tired, really tired. What life is this?' she asked, studying Rory's face for an answer.

'Estella, they will kill us both. Daemons are not welcomed in this underworld. We are the outsiders. If you don't come with me, I will have to leave you'.

'Go, save yourself. I do not want you getting in any trouble because of my reckless behaviour.'

Rory couldn't believe his ears. Estella was hellbent on fighting a war she was unlikely to win. He thought she had gone mad. Rory looked at her quizzingly. 'Estella, your daughter needs you.'

'And that, is why I'm not running. At least she can say I fought with dignity.'

Rory rolled his eyes at Estella's statement. He shook his head in angst. There was little he could do. Rory reluctantly followed Estella back inside his tiny wooden house. To his surprise, Estella walked towards the bedroom, then sat herself down upon the old misshapen bed. Rory's heart was broken. Despite Estella's reluctance to stay, Rory decided to leave. He feared being guilty by association and would suffer the same consequences. He grabbed a black holdall from the back of his broken wardrobe, then stuffed it with various bits of clothes, finally flinging his passport on top. It was clear he was angry with Estella's decision to stay.

'I can't believe you would be so selfish. You have a child to care for. And look what you've done. I, have lived my entire existence under the shadow, hidden for years. Because *you* failed to keep your legs closed, I am forced to leave my home.'

'How fucking dare, you?' Estella couldn't believe he would say such a thing. She stood up to face him.

'You wanted the truth. There it is.'

Estella slapped Rory across the face. She tried to hit him on the head, but he grabbed hold off her hands in restraint. She struggled to wriggle free from Rory's grip, then gave up defeat realising he was far stronger than she was. Estella broke down in his arms. They embraced. Estella wept, but her mind was made. She told Rory to leave her behind. He would travel to Brisbane, Australia. To get there, he would have to travel through Hambleden, a town populated by humans. This was a risk, but one he was willing to take. Rory pleaded for Estella to join him, but she was stubborn and wouldn't budge. She couldn't imagine leaving her baby behind while she travelled to a foreign land. Within minutes, Rory said his farewell and left Estella behind with a broken heart and little hope. Estella promised, they would meet again.

Morning beamed through the walls. Though Rory's house was windowless, Estella's body rhythm knew the hours of the day like a built-in clock. She stirred face down on the bed. Her body could have carried on at rest, but Estella willed herself to get out of bed. As she sat herself up, Estella studied the cold little room, devoid of any happiness. With the baby in mind, Estella hurried herself to Rory's tiny little bathroom. The shower was freezing, exactly how she liked it. Estella may have been on borrowed time but felt she had all the time in the world. She thought about her baby, wondering what Marc was doing. She imagined him beaming with pride, taking to task his fatherly duties. Estella had plans to take down the clan. She was plagued with crazy ideas with ways to defeat the enemy, then settled with a plan to burn the entire house down. It was the only way to escape the hell she had placed her family in. Feeling satisfied with her master scheme, Estella pottered to the kitchen in search of food, hoping the house wasn't empty. Thankfully on arrival, Rory had left several cans of meat on top of the counter. Sheep, and Beef. Estella picked up a can of Beef, slicing it open with her nails. She chucked it down her throat. It was good. It tasted far more authentic than the cheap rubbish she had fed on at Stefan's.

As the day dragged on, a weary Estella settled herself in Rory's cramped lounge. His black dusty sofa reeked of stale cigar, though she never saw him smoke. Estella switched on the television in the corner that was boxier than Stefan's and looked as though it weighed a ton. The human man relayed the news, dressed in a pompous grey suit paired with an awfully bright blue tie.

'It is a state of emergency. Since the implementation of the curfew, the death toll has dropped considerably. However, several bodies were found last

night, bled out with distinctive bite marks around the neck. There is a major military operation underway as the government grapples with the murder statistic.'.

Estella gawked at the television. The humans were disadvantaged, but so, was she. Very soon, she could be the unfortunate soul torn alive, rendered a bloodied death. Estella had to act fast. She got up in a flurry, then ran to the kitchen. In a state of panic, Estella pulled apart each and every draw, praying Rory had matches or at least some gasoline. As she flung the feeble wooden cabinets open, she was disappointed Rory hadn't been more adventurous. Venturing out for the necessary wasn't a good idea. Fearing her plans had been demolished, Estella entertained the thought of meeting Rory after all. Perhaps if she were quick, they would catch the same flight. It could have been so easy. Only, it wasn't. Her own mother would have crossed rivers for her. Estella felt the same duty to her own child, no matter the cost.

THIRTY-FOUR

Marc could no longer ignore the banging to the door. It had continued over five minutes, evidently the caller was persistent. He knew it was his cousin; her scent was like no other. Reluctantly, he levitated down the stairs. Marc pulled the door to his flustered cousin. She looked scared, then dramatically wrapped her arms around him.

'Marc, thank goodness you are here. Acheron and Lucas are dead. So is Elena and Edgar. Achylls was nearly killed, her ribs were crushed to dust. Luckily, she managed to be revived by gallons of Stramus's blood, heeling faster than expected. Apollyon and Ewin were brutally injured, but they're taking rest and likely to make a full recovery within days.'

Runa spoke so fast, Marc found it rather comical. She had given him an entire commentary, little did she know, he had no concern for the vampires back at the Castle. He awkwardly shrugged his shoulders, not knowing what to say. Only he was grateful Lorcan had been spared. Runa was quickly ushered in. The door slammed shut behind her. Marc grabbed her shoulders.

'You must calm down. They wanted a fight, and they got it. The werewolves bargain hard. They don't give for nothing. My only concern right now, is the child.'

'What child?' Runa's mouth fell to the floor.

'She is upstairs. I could do with an extra hand.' He admitted.

'Gosh, I thought the vampires were gravely mistaken. I didn't know it was true' Gawked Runa.

'No, she is as real as the sky itself. A miracle, I must protect.'

'Marc, the vampire's wanted Estella's head on a stick...and the baby. How is it that the child is with you? I mean... that's great.'

Marc pursed his lips, gesturing with his hands. He beckoned to his cousin. The vampires levitated back up the twirling stairs until they arrived at a well-made bedroom. As Marc pushed the door open, Runa was speechless. Placed in the middle of the room, was a gorgeous mahogany wooden cot. Reddish brown, shining splendidly under the candle lights which were sat in wall mounted rustic wicks.

'I made it myself. Thought I'd put some of those wooden slabs to good use. They've been down in the cellar for decades, steadily rotting away.'

'You made that? I didn't know you were so skilled. It's beautiful.'

Runa walked towards the cot. The baby's head could be seen; her tuffs of brown hair stuck above the cot like a bad Mohican haircut. As she peered inside, Runa was taken aback. She cupped her hands to her mouth in disbelief. She was the most beautiful creature she had laid eyes upon.

'She is an absolute joy! But how can this little creature reign so much fear over our species? Five of our men have lost their lives fearing this child to be some kind of monster.'

Runa's voice reeked of disbelief. She thought the vampires were gravely mistaken and had foolishly lost their lives for nothing. The child looked up at Runa with her deep chocolate brown eyes. She appeared content.

'So, where is Estella?'

'Estella is where she needs to be. She has my deepest sympathies. I made her a promise, and I, intend to fulfil it. However, she is no longer my concern.'

'So…she just handed over her child?'

'Not exactly, no. Estella has done the right thing. I admire her courage. Anyway, I don't want you worrying about us. I can handle my own affairs.'

'But Marc, Cerberus will kill the child'.

'He won't. He wouldn't dare come sniffing around here. He has weakened. He cannot step foot on these soils. I have placed a hex. His blood runs like a river.

'You took his blood, to curse him?'

'It's complicated. Cerberus has many secrets. My ancestors guard this home like a fortress. A certain vampire, cannot penetrate its protective wares.'

Runa gulped at her cousin's revelation. She didn't have him down as a sorcerer. Nor had he ever let on that magic was his thing.

'Anyway, are you heading back to Castle Dravenherd? You can stay here with me. She needs a motherly hand, after all.'

'I don't think I can do that. They're expecting my return. Plus, as precious as she is, what if Cerberus was right? That baby could grow up, putting us into bondage.'

'No, she's a good soul. She will treat us like decent creatures, as we do her,' he said.

Marc seemed to be at peace with his decision. Gone was the distressed aura from his energy, replaced with a new vigour for life. He smiled at his cousin. His eyes were happy. The child would be raised as his own. He cared little if she grew to rule over him. That wasn't important. He would teach her all he knew and could only hope she wouldn't grow into an absolute monster. Runa was nervous about the child, but trusted Marc's judgement. She stroked the child's hair. It was so soft, she cooed at Runa's touch.

Runa smiled sweetly. Her eyes lit up as her motherly instincts kicked in.

'She is beautiful. I wonder what it would have been like if I had had a child. If my mother was never bitten. Or if I were the chosen one?'

'I wouldn't worry about that now. For what it's worth, I am sure you would have been a fantastic mother.' soothed Marc.

Runa turned to him. She prepared to return to the castle 'Until we meet again, dear cousin' She embraced her cousin warmly, then wished him well. Seconds in, Runa left the room. Marc heard her leave; the door slammed harshly behind her.

Runa headed back to Castle Dravenherd. Her teleportation was faster than anticipated. Her mind was flooded with grief. Apollyon may have been poorly, but he, was a traitor. Runa hated traitors. She was fond of Estella, and in spite of her betrayal, she couldn't stand the thought of that poor woman being hunted because of his own selfishness. That child would be motherless, and he, was to blame. Runa burst through the castle doors in a flurry. She stormed off to Apollyon's room on the west wing. Located down a lonely corridor, it was unlit, unlike the rest of the castle. Without warning, she flung the door open.

'You traitor. Why would you do this? Does that poor woman deserve this? Does that child, deserve this? Estella was a good friend to us both.'

Apollyon was lying in his coffin unresponsive, the lid halfway covered over. Runa angrily pulled it off. Apollyon's eyes were red and weeping. He looked awful. The massive gash on his face had partially healed, but his wounds had zapped every ounce of energy from his body. He was deathly pale, even for a vampire. To her surprise, he slowly opened one eye.

'Runa, that child is our superior. It will grow to rule the entire underworld. Our people will be shackled. I done what was necessary.'

'You bastard. You're a sorry excuse for a vampire, and an even worse excuse for a friend. That baby is precious. You shouldn't concern yourself with her potential mistreatment of 'our people'. It may not even happen. I guess you are rattled because you won't have the pleasure of slaughtering humans by the droves. Frankly, we need some order. Things are out of hand. If that baby is the only one to stop this carnage, so be it.'

Apollyon's eyes became intense. 'Runa, you're far too emotional. Sometimes I doubt if you are even one of us. You were always so law abiding, too gracious, too fucking morally pleasing. Quite frankly, you bore me.'

'How dare you. You're pathetic. It's a pity the wolves didn't gnaw you to death.'

Runa spat in the coffin. She marched out of the room, slamming the door with a thud.

Back in the great hall, the mood was dark and sombre. The vampires felt defeated by the werewolves but were not prepared to give up easily. Between them all, they had killed at least fifteen but had lost four of their best. Acheron was the head of the board when Cerberus was not around. He had displayed great strength and had defeated many. But was ultimately jumped upon by three. His battered body was a stark reminder of the threat the werewolves placed upon their survival.

'It's a fucking outrage. My husband is dead. What the hell happens now? Those rabid dogs have it coming.'

'Achylls, you must calm down.'

'Stramus, do not tell me to calm down. Four of our people were killed mindlessly because of that pathetic bitch. When I get my hands on her, she will pay for all of this.'

'Achylls, we slaughtered a dozen of those beasts. Unfortunately, we didn't have the numbers to outdo them. As for Estella, she *will* be destroyed. Now please take a seat.' demanded Cerberus.

He had a deep cut above his eye that wasn't healing nearly as fast as it should. In fact, Cerberus's entire eye had almost been plucked from its socket. He looked distraught as he grieved for his niece. Elena was a good vampire. With Acheron gone, Apollyon would fill his shoes as new board member. Cerberus decided that Ewin would take Lucas's place. Tonight, the vampires would hunt again. Apollyon and Ewin were already on the mend and had insisted not to be left behind. Cerberus made plans for 2am. They had less than an hour before the second day of the hunt began. Tonight, was different. After last nights bloodied battle, the werewolves decided to hunt Estella alone. They wanted no further alliance with the vampires and would hunt Estella for their own selfish gain. They had plans to use her and the child as bribery. Cerberus knew their plans and was adamant the vampires had to get to them first.

'Tonight, those filthy dogs will be on the hunt. We *must* outsmart them. I want Estella and the baby back here at the castle, alive.'

'Well, I'm rather pleased to see the back of Lucas. He killed my sister'.

Eyes darted to Bernadette. She sat cuddled in Adrian's arms, stroking his hair and kissing his neck. Cerberus couldn't believe his ears. He demanded she leave the room. Adrian protested. He tried to intervene, but Cerberus wasn't in the mood for reasoning. Lucas was one of his most faithful vampires who had fought for the board for centuries. He wouldn't condone a bad word said about him, but Bernadette was angry.

'Doesn't my sister deserve the same respect? He deceived her, then cut her head off in the hallway!'

'I care little about some human girl, who merely tasted the luxury of our lineage for two minutes. Lucas, was one of my best.' Spat Cerberus.

'You are a heartless beast of a man.'

Bernadette stormed out of the hall. Adrian shrugged. 'Let her be,' said Cerberus. 'We have better things to contend with.'

'She will soon calm down, realising he had done her sister a favour. I mean, let's be honest, Lilith was hideous to look at. She certainly wasn't fit to be a vampire. Did she really think Lucas would take her seriously?'

Achylls's tone was bitter. Talk turned to Marc. No one had seen him since last night. Cerberus wanted him gone. 'He's absolutely useless to us. He may as well be a daemon. Far too emotional.'

Lorcan interjected. 'Cerberus, Marc is a torn man. We cannot judge him in his fragile mental constitution. Frankly, I think he is a great asset to the castle and a true friend.'

'Lorcan, I don't care for your opinion. Marc, is a fool.'

'A fool he may be, but at least he's an honourable fool.' Said Lorcan.

'Who gives a damn. If he took better notice of his woman, this would never have happened' Achylls hurled a glass towards the marbled floor. She seethed as glass shattered. Acheron's death had hit her hard. No one took any notice of her outburst, allowing her to vent her frustrations.

It wasn't long before the vampires set out on their journey. The two injured vampires were already in tow. Despite Runa's earlier antagonizing, nothing would keep Apollyon away from Estella's capture. He was slightly fragile but healed by the minute. The vampires were eight strong and hopeful. Tonight, was cooler than the night before. Not only were they hunting Estella, but their conflict with the wolves would likely escalate if their paths were crossed.

'Adrian, please keep up. I know you'd rather be at the castle with that pathetic woman, but do remember, this is important.'

Adrian wasn't listening. Like a bad smell, Cerberus's voice became an irritant, one he chose to block out. He levitated at his own pace enjoying the night air on his skin, then something caught his attention. There was a scuffle in the trees. Adrian's curiosity piqued. Intrigued, he levitated to the ground with interest. A young face peeked out at him from beneath the bushes. It was a child no older than three. A werewolf. Adrian was surprised to see a child so young out by himself, even if he was a shapeshifting beast. On closer inspection, Adrian realised the child was injured, quite badly actually. Out of nowhere, Ewin came charging along, swiping the child to its stomach.

'I've made it easy for you. That is a wolf. There is no place for sympathy.'

'Ewin? Why did you do that? He was a child.'

'A werewolf, that's what it was.'

As fast as he appeared, Ewin levitated towards some trees before disappearing through the skies, evaporating to a mist. Adrian felt awful, but the child was out of its misery. He took flight to the skies. Adrian levitated through trees. His speed was impeccable. Within seconds he caught up with the others. Ewin still had a satisfied grin on his face. It was kill or be killed. The vampires were merciless.

'We must head out of Glides, and travel further up north. We must search for the town where daemons roam. Unfortunately, it has been so long, the name doesn't come to me. Tonight, we must scale all four corners of the earth.'

Achylls eyed Cerberus as though he were mad 'Where the hell is that?' she screwed up her face.

'I am not entirely sure but am hopeful we will find it.' said Cerberus with great confidence.

'Look who its is' Achylls suddenly exclaimed.

Acheron and Achylls's new recruit had joined the vampires on their hunt. The young brunette who had been left behind at the castle, had followed their scent, and had managed to catch up with her peers. Unbeknown to Achylls, the girl was saved by Acheron who took the fatal blow. The girl squealed with wide eyed excitement at her own ability to levitate and seemed to think it was some sort of adventure circus. She pointed to the hareem of werewolves running riot on the ground. They appeared to be headed in the same direction, though several miles behind.

'Lucinda, I know this is all new to you, but you must contain your excitement.' scowled Achylls.

The vampires eyed the eager wolves. It was a rampage as they galloped the streets in hunt for Estella. Cerberus stiffened his upper lip. He wanted them dead. Every last one of them. And would see to it justice was done for Elena and the others.

'Those vile creatures. Look at them, like a pack of dogs. We must cower or they will soon get wind of us. Quick, shelter behind the trees. Allow them gallop ahead. We must pull back.' he ordered.

The vampires hovered amongst the thick mass of willow trees, cautiously peeping out at the wolves below.

'Cor, what I would do with a bow and arrow right now' hissed Achylls.

'Wouldn't that be a dream. They will surely pay for my cousin's death' said Stramus.

'Be quiet, the pair of you.'

It was four o'clock in the morning. The vampires spanned town after town, scrutinising the major three. They had barged their way through houses, killing anyone in their way. Parks were empty, even the old church was searched. The werewolves had detoured. For the last forty minutes, they had seemingly disappeared from the ground. Ewin recalled them heading up south, but Cerberus was adamant they carried on north. After all, if they were having trouble locating the mysterious daemon town, there was no way a pack of brainless dogs would find it.

'It has been two hours, and we are no closer to finding Estella.'

Cerberus eyed Adrian with venom 'What is your point?'

'This, is a fruitless journey.' Admitted Achylls through gritted teeth. 'We have overthrown every home, killed nearly a dozen humans, and still no sign of that retched woman. I fear those beasts have already gotten to her.'

'Are you mad? We are not giving up that easy. I will search the blue skies if I have to.' Spat Cerberus.

With those words, the vampires carried on levitating through the skies. They shared the same sentiments, but would appease their Master, nonetheless. They had an hour till sunrise. An uneasy feeling settled in the pit of Cerberus's stomach.

THIRTY-FIVE

Marc surveyed the grand mansion he had once shared with the woman he loved. Heath Hall seemed strangely solemn, lacking the vibrant warmth once brimming through its walls. A grave seriousness washed over him. Buried memories danced away in his head. Marc reasoned to himself he would remove all portraits, in particular the large one of Estella at the top of the stairs. But things had gotten easier. The baby had brought joy into his cold heart. She was the daughter he never had, and yet, her stark resemblance to her mother was a constant reminder. It had been several days, but already his bond with the child had deepened. He fed her on blood, she seemed to approve. He read books; she would glare into his eyes as though she understood. Her sleeping patterns were different to his. The child would be placed into her cot by 8pm while he roamed the mansion all night, occasionally leaving her alone to feed on any unsuspecting human he came upon. While Marc slept during the day, she would be awake the entire time, entertaining herself with the hideous stuffed frog he had found in the cellar the. Some days Marc feared for her safety, plotting ways in which she could be hidden in the mansion, away from prying eyes. Sooner or later, they would come looking. Cerberus would insist on a search. Marc knew him well enough.

This evening was like no other. Within minutes of putting the baby to rest, Marc had rearranged the entire mansion. He opened up a centuries old vault, which had been sealed and concealed from the outside world and was previously used for storage. Now, it was a landmine filled with rubble and rubbish; rats scurried between his feet. Unused coffins were amongst the mess, most of which had been broken and destroyed. Marc was old enough to know that vampires had lived underground way before civilisation set in, back when humans had full control. Back then, the vampire community was small and fragile, they had to remain hidden in the shadows. The vault was ten feet underground. The only entrance was through his bedroom wall, concealed by the garish wallpaper Estella had plastered over it with. The vault was never mentioned to the Elders. Thankfully now, his secret would prove to be useful.

It was nearly morning when Estella heard the second knock to the door. She was settled in Rory's bed, but all night she had struggled to sleep. She rolled her eyes in annoyance. The wind was strong and gusty, howling angrily against the front door. Estella tossed and turned, burying her head underneath the oil-stained pillow. Just then, there was a crash to the door. Estella startled. It was as if a car had collided into the house. She leaped out of bed fearing the door had collapsed. Within seconds, voices could be heard. Things quickly spiralled out of control. There was one voice in particular. It was coarse and unsympathetic, ordering the others. Estella panicked. Her worst fears had come true. Fortunately, daemons had a plethora of abilities at their disposal. Quick as a fiddle, Estella vanished from the spot.

'Where is she?'

'Search all the rooms.

The werewolves stormed into Rory's bedroom trampling over the plywood door, shattering it to pieces. Estella counted eight of them. The werewolves were armed. They had firearms as big as houses strapped to their backs, and some tucked under arms, obviously filled with silver bullets.

'She has to be here somewhere. I can smell her. Those daemons, are the world's best tricksters.'

'I can smell her, too. The scent is indescribable.' Said another.

'She has probably camouflaged herself to the wall.' Cried another.

'Blast the place.' barked one, who was bigger and uglier than the rest.

'No, don't' snapped another.

However, it was too late. Within seconds, the spray of silver bullets created such an explosion, the room felt like it was on fire. Estella was stunned. Her mouth fell open, hoping for a prayer. The walls shattered and the bed overturned as bullets drilled their way through Rory's old mattress. The werewolves sprayed the ceiling, too. Although she was unseen, Estella couldn't hide. She became numb as silver bullets riddled her body with such force, she eventually manifested before their eyes. Soon enough Estella fell to the floor in a floppy state, but she was strong and possibly could've healed from silver if she hadn't been sprayed from head to toe. She stirred a little then proceeded to get back on her feet. But it was too late. Disorientated by the effects of silver, she didn't see it coming. One of the wolves crept behind her, staking her in the chest with a massive wooden stake. Estella gasped her last breath as the stake took hold. She clutched her chest. Voice shaky she yelled 'I'm not a fucking vampire, you moron's'.

Estella's hands shook like a leaf. Her body was going into shut down. Four lifetimes flashed before her eyes; memories of her own mother came into play. She looked happy with arms outstretched, preparing to greet her lost long daughter. Estella tensed as her last breath left her body. Her only wish was that Marc cared for her daughter. Estella held her mother's hand. They were reunited at last.

Her mother was reassuring, encouraging her daughter to let go of this world, welcoming her into another. And at that moment, one of the werewolves walked over to her body with a disgruntled look on her face. She was middle-aged with fair hair. She knelt at the body, her eyes scrutinising the corpse. She grew angry at the others. Killing Estella wasn't the intention.

'Well, we do not want bloody daemons taking over' spat a tall man.

'But where is this child they speak of? We were supposed to keep her alive and bring the child as a bargaining tool.'

'Well, there is definitely no baby here. We've searched every room. And this house is tiny. We couldn't miss her if we tried.'

'Well how unfortunate. She is a mother, as am I. There was no need to riddle her with a thousand bullets. Bernard, you promised me before we set out on this quest that she wouldn't be killed. The blonde became angry, surprising the others that she actually cared. All eyes glared at the body. The werewolf-clan left more peacefully than they came. It was already day-break. The sun began to peep through the clouds. On the blonde's orders, the search for the child was to cease for the time being. However, the war with the vampires, had just begun.

A year on since Estella's death, Marc lived a solitary lifestyle. He had become a recluse of sorts, preferring to shut himself away from the outside world. Tuesdays were an exception, and the only day Marc left the confines of the mansion walls. He would stand at the gates, waiting to meet the young vampire with the sad eyes named Lucinda, the girl from the cellar back at Castle Dravenherd. She spoke nothing of the others and refused to say what had happened on that fateful night. The vampires never made it to Health Hall, she said. Whether this were true or not, Marc had no way of knowing. However, he had heard nothing of Stramus. So, every Tuesday like clockwork, Lucinda brought two bags of freshly sealed blood for Marc to indulge on. It was human blood. There were bags stored back at the castle, she said. In spite of Marc's prompting, Lucinda often refused to come inside. Marc found it weird but figured she owed him nothing. This particular Tuesday, Lucinda didn't turn up. Marc waited until a quarter past midnight, like he always had. At 12.30 he grew weary, then headed back inside.

The hybrid child was thriving. She was only a year old, but already taller than most three-year-olds. She often watched Marc at the window, peeping through the thick velvet curtains with her brown floppy hair that sat at the top of her shoulders. Tonight, she noticed Marc's disappointment. She turned to him.

'Do not despair daddy. Mummy says, we will find a way. The war is not over. Humans are still in shackles. Their blood shed spills through the streets, more and more every day. And I'm the one to end it all.'

Marc stopped in his tracks. Cold chills crept up his arms. The child had never spoken. She often smiled for communication, and would occasionally frown if she wanted to be fed. However tonight, Marc's surprise couldn't be hidden. Her vocabulary was superb. Proving far more superior to any human child of the same age. Like a proud father, he smiled as a silent peace settled within.

The End

Printed in Dunstable, United Kingdom

71733276R00194